THE HALF

C000052305

By
Trevor Bloom

A Hookline Favourite

'I wholly enjoyed the fate of the hero with gripping situations and moral dilemmas. I found it increasingly hard to put down, burned a lot of midnight oil'.

'A refreshing lack of idealisation – even of the hero; I believed in the characters.'

'I'd happily read the sequel!'
Book group readers

Hookline Books
Bookline & Thinker Ltd

THE HALF-SLAVE

By
Trevor Bloom

A Hookline Favourite

Hookline Books
Bookline & Thinker Ltd

Published by Hookline Books 2010
Bookline & Thinker Ltd
#231, 405 King's Road
London SW10 0BB
Tel: 0845 116 1476
www.booklinethinker.com

The right of Trevor Bloom to be indentified as the author of this work has been asserted in accordance with the Copyright, Designs and Patents Act 1988.

© Copyright 2009 Trevor Bloom

A CIP catalogue for this book is available from the British Library.

This book is a work of fiction. Names, characters, places and incidents are either a product of the author's imagination or are used fictitiously.
ISBN: 9780955563065

Cover design by **jameshollywell.com**
Printed and bound by Lightning Source UK

For Emma and Nicky,
with love

Characters

Saxons

Aelfric: Ascha's father, hetman of the Theodi
Ascha: Theod, a half-slave
Besso: Ascha's uncle
Budrum: Besso's wife
Saefaru: Wife of Wulfhere
Hanno: Ascha's brother
Hroc: Ascha's brother
Radhalla: Warlord of the Cheruskkii
Sigisberht: Nephew to Radhalla
Totta: Blacksmith
Tchenguiz: Hun slave
Wulfhere: Ascha's rival

Romans/Gauls/Pritanni

Herrad: Octha's companion
Flavinius: Counsellor to Clovis
Rufus Basilicus: Roman auxiliary officer
Syagrius: Governor of Roman Gaul
Quintilius: Secretary to General Bauto
Lucullus: High-born slave

Franks

Basinia: Queen, mother of Clovis
Bauto: Frankish general
Clovis: Overlord of the Franks
Fara: Agent of Ragnachar
Ragnachar: Uncle to Clovis
Sunno: Antrustion
Wacho: Boat master

Others

Eanmund: Half-Dane
Gydda: Jute, friend of Ascha
Kral: Slave master
Octha: Frisian, merchant
Eleri: House slave to Basinia
Dagobert: Frisian, a Frankish agent

Place names

Andecavus	Angers, France
Arduenna	Forest of Ardennes, Belgium
Burdigala	Bordeaux, France
Cambarac	Cambrai, France
Colonia (Agrippina)	Cologne, Germany
Gallia	Gaul, roughly modern France
Gesoriac	Boulogne, France
Levefanum	see Thraelsted
Liger	River Loire, France
Lupia	River Lippe, a tributary of the Rhine
Moguntiac	Mainz, Germany
Noviomagus	Nijmegen, Holland
(Lutetia) Parisi	Paris, France
Pritannia	Britain
Radhallaburh	Radhalla's forest fortress
Rotomagus	Rouen, France
Samara	River Somme
Samarobriva	Amiens, France
Schald	River Schelde
Thraelsted	A slave market, also known as Levefanum
Tornacum	Tournai, Belgium, town of the Salt-Franks
Viroviac	Wervyk, Belgium
Wisurg	River Weser, Germany

Glossary of Terms

Alemani	Germanic tribe
Armorici	Pritanni who fled from Britain to Gaul
Alani	Eastern tribe
Almost-Island	Jutland peninsular
Bacaudae	Lawless bands of slaves and poor peasants
Burgundii	Germanic tribe occupying part of Gallia
Chaussi	Saxon tribe
Cheruskkii	Saxon tribe
Eostre	Spring festival
Faida	Vengeance
Franciska	Frankish hatchet
Gallia	Gaul, roughly modern France
Gesith	War chief's bodyguard
Gesithman	Member of war chief's bodyguard
Heruli	Germanic tribe
Hetman	Tribal chieftain
Mara	Assembly area before hetman's hall
Mansio	Inn
Mischling	Half-breed
Pritanni	Britons
Scara	Frankish army
Seaxe	Saxon long knife
Spatha	Long sword used by horse troops
Suebi	Germanic tribe
Taifali	Saxon tribe
Tiw	Northern god, as in Tuesday (Tiw's day)
Tiwfest	Festival of Tiw
Theodi	Saxon tribe
Vexillatio	Roman troops detached from their parent unit
Walesh	A foreigner

Northwest Europe, 481AD

1

Samarobriva, Roman Gaul   476 AD

The boy sat in a tree high above the forest, his legs swinging. It was hot, the sky blue and without cloud. A fat bead of sweat slid down his neck like a sluggish insect. The boy wiped his eyes and scanned the horizon. He was numb and ached all over, his lower back stiff as a board, but he could not afford to relax. He was the look-out and knew the clan relied on him to keep them safe.

He wet his lips and shifted his position, carefully stretching out one foot and then the other. He rolled his head to relieve the cramp in his neck.

Once more he ran his eyes over the quivering plains.

Nothing moved.

Across the valley, he could see the Roman town of Samarobriva, a few rags of red smoke still hanging over the tiled roofs. Beyond the town, the stone road slashed north, disappearing into nothingness. Far above, buzzards wheeled in their constant search for prey. If he turned his head to the right he could see the tightly furled sail of the clan's warboat *SeaWulf* moored on the river. He twisted and looked down. At the foot of the trees, the crew of the *SeaWulf* had stacked their weapons and lay sprawled in the shade, fast asleep.

He listened; his ears keyed to the sounds of the forest, able to sift out anything untoward, the clank of shields and weapons, running feet.

But he heard nothing.

He drew a wooden carving from his tunic and began to scrape at it with a belly knife. He liked to carve. It passed the time and kept him awake. He would start with a chunk of wood and after a few days he would have a long-handled cup, or a longboat, or a wild animal. He held the carving up and studied it: a young woman with flowing hair and a gentle smile. A good likeness, he thought. He would give it to Saefaru when he went home. He was quiet for a moment, his mind far away. A week since the Theodi had left the homeland to go raiding and already it felt like a lifetime.

He looked down at the sleeping men. The sun had moved and was burning him. Up in the trees it was so hot he could hardly breathe. The air was thick as honey and even the leaves smelled of sunlight. He felt his head nod and his eyes close and he jerked upright with a quick feeling of guilt. You must stay awake, he thought. You must! He lifted his flask, pulled the stopper with his teeth and rinsed his mouth out with water. Replacing the stopper, he looked up, his eyes travelling slowly from left to right across the plains.

He saw movement and stiffened. Hard to make out anything in the haze but then he saw it again, a flicker of motion. He looked away for a moment and then looked again, lifting a hand to his eyes and squinting.

And then he saw them.

Riders!

He blinked and peered again, swinging his head to find a gap in the trees where the foliage was less dense. At least a dozen men, mounted on big warhorses, were swinging round the river bend and coming toward them.

The boy felt suddenly alert, as if his head had been plunged into a pail of freezing water. His mouth dried and he felt a gnawing fear. He twisted and looked down at the ground. The crew were sleeping, oblivious to the danger.

He put his hand to the side of his mouth and screamed, 'Ho! You there below! Riders approaching!'

The cry echoed through the trees and floated gently to the ground. Nobody stirred.

He called again. 'Riders coming!'

Bastards were all asleep. Wake up! Wake up! Damn you.

He peered into the distance. Still coming, and if those horsemen got among the sleeping Theodi, he knew there would be slaughter.

He shouted and waved. Nothing! They couldn't hear him. They'd been rowing all night and were worn out. He felt the panic rise. He screamed and pounded the trunk of the tree with the flat of his hand and waved frantically. Rummaging in his tunic, he found a bone whistle and put it to his lips and blew: a piercing cry, like a bird of prey, the sound scratching at the clammy air. He saw one or two of the clan look up but the rest slept on, their heads wrapped in their cloaks, deaf to his yells.

Come on! Come on!

He looked back. War horses were pounding across the valley floor, black cloaks rippling, lances flashing in the sunlight. Sweet

Tiw! They're coming and we're not ready and they'll be upon us in no time.

He clambered to his feet and shouted again. In desperation, he hurled the wooden figure at the sleeping men. It bounced, and he saw men look up and then Aelfric was on his feet and staring up at him. Almost sobbing with frustration, the boy jabbed his finger at the horsemen.

'Riders!' he yelled. 'Riders coming!'

Aelfric turned towards the north. He put his head back and a moment later words came curling up. 'How many? How armed?'

'Twenty, maybe twenty five,' he screamed back. 'Well armed and riding fast.'

'Romans?'

He looked again. He supposed they might be Romans. How could you tell?

'They're well mounted,' he shouted. 'And they ride like Romans.'

Aelfric swivelled. The boy heard him bellow the war-call and, as the cry went up, he leaned back and closed his eyes, the relief washing over him. He'd done it. He'd warned the clan.

He glanced down again.

Aelfric was striding up and down, booting the men to their feet. He could hear him yelling, Come on lads! Quick now! Move your arses!

The forest floor was alive with running men. Like kicking over an ant's nest, the boy thought as he watched the Theodi grab their spears from the stacks, heft their shields and run to form a shield-wall.

He felt a quick surge of pride. Aelfric was *hetman* and war-leader of the Theodi. Each summer Aelfric took the the clan raiding, crossing the storm-tossed seas in search of loot and slaves and glory. In the boy's view, the *hetman* of the Theodi was without doubt the finest war-leader among the Saxon tribes.

He shifted his gaze back to the riders. They had left the road, riding past Samarobriva, and were coming straight for them. 'Tiw's breath,' he gasped. They know where we are!

He turned suddenly and looked back at the red smoke drifting over the town and felt a nagging doubt. Could that smoke have drawn the horsemen?

On the ground, men were still running with spears and shields. He could hear shouts, and the clank of weapons against shield bosses. The riders were streaming up the slope toward them. The boy felt a flash of resentment. He should be there with them, fighting shoulder to shoulder with his clan. But it was forbidden. He scowled and then forgot his disappointment and wondered if there would be a battle. He clenched his fists and bit his lip with excitement. Unable to bear the tension any longer, he began to climb down, one hand passing over another, horny feet gripping the scaly bark. He reached a lower bough and settled with his back to the trunk. Breathless with anxiety, he wiped the sweat from his eyes and waited to see what would happen.

On the forest floor, Aelfric of the Theodi stood with legs braced, watching the men form up. Powerfully built with a great shaggy head, he wore a studded-leather jerkin held by an ancient Roman army belt. Gold arm bands clasped his wrists and at his feet a boar-crested helmet gaped like an open maw.

'Come on, you bastards!' he shouted, slapping his thigh with impatience. 'Let's go! Let's go!'

He could see the riders now; pressing hard, no sign of flagging. The boy was right, they did ride like Romans. He grimaced. These were dangerous times. The Roman army was not what it once was, but only a fool would ignore well-armed horsemen.

And he was no fool.

Off to his right, Aelfric's kinsman, Besso, was pushing and shoving the men into line. That's the way to do it, Aelfric thought. Old hands in the front rank, beardless youngsters in the wings and rear. The men stood watching him, shield overlapping shield. Some had stripped to the waist to fight. He could see their bare chests heaving. Hear the dry rasp of their breathing. He saw them lick their lips nervously, eyes flicking to the valley, to where the horsemen could now be heard thundering up the slope.

Aelfric put back his head and breathed in deep. Fear had a smoky odour all its own, like a pot of lentils burning. Some of the clan had already pissed themselves. He could see the dark stains spreading down their breeches. But he knew they wouldn't let him down.

Craning his head, he looked for the boy up in the tree. There! A thick tangle of black hair and pale blue eyes glittering in a white and bony face. Just like his mother, Aelfric thought. The boy had seen him and waved. Always wanting to be noticed, that one. Aelfric waved back, his arm scything the air. He'd done the right thing letting him come on the raid. It was thanks to the boy, they'd not been caught unawares. Tiw! What he'd give to have such eyes!

Aelfric tightened his belt a notch. He picked up the helmet and pulled it on, fastening with thick fingers the ties under his chin. He dragged on his leather gloves and then thrust an arm through the strap and hoisted his shield. Flicking off the beaded peace-bands that held the hilt, he drew his sword, feeling the sharp thrill as the blade slipped over the sheepskin lining. She was a good sword, blue-bladed and wave-patterned with a pommel carved from the cold whiteness of wolf bone. With this sword, thirty years before, his father had killed five Huns in a single day.

Aelfric breathed in deep. He lifted the sword and brandished it above his head. The wave-blade snatched at the prickling sunlight, dazzling the men.

'Ready, lads!' he shouted. 'Up spears!'

Sixty spears rose in a dense thicket of gleaming spikes. Holding their shields over their mouths to make the sound bigger, the men roared the war cry of the northern clans.

'Oot! Oot! Oot! Oot!'

The cry boomed through the forest, rolling and echoing like thunder

Grunting with satisfaction, Aelfric turned to face the riders.

A silence fell over the forest, broken only by the dull drone of insects, and the noise of hooves drumming on the hard earth.

***

The Theodi had left their northern homeland ten days earlier. Dipping their oars in silent farewell to the huddle of onlookers on the riverbank, the *SeaWulf* casts off and slides downriver and out to the estuary. Once at sea, Aelfric sets sail for Gallia. He takes them west along the north shore and then turns south past the dreary lands of the Frisian towards the Rhine mouth. Spray in their faces and the crack of sea ropes in their ears, knifing through choppy seas, the sail swelling before a stiff breeze, running fast.

Three days later, they reach Gannuenta. A holy place, the crew tell the boy, a damp and waterlogged island on the muddy divide between land and sea, a place where men pass easily from this world to the next.

The boy stands in the bow as the boat drifts in over the shallows. He is so excited he can hardly keep still. The keel grinds over sand and gravel, and before the oars can be drawn in and the heavy sail taken down and stowed, he has leapt out and is splashing through the shallows, urging the others on.

The Theodi splash their way to the shrine, a wooded grove filled with ancient statues ankle deep in scummy water. The boy watches as his brother Hanno lays food and beer before the Goddess and asks her to look kindly on their raid. Hanno is a true believer and speaks beautifully, his arms lifted high above his head, his voice clear and strong. The boy glows with pride.

A slave is led forward and drowned. The boy runs forward to help pin the slave's body down with branches so he will not rise to torment them. After the sacrifice, the crew trade their dried fish for fresh bread and ham and eggs from the women who come each day to sell their wares to the sea-raiders. A Frisian with long arms and a slack mouth tugs at Aelfric's elbow and offers to guide them to a town in Roman Gallia which he swears, on his mother's eyes, has never been raided.

Samarobriva, the Theodi think with sly smiles, sounds ripe for looting.

Ubba the Frisian leads them south, away from the Rhine, down the coast. They reach the mouth of the Samara just before nightfall and turn inland. The boy takes his turn on the rowing benches. All through the night, he pulls on his oar, numb to the villages and forests that slide past in the night. No sound but the village dogs howling. Their backs bent under a chill and mizzling rain, the crew do not notice the young Gaul, bundled in a cloak under a tree, watching over his cattle. The herdsman is roused by the cold slap of oars. He sees a boatload of sea-wolves nosing through the mist and runs to raise the alarm.

The clanging of the church bell and the raucous eruption of the rookeries tells them they have been seen. Aelfric does what he can and runs the boat bumping into the river bank. The Theodi pour ashore and charge in a heavy-booted stampede toward Samarobriva but, by the time they emerge from the trees, the thick-timbered gates of the town are closing.

When the Theodi realize that their journey has been wasted they go wild. They scream abuse and jeer and bare their arses. The boy joins them, leaping up and down in his anger, hurling every curse he knows. On the walls of the town, stone-eyed farmers stare without emotion while above the jumble of terracotta roofs a thick plume of red smoke already smears the sky.

The boy watches as Aelfric throws his helmet on the ground and stumps up and down. Aelfric swears at the Gauls for having been too quick and his men for having been too slow. The Theodi look shamefaced. Without ladders, they cannot break into the town and they know the Gauls will never leave the safety of their walls while there are Saxon raiders about.

Aelfric orders the crew to search the surrounding farmsteads. They soon return to say that the Gauls have fled, taking their livestock with them. For a town that has never before been raided, Samarobriva was well-prepared.

The drizzle stops.

Wet grasses steam under the rising sun. Midges and horse-flies the colour of iron rise in clouds. The sky migrates from a dove grey to a deep and impossible blue. Aelfric wipes his brow with the back of his hand.

Nothing they can do.

He orders the boy up the tree as look-out. The boy gives Aelfric a grin and shins up the tree as lithe and quick as a squirrel. The Theodi cheer him on and take bets on whether he will fall and break his neck. At the top, he crooks a leg over a branch, waves to show he is up and settles back against the trunk. He scans the horizon in every direction and then takes a piece of wood from his tunic and a small knife and begins to carve.

The Theodi stack their spears and shields. They eat the last of their bread, chewing in morose silence and then they lie down in the soft shade beneath the trees, drag their cloaks over their faces.

And sleep.

***

The riders pulled up when they reached the brow of the hill and saw the Theodi waiting for them in the shield wall. Lodged in his tree, the look-out eyed them with open-mouthed fascination. The strangers' horses were enormous, far bigger than anything in the homeland. Every man carried a lance and shield, an axe in his belt and a *spatha*, the long Roman cavalry sword, at his side. They wore mail shirts or tunics of boiled leather and helmets that gleamed in the sun.

He glanced back at the Theodi. Apart from Aelfric and Besso, they went bare-headed and, while a few had long knives, most were armed only with shield and spear. Compared to the riders, they were wild and rough-looking. They outnumbered the strangers, but he knew men on foot were always ill-matched against men on horseback. If there was going to be a battle, it could go either way and he felt a jolt of anxiety at the thought that he might have to watch as his clanfolk were cut down in front of him.

The riders sat on their horses for a long while, barely moving, their horses shaking their heads and flicking their tails. Then the boy saw one of the riders kick the flanks of his horse and move forward.

Besso moved to Aelfric's side, his lumpy face encased in a battered old iron helmet.

'What are they? Romans?'

Aelfric shook his head. 'They look like Romans. But I don't think they are.'

'Think we'll have to fight?'

'I don't know,' Aelfric said.

Besso pulled a mournful face. 'Guess we'll find out soon enough,' he said.

When Aelfric looked back he saw that a horseman, a slight figure on a clean-limbed bay mare, was walking his horse towards them. Another rider, a burly man on a big thick-necked stallion, kicked his horse's ribs and followed, staying close.

As he approached, Aelfric saw that the lead rider was a young man, little more than a boy, his face angular with a long nose and a wide mouth, high-born by his clothes and weapons. He wore a mail coat and helmet and a dusty riding cloak draped over his back, pinned with a long-tailed gold brooch. Aelfric noted with envy that for all his slightness of build, the young man controlled his horse with a touch that was light and sure.

The side-rider was older, a raw-boned brute with powerful shoulders and a hard mouth. Aelfric knew a veteran when he saw one, yet he noticed the older man held back, as if deferring to his young companion.

The riders stopped, and there was an uneasy silence.

The mare shook her head, jangled her bridle and sighed.

'We are of one blood,' the young man said politely.

The dialect was ugly, the voice thin and reedy, but the stranger spoke with confidence employing the formal greeting of the Germanic peoples. Not Roman then, although Aelfric knew that meant little. The Romans often hired *barbari* to guard their frontiers.

8

'We are of one blood,' Aelfric growled. 'Who are you and what do you want?'

The young man smiled.

'We are Franks, known as the Salt-People,' he said. 'We serve Lord Childeric, Overlord of the Franks.'

His horse dropped her head and began to crop.

Aelfric knew the Franks of old. A southern tribe who had done well from their closeness to the Romans. The Salt-People lived at the Rhine mouth while their kin-tribe, the River-Franks lived upriver. As the Romans had grown weaker, Childeric's Franks had grown stronger, wasting no time in grabbing what they could of Roman Gallia. Even the Theodi knew of Childeric as a bloody and slaughterous war leader.

The young Frank gazed at them, as if unperturbed by their silence. 'Who leads here?' he said mildly.

Aelfric felt a twinge of unease, unsettled to be addressed so coolly by a mere boy. 'I am Aelfric, *hetman* and war-leader of the Theodi Saxons,' he said. 'This is my captain, Besso.'

The young Frank smiled as if the names were familiar to him.

'What do you want, Frank?' Aelfric said curtly.

The boy smiled again. 'Childeric wishes to speak with you,' he said. 'We came to take you to his hall in Tornacum.'

Besso let out a soft gasp. Aelfric frowned. What did Childeric want with him, and who was this boy to tell him, Aelfric of the Theodi, what to do?

The young Frank seemed to sense Aelfric's distrust. 'You would be Childeric's honoured guest,' he said smoothly. 'And of course, your safety is assured. But so you may meet with confidence, I will stay here as hostage until you return. And as you do not appear to have a horse,' he looked pointedly around the forest clearing, 'you may take mine.' He gestured to the big Frank at his side, 'Bauto here will accompany you. But you must leave now. It is a long ride to Tornacum.'

Aelfric saw the shock on Besso's face. No Theod would dare talk to Aelfric that way. The Frank seemed unabashed. He stared at Aelfric, his expression combining a haughty authority mingled with defiance. But there was something more behind those pink cheeks, a touch of cruelty that suggested to Aelfric that this boy was more than he seemed.

Aelfric rubbed his chin with the back of his fist. He was flattered that the Overlord of the Franks wanted to meet him, but had no wish to ride into his lair alone. Yet if he refused the boy's offer he would look a coward. He leaned over and muttered in Besso's ear.

Besso cleared his throat and took a step forward. 'We thank you for your offer. It is most kind,' he said in rich and formal tones. 'We have heard of the Lord Childeric. It is a great honour for my Lord Aelfric to be invited to talk with him.'

The boy nodded, but his eyes never left Aelfric.

'But you should know that among my people, Aelfric is a great war leader,' Besso went on. 'In the northlands he is far-famed. He has hewn limbs and split helms and wielded the wave-sword against our enemies more times than there are hairs on my head.' Besso stroked his thinning hair with the flat of his hand. 'If we are to take a hostage for Aelfric, we must have a warrior of equal rank.'

Besso lowered his voice so that only Aelfric and the two Franks could hear. 'You may be high-born, you arrogant little Frankish shit,' he said, his voice dripping with contempt, 'but you're no more than a boy.' He raised his plump hand and gave a delicate, almost feminine, little flutter in the Frank's direction. 'Come back in a few years, when you're a man, huh?'

With a broad wink at Aelfric, Besso turned and stepped back.

The big Frank swore, his face dark with surprised anger, but Aelfric had eyes only for the boy. He watched as the young Frank struggled to contain his fury. Dipping his head in ironic acknowledgement of the insult, the youth gave Besso a thin and bloodless smile and then turned to Aelfric.

'Aelfric is a great warrior, a noble ring-giver, the most generous of men,' he said softly. 'I meant no disrespect.'

Aelfric waited. Smooth as honey, he thought, but where's the sting?

The Frank looked at him. 'But there is something you should know. My name is Chlodwig, known to the Gauls as Clovis, and I am the son of Childeric, Overlord of the Franks.' He paused and then said, 'And my father is not accustomed to being kept waiting.'

Aelfric pulled at his earlobe. This was different, not at all what he had expected.

'Bring Ubba!' he whispered in Besso's ear.

The look-out shifted his cramped limbs. He watched, not understanding, as Besso walked back to the shield wall and returned with the Frisian guide. By his walk, the boy could tell that the Frisian guide was nervous and seemed reluctant to be drawn from the safety of the shield wall.

When the big rider saw the Frisian, he let out a roar of rage. His fist fell to the hilt of his *spatha,* and he jerked his reins, forcing his horse back. Alarmed shouts rose among the riders, and the line of Saxon spears lurched forward.

The look-out held his breath. He saw Aelfric lift a calming hand and the young rider speak sharp words to the older rider. The boy couldn't hear what was said but the older man seemed to bite his tongue, leaning over his pommel and glowering at Ubba. Bad blood there, the look-out thought. Maybe the strangers don't like Frisians guiding Saxon war bands into Roman Gallia.

Aelfric bent his head and spoke to the Frisian. Ubba looked at the foreigners and nodded. Aelfric spoke to Besso and then seemed to come to a decision. He spoke to the young rider who swung his leg over his horse's neck and slid to the ground and held out the reins to Aelfric. Ascha saw Aelfric take them and then hesitate. The boy shook his head. Everybody knew the *hetman* of the Theodi was a poor rider and uncomfortable on horseback.

The young stranger clapped his hands. At once one of the horsemen spurred up the slope, hurriedly dismounted and knelt on all fours. As the look-out watched, leaning so far out of the tree he almost fell, Aelfric stepped on the man's back and clambered clumsily onto the horse and grabbed wildly at the reins. The big foreigner shouted an order, and the strangers wheeled and rode away leaving the young stranger behind.

The boy watched as the horsemen trotted down the valley, Aelfric bobbing in their midst like a bark on a rough sea. They turned onto the Roman road and went north. The boy followed them with his eyes until they were little more than a dark smudge on the horizon. He felt troubled by what he had just seen, without fully understanding why.

Who were those people, he wondered.

And where were they taking his father now?

2

When Aelfric and the Franks had gone, Clovis the Frank unpinned his cloak and carefully spread it on the dry grass. He unbuckled his sword belt, let it fall and then pulled the helmet from his head, revealing a thick thatch of straw-coloured hair. He placed his sword and helmet neatly side by side on the cloak and then lay down, folded his arms behind his head and closed his eyes.

Besso stood for a while, scratching the bristles on his chin and watching the young Frank, as if lost in thought. He wasn't sure what had just happened, but he was afraid that Aelfric had done something very stupid and they were never going to see him again. He ordered the Theodi to disband and then heaved his belt up over his belly and ambled over towards Clovis. Bending down, he put his face very close to that of the young Frank.

'Make yourself comfortable, my fine Lord,' he said. 'But if you do not return Aelfric to us by this time tomorrow, I promise you by Tiw's holy breath that I will stick those skinny feet of yours into a bonfire and I will burn them to the bone.'

Clovis opened his eyes. He looked up at Besso and gave him a cold smile.

'Of course you will, Besso,' he said softly. 'That's what hostages are for.'

The look-out had heard only snatches of what had passed between the Theodi and the horsemen, but he had seen his father ride away and he realized that the young foreigner had stayed with the Theodi as hostage for Aelfric's life. Passing a rope around the trunk, he half-slid, half-climbed down the tree and then dropped. He landed heavily and fell in an untidy sprawl, his legs numb from the time spent aloft.

He sat and chafed his limbs back to life and then got to his feet, enjoying the prickle of grass under his feet. He found his carving and shoved it in his tunic, gasping as the heat closed in around him. Looking back up the tree, he felt a quick pang of regret. As look-out, every man's life had depended on him, but here on the ground, he was nobody again. Yet he had shown what he could do and that was something they could not take away from him. But now he was desperate to find out what had happened. Who were the horsemen? Where had they taken Aelfric, and who was the young man they had left behind as hostage?

He looked about him.

Beams of sunshine filtered through the trees creating pools of light on the forest floor. The shield-wall had broken up and dispersed. Now the danger was over, the Theodi seemed to be in a boisterous mood. They wrestled and joked, and Ascha could hear them bragging about how bravely they would have fought if only the horsemen had dared to attack.

He was not so sure.

The strangers had seemed had come on boldly and had not been afraid of the Theodi shield wall. He suspected that, against the Theodi, their big horses and slashing long swords would have caused havoc.

He saw Besso, sitting on a log munching an apple and went to join him. Besso looked up as he approached and waved. The boy could see that the apple was mostly rotten, but Besso did not seem to care. He was a big man with a solid neck and a long face who was known to eat almost anything without getting the flux.

'Ha! Ascha. Tha did well, lad,' Besso said in the dialect of the north shore. 'Thi warning meant we were ready for them, although how tha managed to stay awake, let alone see them, I don't know. Does tha want an apple?'

Ascha smiled, delighted that what he had achieved had been noticed, and then spoke quickly, the words tumbling out. 'Besso, who they were and what did they want? And where they have taken my father?'

'Steady on!' said Besso. 'And I'll tell tha everything.'

Between mouthfuls of browned fruit, Besso explained what had happened. The riders were Franks, he said, and were far from where Besso would have expected them to be. Aelfric had gone to speak with the Overlord of the Franks. Besso spoke slowly and solemnly, as was his way.

Ascha bit his tongue and waited as patiently as he could until Besso had finished.

'But why does the Overlord of the Franks want to talk to my father?'

Besso sighed. 'It's always questions with tha, isn't it?'

Ascha stared. Of course, he asked questions. How else could you learn?'

'Well, it's a funny thing,' Besso said heavily, 'but just this once the Overlord of the Franks forgot to take me into his confidence.'

He looked up at Ascha and winked.

Ascha sighed. He hated not knowing what was going on.

'Will my father be all right?'

'Course he will,' Besso said.

'What will tha do now?'

'Wait for Aelfric's return,' Besso said, 'It's all we can do.' He gestured with his apple toward Samarobriva. 'Them Gauls won't pay tribute now they're safe behind them gates. The men are hungry, but I can't send them out to look for food when there are horse Franks abroad. They'd pick them off like flies.' Besso suddenly slapped a hand against his jaw and studied the tiny corpse in his palm. 'I have a bad feeling about this. If it was down to me, I wouldn't be happy until we're at sea again and I can feel the ocean kicking under my keel.'

Ascha sighed with exasperation. Besso was never one to shake the tree if he could avoid it. The Theodi had just seen off a Frankish war band, his father had been taken, and all Besso could think of was getting out.

'And him?' Ascha said, turning to the sleeping Frank. 'What is he?'

Besso blew out a pip. 'Says his name is Chlodwig or Clovis, son of Childeric, which makes him a prince, I suppose. Ubba said he was who he said he was, so Aelfric went with them.' Besso put on the slightly astonished look he wore when people acted differently to what he thought wise. 'I told him he were mad, but tha knows what thi father's like when his mind's made up.'

Ascha looked at his uncle and then at the Frank.

'I want to talk to him.'

'Talk to him, why?'

Ascha wasn't sure why. He was curious and realized that he was also a little envious. The Frank was the son of an Overlord, and Ascha couldn't help but notice how self-assured he had seemed a short while ago. The Frank had ridden up to the Saxon shield-wall completely without fear. Ascha shrugged and said, 'No reason.'

Besso gave him a baffled look and then said, 'Go ahead, but watch thi step. There's more to that one than meets the eye.'

14

The stranger lay on his side and seemed to be asleep, eyes closed, one arm folded beneath his head, thin lips pressed together. An armed guard stood nearby. Ascha ran his eyes over the Frank with a mix of awe and fascination. They were about the same age, the Frank maybe a little younger. He was tall and lean; clean and seemed untroubled by the heat. Ascha noticed that he wore his hair loose to his shoulders, not greased and coiled on top of his head as the Theodi and other Saxons did. His tunic was in a fine and closely-woven material, dyed black, and his helmet and chain mail looked as if they had been made for him. Both had been sand-scrubbed until they gleamed. His sword alone was worth a fortune, the hilt heavily decorated with a rich red metal, framed in gold.

But it was the stranger's boots which struck Ascha most. They were made of soft doeskin, finely stitched and hobnailed, the tops rolled over to show a lining of badger fur. Silver spurs at each heel. Ascha felt a sluggish swell of jealousy pass through him. In the homeland, men would kill for boots like those. Plain to see, this Frank had never had to struggle.

Filled with a sudden anger, he kicked the Frank on the foot. 'Chlodwig, son of Childeric?'

The Frank opened one eye and studied him. 'Ah, the look-out,' he said in a flat and drawling voice. 'And in these parts, I am known as Clovis.'

Ascha was shocked. He realized that Chlodwig or Clovis or whatever he called himself had not been asleep and had been watching the Theodi all along. He would have seen the Theodi fooling in the sun and had listened to what they were saying. He would have seen Ascha come down from the trees and would have known it was he who had had warned the Theodi of the Franks approach. He experienced a vague sense of unease, as if caught doing something he shouldn't.

'What does your father want with Aelfric?' he said.

The Frank sat up and hugged his knees. 'Who wants to know?'

He spoke with a thick Frankish dialect, but Ascha could understand him well enough. For a moment, Ascha considered not telling him, and then said, 'I am Ascha, Saxon of the Theodi clan.'

The Frank looked him up and down. 'You're a Saxon?' he said with surprise in his voice.

'Of course.'

'You don't look much like a Saxon,' Clovis said bluntly.

'Well, I am!' Ascha said.

He was stocky and broad-shouldered, but with his black hair and blue eyes he knew he did not look Saxon. He tightened his jaw, annoyed that the Frank had already succeeded in getting the edge over him.

Behind the Frank, he saw his brother Hroc coming across the clearing, angling towards him. Hroc was the younger of his two half-brothers. He was older than Ascha and had, so Besso always said, his mother's wheaten hair, his father's temper and a cruel side that was all his own. Between Hroc and Ascha there was a raw and mutual dislike, neither knew how it had started and neither cared. It had just always been there. Ascha hated and loathed his brother Hroc almost as much as he adored his elder brother, Hanno. And Hroc equally despised Ascha, never letting Ascha forget that he was younger and of lower rank.

Ascha scowled. Talking to the Frankish prince had been his idea, and he had no wish to share him, least of all with Hroc.

'What does your father want with Aelfric?' he repeated.

Clovis got to his feet, rising in one sinuous movement. The Frank, Ascha saw with dismay, was taller than him by at least a head. Clovis put his fists in the small of his back, closed his eyes and stretched like a cat.

'Why do you care?' Clovis said. 'He is your warlord and makes his own decisions.'

'Because Aelfric is my father,' Ascha said softly.

The Frank paused in mid-stretch, and Ascha noted with huge satisfaction the look of astonishment on the Frank's face. 'Your father is Aelfric, the *hetman* of the Theodi?'

'He is.'

'And your mother?'

Ascha was not prepared for the question. 'What business is it of yours who my mother is?' he said with a sudden burst of anger.

Hroc had come up behind Clovis. He stood with his hands on his hips, leaning forward slightly. Big-bodied and thick with muscle, Hroc wore a *seaxe,* the long knife worn by all freeborn Saxons, stuffed into his belt and carried an axe by a braided leather cord around his neck. Seeing him, Ascha felt uneasy. His brother had a belly-hatred of all foreigners. Saxons were the only people he trusted, and then only so far.

The Frank continued as if unaware that Hroc stood behind him. He swept his arm in a wide arc across the landscape. 'All these are Childeric's lands!' he said in his languid drawl.

16

On the voyage down, Ascha had plagued Besso and Hanno with questions about previous raids they had been on in Gallia. Now, he struggled to remember what they had told him. 'Not so!' he said. 'These are Roman lands. They are open to all'.

The Frank gave him a thin and superior smile. 'They were Roman,' he agreed. 'But Romans no longer rule here. These are our lands. Raid here and you steal from us.'

Hroc stepped forward and pulled on the Frank's arm, spinning him round. 'Tha's lying!' he said. 'Frank land is to the north. This land is Roman, and northerners have raided here for generations.'

'Not anymore,' Clovis said. Taller than Hroc, he held Hroc's glare with bleak indifference. 'They now belong to us. We protect this territory.'

'And if we pay no heed?' Hroc snarled.

Clovis smiled again. 'Ah, that would not be wise.'

'Not wise?' Hroc moved closer. 'And what will you do to stop us, you little turd? The Theodi have raided here for generations. We sail the whale's road and nobody stops us. When we find what we want, we take it.'

Clansmen were beginning to wander over, drawn to the raised voices. Alarmed, Ascha scanned the clearing. Things were getting out of hand. Hroc was spoiling for a fight. Ascha recognized the signs. His first instinct was to leave them to it. What did he care if Hroc slugged it out with the arrogant Frank, but he knew a fight would put his father's life in danger? If Hroc killed or injured Clovis, the Franks would take revenge on Aelfric. They would send men to stop the *SeaWulf* sailing downriver, and the Theodi would die here.

'Come away, Hroc,' he said, laying a hand on his brother's arm. 'Tha doesn't need this.'

Hroc shook him off. 'Go take a piss, little brother. This do not concern tha.'

Anxiously, Ascha searched for the guard but the man had slipped away as soon as he saw Hroc approach. And where was Besso? He was the only one who could restrain Hroc when he was riled.

'You are outsiders,' Ascha heard Clovis say in a grating voice, 'and we will destroy you as we have destroyed all northerners who raid our shores.'

Ascha couldn't help but notice that Clovis had a smile on his lips and his eyes were shining. Ascha stared at him in astonishment. Was the boy mad? Did he have no idea what he was doing? Hroc had been known to knock down an ox with a single blow of his fist and leave it stretched with blood streaming from its ears. But Clovis seemed unaware of the danger he was in. Either that or he was playing some kind of game with Hroc, seeing how far he could push him. But this was a game that could easily spin out of control.

'We raid where we choose,' Hroc roared, spittle flying. 'And we give way to nobody.' He poked Clovis in the chest as if to emphasize each word. 'And...never...to...a... pox-ridden...Frank!'

Years later, when Ascha looked back on the events of that day, it occurred to him that it was the chest jabbing that had done it. Clovis always hated being touched, especially by men like Hroc who he considered lower than an animal. As Hroc went to raise his fist once again, Clovis, his face pale, swatted Hroc's arm away.

'We own these lands,' he said, making no attempt to hide the scorn in his voice. 'So go back to your filthy marshes and eat frogs or fuck your sisters or do whatever it is you bog-folk do. There is nothing for you here. Do you understand, you Saxon prick? Nothing!'

Silence.

Hroc let out a terrifying scream of rage. An axe appeared in Hroc's fist, and Ascha saw the heavy blade arcing down towards the Frank's bare head. Without thinking, he flung himself forward. Ramming into Hroc, he wrapped both arms around his brother's barrelled chest and drove on with all his strength. The force of the rush hit Hroc like a sail-boom, knocking him sideways and hurling them both to the ground with a bone-jarring crash. Somehow, Ascha twisted as he fell and Hroc's crushing weight rolled into him driving the breath from his body in one *whooof* of exploding air. There was a sharp stab of pain as his collarbone gave way and then a tumult of yells. Somewhere far off he heard Besso bellowing. The world was spinning, a dizzy whirlpool of legs and faces and trees and sky. Hroc's face, warped with rage, rose above him. Ascha saw his brother's arm swing back, saw the fist coming and felt a massive blow to the side of his head. There were flashes behind his eyes and a dull roar like an undertow in his head.

And then the darkness slid over him.

***

Ascha's homeland is made up of limitless marshes, wide rivers and mewing gulls. It is bounded by ocean to the north and woods to the south and scattered with *terpen*, the mounds on which the Theodi build their homes to keep them safe from the storm-floods. Dykes hold back the sea, criss-crossing the fields like runes scratched on antler bone.

The Theodi are not a large clan – two hundred and fifty people, all tied by blood and bone – but they know who they are. Long ago they migrated from the Almost-Island and settled between the two rivers. They became guardians of the *hearg*, the sacred pool that lies on their land, and are known by the other north shore folk as the shrine people. The Theodi are proud of their past, and every child is taught the story before they can walk.

The clan fish and they farm. They make salt in the salt-pans and they trade with the summer-traders. Every year the women pack the men off to raid, Gaul usually, sometimes Hispania, or the damp islands, Pritannia or Hibernia. They sail across the ocean and follow the rivers, penetrating deep inland. They fall on isolated villages, loot and slaughter and take their plunder home. Raiding gives meaning to a hard life and provides food and warmth when the rivers freeze and birds fall dead from the sky.

The Theodi view the Pritanni and the Gauls, nations who have allowed themselves to be conquered by the Romans, as weak and wealthy. The clan's northern neighbours – Saxons, Danes, Frisians, Svea, Jutes and Engle – are considered near-kin and are rarely raided. To the east are primitives who worship snakes and live in holes scratched in the earth. These, the Theodi regard as too poor to raid and are left alone.

Ascha grows up as tough as a weed. He has his slave-mother's pale skin and crow-black hair, also her sharpness and strength of mind. But among the Theodi, his broad shoulders, big hands and startling blue eyes mark him as a son of Aelfric.

When he is ten, his brother Hroc takes *waepndag*, the spear-giving festival which marks a boy's passage from child to man. Before a crowd of family and friends, all packed in like salted herrings, the boys line up in Aelfric's great hall. Ascha pushes and shoves his way to the front. As if in a trance, he watches as Hroc and the other boys lay their right hand on the sacred bundle and swear that they will be loyal to Aelfric and the clan.

'In the eyes of Tiw and of this clan, you are now men,' Aelfric says gruffly. 'With this spear and this shield you become whole, a warrior and a free man. From this day forward, the lives of our women and our children will depend on your courage. Remember this for as long as you shall live.'

As the women chant the weapon-song, Aelfric presents each boy with a new spear and shield. The men clash their weapons against their shields, the mothers sniffle happily and Hroc's grin stretches from ear to ear.

Ascha thinks it is the most exciting day a boy can have.

When Hroc comes to bed that night the fire is a dull orange glow, and the floor is thick with sleeping revellers. Hroc thumps Ascha awake. He is drunk and wants to talk. 'I'm a man now, little frog, and tha must treat me wi' respect.'

Hroc talks of what he will do now that he is weaponed. Ascha listens for as long as he can. When his eyelids droop, Hroc kicks him and tugs the blanket away. Unable to bear the cold any longer, Ascha gets up and goes down the hall to where the slaves sleep. He clambers over Tchenguiz, his father's Hun slave, and lies down beside him in the straw.

All that night, Ascha lies awake, thinking.

The next day Ascha goes to where his father sits by the door, his head in his hands, recovering from the drinking of the night before. He waits until Aelfric looks up at him with bleary eyes and then says, 'When will I be given a shield and weapons like my brothers?'

His father looks at him. 'Don't be stupid, boy,' he says. 'How can tha be given a shield?'

'Why not? Hroc and Hanno are weaponed.'

'They are freeborn,' Aelfric says stonily.

'But I am thi son, as are they. We are all of thi blood.'

Aelfric's eyes bore into his. 'Tha's of my blood, but thi mother is a slave,' he says, speaking slowly as if Ascha were deaf or stupid. 'Tha's half-free, a half-slave. Tha can niver carry weapons or a shield. The right to bear arms is denied those who are not free born.'

Ascha stares at his father. His eyes burn and his throat swells. He begins to realize what he has suspected for a long time. He is not and never will be the equal of his brothers. Although the son of the *hetman*, he is slave-born and will never have a spear-giving like Hanno and Hroc. He is a half-slave, trapped in the murky borderland between slave and free.

'But if I am not weaponed, I cannot be whole,' Ascha says, feeling the panic rise. 'I cannot own land. I cannot marry who I choose. I will always be less than my brothers. I have no future.'

His father shrugs. 'It's the law,' he says, rubbing his chin. 'Nothing I can do about it.'

'But you are *hetman*,' Ascha insists. 'Tha can do anything!'

The muscles in Aelfric's jaw tighten. 'Tha is what tha is,' he says. 'And that's the end of it.'

Ascha shakes his head, tossing out his father's words as if they were water in his ears. He feels cheated, as if something precious has suddenly been stolen from him. 'I am thi son!' he screams. 'But without a weapon, I am nothing!'

Aelfric makes as if to leave.

Ascha grabs his father's arm and hauls him round. 'What kind of father does this to his son?' he shouts. 'Tiw's breath! What kind of man is tha?'

Aelfric's fist catches Ascha below the ear and hurls him across the room. He blinks and shakes his head and then gets to his feet and rushes his father, arms flailing. Aelfric takes a step back and hits him again, a hard slap across the face. Ascha flies across the floor and hits the wall with a dull thump.

'Stay down, boy,' Aelfric says, glowering. 'Stay down if tha knows what's good for tha.'

Ascha scrambles to his feet and stands there, chest heaving. His mother comes running. She sees the two of them glaring at each other with murder in their hearts, and her hand flies to her mouth. She screams, a wail of fury and fear, and throws herself between them.

Aelfric stands clenching and unclenching his fists. He points to Ascha but speaks to her, his face flushed with anger. 'Tha should've taught him to accept what he is,' he growls. 'He is not free-born and niver will be. Best he learns that now before it's too late.'

Sobbing with rage, Ascha would have flung himself again at his father, but his mother wraps her arms around him, holds him tight and gives his shoulder a hard squeeze. 'No, Ascha!' she says.

He bites his lower lip but makes no further move.

His mother closes her eyes and opens them again. She turns to Aelfric and in a bleak whisper she says, 'If you ever lay a finger on my son again, as God is my witness, I will kill you and everything you hold dear!'

21

Aelfric's face passes from fury to bewilderment and something else. He sighs, blows air from his lungs and lets his fists drop to his side 'Ach, woman,' he says, shaking his head. 'Sometimes tha pushes me too far and one of these days tha'll regret it.'

And he turns and leaves.

Ascha angrily pushes his mother away. He touches his cheek. There is a burning feeling in his jaw and a taste of iron in his mouth. He is ashamed because she has saved him from a beating. He is surprised to see that she is trembling. Her eyes are bright and her mouth is open and she is panting slightly. He touches her briefly on the arm and leaves.

***

When Ascha came to he was lying on the grass under a small leather tent, his head resting on his own rolled short-cloak. There was a foul and sticky taste in his mouth, and his head throbbed. For a moment he did not know where he was and then he remembered Hroc and the young Frank and he groaned.

The sunlight streaming into the tent told him it was long past daybreak. Flies circled and droned. The air in the tent was stale, heavy and hard to breathe.

He lifted a hand and gasped as the pain hit him, a blunt ache that began at his cheek, ran along his jaw and down his neck.

'Tha's awake, little brother?'

A face appeared at the end of the tent, rimmed in sunshine. Hanno, Ascha's elder brother, was tall and lean with yellow hair and an easy smile. He was a poet and a warrior, everything Ascha admired in a man.

Hanno came in and sat down, folding his long legs beneath him. Despite the oppressive heat, he looked as fresh as a daisy. He pulled out a flask and offered it to Ascha with a giant smile. Ascha took it, pulled the bung with his teeth and upended the flask. The water was cold and fresh, and he drank greedily.

He blinked and peered at Hanno with gummy eyes.

'What happened?' he mumbled, the pain rolling over him in a bone-softening, swell.

Hanno gave a dry laugh. 'Tha stopped Hroc from cracking that Frank's skull and avoided a bloodbath. That's what happened.'

Ascha groaned. 'Where's father?'

'He's back and is well.'

'And Hroc?'

'Kicking his heels in the forest somewhere,' Hanno grinned. 'We were lucky. If Hroc had killed that Frank, they would have slaughtered us all before we reached the river mouth.' Hanno gave Ascha a vacant smile. 'Odd thing is, he blames tha. He thinks tha humiliated him in front of the clan.'

Hanno laughed suddenly and slapped his thigh.

Ascha thought Hanno had everything a man could want: high rank, good looks and the lazy charm that women adored, but he often found his brother's easy-going nature irritating. For all his viciousness, Hroc knew what he wanted and fought to get it.

Ascha tried to sit up but groaned once again as the pain hit.

'Easy, now,' Hanno chuckled. 'Tha took it on the jaw and probably cracked a rib or two when tha fell. Besso thinks thi shoulder may be broken. It will mend soon enough and is unlikely to ruin your chances with that girl of yours back home.'

Ascha missed Saefaru more than he cared to admit. He would give anything to have her here by his side. He snuffled the air. He could smell the thick red-black aroma of roast meat.

'I'm hungry,' he said, closing his eyes. 'Is there any food?'

***

Ascha spends his last evening before the *SeaWulf* sails with Saefaru. They sit together on the riverside and watch as the *SeaWulf* is turned, ready for the morning tide. It was he who carved the prow, a long-necked dragon with gaping jaws and wild eyes, a hard ridged spine and flared nostrils. He is proud that his prow dragon will lead them to Gallia and bring them home again. He will sleep under the stars, he will hear the crash of spears on shields. There will be plunder and comradeship, a chance to make his father proud of him.

'Will you miss me?' Saefaru says, poking a finger between his ribs.

She asks him the same question whenever they meet. Since spring, their feelings for each other have turned from friendship into something more, although nothing that either of them could put a name to. Her father disapproves, thinking Ascha is unworthy, but Saefaru takes no notice and Ascha loves her for it. He likes being with her. She is warm, high-spirited and good to be with. She draws him out of himself and makes him laugh. When he is with her he feels complete, less of an outsider.

Saefaru is on her feet, pulling him up, urgent now. 'Come, Ascha,' she says. 'Quickly.'

Off to the west the sun is dropping below the horizon, the sky going from purple to the colour of pewter. He goes with Saefaru, her slim hand in his, back into the soft darkness.

3

Ascha slept and half-slept. It was mid-afternoon when he opened his eyes again. His shoulder and jaw were still throbbing, but the pain was less. He sat up. The air in the tent was stifling, as if someone was kneeling on his chest. On the grass beside him lay a plate of greasy meat, speckled with flies.

He ate quickly, stuffing the food into his mouth and wiping away the grease with the back of his hand. Then he got to his feet and went outside.

He breathed in and was immediately struck by the silence.

Across the clearing the Theodi were ranged in a half circle before his father. Aelfric stood with his feet planted firmly in the dust and seemed to be addressing them. Besso, Hroc and Hanno were by his side. The young Frank, Clovis, sat on a log, chewing a thumb nail and fidgeting. He seemed unhurt. Every so often, he looked up and listened with a bored expression before returning to his thumb. Behind him stood the big Frank wearing full war gear and a watchful expression. Plain he had no intention of letting his young master out of his sight again.

The Franks were some way off. They had dismounted and laid down their spears and stood loosely, talking among themselves. A pack mule stood blinking in the shade under the trees. It carried two small iron-bound chests on side-cradles. Ascha gazed around him in wonder. The hostility between the Saxons and the Franks seemed to have burnt off like a midsummer mist. Something significant had happened while he was sleeping and he was furious that he had missed it.

There was a sudden shout and the harsh clang of iron on iron. Spears rattled against shield bosses. Birds rose and wheeled above the trees. The Franks looked up. The Theodi, it seemed, had come to an agreement.

Ascha crossed the clearing and pushed through a shoal of bodies to the front. The men seemed in high spirits, and he guessed the meeting had gone well. They turned and nudged each other to let him through.

A Theod gave him a half-smile, pulled a long face and shook his head.

'What?' Ascha said.

'Nothing,' the man muttered and looked away.

Ascha felt unnerved. His jaw was throbbing and the pain in his upper body had returned. He could only guess what he looked like. Shoulders hunched and arms crossed, a welt on one cheek, skin grey with pain.

Aelfric and Besso looked up. Ascha was shocked to see how weary his father looked. Aelfric seemed drained, his expression resigned. He stared at Ascha and then turned and with half-closed eyes said something to Besso. Besso came and took Ascha by the elbow and pulled him to one side.

'Besso, what's going on?'

'Thi father says the Franks want a pact,' Besso said. 'He says they will give us silver if we go home and agree not to raid Gallia.'

'The Franks will give us silver not to raid?'

'Roman silver, all hacked and ready for sharing.' Besso nodded towards the mules.

Ascha let out a low whistle. So that was what had put such stupid grins on their faces. He thought for a moment. 'And does Aelfric want this?'

Besso nodded. 'He said the Franks are too powerful. This way we take their treasure without a fight.'

Ascha fumed. How could he have slept through this? The Franks were going to pay them to go away?

'And if we don't accept.'

Besso shrugged his shoulders, 'We've already agreed. It's done. The Theodi are now allies of the Franks.' He put his head back and laughed, exposing blackened teeth.

'What do we do now?'

'We take the Franks' silver and go home,' Besso said. He paused. 'Thi brother, Hroc, and others were against the pact. They thought we should not tie ourselves to the Franks, but thi father and most of us thought it was a good offer and we should accept. Aelfric said the Franks now own this land. They are working with the Romans and if we hadn't accepted, the Franks would destroy us.'

Ascha tried to make sense of it all. He knew Hroc hated the Romans and the Franks and would have seen the alliance as a trick. He was sure that Hroc would have preferred to take the war-road, but with chests of Roman silver in plain view, he'd been easily overrruled. But what really shocked him was the realization that the Franks were now working with the Romans. And the Franks seemed to have the upper hand. That, he realized, was why they had helped the Gauls in Samarobriva. All his life he'd heard stories of how powerful the Romans were. But now the Romans' strength was waning and the Franks were taking over. Ascha had a feeling of being on the edge of great change and the young Frank, Clovis, was right at the heart of it.

'But if not Gallia, where will we raid?' Ascha said. The Theodi had raided Gallia for as long as he could remember.

Besso shrugged. 'Pritannia,' he said. 'Where else?'

Pritannia! His mother's country, a hard voyage, beyond land-sight. Lose your bearings and you might find yourself adrift in a rimless sea. He shuddered.

A sudden bellow from the front. 'I would address this assembly!'

The voice was unfamiliar. Men bent their heads to see who spoke. When they saw it was the big Frank with the red face, there was a murmur of surprise and then silence.

'I am Bauto, Commander of my Lord Childeric's royal guard,' the big Frank said. 'I am happy there is now a pact between our peoples.'

Besso scratched his beard and rolled his eyes at Ascha. Odd to think of the grim Frank as ever being happy.

Bauto went on, his voice a low growl. 'But before this pact becomes law, there is one thing we must resolve.' He paused and then turned and spoke directly to Aelfric, 'We demand one of your sons as hostage, to join us and fight alongside us for as long as there is a peace between our nations, his life to be forfeit should this pact be broken.'

Stunned, Ascha whirled on Besso, 'Is he right?' he said. 'Can they ask such a thing?'

'They have the right,' Besso said sourly. 'How else can they be sure we will keep our side of the deal?'

Ascha looked at him aghast. They were going to send away one of his brothers to live among strangers? He swivelled. Hanno stood next to Aelfric, tall as a sapling, his handsome face framed by two thick braids of yellow hair. Hroc stood apart. He had that surly look about him that Ascha knew so well, chin up and lips clamped tight.

'Who will my father choose? Hanno or Hroc?' he whispered, hoping with all his heart it would be Hroc.

Besso turned and spat into the dust. 'Hanno is first-born and will be *hetman* when your father dies. Your father will choose Hroc,' he said solemnly.

Ascha breathed out with relief. He felt a quiet satisfaction that Hroc and not Hanno would go. Serve him right, he thought, for all those years Hroc had made his life a misery.

'Does he know?' Ascha said, but Besso didn't answer.

A man elbowed Ascha in the ribs. 'Tush! It's thi father's turn to speak.'

Aelfric took a step forward. He stood with his head bowed, rubbing the back of his neck with his hand.

'I have two sons.' Aelfric said, in a voice so quiet the men at the back struggled to hear. 'They are fine men, good fighters. I am proud of them both.'

He paused and examined something in the dry grass with his toe.

The crowd waited.

'Hanno is my first-born and will succeed me when the black raven comes for me. He has a wife and children.' A southerly breeze filled the treetops and rustled through the grasses, promising relief from the heat. The men stood without moving, a hard business to watch a man choose between his sons.

Ascha studied his brothers. Hanno seemed detached, as if unable to believe that he could suffer at his father's hands. Hroc managed somehow to look angry and puzzled at the same time. He glared at Clovis and Bauto with eyes that were hard and bright. His fists, Ascha saw, were clenched.

'Hroc is my second-born,' Aelfric went on. 'He is a great fighter and if Hanno dies in battle, he will become *hetman*. He has no family of his own.' Hroc's brows knitted together. He tugged on his beard and frowned. 'Hroc will go with you as hostage,' he said. 'He will fight alongside you and learn your ways. Hroc will uphold the honour of the Theodi.'

A pent up sigh escaped from the Theodi and then all eyes cut to Hroc. A look of unspeakable horror had passed over Hroc's face, and it was plain to all that Hroc had assumed that it would be Hanno who went as hostage. Ascha watched Hroc struggle to come to terms with his father's decision. He stood pale with fury, his knuckles clenched.

'No!' he said. 'Tha's my ring-giver, my own father. I will be loyal to tha in all things but I will not do this. I will not go with these people as hostage.'

The air was thick with silence and then the crowd erupted. They cheered and shouted and stomped their feet with approval.

For a moment, Aelfric seemed stunned. His jaw gaped, and he seemed uncertain how to react. Then his head snapped back. 'Tha's my son and tha owes me loyalty,' he roared, his face reddening. 'Tha will do as I say. Tha will go with them!'

Hroc furrowed his brow and shook his head. 'This pact is a bad business. I am not a slave to be told by the Franks where I may and may not go. I will not rot my life away in Frankland. I would sooner die.'

The Theodi went mad.

They hammered their spears against their shield bosses. Whooped and laughed. Ah, this was how a warrior spoke. Ascha watched in astonishment as the mood of the clan changed. Besso always said that the assembly brought out the best and the worst in men. But behind the yells of those supporting Hroc, he heard the angry shouts of those who felt threatened by Hroc's breach of trust. Without a high-born son to underpin the exchange there would be no alliance. No booty.

Men hurled abuse. One Theod took a swing at another. Things were turning ugly. Ascha backed away, fearful for his damaged shoulder. Some of the Franks had already mounted and were getting ready to leave. Off to one side, the big Frank was arguing with Clovis, and Ascha guessed that he was appealing to Clovis to leave. Clovis didn't move. He seemed unafraid, watching the milling Saxons with a look of savage delight on his face.

Sweet Tiw! He's enjoying it, Ascha thought.

In growing alarm, Ascha watched the Theodi brawl among themselves. Aelfric and Besso pushed their way through the throng, bellowing in men's faces, shoving them apart.

The brazen clangour of a trumpet split the air. The Theodi fell silent. They turned to see Clovis standing on a shield held by two Franks. Clovis waited until the din had subsided and then he spoke.

'Aelfric,' he said in his thin reedy voice. 'Do you not have another son? Is not Ascha the look-out also your son?'

Ascha's mouth dropped open. What did the Frank just say?

He sensed that everybody had turned and was staring at him. Clovis scanned the crowd. He saw Ascha and beckoned him. Ascha hesitated, wanting to hide, and then reluctantly took a step forward. Men turned and stood aside to let him pass. His father watched without saying anything, as if unable to stop matters slipping out of control.

'What of this one, my Lord Aelfric?' Clovis said, jabbing a bony finger at Ascha, his shrill voice tinged with triumph. 'Is he not also your son?'

Aelfric grimaced. He glanced at Besso and then growled, 'He is my son but he is not my son.'

A wicked smile spread across the Frank's face and one eyebrow arched. A riddle! Clovis put his head on one side and looked at Ascha as a bird might a worm. 'How is he your son and yet not your son?' he asked softly

Aelfric shook his head, and Ascha saw the slow fury behind those grey eyes.

'Ascha is not freeborn,' Aelfric said.

'The son of the *hetman* is a slave?' Clovis said, incredulous.

Silence, a shared sense that some things should not be aired before outlanders. It was Besso who eventually spoke.

'The boy's mother is a slave,' he said with slow deliberation. 'Aelfric is his father, which makes him a half-slave. By law, he is not a freeman and cannot inherit or bear arms.'

'Ascha the look-out is a half-slave?' Clovis said disbelievingly. 'Yet he warned you of our coming and he saved my life when your freeborn son would have gladly taken it. And he saved your life, Aelfric, which would have been forfeit if Hroc had killed me.'

Neither Aelfric nor Besso had an answer to that.

When Clovis spoke again there was a brittle edge to his voice: 'Aelfric, it seems to me that your half-slave son is worth more to you than your freeborn son who is bold enough to defy his father and his clan.'

Hroc swore, and his hand dropped to his sword. Besso and Hanno moved to Hroc's side. Hroc's face darkened, but he allowed them to hold him back. The Theodi were silent, confused as to the direction things were going.

Clovis thought for a moment and then said. 'I will take Ascha the half-slave as hostage for the pact.'

Uproar.

For one brief moment, before the fear took hold of him, Ascha felt a flutter of joy. The Franks wanted him, the half-slave, not his free born brothers.

'Lord, we cannot take him,' Bauto shouted. 'He's not worthy. We must take the second son or there is no pact!'

'Bauto, I am the son of Childeric, if I accept him, then he must be worthy,' Clovis said. He spread his palms wide and smiled at his own cleverness.

'Your father will never agree to this,' Bauto said.

'My father won't care, one way or another,' Clovis said. He folded his arms and said that he was no more prepared to accept Hroc than Hroc was prepared to come, but he would take the boy.

Nobody spoke. All eyes on Aelfric. The *hetman* of the Theodi rubbed his chin with the back of his fist and ground the toe of his boot into the dust.

'Father?' Ascha said, but Aelfric's huge head was bent low. In mounting desperation, Ascha sought Hanno's eye but Hanno pulled a sad face and gazed over the tree-tops. Hroc, furious with everyone, turned on his heel and left. When Besso blew his nose and refused to look him in the eye, Ascha knew.

Aelfric looked up.

He stared at Ascha for a long time while Ascha stood without moving, his heart hammering against the wall of his chest. He watched as his father tugged at his beard and then breathed in deep and blew the air from his cheeks.

'So be it,' his father said. 'Ascha, son of Aelfric, goes to the Franks as hostage for the pact.'

As the full weight of his father's words hit him, Ascha felt his belly heave and he retched, splashing his britches and feet with his own filth. He wiped his mouth with the palm of his hand and bit his lower lip, stifling a sob. He would not let them see him weep.

In the years to come, Ascha would often go over in his mind what happened that day. Feeling as if a lump of ice had chilled his spine and left his body numb, he watched as arrangements were made for him to go with the Franks. He could no longer feel the pain in his neck and jaw. He kept thinking and hoping that at any moment his father would change his mind. Surely, they were not going to go through with this? They were not going to leave him here? An outcast among strangers?

The Franks unstrapped the chests of silver and placed them on the ground. Bauto went to one of the chests, pulled an axe from his belt and knocked out the metal pin that secured it. He threw back the lid and pushing his hands deep inside, held up two handfuls of silver and let them trickle through his fingers. The silver glinted in the sunshine, tinkling like water as it fell. The Theodi surged forward, eager for a look. They crowded around the chests. There was laughter and a hum of excitement.

Ascha stood apart, his arms wrapped around his shoulders. This couldn't be happening!

He was dimly aware of mounted Franks moving off into the forest, riding with a sense of purpose, as if knowing what they had to do. He saw Bauto murmur a few words to Aelfric who nodded and then turned and called out a single name, 'Ubba!'

Ubba the Frisian who had led them to Samarobriva suddenly sprinted away. He ran full tilt across the clearing and plunged into the forest. But the Franks were already there before him. Ascha saw Frankish horsemen working their way between the trees, lances raised. They cut the Frisian off and drove him back to the clearing.

Ubba stood with his head swivelling and eyes wide with terror. Ubba saw a gap between the Franks and went for it. Immediately, two riders on the other side of the clearing spurred their horses.

'What's the betting he don't make it,' Ascha heard someone mutter.

The Theodi watched in silence.

The Franks rode hard, kicking at their horses' flanks with their heels. Ubba looked over his shoulder once. He screamed when he saw what was coming. The lead Frank's *spatha* flashed and with a twist of the wrist, cut back and up. Ubba's head lifted from his torso, turned slowly in the air, and bounced across the grass.

A low murmur broke out from the Theodi. Ubba was the last barrier between them and the Frankish silver. Now they could go.

Ascha shivered, his flesh deathly cold. This was no dream, this was real. He had no idea why Clovis had chosen him. All he knew was that by taking him, Clovis had resolved a dispute that might have split the clan. His exile was a small price to pay for Frankish tribute. The Theodi, he thought bitterly, had reason to be grateful to Clovis of the Franks.

The sun was beginning to dip towards the horizon as the Theodi made ready to go. The crew slung their shields and cut poles to carry the silver chests. One by one, they came to take their leave. They murmured a few words, clapped him on the back, sending the pain jolting through him, and then moved, anxious to be away. The silver would not be shared until the *SeaWulf* was at sea. Some left without saying goodbye, and Ascha wondered if they were ashamed of what had happened.

Besso wrapped Ascha in his fleshy arms and tried to make a joke of it but gave up when he saw Ascha's face. 'Be strong,' he whispered. 'Tha knows tha can survive this.'

Hanno ruffled his hair and held him close. He drew a double-sided comb from his tunic which Ascha had carved for him from antler bone the previous summer and handed it to Ascha. Ascha took it, feeling his eyes mist. How would he survive without Hanno looking out for him?

Hroc couldn't face him. 'Watch thi step, little brother,' he said gruffly and left without a backward glance.

His father stood some way off, his shaggy head resting on his shoulders like a rock. Ascha screwed both fists into his eye sockets, grinding them round and round and then went over to him.

'Father?' he said in a small voice.

Aelfric turned towards him and they moved together in a clumsy embrace. The pain surged but he made no attempt to break away. Later, there would be many times when Ascha would try to relive that moment. What was said and not said. He remembered hoping that his father would have a change of heart. But what he would remember most was the scratchy feel of his father's shirt against his cheek, and the warm odour of leather, sweat and woodsmoke, his father's smell.

Aelfric's hands fell to his sides and his shoulders sagged. There were deep lines around his eyes, and Ascha thought he saw sadness there. He wondered what his father would say to his mother. How would Aelfric tell her he had sent her only son into exile? He had a sudden picture of his mother standing on the foreshore, her slight form bundled up against the wind, watching and waiting for him to return.

His father patted his cheek and turned away. Ascha watched him go, consumed with misery and at that moment he felt a deep disgust and hatred for his father and knew that as long as he lived he would never forgive him.

The Theodi moved out. Ascha could hear them laughing as they tried to keep their footing on the steep slope, the silver chests swinging wildly. They ignored the Gauls silently lining the ramparts of Samarobriva and headed down to where the *SeaWulf* waited to take them home.

Ascha watched them go. When he could see them no longer, he walked slowly back to where the Franks sat waiting for him on their big horses. He stood without a word until one of the troopers grunted, scooped him up and sat him on the bony hindquarters of a mule.

Then, as the sun began to drop towards the horizon, Clovis led them down the valley side and north towards Tornacum.

4

They travelled north. Dusk was falling when they came to a fork in the road. Without breaking step, Clovis and an escort of four Franks broke away, leaving Bauto and the remaining Franks to ride on.

Ascha felt a sudden jolt of panic.

'Where are they going?' he called to the Frankish trooper riding beside him.

'Tornacum.'

'Then where are we going?'

'You'll find out soon enough,' the trooper said.

Until he saw Clovis ride away, Ascha had given no thought to what the Franks would do with him. He had assumed he would serve his hostage-time with Clovis and it came as a shock to realize the Franks had other plans. He felt sick to the pit of his belly. Some of it, he knew, was hunger and the pain of his shoulder, but the rest was fear.

It was almost dark when Bauto led the Franks off the road. They went down a dirt track overgrown with weeds to where a settlement of cabins and roughly-hewn huts stood on the edge of a marsh. Even in the fading light it looked dismal, drained by a ditch that brimmed with foul-smelling water. Pigs rooted in the mud. Armed men watched as they rode up. No women.

'What is this place?' he said to one of the Frankish troopers.

'The barracks for the *scara*, the army of the Franks,' the Frank said. 'It's where the Overlord's Antrustions are billeted.'

'Antrustions?'

'The Overlord's own personal guard. High-born men, hand-picked for their fighting ability and their loyalty to Childeric.'

Ascha could hear the pride in the man's voice. 'Why have I been brought here?' he said.

The man snorted. 'Because you're now a hostage, and this is where Childeric keeps his royal hostages.'

He thought about that. A royal hostage! Was that what he was? 'What kind of men are the hostages?'

'Foreigners, all of them,' the Frank said sourly. 'The sons of warlords and princes. We hold them to guarantee the peace between us and their own nations. If war breaks out, both sides know the hostages will die.'

'But why here?' He flung the question, anxious to know what his future would hold.

'Hostages serve in the Overlord's *scara*,' the Frank said. He leaned over his horse's neck and spat in the mud. 'That way they can be useful, and the Antrustions can keep an eye on them.'

Hostages and Antrustions sounded unlikely bed-fellows. He imagined the rivalry would be bitter: neither side willing to extend the hand of friendship to men who might one day become their enemies. And then another thought struck him. He was unweaponed. He would not be allowed to serve in the Frankish army.

They rode into the camp. Ascha slid off the mule and waited. Eventually, one of the Franks jerked his head, and Ascha followed him. The man took Ascha to one of the barrack huts. The hut was full of bunks jammed close. Weapons and kit hung on the walls and a sheaf of spears stood by the door. There was a musty smell of packed bodies. A few men stopped talking and watched him. By their clothes and their hair, he knew them to be foreigners and assumed they were the royal hostages.

'We be of one blood,' he murmured courteously.

They said nothing. No smiles.

The Frank waved him towards a bunk at the back and left. Ascha flopped down and closed his eyes. His head throbbed and his shoulder ached. Never in his life had he felt such loneliness.

Slowly, he twisted his head. The hostages sat on benches or their bunks talking about weapons, girls and beer in Frankish or their own dialects. Ascha watched them carefully. One of the hostages, a big man with tattooed shoulders, glanced at him and Ascha looked away.

He was adrift among strangers.

It was several days before the camp learnt that the new hostage was both Saxon and slave-born; a mix toxic enough, Ascha discovered, to unite the hatred of hostages and Antrustions.

The Franks loathed Saxons as bandits who had terrorized the coastlands of Gallia for generations. And as the half-slave son of a poor tribal *hetman*, he was despised by the royal hostages who saw his presence as an insult to their rank.

His new companions soon made their feelings felt. Wherever he went, Ascha was goaded and jeered at. He was waylaid, tripped and beaten, his food knocked from his hands, his tools scattered and his work sabotaged. At night he lay in his bunk, his body coloured with bruises and choked back the sobs. He was alone and friendless and there was nothing he could do to stop the torment. Had Clovis intended some cruel joke, choosing him and then dropping him among those most likely to scorn him?

Drifting off to sleep, he took comfort in thoughts of home. He pictured the small figure of his mother waving farewell from the riverbank as the *SeaWulf* slipped to sea and he thought of Saefaru, her golden hair billowing, waiting for him as she had promised she would.

Ascha withdrew into himself. He spoke to nobody and nobody spoke to him. He soon found work, carving bowls and spoons and ladles with long and finely worked handles, but took no pleasure in it. The flesh fell from his bones, and he grew pinched and thin. He no longer washed and shuffled about the camp with his eyes downcast like a walking ghost. His hair grew lank and the skin on his arms and legs felt dry and scaly to the touch.

Every day when his work was finished, he would go and sit by the main gate. He liked it there because it was the busiest spot in the camp, and the safest, the one place where he knew he would not be attacked. He would whittle and go over in his mind what had happened outside Samarobriva. Rage and disappointment gnawed like a rat at his innards. How could his father have cast him out? What had he done to deserve such punishment?

But he had no ready answers.

He took comfort from watching the daily comings and goings of the Frankish troops and the Roman traders who came to do business with them. He saw how much more attached the Franks were to their land in Gallia than the other Germanic nations, and how determined they were to hang onto it. As a half-slave he had always had a keen sense of where power lay and, almost without realizing it, he noted things that others missed. As the weeks passed, he developed a grudging admiration for his hosts, their hunger for power and their single-minded love of war, but their dependency on the Romans intrigued him. It was almost, he thought, as if a young man had inherited land from an old and feeble uncle, but still wanted the uncle to show him how to run it.

One day Ascha was cornered by a gang of Antrustions. They were led by Sunno, a big-boned Frank from Camarac whose brother had been burnt alive by raiding Saxons as a sacrifice to Tiw. Sunno and his friends circled Ascha and watched him, thumbs in belts.

'Let me pass,' Ascha said.

Sunno glared at him, his face dark with hatred, and then they laid into him. He stood his ground and fought back, trading blows for blows. They knocked him to the ground. Each time he got up, they knocked him down again. After a while, Ascha curled himself into a ball and waited for them to finish. They beat him and kicked him so savagely he thought he would die. When they were done, they tossed him into a latrine pit and went away, their arms draped over each others' shoulders, laughing fit to bust.

Wet through and stinking, Ascha limped back to the barracks. He stank so bad the hostages threw him out. He crept into the barn and lay down in the straw. He was covered in bruises, his eye was swollen and two of his teeth were loose.

That night he lay awake, thinking it through. The attack had jolted him from his torpor. He realized that as a Saxon and a half-slave he was doubly cursed. Clovis had forgotten him and he was on his own. Without protection, he knew he would die in this place. He had to make himself more valuable to the Franks alive than dead. He went over in his mind everything he had learnt. He had to find a way to make himself useful.

The next day Ascha took a knife and sawed away at the tightly coiled topknot that marked him out as a Saxon. He shaved the back of his head to the crown and braided his side locks in the Frankish manner. Then he went and asked leave to speak to warlord Bauto.

Bauto's Antrustion bodyguard took one look at him and knocked him to the ground. He got up, spat the blood from his mouth, and asked again. The Antrustion stared at him, shrugged and went away. For two days he stood in the hot sun without food or water. At night, he curled up outside Bauto's tent, rising before dawn to resume his place. On the third day an Antrustion came out, snapped his fingers and he was ushered in.

Bauto ran his eye over Ascha with a look of cold distaste.

Ascha waited, barefoot, pale and wasted, his clothes fouled.

'What do you want, boy?' Bauto said.

Ascha paused and then he spoke, a rush of words without stopping for breath. When he had finished Bauto leaned back in his chair and looked at him. 'You want me to give you weapons and to train you as I would a Frank,' he growled. 'You mad or stupid?'

'Neither,' Ascha said. 'You need fighters. Frankland is surrounded by enemies and you need every man. I am young and I will learn fast, faster than any Frank. Teach me to fight, and I'll serve you well.'

The warmth of Bauto's hut made his head swim. He felt light-headed from hunger and weariness and had to steel himself to avoid falling.

'You're slave-born!' Bauto growled. 'By rights you shouldn't even be here.'

'But I am also an outlander with no ties. I can do for you what others would not. I can be useful.'

Bauto shook his head. 'Saxons are animals, terror raiders who come like wolves in the night to slaughter and maim. Why would you be any different?'

Ascha bit his lip. He had thought long and hard about this moment and knew that he could not afford to be squeamish. 'I'll be more loyal to you than any man in your army,' he said quietly. 'I will do anything you want.'

'Is that all?' Bauto said, with a sneer.

'I ride well.'

Bauto raised an eyebrow. 'That is of some use,' he said grudgingly. He put two big hands on the table and leaned forward. 'Any more?'

His last shot. He breathed in deep and let it go. 'I speak Latin as well as any high-born.'

Ascha had grown up with an ear for the different north shore dialects, but Latin had always been a secret language, used only when he and his mother were alone. The language of heaven his mother called it.

Bauto looked at him, 'What of it?'

'If you are to conquer Gallia, you will need people like me.'

Bauto looked at him, his eyes narrowing. 'Who says we have plans to conquer Gallia?'

'It must happen. Rome is like a corpse rotting from within. It's only a matter of time before the Franks take their place.'

Bauto waggled his head.

'You'll need men who can speak Frankish and Latin,' Ascha said earnestly, his chin lifting. 'Men you can rely on.'

Bauto frowned. 'But the Romans and the Gauls will learn Frankish.'

'They won't,' Ascha said. He had thought about this and spoke with conviction. 'There are too few of you and too many of them. If you are to conquer Gallia you must think as they do.'

'Why should I think like a Roman?' Bauto said. 'We rule here now. They do what we say.'

Ascha shook his head, the excitement rising. 'Na, Lord. You think you do but you rule in name only.

Bauto gave him a long and thoughtful stare. 'How so?' he said softly.

Ascha hesitated. His mind worked fast, pulling together what he had seen and what he had heard, making sense of it all. He struggled to find the words. 'You have taken over the Romans' lands but they hold you like this.' He cupped his hand and squeezed it. 'You rely on Romans to manage your affairs, Romans make your laws and collect your taxes, Roman merchants control your trade, and your great estates are run by Romans. They have lost power, sure enough, and they have lost their lands, but they have adapted. You cannot rule without them.'

Ascha paused, surprised by the strength of his words. But he knew he was right. He could feel it in his bones.

Bauto laid one thick finger across his lips and tapped them lightly. 'Perhaps it's as you say,' he said. 'You're an outsider and see things others don't.' He shrugged. 'It doesn't matter. The Romans will do what we tell them.'

Ascha saw the opening and went for it.

'You think so? The truth is they despise you! The Romans think of you as barbarians. They laugh at you, but they…' he paused to think of the word, '…they manipulate you as they have always done.'

For a moment he thought he'd gone too far. Bauto rose to his feet, his face flushed and his fists bunching. Then he frowned and looked thoughtful. He cast a wary eye over the Roman clerks working with their heads down at the back of his tent and scratched his chin.

'Yes,' Bauto said. 'They do, don't they.'

The next day, two Antrustions came and brought Ascha to Bauto. The Frank handed Ascha a message tablet in a wooden case.

'Take this to Lutetia Parisi and give it to Silvanus Vegetus, merchant. He lives close by the baths in the north of the city. The Antrustions will give you a horse.'

Ascha nodded and mumbled a few words. An Antrustion tapped him on the shoulder and led him away. Bauto did not bother to look up.

Ascha rode all that day and most of the next and reached the city before nightfall. Lutetia Parisi sat on a low hill with a river to the north and mud flats and marsh to the south and east. The merchant lived in a small red-roofed house near the river. Ascha dismounted and walked up a gravel path and pulled on the bell. A slave opened the door, asked his business and then closed the door in his face.

Ascha cursed, but was forced to kick his heels outside the door. The slave came back and admitted him. Ascha threw him his cloak with a look of contempt and went inside. The house smelled of damp and cooking, and he realized with some surprise that he was hungry. He had been so anxious to get to Parisi on time that he had not eaten since he had left Tornacum.

Silvanus Vegetus was bald and thin as a rail and wore a serious expression. The merchant took the message Ascha handed him, turned it over several times, and then broke the seal with his thumb and began reading. Ascha turned to go. The merchant called him back and pressed a copper coin into his hand. Ascha thanked him and left.

Down by the river he found a stall and bought a meat pie. He ate the pie standing up with hot meat juices running through his fingers and dripping onto his chest. When he had finished, he wiped his hands on the seat of his britches, mounted and turned his horse north.

After that, Bauto gave Ascha other messages to carry. Ascha rode as an official Frankish messenger to all the leading towns in Roman Gallia. The letters he carried were mostly routine demands for grain, wine, woollen socks and cloaks for the Frankish army. He delivered them to traders, lawyers and Roman officials. It wasn't long before he guessed that some if not most of the people he visited were spies in the pay of the Franks. Sometimes they asked him to wait and then he was given a letter to bring back to Bauto.

As the weeks went by, Ascha began to form opinions on the Romans he met. He took a view on whether they were honest or corrupt, whether they had genuine information to pass on or were inventing news they could exchange for Frankish gold. At first, he found them wary and cautious but as they got to know him, they began to loosen up. He spoke their language and he knew they saw him as different to other barbarians. Sometimes, when he judged it was safe to do so, he asked them questions about their trade. He kept his eyes and ears open, remembered the gossip he picked up about Roman dignitaries, and never forgot to count the Roman troops he passed on the road.

He told Bauto everything he learned, listing his observations and adding further impressions when he thought them relevant. The Frank listened carefully, his forefinger tapping his lips, taking it in.

Ascha was pleased. He was making himself useful.

One afternoon, a tall Antrustion captain with ice-blue eyes, a drooping moustache and his skull shaved close, came to the hut where Ascha slept.

'I am Lothar,' the Antrustion scowled. 'And I've been ordered by Bauto to teach you to fight. Tiw help us all!'

Ascha threw himself into war training. He enjoyed the exercise: the long runs each morning, the wrestling and the tugs-of-war. But most of all he loved working with weapons. It was what he had been waiting for all his life. He worked hard to master his new craft: the downward cut from shoulder to chest, the hard stab at the side of the neck, the sharp thrust to head or belly or groin.

'All men flinch from a cut to the face,' Lothar said. 'Their face is who they are. Strike through the mouth and the day is yours!'

Lothar taught him to handle the spear and the *seaxe*, the long bladed single-edged knife worn by all Germanics. He showed him to throw javelins and lob slingshot, how to wait until the last moment before hurling the *angon*, the Frankish barbed spear, so it would punch through an enemy's shield and maim. He learnt to use shields: the small one for fast-footed close work and the big war shield with its heavy iron boss for battle. To parry, feint, lunge and block, using either hand equally. 'If your right arm is injured you must be able to kill with your left or you are dead,' Lothar shouted.

But of all the weapons he worked with, it was the *franciska* he loved the most. The Frankish tomahawk had a long shaft and a sensuously curved blade – like a woman's back, Lothar said.

'In the right hands, the *franciska* is deadly,' Lothar told him. 'Look after her as you would your sister and keep her by your side at all times.'

Ascha took him at his word, and the *franciska* became his weapon of choice. He practised every day, swinging the blade until it became as much a part of him as his arm. He was not a natural killer, but he was fast and he was agile. With his speed and nimbleness, he found he could overcome opponents bigger and stronger than himself.

His skill was eventually noticed and the Franks, a heavy-witted people seeing a link between his trade and his dexterity with their national weapon, took to calling him the Carver. Ascha didn't mind. Better to be known as a Carver than a Half-Slave.

As weeks turned into months, the Franks saw that Ascha was now under Bauto's protection and left him alone, while the hostages learnt to accept him as an exile far from home, like themselves. Ascha no longer thought of himself as a Theod but as a hostage in Bauto's army. The memories of what had happened that day at Samarobriva began to fade

With a *seaxe* in his belt and a *franciska* swinging from his hip, Ascha felt and acted differently. For the first time in his life, he was proud of who he was. He was working for Bauto and he walked with his head held high. If he had doubts about what the Franks wanted in return for arming and training him, he put them to one side.

'Y'know, for a bare-arsed Saxon ditch-dog, you're not so bad,' Gundovald the Goth told him one night as they sat around the fire grilling sausages. And with a booming laugh Gundovald slapped him on the back so hard he thought his lungs would burst.

One day, when Sunno the Frank tripped him as he was re-wheeling a cart, Ascha turned, his blade already drawn. But this time he found he was not alone. Gundovald and the hostages smilingly drew their weapons and watched his back while Ascha and Sunno fought it out.

The fight was fast and bloody.

Sunno went down with Ascha's *seaxe* wedged between the bones of his forearm and a *franciska* caressing his throat and was carried off screaming like a girl. Ascha pounded his chest, raised his arms and roared his joy.

He had become a warrior.

And he had survived.

5

Andecavus, Roman Gaul, five years later
481 AD

Just before sun-up and the first pink flush of dawn was colouring the sky. In a drowsy blur Ascha heard birdsong and sensed the stirrings of the early risers. His body still ached from the clash with the Herul and he'd slept badly, his rest broken by the screams and groans of the wounded. He rolled over and opened his eyes. He seemed to be the only one awake, the other hostages still wrapped in their blankets.

A man was coming towards him, skirting the smoking campfires and stepping over the sleeping men. Roman, he guessed, the wrong side of forty, dressed like a clerk and peering about as if he was looking for someone. The man stopped when he saw Ascha.

'Are you the Saxon?' the Roman said in thickly-accented Frankish.

'Who wants to know?' Ascha mumbled drowsily.

'I am Quintilius, secretary to general Bauto and I'm here on royal business,' the Roman said, wrinkling his nose.

Ascha pursed his lips. They all stank, of blood and sweat and death. Nobody had washed for days. He pulled himself up on one elbow and rubbed a hand across his chin. 'I'm the Saxon,' he said. 'What do you want?'

'You must come with me.'

'Why?'

'Lord Bauto wants to see you.'

'Bauto wants to see me?' He could hear the surprise in his voice. He had not seen Bauto in years. Was this some kind of joke?

'He has received despatches. They concern you.'

Ascha gazed at the Roman in amazement.

Quintilius tightened his mouth with impatience and walked back the way he had come. He stopped a little way off and looked at Ascha expectantly. Ascha sighed and shook his head. He got to his feet, scooped up his cloak, wrapped it around his shoulders and followed.

***

Ten days earlier, a war band of sea-raiders led by Eberulf the Herul had landed at the mouth of the Liger. Using an island in the estuary as a base, Eberulf sends his raiders sweeping through Roman Gallia spreading terror and destruction. They sack the towns and villages and fire the fields and leave the province a smoking wasteland. When the Herul reach Andecavus they destroy the city in a storm of fire and slaughter.

Syragrius, imperial governor of the last Roman enclave in Gallia, has too few troops to defend his dwindling territory and sends riders to appeal to the Franks for help. Bauto calls up the *scara*, the Frankish army, and leads them with five hundred Antrustions and the royal hostages out of Tornacum, heading south. They reach Lutetia Parisi and take the stone road to the west.

A week later the Franks reach Andecavus. A pall of greasy smoke covers the town. Bodies litter the streets and the sweet stench of death hangs on the air. The Franks trudge through the smouldering ruins in silence. On the other side of Andecavus they find a detail of grim-faced Roman horse soldiers waiting for them under the trees. Bauto shakes hands with the Roman commander, a young officer with a sharp nose and dark curly hair, and then the Roman turns his horse and leads them along the river westwards. The Romans have sent scouts fanning out in search of the Herul, and the raiders are not difficult to find. Burdened by laden oxcarts and lines of stumbling captives, their retreat to the river mouth is slow.

The allies gain on them by the hour.

The air is heavy and the sky cloudless. The sun glistens on spear points and helmets, pricking eyes and flaming the men's pale northern skin. A month earlier, Ascha thinks, and this desert of dry earth and burnt stubble would have been a sea of soft-swaying wheat. Now the dust rises up in clouds, stinging their eyes, drying their throats and rubbing their shoulders raw.

He drops out of the column. Lowering his shield, he lets his pack fall to the ground. He drags off his helmet, touches his brow and winces. The iron rim has chafed, and the skin is sore and weeping. He put his fists against his lower back and with a little gasp arches his spine. He yanks out the stopper from his flask and dribbles some water onto a neck cloth and roughly swabs the dust and muck from his face.

'Shift your arse, Saxon. We haven't got all day.' Gundovald's voice.

With a sigh, Ascha pulls on his helmet. He picks up the heavy shield and pack, hoists them on his back and runs to join the column.

Ascha and the hostages trudge over the crest of a low rise. Far off on the plain, at a point where the old Roman road disappears into a clump of scrub pine and oak, a mass of people, carts and animals are slowly grinding toward the coast. He can hear the rumble of wagons and see the shimmer of iron weapons and smell the salt-tang of the sea.

When the Heruli realize they cannot escape, they turn. Tall men with pale hair and hungry faces. They form a wall of shields and yell defiance.

Trumpets bray. Captains bellow. Horses thunder by in a cloud of dust. Ascha tightens his grip on his shield. Now they've got them.

The Franks move up. Weapons clank, harness rattles, and there is a steady tramp of feet.

When they are no more than twenty five paces away, the Franks face the Herul. The shouts and yells fade away. No sound, not a whisper. Ascha fronts his shield and draws his *franciska*. Stiff with tension he waits with the other hostages. He breathes in and tries to keep calm. This is the hard time, the moment before a battle. His mouth is dry, and he feels the cramp of fear in his guts. He breathes in as deeply as he can and lets it out in a long shuddering rush.

The horns blow, and the Herul scream their war song. With a shout, the Franks run forward and hurl their *angons*. Ascha watches, fascinated, as the javelins slowly arc and drop on the Herul. Men fall impaled, and Heruli shields bristle with Frankish lances. Frantically, the Herul hack at the spears, trying to cut themselves free of the encumbering *angons*.

The horns blow once more and the Frankish front line moves off. They charge, plunging headlong into a murderous thicket of axes, spears and swords. Leaping onto the *angons* trailing from the Heruli shields, they uncover the Herul like snails on a thrush's anvil. Axes sweep and spears lunge. The air is full of men's cries and the clash of iron.

After a short and fierce battle, the Heruli shield wall begins to give. Those at the rear turn and flee. A gap opens and the Franks pour through like a winter torrent.

46

Eberulf holds out to the last, surrounded by his sons, their shields overlapping, tired blades swinging low.

The Franks close in like dogs around a boar.

Ascha hears Bauto shout, 'Five solidi to whoever brings me Eberulf's head!'

Eberulf hears it too. He grins and his axe flashes. An Antrustion goes down and another leaps in to take his place.

With a wild yell, Ascha rams his shield into a Herul's face. He hacks with his *franciska* and sees the man fall away. Another Herul rushes him. Ascha parries and then chops at the man's leg. He hears a half-choked howl, and the Herul topples back. Ascha swings and feels the crunch of bone as the hatchet bites deep.

He turns and catches a glimpse of Eberulf fighting for his life but loses him again in a crush of bodies and jabbing spear points. And then suddenly the field clears and Ascha sees the warlord of the Herul, eyes wild, his face and beard flecked with blood.

'How now, you old bastard!' Ascha screams.

And the *franciska* swoops.

Quintilius walked on without looking to see if Ascha followed. He led Ascha through a jumble of supply wagons, past the cages where the last of the Heruli sat in wretched huddles waiting for the slave buyers, and out beyond the grave pits which stank of death. They came to a small field of sun-bleached grass. Ascha looked about him. Half a dozen double-poled tents for Bauto and his captains, shaded by trees. Outside the biggest tent Ascha saw a tall staff with six black horsetails. Bauto's standard.

Antrustions barred the gate to the field. Heavy hard-looking men in dark horse-hair crested helmets, carrying long-leafed spears. Ascha tensed, recalling the misery of his first months in Tornacum, but the Antrustions let them pass without a word.

Bauto was standing outside his tent. He was stripped to the waist. A slave with a thin face and frizzy black hair stood by him holding a bronze ewer. As they drew near, Bauto dipped his head and the slave poured water over the warlord's head and shoulders. Bauto cupped his hands and washed, using a nubbly finger to clean out his ears and nose and then hawked loudly and spat to one side.

Ascha was pleased to see him again. Bauto had met his father and knew the world he came from. Ascha looked him over. Bauto hadn't changed. Middle-aged, but the body was still hard-muscled, skin the colour of old oak, with just a hint of softening around the belly. A scar branched like a deer antler down one arm. Like all high-born Franks, Bauto shaved the back of his head. Only Frankish royalty had the right to wear their hair long.

Above the trees, the sky was shifting to a dove grey. The hostages would be up and about, preparing for the day. From one of the tents Ascha heard the low gurgle of a woman's laugh.

The slave picked up a towel and began to dry Bauto's back with quick efficient strokes. Quintilius took this as a signal. He stepped forward and put his hand to his chest in a lack-lustre Roman salute.

'I have brought the Saxon, Excellency.'

Bauto looked up. Quintilius was dismissed with a jerk of Bauto's jaw, and Ascha felt hard blue eyes fall on him. Bauto looked at him as if seeing him for the first time.

'It's been a while,' Bauto growled.

'It has, Lord.'

'You've changed, filled out a bit. Put on a bit of muscle. You used to be a gawky wretch. Life as a Frank must suit you.'

Ascha nodded. 'Suits me well enough.'

Bauto rotated his finger in a slow circle above his head. 'And you wear your hair shaved now, like a good Frank? Not like some top-knotted barbarian, huh?'

Bauto's mouth lifted at his own joke. He took the shirt the slave handed to him, dragged it over his head and stuffed it into his breeches. He buckled on a heavy war belt and then sat down and pulled on his boots.

'And these days you bear arms,' he said, 'like an honest freeman?'

Ascha bent his head. 'I do, Lord.'

Bauto grinned. 'And if Eberulf were alive he'd say you know how to use 'em, eh?'

Ascha gave him a wide grin. 'I think he would.'

Bauto waved the slave away. 'Na, you fought well, lad. Earned your gold...'

'Thank you, Lord.'

'...for a Saxon half-slave, you sure know how to fight. Put us freeborn folk to shame.'

Ascha stiffened. He felt his cheeks flame but held his silence.

Bauto watched him and then slowly dipped his head.

'Yes, you've come a long way, boy,' Bauto said. He leaned to one side and spat again into the dust. 'Come so far that maybe you've forgotten your mother was a slave, huh?'

Ascha held his eyes. 'I've not forgotten.' How could he ever forget? It lived with him each and every day. No matter what he did, he would never be good enough. He would always be the half-slave, never the equal of a free man.

'Did you know that a German called Hwadaker is now emperor of Rome?'

'No.'

'When barbarians become emperors, slaves become warriors, women rule and pigs fly. That's when the world turns upside down. Ain't that right?'

'If that's how you see it,' Ascha said sourly.

'Oh, I do, boy. I do.'

Bauto scratched his chin and seemed satisfied with whatever point he was trying to make. He picked up a message tablet from a brass table and tapped it against his palm.

'I've just received despatches from Tornacum,' he said. 'Childeric is dead and his son, Clovis, is now Overlord.'

Ascha's jaw dropped. 'He can't be,' he said. 'He's no older than I am.'

Bauto gave him a sly glance. 'That's thrown you hasn't it? Well, he is and he's sent for you, wants you to ride to Tornacum. What do you think of that?'

Ascha was stunned. He stared at Bauto. 'Why does he want to see me?'

Bauto opened the pouch on his belt. He took out a bone pick and began to scrape the line of black from his nails. 'You really don't know?'

'How would I know?'

'You wouldn't be lying to me now, would you?' Bauto said, tapping the pick against his teeth.

'I've never lied to you.'

Bauto gave him a thin smile and put the pick back in his pouch.

'Maybe he wants to thank you for saving his life when that fool of a brother of yours would have dashed his brains out. How do I know what he wants? All I know is that you have to be in Tornacum before the week is out.'

Bauto held out the message tablet, and Ascha took it.

'Take my report of the fight with the Herul to Clovis. If he asks, tell him it was a glorious victory over the enemies of Frankland.'

Ascha hadn't expected this. He had no idea why Clovis wanted to see him and nor did he care. He'd not seen the Frank in five years.

49

Where was Clovis when he needed him? Overlord or no, Clovis could go hang.

'And if I don't?' Ascha said quietly.

Bauto looked at him. 'Don't what?'

'What if I take the horse and go elsewhere?'

Bauto leant forward. Hard fingers gripped Ascha by the jaw and dragged him close. He could see the blood vessels in Bauto's eye and smell the garlic on his breath.

'What will you do?' Bauto said with a sneer. 'Go join the *Bacaudae* in the forest. Spend the rest of your life scrabbling for roots and robbing travellers. Is that what you want?'

Ascha held his gaze for a moment and then let his eyes fall. The last thing he wanted was to join a band of rebel slaves.

Bauto scowled and pushed him away. 'For reasons best known to himself, Clovis took you as a royal hostage,' Bauto hissed. 'But I was the one who made you a warrior. I trained you and I gave you weapons when your own people wouldn't give you the time of day. Remember! Without us, you are nothing!'

Ascha was beaten. 'I know it,' he said.

'And don't forget, we own you. Go missing and the pact between our peoples is over. Do I make myself clear?'

Ascha nodded. He supposed he should feel grateful to the Franks for arming him but he'd given them good service and he knew well enough that the Franks rarely did anything without good reason. He took the tablet and slipped it inside his tunic. 'I'll not fail you,' he said.

'The roads are not secure and there are many – Romans, Franks and *Bacaudae* – who would think it worthwhile to kill a royal messenger. Ride fast during the day, lie up at night and if anyone tries to stop you, kill them and ride on.'

Ascha turned to go.

'Just one thing...'

'Lord?'

Bauto thought for a moment. He looked over his shoulder at the Antrustions and then back to Ascha. He beckoned him to come closer and put a hand on the back of Ascha's neck.

'I meant no harm, boy' he said lowering his voice. 'It's not been easy for you, but you worked hard and you did what you could. You learned to fight like a Frank and you've been loyal. Never betrayed us to those murdering wolves you call your kinfolk. And your father kept his word. Your clan haven't raided us since you

50

were hostaged.' Bauto chuckled. 'Never thought he would keep the pact, but he did. He must want to keep your young bones alive, eh boy?'

Ascha glanced away. He didn't want to hear about his father. His father had abandoned him and left him to rot in exile. He hated his father. At the other side of the field, one of the mules had kicked a warhorse. He could hear the mule driver pleading with the Antrustions. There were raised voices and the meaty sound of a fist striking flesh.

Bauto leaned forward. 'Maybe Clovis was right. He saw something in you. Perhaps I was wrong to oppose the pact with your clan.' He shrugged. 'But listen to me, boy.' Bauto leaned in. Ascha felt the breeze lift, saw the horsetails stir. 'Be careful how you deal with that young butcher. Our new Overlord is not like other men. Too many of his enemies, including his own family, have felt the strangler's bowstring. Keep your wits about you and watch out for that she-wolf his mother.' Bauto threw another glance at the Antrustions. 'Now go,' he said. 'Get out of my sight!'

Ascha blinked, looked away and tried to collect his thoughts.

When he looked back, Bauto had gone.

Back in the lines, the hostages were sitting around the fire, their feet outstretched watching Gundovald cook. There was the sound of fat sizzling and the aroma of bacon.

'What did the old man want?' Gundovald said.

'I have to go to Tornacum,' Ascha said, his voice toneless.

There was a clamour of surprised voices.

'Why?'

'Childeric is dead, and Clovis is Overlord. He wants to see me.'

'What does the Overlord of the Franks want with the likes of you?' Hortar the little Alaman said crossly.

Ascha said nothing. He didn't know what Clovis wanted but he had a strange feeling that, one way or another, his life was about to change. His heart was thumping and his palms felt clammy with sweat. He was aware of the hostages watching him.

'When do you have to go?'

'Today.'

There was silence. Immediate departure was not a good sign.

'He must have told you something?' Gundovald said.

Ascha shook his head. 'He told me nothing. He doesn't know himself. I must make the best of it.' He could see they didn't

51

believe him, but it was true. 'At least it means I won't see your ugly faces for a while.'

'Likewise,' said Friedegund cheerily.

Hariulf the Burgundian waved his bread in the air, his mouth full of bacon. 'Maybe he's going to reward you for taking out Eberulf,' he said, fat sliding down his chin.

Somewhere a horse whickered softly. Beyond the trees there was the harsh and insistent clangour of an armourer repairing weapons. *Clang! Clang! Clang!* The noise stopped and then started again.

Ascha shook his head with a rueful smile. 'I don't think so.'

'Myself, I think perhaps our new Overlord seeks your advice on how to conquer Gallia.' Atharid the Thuringian said, one finger tapping the side of his nose.

'Na, he send Ascha to Ravenna as ambassador to the Romans,' Friedegund the Suebian chortled. They laughed along with him, slipping into the familiar routine of casually traded insults.

Ascha picked up his cloak and flung it over his shoulder. He tossed his tools and a few possessions into a blanket and tied the corners in a thick knot, moving with the nervous haste that comes before sudden departure.

'When will you be back?' Gundovald asked quietly.

He blew out his cheeks. 'Two weeks, a month, perhaps longer.' He tightened his belt. 'Save my share of the loot for me. If I don't come back, divide it among yourselves.'

The hostages exchanged glances.

Friedegund said, 'You'll miss the piss-up.'

He nodded. The Romans had promised them a feast to celebrate the destruction of the Heruli. They'd talked of little else.

'Wine, food, beautiful fat-bottomed girls,' Friedegund said, his voice wistful.

Ascha smiled but said nothing.

Gundovald wiped his mouth with the back of his hand, ran both palms down the front of his tunic and slapped his thighs. He stood up, held out both arms and wrapped Ascha in a huge bear hug. They stayed like that for what seemed a long while, patting each other gently while the others stood in silence and watched them.

'Goodbye little Saxon,' Gundovald said. 'Try to stay alive.'

Ascha took a few moments to lace his helmet to his belt, his fingers fumbling with the cord.

Then he picked up his bundle and left.

6

The Great Hall of the Franks, formerly the imperial Basilica, was a huge brick-built building that overshadowed the hovels and cramped alleys of the town and dominated the landscape as far as the eye could see.

Ascha dismounted and tied his horse to a rail. He took his bundle and sat on the steps. He sat there for a long while, watching people pass in and out and then he got to his feet, climbed the steps and went through a pair of iron-braced doors into the hall.

As he stepped inside, his head lifted. A massive timber roof straddled the hall like an upturned boat. A double row of high windows ran along two immense walls to a back wall which was blunt and curved like a ship's bow. Old Roman statues lined the sides, and threadbare tapestries covered the brickwork. Overawed, Ascha gazed. In all his life he had never seen such a wonderful building. His father's long hut could fit in here five times over.

The hall was tightly packed: landowners, slave traders, Frankish warlords, merchants, moneylenders, agents. A hubbub of voices rose and fell like the ocean swell. He heard the crisp Latin dialects of the Gauls and Hispani, the sing-song lilt of the Pritanni, driven out from their island by Saxons, the strange throat-clearing sounds of the eastern traders – Syri, Greeks, Phoenicians and Jews in their caps and long woollen gowns. And beneath, like a dark undertow, the bristling dialects of the Germanic tribes that now ruled Gaul: Franks from the Salt and River confederations; Frisians from the Rhine mouth; Burgundii, Thuringii and Alemanni. And the much travelled, much tattooed Western Goths.

He pushed through the crowd to the far end of the hall, eyes taking it all in. The air was warm and heavy and already he could feel his shirt glued damply to the small of his back. A heavy goat-hair curtain screened the bow of the hall but, through the gap, he could see clerks working at long tables. Scrolls and books lay on the floor or were stacked in racks against the wall. As he watched, clerks went soft-footed to the racks and brought away rolls of parchment, each as big as a child, which they laid on the tables, weighing the corners with stones. Clerks wrote on the parchment with slender-beaked pens which they dipped from time to time into great ink pots of solid brass.

Ascha stated his business to a yellow-haired captain of Antrustions. The captain glanced at Bauto's seal on the letter-tablets and directed him towards a row of benches filled with people waiting to see the Overlord.

It was hot and the sweat was running down his neck. He looked for a seat but it was clear that nobody was going to make room. He lost patience and angrily shoved in between a Frankish merchant and a Gaulish landowner. He dropped his bundle on the floor and pushed it underneath the bench with his heel. The Gaul glanced at him sideways, took in his travel-stained clothes and greasy bundle, and grimaced. Ascha was dog tired and didn't care. He lay back against the cool stone, pulled his cap down over his eyes, and dozed.

He woke to stillness. For a moment he forgot where he was. Silence filled the hall like mist in a valley bottom. The crowd had stopped talking and were craning their necks, peering towards the door. The Gaul was already on his feet, his face lit with excitement. He turned to Ascha and beamed.

'It's the new Overlord. He's coming!'

Ascha got to his feet. The crowd broke into a murmur and pressed forward. He heard the measured tramp of marching feet, and then the crowd parted soundlessly before a column of Antrustions - big, heavy-boned men, picked for their build, wearing leather jerkins and horse hair helmets. They marched the Roman way, eyes forward, cleated boots slamming down on the stone floor in a steady pulse, wave after wave, the rhythm of heartbeat.

Behind them came two young women scattering flower petals from bronze bowls. There was a pause and then Ascha heard a sharp intake of breath from the crowd as Clovis came into view. The young Overlord walked slowly, long arms hanging loose, cold eyes flicking from side to side, his hair thick and long. He wore a fixed and serene smile, occasionally lifting one hand in greeting.

But it was the Overlord's clothes that struck Ascha most.

The new Overlord of the Franks was dressed like a Roman emperor; a silk tunic in red and green with a gold torc around his neck, as thick as a man's thumb. He had draped a rich purple cloak heavily embroidered with what looked like a swarm of golden bees across his bony shoulders and pinned it with a golden long-tailed brooch. From a belt studded with jewels, hung a sword decorated with neat lines of small red stones. Sell his clothes and you could live in luxury for the rest of your life, Ascha thought. Behind Clovis walked a young boy carrying a gold staff on a silk cushion, followed by a gaggle of Antrustions and royal officials.

Ascha imagined he saw Clovis give him a faint smile, and then the Overlord's eyes went blank. The column marched past and Ascha heard their footsteps fade. There was a lull and then the hum of voices surged once more. Ascha sat and blew out his cheeks. He looked down at his clothes and ran a shy hand over his tunic's coarse homespun. He had never imagined it would be like this. He was out of his depth here. He felt envy and resentment, tinged with a touch of awe.

'Tiw's breath,' he muttered to himself. How could the skinny Frank he'd met at Samarobriva have turned into this young prince?

So much wealth.

And so much power.

The line of delegates waiting to see the Overlord moved slowly. Bored, Ascha turned to the landowner by his side and asked him how long he had been waiting. The Gaul was young and plump with a face as soft as yoghurt. He went by the name of Verecundus and had come every day for a week to ask the Overlord's help in settling a boundary dispute. Verecundus seemed to know everybody. Overjoyed to find the filthy barbarian spoke his language, he was happy to point out the dignitaries and give their reasons for being there.

A middle-aged Roman with an ulcerous leg had come to complain that the Frankish Lord billeted on his estate had drunk his cellar dry, abused his daughters and carried off all his slaves.

They both laughed at that.

An old woman with a pale and bloodless face was Genovefa, a holy woman. She was accompanied by a moon-faced drab, similarly dressed in a black gown, who sat clutching an elaborately painted wooden box.

'What's in the box?' Ascha said.

'The toe of Saint Jerome,' Verecundus whispered. 'It's a gift for the Overlord.'

Ascha tried to look impressed but found it hard. 'Does Jerome not need his toe?'

Verecundus looked at him in astonishment. 'Jerome,' he explained, was a holy man, and had been dead many years. Genovefa had come on a sacred mission. She was here to convert the Overlord of the Franks to the true faith.

'Clovis is a Tiw-believer,' Ascha said. 'Why would he change his beliefs for her?'

Verecundus tapped the side of his nose and winked. 'It's easier for Clovis to rule over Gallia if he shares – or appears to share – our faith.'

'And that one?' Ascha pointed to a dark-faced Frankish nobleman with hair brushed straight back from his brow who made no secret of his impatience at being kept waiting.

The Gaul's round face broke into a scowl. 'That is Fara, agent to Ragnachar, the Overlord's uncle,' Verecundus said stiffly. 'His master had expected to become Overlord, but Clovis beat him to it.'

Ascha was curious and would have asked more but at that moment, the curtain was suddenly drawn back, brisk as a weaver's shuttle, and a high-born Roman official appeared. Fifties, Ascha guessed, middling height and overweight but with a high forehead and intelligent eyes. Under one arm, he carried a leather writing tablet, worn smooth from years of use. The delegates shuffled and stretched and tried to catch his eye.

'Who's he?' Ascha said.

'Flavinius,' Verecundus said. 'Counsellor to the Overlord.'

Something in the Gaul's tone suggested a measure of respect. 'Is he important?'

'Very. He has the Overlord's ear. They say Clovis does nothing without running it past Flavinius first. His knowledge of the law is unrivalled.'

Ascha looked at Flavinius with interest, plain to see that this Roman had no problems working for the Franks. Flavinius scanned the line of dignitaries. He saw Ascha, pointed and crooked a finger.

'It's you! He's calling you,' Verecundus said excitedly.

Ascha scrabbled under the bench for his bundle and got to his feet. At once there was an outcry from the delegates. Someone pushed in front of him. He recognized the Frank that Verecundus had said was agent to the Overlord's cousin. The Frank was lean and wiry and bore a hooked nose like a blade. A livid white scar ran across his left eye. Around his neck he wore an embossed seal which he now held up in front of Ascha, if it were some kind of talisman.

'Out of the way, boy!' he snarled. 'I am Lord Ragnachar's man and I take precedence here.' The man's eyes were black as soot.

A strange odour, like some exotic perfume, filled the air.

'Not today, my Lord Fara,' a smooth voice cut in, and Ascha felt Flavinius push his bulk between them. Flavinius took Ascha by the elbow and steered him toward the curtain. As he was led away, Ascha glanced back over his shoulder and saw the nobleman's face gripped in a dark scowl.

Flavinius ploughed through the clerks to where a small door was set in the back wall, guarded by two Antrustions. Flavinius rapped twice, opened the door and beckoned Ascha with a cupping motion of his fingers.

Ascha breathed in deep. He ran his fingers through his hair and followed the Roman inside.

Despite the heat outside, the chamber was cold and dark, the air thick with the smell of dog. In one corner, a fire struggled to give off heat. After the noise and bustle of the hall, the room seemed deathly quiet. Clovis was sitting in a chair, his legs outstretched and his boots propped on a table. He got up and greeted Ascha with all the appearance of warmth.

'My Saxon friend, let me look at you!'

He took Ascha's hand and squeezed it. His palm was moist, his fingers as soft and smooth as a girl's.

'It's been a long time,' Clovis said, looking him up and down.

'It has,' Ascha agreed.

'You look good, all grown up and carrying weapons.'

Despite himself, Ascha smiled. It always pleased him when his arms were noticed. He might not be free-born, but at least he looked free.

They scrutinized each other without speaking. Clovis was heavier with a long jaw and sharp cheekbones, the bony face softened by hair that was long and curled, the privilege of royal rank. He had taken off his heavy cloak and thrown it in a dishevelled heap on the table.

Clovis smiled and laid a hand across Ascha's shoulders. 'How was your journey?'

'Fine,' Ascha said. 'It's a good road.' He felt ill at ease. What was he doing here, talking to the Overlord of the Franks? Out of the corner of his eye he could see Flavinius at the back of the room, watching them.

'All the same, you must be tired. It's a long way from Andecavus. Have some wine. It's one thing these Romans do well.' Clovis gestured to a bench.

Ascha sat, his bundle between his feet. Clovis turned and bawled for wine. Almost at once, two women came in from another room. An old crone dressed in black, her eyes a mesh of wrinkles, carried two glass goblets on a small tray while a girl hefted a jug of wine on one shoulder. The girl was young and shoeless with green eyes and a hard mouth. The old woman put the goblets on the table and the girl poured the wine.

Ascha looked her over. She was pretty, probably a slave. He saw that her hand trembled slightly as she poured and he wondered why she was nervous. The girl filled both glasses and then let out a faint sigh, as if relieved she had not spilt any.

Ascha thanked her, and she smiled and padded away. He lifted the goblet to his lips. He had never drunk wine from a glass before. Glass was rare, fit only for the rich and high-born. The smell of fruit filled his senses. He sighed. This was a world away from the rot-gut the troops were given. He filled his mouth and swallowed and almost immediately felt himself relax. He smacked his lips. Maybe Bauto was wrong. There wasn't anything to be afraid of here. He would have a drink and a laugh with Clovis, and then he would go back to camp. He would have plenty to tell the hostages. And if he was lucky, he might still be in time for the victory feast.

He was aware suddenly that Clovis was watching him. Clovis smiled and bent his thin nose over the rim of the glass. 'So, you're a warrior now?' he said. 'Trained to kill!'

He pronounced the words in a slightly mocking way that Ascha didn't care for.

'Yes,' Ascha said. 'And you are the Overlord of the Franks.'

There was an awkward pause and then they both laughed uneasily. They drank some more and sat without speaking.

And then Clovis said, 'Of course, at the moment my lands in Gallia are small. A few towns here and there, scattered colonies of settlers. But one day, I will rule over an empire that will stretch from the Rhine to the Roman Sea.'

Clovis spoke with quiet determination, and Ascha saw that he was serious. He was not surprised. Every Frank he'd ever met believed that they were the natural heirs of Rome.

Clovis picked up the jug and filled Ascha's glass. 'So, Bauto still lives?'

'Lives and prospers.'

'It's strange. I see so little of him these days. Sometimes I think he avoids me.'

'I'm sure he doesn't.'

'Yes,' Clovis muttered darkly. 'I'm sure he does.'

Ascha took a gulp of wine. 'I think Lord Bauto prefers the life of a soldier to life at court,' he said, suddenly affable.

Clovis looked at him and nodded. 'Yes, that must be it,' he said, unconvinced. 'Has he dealt with those Heruli pirates?'

Ascha tossed back the wine and rasped his tongue against the edge of his teeth. 'He did exactly that! Your army has achieved a glorious victory, and the Heruli were annihilated.' He bent and rummaged in his bundle, found the birchwood writing tablets and handed them to Clovis.

'Flavinius!'

Flavinius rose ponderously to his feet and came and took the tablets away.

Ascha jerked as he remembered. 'And to celebrate his victory, Lord Bauto has sent you a gift.'

'A gift!' The cold eyes glittered.

Ascha picked up the leather sack and handed it over. Clovis opened it and peered inside, recoiling as the stench hit him. 'A valuable gift indeed,' he murmured. He pulled out a human head by its topknot and held it aloft. A middle-aged man, fat-nosed and thick-lipped. Hacked off below the jaw-bone. One eye was gone, smashed by a blow to the side of the face, the other stared without seeing. The hair filthy with mud and blood, the teeth broken and the eyelids black.

'It's Eberulf, isn't it?' Clovis said, squinting. 'He and my father used to be friends. My father offered him terms but he refused. Now look at him, crow-food.'

He threw what remained of Eberulf to the floor. The head bounced and rolled and came to a halt under a bench leaving a bloody trail across the flagstones.

'Flavinius, take that thing away and stick it on a spike at the gate.'

Flavinius picked up the head up and silently withdrew.

'Now, do you know why I summoned you?' Clovis said softly.

'No,' Ascha said. He tried to hold the Frank's gaze but looked away. He was beginning to find the young Frank's confidence unnerving.

'Oh, take it easy! You're among friends.' Clovis gave Ascha's shoulder a quick squeeze. Reaching back, he picked up a scroll from the table and with a snap of his wrist unrolled it on the floor. He knelt and stretched over the parchment, unfolding the rips and smoothing the tears. Then he sat back on his heels, put his hands on his thighs and looked up at Ascha.

'I know it's been a while since we met, but you've not been a stranger to me.'

'What do you mean?'

'I have had reports on you.'

Ascha looked at him. 'What kind of reports?'

Clovis smiled. 'They tell me that you are skilled with weapons, ambitious, adaptable and loyal, if resentful about the, ah, injustice surrounding your birth. You are hard-working and resourceful, although at times headstrong, and you keep the hostage laws. Oh, yes, and for a backwood's barbarian, you are quick to learn.'

He felt as if someone had crawled inside his head, carefully examined all his thoughts, and left.

'Can you read a map?' he heard Clovis say.

'No.'

'Then I will show you. Come!' The Overlord patted the floor beside him.

Ascha glanced at Flavinius who studiously avoided his eyes. Slowly he went down on his knees beside Clovis, taking his wine with him. He blinked at the cat's cradle of scrawls and lines and coloured scratching that covered the parchment.

Clovis pointed with a long forefinger. 'This shows you the world as a hawk might see it. Here is the Great Ocean and here the Roman Sea. The Romans still control Italia but they have lost Hispania and have given up the island of Pritannia because they could no longer hold it.' Clovis jabbed with his finger as each country was mentioned. 'Up here below the Rhinemouth are the lands of the Franks. The Frisians are above the Rhine, Thuringii to the east, and way up there, your homeland. But this is the real prize.' He ran his hand in a wide circular movement over the map and looked up at Ascha. 'Gallia! The richest and most fertile land of all.'

Clovis jumped to his feet. He went to the table, picked up the wine jug and slopped more wine into Ascha's glass. Some of the wine spilled, staining the map.

'Ascha, tell me! How long have you lived among us?'

Ascha thought for a moment. 'Five years.'

Clovis looked surprised. 'As long as that?'

He nodded. Five years since his father had walked away and left him among strangers.

'And in that time we have treated you well. You have been an honoured guest amongst us?'

Ascha looked to see if he was joking and saw he was not. 'That's one way of putting it,' he said dourly. He waited, wondering where all this was going.

Clovis went to the fire. He paused for a moment, staring deep into the flames.

'You will have learnt during your time with us that the Franks are different from other nations. We are an unusual people, Ascha. We straddle two worlds: the world of Rome and the world of the north.'

Ascha got to his feet. Clovis turned to face him, his eyes hard and bright.

'Ascha, the Romans' day is over. Their power is fading,' he said. 'I believe it is our destiny to build a new empire. We Franks will rule this land as the Romans ruled it before us.'

Ascha pulled on the wine. 'And what of the other great powers? The Goths, the Burgundii, Alemanni.'

'What of them?'

'They all want their slice of Roman pie and they won't let you have Gallia without a fight.' He had discussed this many times with the hostages and knew their nations resented the Franks' ambitions in Gallia.

The Overlord's face curled into a sneer. 'But they lack our will. And they do not understand what made Rome great. We Franks, we know Rome.'

That, of course, was the key, Ascha thought. The Franks had lived alongside Romans for generations. They had learnt from their imperial neighbour, taken what they wanted and thrown away the rest. Compared to the Franks, the other Germanic tribes were primitive barbarians.

'They'll fight you all the way,' Ascha said.

Clovis put a reassuring hand on his arm. Ascha saw that the Overlord's nails were raw and bleeding, bitten to the quick.

'I know there are barriers to overcome,' Clovis said with icy deliberation. 'But if we are bold, if we choose our alliances wisely and if we take our chances as they arise, we can shape our future. We can become masters in the west. We will take over the rest of Gallia and force that old bastard Syagrius to come to terms. Then we will defeat the others one by one, and Gallia will be ours. I shall unite the Frankish and Roman people, Ascha. Think of it! One nation and one people, under Frankish rule.'

Mad as a box of rats, Ascha thought. But he was impressed all the same. If anyone could take over from the Romans it would be Clovis and his Franks. He knew the Frankish army, the *scara*, from the inside and understood what it was capable of. The Franks were tough, and they knew what they wanted. With Clovis as Overlord, they would have the will and the means to conquer. Perhaps, one day, Clovis would rule over Greater Gallia.

There was a commotion outside.

'What now?' Clovis said.

A woman swept into the room, her silk cloak billowing like a sail.

'Mother,' Clovis said, getting to his feet. 'How nice to see you.'

Ascha snapped to his feet. Basinia! Childeric's queen.

She was late thirties, nudging forty. Coiled blonde hair, a wide brow and a mouth that was mean and downcurved. Still beautiful, but in a hard and brittle sort of way. Her dress was silk, the colour of the sea, tightly belted. Across her forehead she wore a head-band of woven gold thread. Earrings, brooches and dress clasps, all gold.

The queen put her face up to be kissed, patting her son's cheek with detached fondness. Her eyes fell on Ascha and surveyed him coolly. When she was done, she turned to Clovis and raised one arched eyebrow.

'The Saxon I told you about, Mother.' The Overlord examined his knuckles, chose one, and chewed it. 'He brings news of Bauto.'

'Which is?'

'The Herul are destroyed.'

'Good!' she said.

She took a white linen kerchief from her sleeve, shook it open, and laid it on the bench. She straightened the kerchief fractionally and then sat down, her dress rustling like leaves blowing over an open grave. She looked up at Ascha.

'I understand your father is a warlord among the Saxon people.'

'My father is Aelfric, *hetman* of the Theodi.'

'And your mother?'

He hesitated. 'She is *Walesh*, a foreigner.'

'You mean she is a slave,' Basinia said in a matter of fact tone. She looked down at her knee and smoothed the silk of her dress with long languid strokes.

Ascha swallowed. He tipped his head. 'Yes, lady.'

Basinia's looked up. Her eyes travelled over him, sifting him like flour. 'Then you must be a *mischling*. A half-slave!'

He felt a chill run through him. What in Tiw's name was going on? 'That is what the law calls me,' he said coldly.

She nodded. 'Life as a half-slave must have been hard,' she murmured.

'Hard enough.'

'Made you what you are, perhaps?'

'Perhaps.'

'Harder still to have been a hostage, an exile in a foreign land.'

'I survived,' he snapped. Calm down. Don't let her get to you. He sipped some wine and used the moment to force himself to breathe more slowly.

She watched him and he could see the thoughts passing through her mind.

'Bauto trained you as a warrior and gave you weapons even though you were a half-slave?' she said.

'You know he did.'

'He took a big risk.'

'I don't think he sees it like that.'

Basinia thought about that and then she gave Clovis an almost imperceptible nod. She turned back to Ascha and motioned for him to sit.

'Has my son explained what we are trying to achieve here?'

'Some. But I don't see what it's got to do with me?'

Basinia brushed a speck of dust from her dress. 'For reasons I do not completely understand, my son thinks highly of you, so I will tell you.' She shifted in her seat and crossed her hands in her lap. 'There is one obstacle which might defeat our plans.'

'Lady?'

'The north shore tribes.'

'They are the single biggest threat we face,' Clovis added.

He looked at them both. 'Why? The northern clans are few, and they are poor. They raid because life is hard and they'll starve if they don't. You can buy them off as you bought off the Theodi. Or destroy them as we destroyed the Herul at Andecavus.'

'So you would think,' said Clovis. 'But the world is changing. There is talk of an uprising. The tribes are uniting to form a confederacy of all the Saxon and northern tribes. If that happens they will sail as one. Fight as one. It will mean not one or two boatloads of raiders, but twenty, thirty making landfall on our coast. We could not withstand them. They would devour us.'

Ascha shook his head. 'Northerners are simple folk. They're not going to unite. They couldn't agree to milk a cow, let alone build a fleet.'

'Then let me explain,' Basinia said, her tone suddenly sharp. 'A confederacy of northern sea-raiders would unleash terror across Gallia. While we deal with the sea-raiders who threaten our rear, the other Germanic nations, the Goths and those vicious bastards, the Alemanni, will attack us from the south and east. We would be crushed between the wolves of the forest and the wolves of the sea. Our very survival would be threatened.'

There was an edge to her voice he'd not heard before. He wondered if it was fear.

'What has this to do with me?'

'We think you can help us.'

He laughed. 'I don't think so.'

Basinia said, 'The confederation is led by a Saxon tribe.'

'Which tribe?'

'The Cheruskkii.'

Ascha's mouth fell open. 'The Cheruskkii?'

'You know them?'

Of course he knew them. The Cheruskkii were *Waldingas,* forest people. He nodded. 'Their lands lie upriver from ours.'

'In the past they were of little account but something seems to have changed. A new war chief perhaps? They have become very powerful,' Basinia said.

'It's not my concern,' Ascha said, but he was troubled all the same.

Clovis glanced at his mother. 'We have heard that one tribe is holding out against the Cheruskkii. They have refused to join and have become a rallying point for those opposed to the confederation.'

Ascha felt the blood drain from his face. 'Which tribe?' he whispered.

'The Theodi! Your father's clan,' Clovis said bluntly.

Ascha took a gulp of wine. The world was closing in, boundaries washing away. Now he knew why he had been summoned. How could he have been so stupid as to think that Clovis had wanted nothing more than to talk of old times. 'I am a Frank now,' he said. 'This does not concern me.'

'I disagree,' Clovis said. 'I think it does.'

Basinia went on. 'The Theodi are small but they are a holy tribe and they have influence.' Her voice was soft, as if she were addressing a child or a lover. 'Your father is stubborn and has resisted all invitations to merge, but the Cheruskkii are unlikely to tolerate his refusal much longer. If the Theodi join the confederation, there will be nothing to stop the Cheruskkii taking the tribes to war.'

He had a sudden picture in his mind of his father before the shield-wall at Samarobriva. Feet rooted in the dust, as iron-willed as a mule. 'My father would never join,' he said with a bitter laugh. 'It would mean breaking the pact he made with the Franks.'

'But if he doesn't,' Basinia said quickly, 'the Cheruskkii will move against the Theodi.'

Ascha hadn't thought of that. He sat on the bench and rested his chin on his fist. The Cheruskkii and the Theodi had always been friendly, but he knew that if it came to war the Theodi were few and would not be able to last out for long.

He sucked his tooth. 'What do you want of me?' he said.

'Information.'

'You have spies.'

'We need someone we can trust,' said Basinia. 'A Saxon, not an outsider. We need to find out what the tribes are planning. Will they invade and where will they land? How many ships? How many men? When will they come?'

'You want me to become a spy against my own people?'

'No,' Clovis said brutally. 'But you can save them. Do you want to see the Theodi destroyed?'

That shocked him. Was that what this was about? The destruction and slaughter of his clan? He was the son of a slave, and the Theodi had never taken him as one of their own. He owed them nothing. And yet he knew it wasn't that simple. Despite everything, they were still his kin, his blood.

Basinia moved closer. She laid her hand on top of his. Her eyes were grey, the colour of ashes. He could smell the oily sweetness of her perfume. He wished he hadn't drunk so much. He was giddy, and his head felt as if it were stuffed with wool.

'Help us, and we will reward you,' Basinia said. He could feel her stroking the back of his hand. 'You will be wealthy. You can buy whatever you want. Land, women, fine clothes, and you can go home.'

Home, he thought bitterly. That was rich. Home was the one place he had never felt at home.

But the thought of reward made him think.

'The clan won't trust me. I have been too long with the Franks.'

'They will suspect nothing,' Basinia snorted. 'You were a half-slave, a simple woodcarver. You were never a warrior.'

And at that, his head begin to clear. Going home would mean going back on everything he'd worked for. But if he did, he would be well placed. The Overlord and his mother needed him. Do this, and they would be grateful. He could ask for anything.

'You want me to find out whether the Cheruskkii will attack Gallia?'

'We need to know if there is going to be an uprising of the northern tribes. If there is, we need to know when and where they will attack. You must find out who leads the Cheruskkii and, if you can, you must kill him. He is a threat that has to be removed.'

They wanted him to be a spy and an assassin. 'I'd be on my own, without weapons.'

'It will be dangerous, there's no denying,' Clovis said.

'How will I get the information back to you?'

'One of my agents will contact you.'

'How will I know him?'

'He's a Frisian. He will find you.'

'How much time do I have?'

'Not much. If they're going to come, they'll come next summer.'

Ascha breathed in deep. This was not what he had expected but he knew with every fibre of his being that he held his future in the palm of his hand. He would never get a second chance. But what did he want? Wealth? Land? Women? All that, of course, but there had to be more. Think man, think!

And then it came to him.

He was a half-slave, caught in the hazy twilight between slave and free. He had struggled with the shame of it ever since he could remember. All he had ever wanted was to be whole, the same as his brothers. The Theodi would never give him that, but Clovis could. Clovis was Overlord of the Franks. Clovis could do anything.

'I'll tell you what I want,' he said.

'Be my eyes and you can have anything,' Clovis said. He had pulled his heels up onto the bench and sat with his knees hunched under his chin, chewing his nail.

'I want 100 solidi.'

There was a brief pause. 'Agreed!'

'And my freedom.'

Clovis and Basinia looked at him in astonishment. 'You're not a slave,' Clovis said. 'You're half-free. We would never have armed a slave.' He spoke with disgust, the very idea abhorrent.

'I know, but it's what I want,' Ascha said. 'I want you to make me a free man. I want there to be no doubt.'

Clovis walked away shaking his head. 'I know of no procedure for making a half-slave into a free man,' he said. 'The law does not allow it.'

'You owe me!' Ascha growled.

For the first time, it occurred to him how closely interwoven their lives were. If he had not saved the young Frank's life at Samarobriva, Clovis would never have become Overlord and he would never have become a hostage.

Clovis seemed to think the same. He nodded slowly. 'Very well,' he said evenly. 'Do this and I will declare you free. After that, any man who calls you half-slave will be flogged until his back is raw.'

Ascha saw the Overlord give his mother a thin smile. A bargain!

'Swear it!' he said furiously.

Clovis paused. 'I swear it.'

'On your father's grave.'

Clovis scowled.

'I swear this on the blood of my dead father Childeric and on his grave. May I join him in the cold earth and stones take the place of my eyes if I break this sacred oath.'

Ascha drained his glass. He sat for a long time staring into space. Could he trust them? Of course not! Bauto, the old dog, had been right on that count. But it was worth the risk. Pull this off and he would be a free man. He would be whole. He wasn't so stupid as to think it would be easy. But he knew he was ready. He'd been ready all his life.

Ascha put down the glass and stood up. A log shifted in the fire, sending out a flurry of sparks and a sudden gust of heat. Outside, in the hall, there was a burst of raucous laughter, like a sail tearing.

'Make the arrangements,' he said, 'and I'll do it.'

After that things moved quickly. Flavinius put Ascha up at his house across the river and arranged for him to travel overland as a woodcarver. Flavinius took away his Frankish army clothes and weapons and replaced them with a rough coarse-weave tunic, a short hooded cloak and the kind of soft cap that craftsmen wore. Flavinius gave him an old satchel, his tools, a blanket and enough flour and hard biscuit for a month.

Unable to sleep for excitement, Ascha spent the night drinking beer with Flavinius. Neither of them spoke much. Flavinius told him briefly what he might expect to find on the road and then they lapsed into silence. Ascha's thoughts were of the future and, if Flavinius had any opinions on what Ascha had agreed to do, he kept them to himself.

The next day Ascha went down to the city gate, strode past the grinning skull of Eberulf the Herul, and headed east.

7

Ascha set a brisk pace, following the old military road that ran from Gesoriac on the coast through Tornacum to the Rhine. He knew he didn't have long before the rainy season arrived and the dirt roads on the other side of the Rhine would become quagmire. He pushed himself hard, switching between running and fast marching, as he had done in his army training. He met peddlers and tattered hawkers, their wares piled high on their backs, farmers moving their bleating livestock and women selling eggs by the roadside. They gave him no trouble. Sometimes, he came across groups of Frankish settlers, surly men, hollow-eyed women and grimy-faced children trekking south in oxcarts that yawed and pitched like boats in a storm.

One day he encountered a Frankish war band. He lifted a hand in friendly greeting and stepped aside to let them pass, but they tramped on without a sideways glance. They were swathed in deerskin, their clothes stiff with dirt and grease, and led by a warlord with white-bristled cheeks who rode a shaggy pony and glared at him with eyes as hard as flints.

He came to a sordid village high in the forest they called the Arduenna. Smoke and the smell of cooking drifted on the evening air. A sullen knot of villagers watched him from the side of the road. They asked him where he thought he was going in such an all-fired hurry. He shrugged and said to the Rhine. You an escaped slave, they asked. When he said he wasn't, a villager picked up a stone and pitched it at him. He kept on going.

He went on, moving up through the high country, working his way east. At nightfall he left the road and found a sheltered spot beneath the trees. He sat and ate his bread and then rolled himself in his blanket. He listened for a while to the cry of the wolves, his fingers laced behind his head, and then he slept.

A week after he left Tornacum, he came to a wide valley. A stiff wind was blowing and a cold rain clicked on the leaves. He looked down on a sluggish pewter-coloured river and knew he had reached the Rhine.

Flavinius had spoken of the Rhine as the edge of civilization, beyond which lay darkness and barbarity.

'One winter, when my grandfather was a boy, the Rhine froze.' Flavinius had said. 'The barbarians crossed over in their thousands. Vandals, Suebi, Franks and Alemanni.'

The Romans were unable to hold the barbarians back, Flavinius said. Their lines gave way, frontier posts were abandoned and farms and border towns overrun. The great landowners fled and the poor were left to fend for themselves. Barbarian lords took over the great estates and the Gauls found themselves ruled by new masters.

Ascha was half way up a wooded hill when something made him stop. He turned and looked back. Three riders were coming round the last bend in the road. He felt a sudden tingling in his spine, the barest sensation of danger. He walked on, eyes on the ground. The riders rode past, splashing him with wet muck. He saw that they wore long Frankish cloaks and sealskins, the hoods pulled over their heads. They had gone some way up the hill when one of them pulled on his reins, turned and walked his horse back toward him. The man pushed his cloak off his face. Ascha saw that he was an Easterner, dark-skinned and black-bearded, carrying a long sword on his hip. There was the glint of mail beneath the man's cloak. The rider came up close forcing Ascha off the road. He felt the man's eyes upon him, taking in the mud speckled clothes, the soiled boots, the dark hair cropped short under the grubby cap. The gaze lingered on the satchel at Ascha's hip.

'What are you?' the rider said in a guttural accent.

'No-one, Lord.'

'What's in the bag?'

'Tools.'

'What kind of tools?'

'I'm a woodcarver.'

The man gave a derisive snort. 'Where you from, Carver?'

The other two riders had stopped. They turned their mounts and rode slowly back, moving apart as they came, filling the road. One said something, and the other laughed. Ascha had a bad feeling about them. He looked about. Thick woods on one side of the track and, on the other, the ground fell away sharply. The rain started up again, pattering on the leaves above his head.

The first rider shouted at him. 'Answer me! Where you from?'

'From my village, Lord.'

'And where, damn you, is your village?'

'Over there,' Ascha said and gestured with one slack arm to the mist shrouded hills behind.

He knew as soon as he spoke, that it didn't sound right. The man looked to where he pointed and then back at him. 'You're lying,' he hissed, and his fist dropped to his sword.

Ascha snatched off his cap and waved it under the horse's nose. The horse reared and squatted back on its haunches and took a couple of steps back. Ascha scrambled under the horse's neck and ran to the side of the road and leapt over the bluff. He hit the ground and slithered down the bank in a wet slurry of mud and leaves and gravel. He rolled and slid a good way. He looked for something to hide behind, made a grab for an overhanging branch and ducked beneath the tree's exposed roots. He lay there, chest heaving, quiet as a mouse. There were shouts from the road and he wished he'd gone further down. Above him, he heard the jingle of a bridle and a horse blowing. Stones and gravel rolled past his ear. There was a creak of saddle leather as a rider leaned forward, looking for him. By the sound he guessed they had moved down the road, looking for a way down the slope and then he heard them coming back.

Ascha lay on his stomach, waiting, hoping they wouldn't dare follow with the horses.

'Said he was a woodcarver,' he heard the first man say.

'We're not looking for a pox-ridden woodcarver.'

'I think he was lying,' the first man growled, annoyed his judgement was in question.

'Well, he's gone now,' the third man said.

Ascha lay listening. The first two were foreigners but the third man was a Frank and high-born. And he knew the voice. Ascha felt his senses jangling. Where had he heard him before?

'If he was woodcarver, why did he run?'

'You probably scared the shit out of him,' the Frank said.

With a start, Ascha recognized him. The Frankish lord he had clashed with in the Great Hall. Lord Ragnachar's man. He held his breath while the rain soaked him to the bone.

A grunt and another curse, a rock came skittering past. After a while the Frank said, 'We've wasted enough time, let's go!' They pulled their horses back and Ascha heard them splashing through the puddles as they trotted away.

When he could hear them no more, he slid down the valley side on his back and heels, stones clattering beneath him. He came to a stop at the bottom and lay there for a moment, gasping for air and listening. He looked up at the ridge in both directions. No sign of them. He wiped his mouth with his arm. What in Tiw's holy name was Ragnachar's man doing out here? And who was he chasing? Whoever it was, he wouldn't last long once those three got hold of him.

And then it occurred to him. What if it's you they're after? He shook his head. No, not possible. Clovis had no reason to send men after him, and besides, a troop of Antrustions was more his style. And the Overlord was unlikely to reveal his plans, and not to his uncle Ragnachar if Verecundus was to be believed. Ascha chewed it over but could make no sense of it. How much do you want this, he thought? You want it enough to die for? Because you'd better!

A sheep trail led through the trees. He scanned the valley rim for a while, then turned and followed the trail north.

The rain stopped and the clouds began to lift. A cold sun shimmered over the valley, splashing the woods in a golden honey-coloured light. He came across a small settlement by the riverside. Nothing much, a sprawl of cabins and a landing for boats. Thin gasps of blue smoke gusted, and there was a stench of ship's caulk. He'd found a crossing point. Flavinius had refused to give him money. You won't need solidi where you're going, he'd said. Now he had to find a way to get across the Rhine.

He saw some men caulking a boat and asked them for the boat-master. A watersider with pock-marked cheeks jerked his head towards the jetty where a river man was driving wedges into an oak log.

'That's him. That's Wacho!' the watersider said.

The boat-master was a Frank, his workers mostly Gauls. He supposed that was how it was these days. Wacho was a big man running to fat with a bald head and a large nose. When Ascha walked up, he was gnawing a hambone. A small ship lay alongside the jetty, its spindly mast scratching the sky's grey underbelly.

'We be of one blood,' Ascha said.

The boat master looked at him without replying. Ascha looked at the hambone. He hadn't eaten for two days and was hungry.

He tried again. 'She's a fine ship!'

The ship was sturdy rather than beautiful but she was northern built. Long strakes overlapping like roof tiles. A good waxed sail. Six oars, four in the bow and two behind the cargo space. She'd ride the water well, he thought, sliding over the waves like a swan not ploughing through them as did the fat-arsed Roman and Gaulish vessels.

'I'm looking to go across.'

The Frank gave him a hard stare. 'An' you can pay f'that?' he said.

I'm a woodcarver.' Ascha said. 'Best there is. Take me across and I'll cut you your own prow-head. Gods, serpents, boars, dragons or hell-fiends, you name it, I'll carve it.'

'What do I want with a prowhead?' the Frank said. 'This is is the Rhine, not the ocean, an' my *Clotsinda* ain't no war ship.'

'River squalls can be treacherous. A prowhead will protect you from bad river spirits and keep watch over you while you sleep. It will bring you good fortune.'

The master peered at him and scratched the side of his face, thinking it over. He turned and tossed the hambone into the water. Ascha watched the bone arc through the air and sink through a ripple-whorl into the silt.

Wacho agreed that Ascha could carve a prow for the *Clotsinda*. They would be sailing the next day when the passengers Wacho was waiting for arrived. If Ascha didn't finish in time, they would sail without him. In the meantime, he could dip into the watersiders' rabbit stew and sleep with the other unmarried men in the cow shed.

Ascha spent a long time grinding his chisels against his slate stone, testing the edge with his thumb. When he was done he went to the rivermen's wood yard and found a block of unseasoned oak as high as his shoulder. He sketched out a dragon-monster with chalk, rubbing out the lines and redrawing them until he was satisfied. Then he picked up a mallet and began to carve.

Ascha worked fast, lopping off corners and gouging great chunks. He chiselled the head, cutting deep bulbous eyes to see hazards in all weathers. A beak of a mouth, hard and terrifying to drive away the river demons, and a spiralling and serpentine body, thick as a man's thigh. As he carved, chips of oak flew from his blade, like sparrows before a storm.

Ascha lost all sense of passing time. Once he looked up and saw a group of the riversiders' children watching him. They were in rags, the little ones naked, bellies stretched tight and skin shadowed with dirt. He spoke to them but they shook their heads, their toes kneading the mud like dough.

***

He is eleven when he discovers he can bring life from wood and stone. His mother and Hanno encourage him with words as warm as milk. Hroc sneers and tosses his tools in the midden. One day his father comes into the workshop. He bends his big head under the lintel and frowns into the gloom. He pokes the chisels and stone punches on the bench with a thick finger so they clink and runs a hand over a bench floury with dust.

'They say tha has the gift,' he says gruffly. He picks up a carving of a bear and holds it up to the light.

Ascha waits.

'I was a carver once,' his father says after a while.

'Tha, a carver?' Ascha says, not believing.

'My father died suddenly and I became *hetman*.' Aelfric gives Ascha what might have been a smile. 'Perhaps tha's inherited thi gift from me?'

'Perhaps,' Ascha says. The thought that his father might have been a carver has never crossed his mind but he can hear the regret in his father's voice and senses what might have been.

'A good likeness,' Aelfric says handing him back the bear. 'But tha'd do better with limewood.'

Aelfric turns to go. He pauses at the door, his hand on the latch.

'Remember, lad, the spirit of a carving lies in the wood. Without it thi work has no life. It will be as cold as the grave. If tha's to become a carver tha must free the spirit. Free the spirit within!'

And he is gone.

***

Late in the afternoon and a flatbed mule cart came trundling down the river path. Ascha looked up. Next to the mule driver sat an old man with a grey beard and a gown the colour of tree bark. A young woman was in the back with a shaven-headed slave boy. Trotting behind the cart came another slave, a big fellow with the build of a wrestler.

Wacho ran his hands down his shirt and went to greet them. He shook hands with the old man and helped him down. They talked and threw sharp glances at the black clouds roiling in from the north. Ascha reckoned they were deciding whether to leave, and risk getting caught in the storm, or wait until the following morning.

As he watched they seemed to come to a decision. Wacho took the old man by the elbow and led him towards the cabins. The girl hitched up her skirts, jumped down and followed them, stepping over the puddles. With a squeal of iron on wood, the two slaves dragged the chests off the cart and laid them down in the mud. The driver climbed back on the cart, whipped the mule and the cart went bouncing back the way the way it had come.

Ascha turned back to his work. They wouldn't be sailing until the following day. He had time to finish the carving.

Dusk fell and the rivermen gathered at the water's edge. They dragged dead limbs from the forest and threw them on a fire until the flames clawed high. The rivermen sauntered up and down in the half-light, cracking crude jokes and laughing.

The riverman with the pockmarked face brought Ascha a mug of beer. His name was Baculo, and he was a Gaul from the Roman enclave at Moguntiac, cut off when the Franks overran the territory thirty years before. He smiled a lop-sided grin and settled in the mud by Ascha's feet, watching him with his head tilted, like a heron wading for frogs.

The sun dipped and the dusk gave way to night. In the twisting firelight, Ascha's prow monster came alive. The long neck coiled and the beaked jaws snapped and snarled. The river folk grew silent. No sound but the crackle of the fire and the dull slap of the waves.

When the prow was finished, Baculo helped Ascha carry it over to the *Clotsinda*. The two of them raised the prow high and then, on Ascha's gasped command, let it drop.

'Gently! Now!'

The prow head slid neatly over the prow stem. Baculo grinned with blackened teeth. Ascha was pleased. Wacho hadn't given him much time, but the work was good and he had his passage across the Rhine. He picked up the mallet and a handful of spikes and began to hammer them into the prow, pinning the prow-monster to the stem.

Just then he saw the old man and the girl leave their hut. He paused and watched them walk arm in arm across the mud flat.

'Who's the greyhair?' he said to Baculo. He spoke in Frankish not wanting the Gaul to know he knew his language.

Baculo snickered. 'Octha the Frisian,' he said. 'He is a merchant from downriver.'

'And the girl?'

Baculo shrugged. 'Herrad. Octha say she is his niece.'

'And is she?'

'Maybe, maybe not.' Baculo said and tapped the side of his nose knowingly.

Ascha wasn't sure what to make of that. 'Where are they going?'

'Levefanum in the Rhine mouth. Octha comes upriver to Colonia twice a year to trade. Now he go back.' Baculo looked over his shoulder and lowered his voice. 'Master say they keep all their gold in those boxes. Master say they rich, really rich.' He giggled and winked at Ascha.

Ascha watched the merchant and the girl walk to the water's edge. One of the merchant's legs was twisted, giving him a dragging gait, like an injured crab. The girl supported him, the old man's weight resting on her arm, their heads together. Ascha saw her put her head back and laugh and, a moment later, he heard the merchant's answering chuckle. He was filled with a sudden feeling of loneliness and envied their closeness.

He watched as they reached the end of the mudflat and turned back towards the fire. He finished hammering the last spike into the prow-monster's neck and stepped away. A cheer went up from the river people and he smiled. The merchant and the girl stood watching him, firelight flickering across their faces.

'A fine piece of work,' the merchant said. 'You've a good eye, son.'

He spoke with a Frisian twang. Ascha thanked him and they exchanged names. The merchant was bald with a swathe of curly grey hair on the sides and back. A burnstone amulet strung on a cord around his neck. Watery eyes, blotched cheeks and a dry frizzy beard, but the voice was strong and friendly.

The girl stood with her hands on her hips studying the prow-head. He had an impression of an oval face, green eyes, a firm mouth and a high smooth brow like an upturned bowl. Her hair was long and dark, falling thick around her ears. A wide-sleeved and hooded dress in blue wool gathered at the waist over a white linen blouse. She was his age, he thought, maybe younger.

The merchant turned to say something to the rivermen and the girl suddenly hitched up her skirt, grabbed a rope and pulled herself up onto the boat. He held out his hand to help her, but she frowned and shook her head. He could see that she was agile and strong, her limbs tanned brown by the sun. She ran a hand over the prow-monster's head and rubbed the beast's scaly neck, stroking and patting the monster as if it were a hound. He watched her, his mouth drying.

'You carve well,' she said.

'It's nothing.'

'No, it's not nothing. It's something! Few can carve like that. You have a gift.'

She spoke Frankish but with an accent he couldn't place. And she was not the merchant's niece, he was sure of that. He caught himself staring at her and felt unsettled, not sure of what to stay. The girl looked at him and smiled.

The merchant called out to him, 'You travelling with us tomorrow?'

Ascha dusted off his hands and jumped down from the boat. 'Yes, at least until we get across the river. I live over there.' He pointed vaguely to the river's far bank. All being well, the merchant would assume he was a river-Frank or maybe a Thuringian.

'How long since you been home?'

'I don't know.'

'You don't know.

'Maybe five years.'

The merchant whistled. 'Five years is a long time.'

'Yes.'

'But you shouldn't be travelling right now,' the merchant said. 'It's not safe.'

'Why not?' Ascha said, suddenly alert.

'Because there's trouble brewing among the Saxon tribes, that's why.'

The girl went to the merchant. She put her arm through his, laid her head briefly on his shoulder and then broke off and wandered away. Ascha watched her go, his eyes following the roll of her hips.

He looked up and saw that the merchant had noticed the object of his gaze. He felt his neck burn. 'What kind of trouble? ' he said.

'Seems the Saxons have a new war leader, and he's been stirring them up,' the merchant said.

Ascha frowned. If the Cheruskkii had a new warlord that would explain much. Men would follow a strong warlord, especially if he was successful in battle.

'What's his name?'

'Radhalla.'

'Radhalla, the Cherusker?'

'You know him?' Octha said, not bothering to hide the surprise in his voice.

Ascha recovered quickly. 'Heard of him. Tavern stories, mostly.' He tried to remember what he knew about Radhalla. He and his father had once been friends. They'd fallen out and now it seemed Radhalla was running the Cheruskkii confederation. Strange that Clovis had said nothing. Maybe he hadn't known, but he wouldn't bet on it. The Franks were good at finding out who their enemies were.

'Whatever you've heard is probably true,' the merchant went on. 'He's ruthless – they say he killed his brother to become *hetman* – but he's also tough and as crafty as a wolf. The Iron Plough they call him.'

Thoughts whirled in Ascha's head. This put the stand-off between the Cheruskkii and the Theodi in a very different light. Radhalla, the Iron Plough? Sweet Tiw! Did the Franks expect him to kill his father's old friend?

'You seem to know a lot for a Frisian river trader,' he said.

'I'm Frisian-born, but I served with the legions for nearly twenty years,' Octha said cheerfully. 'A Goth spearman opened my leg to the bone and I was left like this.' He slapped his twisted limb. 'I was invalided out and set myself up as a river trader on my retirement pay.' He pulled his mouth down. 'It's not a bad life, but I miss my army days.'

But Ascha hadn't time for the merchant's army stories. 'This Radhalla, what do you think he wants?' he asked bluntly.

The merchant rolled his eyes. 'You ask too many questions, boy,' he said with a touch of annoyance.

'My ma always said I needed to know the answer to everything.'

'Well, she wasn't wrong.'

The merchant seemed mollified. He threw his hands up in the air and let them fall. 'Radhalla wants to unite all the northern tribes into one. The Franks united over fifty years ago, and they now control most of upper Gallia. Radhalla probably thinks he can do the same for the Cheruskkii. So far, it seems to be working.'

Ascha turned casually and looked for the girl. She was sitting on the landing with her hands folded in her lap, staring into the water. From time to time, she brushed her hair from her eyes and pushed it behind her ear. She seemed lost in thought. He wondered if she was listening.

'But what if the tribes don't want to join?'

The fire was dying now, the river folk drifting to their beds. With a grunt, the merchant sat down on the deck next to the girl and leaned back against her. She took his weight and they sat facing in opposite directions, supporting each other. The merchant blew his cheeks as if gathering his thoughts.

'Radhalla always gives them a choice. They can join and be absorbed into the Cheruskkii, or he drives them off their lands into exile. Either way he wins. He acquires wealth and territory. His fame spreads, and men flock from all over the north to join him.'

'You think Radhalla will use his power to negotiate with the Romans?'

The merchant sighed. 'You don't let up do you boy?'

'Well, what do you think?'

'What do I think of what?'

Ascha closed his eyes. 'What's Radhalla's aim? Will he negotiate for tribute or will he take the confederation to war?

'How do I know?'

'Your best guess then.'

The merchant looked at him. 'I think he'll fight. The only question is when.'

He suspected the old man was right. An uprising against the west seemed likely. The girl shifted. She produced an apple from her dress and a small bone-handled knife from her sleeve and began to peel the fruit, cutting thick slices and putting them into her mouth. She gave a piece to the merchant and offered one to Ascha. He looked at her and then took the apple from her fingers.

She looked up at him, unsmiling.

'And what do you think, Carver?' she said. 'Does the thought of a Saxon uprising keep you awake at nights?'

There was a sharpness in her tone that caught him unawares. For a moment, he was afraid that she might suspect he was Saxon-born, and then he relaxed. He looked like a Frank and spoke like a Frank. Why should they think him anything but what he said he was?

'The Saxons are barbarians,' he said dismissively. 'When they've filled their boats with loot, they'll go home.'

The girl leaned forward, eyes hot with anger, her hair sliding across her cheek in a thick black wave.

'Dear God, man, you think those murdering savages have a right to raid?' she spat.

He shrugged. 'It's what they've always done.'

She was on her feet, glaring at him, her face flushed and her eyes filling with tears. 'The Saxons are wolves who spread terror and bring misery to all. They slaughter everybody, women and children. They are a disease. And if we don't deal with them before they unite, they will destroy us all.'

Ascha stared, dumbfounded by her vehemence. Behind him, he heard the merchant's dry cough.

'Herrad loathes all Saxons,' the merchant said softly. 'And with good reason. Her sister, Prydwen, was taken by Saxon raiders three years ago. Herrad hasn't seen her since. She is probably a Saxon slave now. Or worse.'

Ascha felt his face redden. 'I'm sorry,' he said. 'I didn't...'

The girl gave him the barest nod and looked away.

He cursed, riddled with a sudden feeling of guilt. Feeling suddenly ashamed, he turned back to Octha, 'But how can you destroy them?'

'It wouldn't be easy. The Saxons are fast and go where they please. They can raid and be long gone before they are discovered. And the legions today are only a shadow of what they once were. The only way you can destroy them is from within. You have to know where and when they will strike. And when you know that, you bide your time and you wait for them and then, when you are ready, you hit them as hard as you can.'

And the merchant smacked his fist loudly into his palm.

No doubt Clovis saw it that way too. The Romans were almost spent, but the Franks could do it. They were brutal enough and they had the will. All they needed was the right information. Which he supposed was where he came in. The sooner he found out what Radhalla was planning, the sooner he got what he wanted.

He glanced at Herrad. She caught him looking and held out a slice of apple. A peace offer? He hoped so. He took the apple. She gave him a faint smile and he smiled back. At that moment, he felt something he had not felt for a long while. A sense of well-being that, if not quite happiness, was close enough.

Later that night the boat master sought Ascha out in the cowshed where he slept with Baculo and the other rivermen. Wacho had been drinking and the sourness of his breath washed over Ascha like the stench of rotting meat.

'I'm grateful, Carver. That was good work you did for my *Clotsinda.* Help us with the rowing tomorrow and I'll take you to the other side. But keep your head down, if you know what's good for you.'

Ascha nodded. He was not interested in how Wacho and the rivermen earned their living.

'Course, he keep his head down, master.' Baculo said. 'He dreams a doin' jig-a-jig wi' the merchant's niece.'

The men laughed and hooted and pounded the cattle stalls in their glee. Wacho lowered his head and grinned, his teeth bright in the darkness.

Ascha pulled his cloak over his head and tried to sleep. Sometime after midnight he woke and heard men talking. He thought he recognized Wacho's voice and possibly that of Baculo. He must have fallen asleep again because he dreamt of his father, saw him clearly, his massive head and thick hands. His father was trying to speak to him, to tell him something, but he couldn't make out the words.

8

The next day was sunny with a hard-edged brightness. Ascha got up and made his way to the landing. He watched as the rivermen loaded the *Clotsinda*, rolling casks of wine down the plank and stacking the boat with jars of oil, sacks of grain and hides. A fresh breeze was blowing raising white caps on the river and dashing spray high over the riverbank. Wacho paced up and down, shouting angrily. When they were done, the rivermen tossed their cargo hooks in a jangling heap, threw a tarpaulin over the cargo and tied it fast with seal hide ropes.

The merchant arrived with the girl. Ascha went forward to meet them. Octha shook his hand warmly, and the girl smiled and raised a hand in greeting. She wore the same blue skirt as the night before. The skirt was wet from the spray and he noticed how it clung damply to her legs.

The two slaves carried the merchant's chests and put them in the boat, stacking them by the mast. The merchant took a seat in the stern and the girl joined him. She carried a blanket over one arm and a leather bag. The rivermen took their places. Wacho gestured to Ascha to take an oar in front of the cargo mound, but the merchant wouldn't hear of it.

'Carver, come and row back here,' he said, 'and we can talk.'

Wacho scowled and opened his mouth to say something but then let it go. Ascha stepped into the boat behind the cargo. He laid his satchel and blanket roll between his feet and grasped an oar. Baculo took the other. Wacho was the last to come aboard. He jumped onto the stern and took hold of the steering board. The sail bellied with the wind, and the ropework crackled. A watersider pushed them off. Six oars sliced into the thick water, the prow monster snarled and *Clotsinda* drew away.

Ascha and the other oarsmen fell into a steady rhythm. He watched the settlement as it grew smaller and thought he saw movement. He looked again and saw three horsemen moving slowly along the mudflat. He watched them ride between the cabins of the rivermen, slowly separating and then coming together again. They stopped at the water's edge. Ascha peered. They were the same three men he'd met on the road two days before, he was sure of it.

The merchant's voice cut across his thoughts. 'They friends of yours?'

'No,' he said. 'They're no friends of mine.'

They both watched the horsemen until they could be seen no more.

The *Clotsinda* made good headway, six sweeps plashing as one. Ascha put his back into the rowing, watching with pleasure as the Rhine slid by. Green wooded slopes, studded with white-washed houses that gleamed in the sun. After so many days on the road it was good to feel the wind in his hair and the spray in his face. Mid-river, and the wind blowing strong, Wacho barked a command. The rowers pulled in their oars and allowed the wind to drive the *Clotsinda* north.

Octha was a good travel companion. He told stories of his army days, of the people he knew, and his life on the Rhine. He pointed out to Ascha the old Roman frontier posts, the walls crumbling and long-abandoned, greenery invading where legionaries had once gamed and slept. Ascha listened with half an ear and kept his eyes on the girl. She had settled back on her elbows to watch the river unroll, her hair blowing free. The slaves stood by the mast, as if guarding the merchant's chests. Only the smaller slave spoke. The other listened, occasionally gesticulating with his hands. The big slave, Ascha decided, was a mute, as dumb as stone.

The sky darkened and the air turned damp and cold. Talk faded. The girl unfolded the blanket and laid it across Octha's shoulders. She took bread and cold meat from her bag and gave it to Octha. She prepared more food and handed it to the two slaves.

'Carver, will you eat with us?' she asked. He thought for a moment and then nodded and took the food she offered, noticing she did not offer Wacho or Baculo. Ascha ate and leaned back against the strake, closed his eyes and allowed his mind to drift. He thought of his village and tried to imagine the welcome he would receive. He felt a sudden overwhelming yearning to see his mother again, a feeling so strong it brought tears to his eyes.

He woke with a start disturbed by a strange sound, a muffled groan accompanied by a gurgling noise like water sluicing through a dyke gate. He looked up. The big slave stood with his arms wrapped around Baculo who was on his feet, holding onto the slave, as if to stop him falling. Sunlight flashed on a blade that plunged again and again into the slave's side. The slave half turned towards the girl and cried out what might have been a warning. His knees buckled and he fell. The young slave boy had pressed himself against the side of the boat, eyes wide with horror, gibbering with fear.

The girl stood between Baculo and the merchant, brandishing her little knife and jabbing at the Gaul's face.

'No,' Ascha heard her shout. 'No, you will not!'

Baculo cursed her in gutter Latin and whipped back his head to save his eyes. 'Out of my way, girl,' he shouted and jinked looking for an opening. The merchant gazed up at them both, his jaw dropping in lolling disbelief.

Ascha's hand went for his *seaxe* before he remembered Flavinius had taken it. He swore. Baculo feinted with his knife and then punched the girl in the mouth. She reeled back. Ascha came up behind Baculo. Scooping up a cargo hook he swung it in a single fluid movement into the Gaul's groin. Baculo's scream shredded the air.

Behind the girl, Wacho left the steering-board and moved towards the merchant, *seaxe* already drawn. He seized Octha with a beefy forearm, dragged him up, and laid the edge of his knife against the old man's throat. The girl shouted out in fear or anger and slashed, opening the boat master's forearm to the bone. Wacho grunted but continued to grip the merchant tight.

Ascha pulled on the cargo hook, but Baculo's thighs had clamped shut, trapping the hook. Ascha stepped over Baculo's writhing body, grabbed the girl by the arm and dragged her away.

He stood facing Wacho with knees slightly bent, arms in front of his chest, head lowered. Octha was choking, his eyes rolling up in his head.

'I told you to stay out of it!' Wacho snarled.

'I know you did,' Ascha said.

'This is not your fight.'

'No,' Ascha agreed and took a step forward.

'Come any closer, boy, and the old man dies!'

Ascha let his arms drop. 'Then kill him,' he said. 'I met him yesterday.'

Wacho frowned. The *seaxe* lifted. Ascha kicked Wacho on the knee with the side of his boot and then hit him in the face with his elbow. The boat master grunted. Ascha hit him on the nose with the heel of his hand and heard the bone crack. Wacho released Octha who dropped to his knees. The girl rushed to help him. Ascha moved in fast, knowing he had to put Wacho down. He punched the boat master in the throat and drove his fist into Wacho's ribs. Wacho gasped and let the long-knife fall with a clatter on the deck. Wacho stumbled back with his hands to his face, blood streaming from his nose. Before Ascha could do anything, the boat master half-turned, lost his footing and toppled into the river.

'Carver!' the girl shouted.

Ascha swivelled.

Baculo was on his feet, his breeches drenched in blood, advancing with murder in his eyes. Ascha bent and came up with Wacho's *seaxe*. As the Gaul lunged, he parried and seizing Baculo by the hair, forced back his head.

He paused, remembering the beer Baculo had given him the night before.

And then he cut his throat.

They heard feet scrabbling and two rivermen appeared above the cargo mound. Their eyes widened when they saw the bodies of Baculo and the slave. Ascha called out to them that Baculo was dead, and their master probably drowned. He said that if they rowed the *Clotsinda* to the next landing, they would come to no harm and would be free to take Baculo's body and go home. When the rivermen realized that Wacho was gone, the fight went out of them. The attack, they said, was Wacho's idea. Wacho had planned to kill the merchant and dump him overboard. They said nothing of what would have happened to the girl.

When the rivermen had slid back the way they had come, Ascha went to the girl.

'Are you all right?' he said.

She nodded. She seemed stunned but unhurt. He saw that the hem of her skirt was spattered with the slave's blood.

'We have to get off this boat in case the crew change their minds,' he said.

She nodded again. She went to the big slave and closed his eyes, stepping over Baculo's body as if it were dogshit. She spoke softly to the slave boy who was curled up on the deck trembling. She ran a hand through the boy's hair, patted his cheek and then went to Octha. She wrapped the merchant in a blanket and made him comfortable. She and Octha exchanged a few words and then she stood and attended to the boat. Ascha watched as she checked the sail, adjusted the sea ropes and then took hold of the steering board and turned the boat toward shore. He made no move to help. He felt drained and weary. He'd never before killed a man who was not his enemy and he was surprised at how much it shocked him.

They borrowed a spade from a local farmer and buried the slave on a wooded rise overlooking the river. When it was done, Ascha dropped the spade and prepared to leave.

Octha was sitting on one of the chests, his elbows on his knees, staring at his feet. He seemed stunned by what had happened. He looked up as Ascha approached.

'They would have killed us,' he whispered.

'Yes,' Ascha said.

'I've known Wacho for years, always thought of him as my friend.'

'What will you do now?'

'The farmer will put us up for the night. Another boat will be along in the morning and will take us downriver. We'll be at the Rhine mouth in three days.'

Ascha could see Herrad and the boy looking down at where they had buried the big slave. Her hands were clasped before her and he saw her lips moving. He wondered if she was praying.

'And you?' the merchant said.

'East,' Ascha said. 'I'm going home.'

The merchant pushed down on his thighs and got to his feet. 'Then we go in opposite directions,' he said.

Ascha nodded. Unlikely they would ever meet again. The merchant seemed to have the same thought. He paused and looked at him directly.

'Where did you learn to fight like that, boy?'

'Picked it up here and there,' he said quietly.

'Here and there?'

'Yes.'

'And you're a woodcarver?'

'Yes.'

'And where did you say you were from?'

'I didn't.'

The merchant took Ascha's hand and looked him in the eye.

'Whoever you are, I wish you a safe journey. Remember my name: Octha the Merchant. On this river, everybody knows me.'

The merchant dipped his head, took off his burnstone and put it around Ascha's neck. 'I want you to have this,' he said. 'Its magic will protect you.'

'I don't need it.'

'Don't argue, boy. It will do you a lot more good than it will an old fool like me.'

Ascha ran a thumb over the amulet. The amber was rich in colour and smooth to the touch. He looked at Octha, nodded his thanks and moved away. At the edge of the clearing he turned, struck by a thought.

'Old man, can I ask you a question?'

'Of course.'

'What's in the chests?'

The merchant looked back at the two boxes.

'Glass,' he said.

'Glass?'

The merchant raised his shoulders. 'Colonia is the only town in upper Gallia where Roman glassmakers can still be found. There are four dozen wine goblets in those chests. Exquisite things. All wrapped and packed like a babe in the womb.'

'What will you do with them?'

The merchant rubbed a thick thumb against his fingers. 'Sell them, of course! I know men who will pay good money for such luxuries.'

Ascha shook his head. Two men, three if you counted the slave, had died for a box of glass. He walked over to the girl.

'I've come to say goodbye,' he said.

Herrad looked at him, and he saw her eyes drop to the burnstone around his neck. She turned and walked with him a little way up the hill. They stopped and faced each other. 'Maybe you should stick to carving flowers and animals,' she said with a smile. 'Your sea-monsters are too ferocious for this world.'

He said nothing.

She held out her hand, and he took it. Her skin was cool and her eyes seemed bottomless. Ascha glanced back at the merchant. Octha was talking to the farmer. He could see him waving his arms and pointing to the river; boasting about the fight, as likely as not. Herrad smiled at him, and he at her, and then she leaned forward and kissed him lightly on the cheek. It was over before he knew what had happened.

'Goodbye, Carver,' she said.

At the top of the valley he looked back. He could see them both far below, the stocky figure of the merchant in his robe next to the slighter form of the girl. He waved and then a soft rain began to fall and he lost them.

9

He struck east, moving up the valley of the Lupia from the Rhine. The going was slower, but he pushed on as fast as he could. He crossed the watershed and moved on down until he found the headwaters of the Wisurg which he knew would lead him home. He thought about what the merchant had said about Radhalla. The thought of confronting the Cherusker troubled him.

One morning on waking, he had a sudden memory of the girl standing before the mast, her knife flashing in the sunlight. The picture was so vivid, he almost gasped.

He came to a village deep in the forest on the edge of Saxon territory. He dropped to one knee, snuffling the air and then walked on warily. The village was a scene of desolation, huts and granaries burnt to the ground, timbers charred, the ash still smouldering. In the fields cattle lay dead, their legs pointing to the sky. Smoke drifted.

He walked on, scanning the trees, fearful of what he might find. On the other side of the village, he came across a group of peasants digging a grave pit. There was a chill in the air and their breath came out in smoky plumes. They watched him approach, staring with eyes that were bleak and empty. Close by, a dozen bodies lay in the mud, wrapped in sacking, waiting to be put in the ground.

'We be of one blood,' Ascha whispered.

'One blood,' they said.

'Who did this?'

They made no answer. He asked again, and a villager murmured, 'Cheruskkii. They came yesterday. They said we must pay them tribute or they would be back.'

Ascha blinked and looked towards the north. He had never known Saxons to raid so close to their own homeland. He felt a dark premonition that something bad was going to happen.

He went on, each day much like another. The days grew cooler and the nights were cold. He stuffed his boots with grass and tied his blanket around him. The road turned into a droveway and then into a river track that petered out as the river neared the sea. One afternoon, he lifted his eyes and saw a grey horizon studded with *terpen*, the grassy mounds on which the north shore folk built their homes to keep them above the storm flood. Like scabs on a pig's back, he thought. Rooks cawed and seagulls mewled. He was bone-weary, hungry and his feet ached.

But he was home.

He came to the hedge which marked the village boundary. A cold rain fell, and mist blotted out the estuary. He had forgotten how bleak the homeland was. When he thought of the green woods and rolling plains of Gallia, the lands of the Theodi seemed grey and desolate.

He ate his last piece of bread, took a sip of water from his flask and then sat and watched the pale wood smoke drifting over his village. He felt nervous, unsure of what to expect. Would his people remember him? Would they know who he was? What would he say when he faced his father again? He clenched his jaw and went over in his mind what he had to do. Keep your ears open for talk of war. Count the long ships that pass down the Wisurg. Take note of the tribes that join the Confederation.

After a while, he got to his feet. He scraped the thick mud from his boots on a clump of grass and walked on.

Scabby-kneed children stood barefoot in the street and stared at him. Dogs snuffled his cloak. He walked down dank and narrow alleyways, twisting through huts and outbuildings, breathing in the acrid tang of his birthplace, a sour mix of salt marsh, wood smoke and human waste.

His father's hall lay in the middle of the *terp* surrounded by a rough palisade. The hall's roof curved like a saddle, and the boards were peeling, the chinks daubed with mud. A doorway was carved with painted animals, birds and flowers, his own work.

He lifted the bar of the gate and stepped inside. Blood was pumping into his chest, and his mouth was dry. A woman emerged from the house. She walked to a garden, furrowed with vegetables, picked up a hoe and began to work. He watched her without moving, a lump in his throat. She seemed smaller than he remembered, the hair greyer beneath the linen cap.

And then, as if disturbed by some foreboding, she turned and looked straight at him, one hand raised to shield her eyes. Slowly, so as not to alarm her, he stepped away from the shadow of the palisade. The woman's eyes travelled over him for what seemed a long while and then she suddenly stiffened, and a hand flew like a little bird to her mouth.

'Hello, Ma,' he said.

The hoe slipped from her fingers and rattled on the ground.

They hugged and held each other for a long time. Ascha felt as if a great weight had been lifted from his shoulders. He kissed his mother, and she wound her arms around his waist and squeezed him tight.

'You look older,' she said. 'And your clothes are different, and what have you done to your hair?'

He laughed and ran a hand over his head. His hair was growing out but was still short.

'I thought I would never see you again,' she said. 'Look at you, all grown up!' She gave a sound that was somewhere between a sob and a laugh.

'It's good to be home, Ma,' he said. He put his arms around her shoulders and pulled her close.

'Go inside and I'll get you something to eat,' she said. She grasped him by the elbow and pushed him towards the door.

He stepped inside and peered about nervously. The hall was much as he recalled, dark and double-aisled, one end given over to cattle and separated from the living area by a wicker screen. Around the walls were benches, beds, a salting tub, water buckets, troughs, a table and his father's chair. A planked floor was strewn with rushes, the walls bare but for brightly-woven blankets and his father's war harness. Mail coat, shields, helmet and sword burnished until they shone. A fire glowed in the sandbox, and he could smell the burning pine. He ran a hand down the length of the table and touched the back of his father's chair with the tips of his fingers. He breathed in the musky smell of home and, as the memories came rushing back, his eyes misted.

His mother gave him eggs cooked in sage, boiled meat, cheese and bread washed down with sour milk. He ate hungrily. When he had finished, she sat him down by the fire, held his hands, and told him of his father's death.

'He was travelling,' she said, speaking in Latin as she always did when they were alone. 'He fell from his horse and broke his thigh. They brought him home and put him to bed, but he caught the wound fever. He was sick for a long time. Towards the end he had pains here,' she touched her chest. 'I treated him as well as I could, but nothing seemed to work. One day I left him for a moment and when I came back he had changed. He was very pale and his skin was wet, as if greased with goose fat. I touched him on the shoulder and he just toppled over. When I felt his wrist, he was dead.'

Ascha looked at her. His father was dead? He felt cold all over.

'I had no way of telling you,' his mother said helplessly. 'I didn't know where you were.'

'When did he die?' he said.

'About a month ago.'

He tried to remember where he would have been, probably marching to fight the Herul. The breath came out of him as if he'd been kicked by a bull. He forgot his hatred and the burning anger he had tended for five long years. His eyes prickled, and he walked away so his mother wouldn't see. He blundered into the yard not knowing where he was going. He bit his knuckle and ground his fist into his eye socket. It was as if someone had reached in and ripped away some innermost part of him. Had there been no sign of Aelfric's departing spirit? No shadow?

And then he remembered the dream at the river crossing, his father calling to him.

His father had not forgotten him.

His mother followed him into the yard. She put her arms around him and held him. He turned and wrapped his arms around her shoulders.

'He grieved for you,' she said. 'He grieved every day. He felt he had no choice but to send you away.'

Ascha shook his head. 'Did he have a warrior's burial?' he said thickly.

She nodded. 'Your father's sworn-men paid him full honour.'

His father had been buried in full war gear in a felt shroud with spears and shield, his second best sword and his favourite *seaxe*. A horse had been killed and planted in the soil with him. Food and a bucket of ale had finished the corpse dressing.

'Your father always liked his beer,' his mother said.

He laughed at that and the tears welled up again.

'Folk came from all the neighbouring tribes,' she said. 'It was a good funeral. Hroc insisted.'

'Hroc?'

She looked at him. 'Hroc is *hetman* now,' she said.

He couldn't believe what he'd heard. Hroc was *hetman?*
She nodded.
'But he is not firstborn. And he was not my father's choice.'
His mother led him back into the hall and sat him down. She
paused and then said, 'Since you went away there has been a lot of
trouble. The Cheruskkii have become very strong.'
'I know, Ma. I know all about the Cheruskkii.'
She nodded, accepting without question that he knew. 'They
wanted us to join them. They thought that having us aboard would
make their war lawful. Your father was against it. He thought it
would be the end of who we were.'
'What happened?'
'There was a raid. Two young boys and a girl were taken. A man
was killed. Your father suspected the Cheruskkii, but they denied it.
He was already sick by then. He was dying and he knew it. But
before he died, he decided he would make Hroc *hetman.*'
'But why Hroc?' Ascha said, the bitterness flowing out of him.
'Hanno had the birthright.'
'Hroc knew the Cheruskkii. He was friends with Sigisberht,
Radhalla's nephew, as your father and Radhalla were once friends.'
She looked at him, her eyes far away and glistening. 'And he was
always the stronger.'
'But Hroc can't be trusted. He nearly got us all killed at
Samarobriva.'
'He's a hothead sure enough, but your father thought that if he
was *hetman* we would have a better chance.'
Ascha struck the table with his fist, sending the plates jumping.
'It's not right, Ma!' he yelled.
She frowned. 'What's not right?'
'My father named Hroc as hostage, but Hroc refused to go. It split
the clan.'
'That's what they told me.'
'So the Franks chose me even though I was not free born.'
She laid her hand on top of his as the understanding dawned. 'You
mean you needn't have gone away,' she murmured. 'You needn't
have become an exile.'
She wound her arms around him and held him close. He felt a
slow fury at the futility of it all. All those wasted years, and he
would never see his father again. Aelfric would never know what
he had become.

When he was calmer, he pulled away from her. He wondered what Hroc would do. Would his brother come to terms with the Cheruskkii or would he hold out? But he already knew the answer to that. Hroc would never give in to the Cheruskkii. That was why Aelfric had chosen him rather than sweet-natured Hanno. One thing he was sure of. With his father dead and Hroc *hetman*, there was nothing to keep him here. Maybe when all this was over, the Theodi would let him take his mother and return to Frankland. They could start a new life there.

'And Hanno?' he said.

'He took it very badly. When Hroc became *hetman*, Hanno left the clan and went to live among the Taifali, his wife's people, across the river.'

He looked at her, taking it all in. 'And where is he now?'

'He's here,' she said simply. 'He came back. He said he'd thought it over and wanted to return to the clan. He was prepared to accept Hroc as war leader and would serve him loyally. Blood was thicker than water, he said.'

'And what do you think'.

'He always was weak,' she said.

They came as soon as they heard. Hanno first, his face flushed from running, lean and tall as an elm, clean-shaven with a mane of tawny hair, but as gentle and placid as a large dog.

'Tha's grown, Ascha. Tiw's will, and tha has come back to us.' Hanno hugged him and ruffled his hair and punched him playfully on the upper arm as he used to when Ascha was a boy.

Ascha grinned and punched him back, delighted to see him.

Behind Hanno came Budrum, his father's sister, throwing her flabby arms around his neck and covering him with kisses. Besso, bending low under the lintel, his long face breaking into an unaccustomed smile. And Tchenguiz, his father's Hun slave, his short square body and skin the colour of walnut, squeezing Ascha so hard he thought his chest would burst.

'Ha! Ascha! Tha's home at last.'

Hroc came later.

He entered the hall, filling the doorway, and slowly surveyed the room. When his gaze settled on Ascha, he looked at him, his eyebrows knitted, as if he were a stranger. Hroc was not as tall as Hanno but his chest and arms were as powerful as a bull. He wore a full beard and his hair, the colour of wheat, coiled and knotted on the crown of his head. He walked up to Ascha and looked him up and down. Ascha tensed. He felt the muscles in his shoulder stiffen and his mouth go dry

'I am glad to see tha alive, little brother,' Hroc said softly. 'Welcome home.'

Two days later he and his mother went to visit his father's grave. They carried food and a pitcher of beer, sustenance for Aelfric in the next world. Aelfric's grave was a whale-backed and grassy hummock overlooking the estuary. While his mother swept out the mourning booth, Ascha sat and tried to recall the man his father had been. Soft drifts of childhood memories blew through his head like autumn leaves. He remembered his father telling drunken war stories, his big face creased with laughter. And he remembered him standing before the shield wall, sword in hand. But his mind kept returning to his father's boot grinding the dust as he decided which of his sons to send away.

He placed the food in the booth and stepped back. A son's duty to bring meat to his father, he thought ruefully. And he'd always been a good son, hadn't he? Always done what was needed. But tha never gave me a chance, did tha? I was the son of the slave-wife. Good enough to serve at table, to empty the shit-bucket and to clean out the pig-sty. Good enough to work from dawn to dusk on the farm. Good enough to give to the Franks as hostage. But never good enough to bear arms or to treat as equal to his brothers?

For years he had hated his father so much that it came as a surprise to discover that his feelings had changed. The hatred he had harboured had not gone but it had faded, leaving only sadness in its wake. And something else besides, relief maybe or maybe regret for what he had lost. He wouldn't have wanted to see the guilt on Aelfric's face when he met the son he had sent away. We are born and then we die, Ascha thought. And when we die, everything dies. All our hopes and fears, gone as if they had never been.

He looked up.

Out in the estuary, the sea was cold and grey. Seagulls shrieked. There were boats on the river but no warships. The thought crossed his mind that apart from the *SeaWulf* hauled up on the riverbank, he'd not seen a single war boat pass down the river since he had arrived. If the Cheruskkii were planning an uprising, there were few signs of it. That morning he had gone for a run along the river, to the edge of Theodi land in both directions.

Nothing.

He took the jug of beer from his mother. Holding it in both hands, he whispered a prayer to Great Tiw for Aelfric's spirit and then poured the beer over his father's grave, shaking it free of the last drop.

10

Early the next morning he pulled on his boots, cut himself a piece of cheese and stuffed two hard boiled eggs in his tunic. He led Caba, his father's mare, from the stable and saddled her. The mud in the yard was frozen, and the mare put down her hoofs cautiously, chewing the bit and fretting in case she slipped. He gentled her, whispered in her ear and blew in her nostrils. Vaulting onto the mare's back, he went off at a swinging trot through the village.

He took the horse down the terp-side and out to the fields. It had been raining and the ground was soft underfoot. When he reached the meadows, he let her have her head. She snorted, flicked back her ears and was off, galloping in a thunder of hooves and flying mud. He rode for a while and then took the track that led out to the river mouth.

The river was wide and empty, still no ships. If the Cheruskkii were gathering warships for a raid, they weren't doing it in the estuary.

He rode for most of the morning. Far off he could hear the distant boom of the surf and the hiss of the marsh grass. He pulled in and let the horse crop while he shelled the eggs and ate them and the cheese. He filled his lungs with sea air and rolled his neck and felt the tension ease from his shoulders. Tiw! It was good to be on a horse again. If only his life could always be like this. He went on, taking Caba across a stream and up the other side and out onto the moor.

And then, by a stand of wind-stunted trees, he saw movement.

There were men coming down the track, maybe a dozen, slouching along with spears and lances and big war shields. He watched them for a while and then he turned the horse and rode back some way, before swinging round. He saw a break in the trees and made for it, ducked under a branch and came out through the weeds and dead grass ahead of them. The men were already coming into view. He could hear muffled voices and the chink of metal.

When they saw him they stopped and watched him, fingering their weapons. They were filthy with matted hair and carried blanket rolls and sacks over their shoulders, every man armed with wood and iron. Even from where he sat, he could smell their sweat, like a pail of armpits. One of them stepped forward. Scrawny-thin and dirty with hair that was long and filthy, he wore an iron helmet and a sealskin pinned with a thorn.

'That's far enough!' Ascha said.

The man gave him an easy smile. 'We be of one blood,' he said.

'One blood.' Ascha said curtly. 'What are you and what are you doing here? This is Theodi land.'

'We're travellers, friend.' The man said, the accent more Danish than Saxon.

'Where do you think you're going?'

'Nowhere.'

'You're going nowhere?'

'We're heading south.'

'Why?'

'To join the Cheruskkii.'

'The Cheruskkii? You're a long way from the road.'

The stranger studied him. 'You could be right.' His eyes fell on the mare. 'That's a good horse you got there, friend,' he said. He scratched the back of his neck and muttered something to the other men and then took a couple of lazy steps forward. 'Now, tell me,' he smiled, 'how do we find the road?'

Ascha twisted in the saddle and pointed. 'Go to the river and follow it south.'

He'd not seen them move yet they seemed closer. They had moved off the track and were coming towards him, trying to outflank him.

Ascha shouted, 'Stand back!'

The stranger was lithe and quick. He made a grab for the mare's headstall. Ascha kicked him in the face and pulled the horse around, hammered his heels and charged straight at them. The mare's shoulder caught one man and sent him flying. The others scattered. Ascha rode through and out the other side. When he was beyond them, he pulled up and looked back. The leader was sitting in the mud nursing his jaw, the rest of them watching him.

He followed them until they left Theodi territory. Northerners, he knew that much, but not Saxons.

Radhalla was casting his net wide.

On his way back to the village, he went over what he knew.

One, Radhalla was now war leader of the Cheruskkii nation.

Two, he was assembling a confederation of Saxon tribes, dominated by the Cheruskkii.

Three, he was recruiting. Not just Saxons but from tribes across the north.

Four, the attack on the Thuringii meant he was already raiding beyond Saxon territory.

Ascha sucked in air between his teeth. He had no idea what Radhalla planned to do but it looked as if Clovis had been right to be afraid. An uprising seemed inevitable. Invasion by land was possible, but unlikely. The journey was long and dangerous, and Radhalla had no way of transporting an army across the Rhine or bringing them back. Which left by sea. Yet, since his return he had not seen a single Cherusker, let alone a Cherusker warboat. Clovis had said that the Theodi were threatened by the Cheruskkii. He was beginning to wonder if Clovis had lied to persuade him to return home.

He clicked his tongue. He needed information, and the only way to get it was to find out for himself. And that meant going to the lands of the Cheruskkii. The thought made him nervous. Even if Radhalla had no plans to move against the Theodi, a Theod could not consider himself safe among the Cheruskkii.

He kicked the mare's flanks and trotted down the road. In the fields, dark figures were moving, men busy with the winter ploughing, women carrying water, children driving goats and sheep to graze.

When he got back to the farm, he found Tchenguiz squatting cross-legged on a bench, mending a harness.

'Good ride?' Tchenguiz said.

'Good,' he grunted, swinging his leg over and sliding off the mare's back. 'I went out to the point and down the river as far as muddy beck.' He hesitated and then said, 'There were armed men on the moor.'

Tchenguiz stopped what he was doing. 'We see them sometimes.'

Ascha felt a flush of anger. 'I remember when no man would cross our land without our say.'

Tchenguiz stood up, unstrapped the saddle, laid it on the ground and threw a blanket over the mare. 'That was a long time ago,' he said, 'before your father died.'

His voice sounded flat and without emotion.

'Where are my brothers?'

'Hroc is in north field. Hanno went upriver to buy a cow.'

Odd, Ascha thought. They didn't need another cow. Since his return, he'd seen little of Hanno. His brother seemed distant, as if he had things on his mind. Ascha was beginning to wonder if he still bore a grudge.

Tchenguiz sat back down on the bench. Ascha hesitated and then went over and squatted down beside him.

'Tchenguiz, does tha miss my father?' he said.

'Ha!' Tchenguiz said and gave one of his strange barking laughs. 'Aelfric was good man.'

Tchenguiz had a flat nose and powerful shoulders. He wore a thin beard, no more than a few hairs on his chin, and a patched woollen poncho. Aelfric had trusted the Hun and given him freedoms he would give no other man, slave or free. In another life, they might have been friends. When Ascha was growing up, it was Tchenguiz who had taught him to ride and to shoot with the bow. Tchenguiz he went to when the other boys kicked him and spat at him for being a half-slave. Tchenguiz understood what it was not to be free and, Hanno apart, he was the only man Ascha knew would never hurt him. He felt close to the Hun, as if they shared a deep secret. But he also remembered times when he had treated the Hun badly. Caught between slave and free, he'd often taken out his frustrations on Tchenguiz. They had been friends all his life, but never equals.

'Was tha with him when he fell?'

The Hun nodded.

'What was he doing? Hunting?'

'Na, he go see Radhalla.'

Ascha glanced at Tchenguiz but the Hun kept his head down, busying himself with the harness. Strange, he thought. His mother had made no mention of this.

'Why did my father go see Radhalla?'

The Hun looked up at Ascha. 'Your father wanted to make things better between Cher'skkii and Theodi. I tell him not to go. But he not listen to me. Always he know better. I tell him, Radhalla is bad man.'

Ascha peered at Tchenguiz. 'And he fell from his horse?'

Tchenguiz nodded. 'Caba throw him, and he go down.'

Ascha frowned. His father's nervousness with horses was well known, but this puzzled him.

'But the mare seems gentle enough.'

'Ha, Caba very gentle,' Tchenguiz said. He picked up a brush and began brushing the mare's flanks.

Ascha thought for a moment.

'What happened? Did something scare her?'

Tchenguiz put down the brush. He looked down at the mud and then up at Ascha.

'We in forest riding home,' he said. 'All of a sudden, Caba rear and throw Aelfric. She run away. Next day when I find her, she very frightened and saddle slip to here.' He held his hand a little way off the ground. 'Take me long time to calm her.' There was a flash of anger in the Hun's eyes. 'Long time!'

'Was she hurt?'

Tchenguiz nodded. The thought had occurred to him also. 'I look. At first I see nothing. Then I find big wound on her rump, like this.' He put his forefinger and thumb almost together to form an egg-sized ring.

'Insect bite?'

Tchenguiz looked at him. 'Not insect.'

They held each other's gaze. 'A stone, then?

'Ha!' Tchenguiz said with a small sigh.

They held each other's eyes.

Slingshot!'

'Maybe.'

'And tha saw nobody.'

Tchenguiz shook his head. 'It was forest, almost night.'

'What does tha think happened?'

Tchenguiz shrugged. 'We in Cher'skkii lands.'

Ascha stared at him without blinking. He knew Tchenguiz was holding something back.

'Does tha think Radhalla killed my father?'

Tchenguiz looked at him. 'I am slave. I do not think.'

Stung, Ascha grabbed him by the shoulder. 'Yes, tha does, Tchenguiz,' he shouted. 'Slave or no slave, tha believes Radhalla killed my father.'

He let go the Hun's arm. Tchenguiz looked at him, his face blank. Neither of them spoke.

Ashamed of his outburst, Ascha closed his eyes and rubbed a knuckle against his nose. He had overreacted. He should learn to control his temper. 'What happened?' he said in a softer tone.

'Thi father hurt bad,' Tchenguiz said. 'He break his thigh and hit his head. We fix his leg and bring him home. He sleep a lot. No eat, no talk. He not know me. Only know thi mother. Sometime he talk to her, like this.'

Tchenguiz pushed out his jaw and let out a strange whimper, like a sick animal.

The homecoming feast was Hroc's idea. The beer buckets were taken down and scalded, tables set up in the hall, crisp linen sheets laid white as a fall of snow. A sheep and a pig were slaughtered. The women baked, and the men brewed beer.

Ascha arrived late. He had gone for a long walk along the riverbank, brooding over what Tchenguiz had told him. By the time he entered, the hall was dark and crowded, filled with the smell of wood smoke and roasting meat. The free men sat at the tables while the women and children sat on benches around the walls. Dogs weaved between them like flies over a cowpat. He saw his mother ladling ale into drinking-cups which Budrum passed along. Sweating slaves staggered between the tables carrying trays laden with food and drink.

As soon as they saw him, Ascha was swept along on a tide of welcome, hugged and backslapped and enfolded in brawny arms, his back pounded until it ached. The women were excited and twittered like birds. The men shyer, their faces cracked with grins. They came up to him stomping their boots and told him he hadn't changed a whit. Others said how different he was from the boy who had gone away. Children peered at him and wondered who the stranger was. And all the while his mother held his hand so tight he thought it might break.

Ascha basked in their happiness. But he noticed how his exile had been like a death, mourned and then put aside. Not forgotten, but barely remembered. He saw his brothers dressed in their finest and watched with growing resentment as Hroc took his seat in his father's chair. He had hoped Hroc would say something about what had happened at Samarobriva, but after a while he realized that Hroc would never feel remorse. Hroc had done what he wanted and that, for Hroc, would always be enough.

Hanno looked up and called him over. Ascha hesitated. As a half-slave, he could not eat with the freemen on the high table, but then Hroc waved and patted the bench beside him.

Grinning, Ascha took his place between his brothers.

Later, when everybody was woozy with food and beer, they called for Hanno.

'Tell us a story,' they roared, stamping their feet and whistling.

Ascha clapped and cheered along with everybody else, remembering how his brother could catch a poem by the tail and spin it, weaving a story that would charm the very birds from the trees.

Hanno got to his feet. He raised his hands and asked for quiet. He wore a red woollen tunic, his hair washed and gathered in a horse's tail that whispered down his back. He waited until there was silence.

'Today is a special day,' Hanno said in sombre tones. 'We are gathered here to welcome home my brother, who was cruelly taken from us by the Franks.' He turned to Ascha and placed a hand on his shoulder. 'But now Ascha has returned to us. My heart fills with joy to see tha here once again, back with thi own people, back home where tha belongs.'

They let rip, feet stamping and knuckles rapping.

Ascha beamed.

'But life is not all joy,' Hanno said. 'Not long ago my father died. Aelfric was our *hetman* for many years. He took us on raids across the sea and led us against our enemies. He forced the Franks to pay us tribute, and we came home rich in slaves and war-loot.'

Ascha took a sip of beer and glanced around. The Theodi were nodding, caught by the moment.

'Under Aelfric's wise leadership we were blessed by Tiw. We traded with the outlanders who crossed our lands and we grew wealthy. We forgot the taste of hunger. They were good years.'

The fire crackled and spat and a log shifted. Ascha swept the room. The Theodi were watching Hanno, mouths open. He was aware of Hroc sitting beside him, drinking in every word.

Hanno lifted his hands. 'We are *Aelfricingas*, the people of Aelfric, and we mourn his death,' he said.

'We mourn his death,' the Theodi intoned.

'Since Aelfric died, times have been hard,' Hanno continued. 'We suffered when the storm-surge flooded our fields. We suffered when the harvest failed. We suffer still from the threat of war.'

'We have suffered,' they murmured.

The wind gusted, rattling the shutters. A thick plume of smoke tumbled into the hall and slowly uncoiled, stinging Ascha's eyes. He held his breath, every eye in the hall on Hanno.

Hanno lowered his arms and then lifted one hand. 'Why, brothers and sisters, do we endure these hardships?' He paused and looked about him. 'I will tell you why. Since Aelfric's death, the Theodi have turned away from Tiw. His face no longer shines upon us.'

Hanno lifted both arms high in the air and put back his head, his voice rising.

'People of the Theodi, I say to you now, we must turn back to the path of Tiw before it is too late. We must take the God of the Theodi once more into our hearts. Trust in Tiw and with his divine help, I promise you, we shall be a holy people once more.'

Silence but for the crackling of the fire and the wind whistling through the rafters. Hanno stood, eyes glittering, and then abruptly sat down.

The Theodi looked to one another uncertainly.

A crash as a bench tipped over.

Hroc lurched to his feet, beer in hand. He took a step, nearly stumbled, and then leaned on Ascha's shoulder for support. He swore beneath his breath and then flung his arms wide.

'My friends! I am a simple man and I do not have Hanno's way with words, but I will say this. While there is beer in the bucket and meat on the table, while there is food enough to give our little ones plump cheeks and warm bodies, while our women have kind hearts and fat arses, we will remain true to who we are. And bugger what Tiw thinks! We are Theodi, the people of the pool! We shall survive. And one day, I promise you, we shall prosper once again.'

The crowd went wild, laughing and thumping their feet on the floor. Ascha glanced at Hanno. His brother was staring at Hroc, his handsome face twisted into a look of dark fury. His father had been right, he thought. In times of crisis, what the clan needed was the leadership of a pig-headed brute like Hroc, not a god-fearing poet like Hanno.

Hroc raised the beer horn. Turning to Ascha, he dragged him to his feet, breathing warm beery fumes into his face.

'Welcome home, little brother,' he bellowed. 'Welcome home!'

After the feasting, the trestles were taken down and the benches pushed back. The clan danced to the thrum of the bowstring and the rap of the skin-drum, floorboards squawking like wet hens.

Besso got to his feet. He hitched his belt up over his belly, cupped one hand behind his ear and sang, slapping his thigh to keep time. He sang the old songs, of long raids across the sea, of friendship and battle and the joy of returning home, laden with loot, to a woman's warm welcome. His voice was rich and deep, like old oak steeped in honey. Once, Ascha would have listened to Besso all night, but now he felt on edge. He had to keep in mind what he was doing here. He had a job to do.

He felt a tug at his sleeve. It was Hroc. His brother pulled him by the arm, drawing him away from the noise and the press of bodies.

'How does tha find us?' Hroc yelled.

'I feel like a ghost,' Ascha said. 'Nothing is what it was.'

'Maybe tha came back to the wrong place.'

'Maybe I did.'

They smiled at each other without humour.

'The young Frank,' Hroc said, 'that little piss-pot we met at Sam...'

'Samarobriva.'

'They tell me he's now Overlord of all the Franks?'

Ascha nodded. 'He is.'

Hroc shook his head. 'Tha should have let me kill him when I had the chance.'

Ascha pursed his lips. If Hroc had killed Clovis, life would have been different for all of them. 'Tha's right, I should have,' was all he said.

'Does tha think the little bugger will take the Franks to war against the Cheruskkii?'

'Why would he?' Ascha said, his words tinged with venom.

For a moment there was no expression on Hroc's face, and then he gave Ascha a grim smile. 'Tha's right,' he said. 'Why would he?' He grinned and slapped Ascha hard on the shoulder. 'Now tha's home, we must go hunting. Boar! That's the thing. There's a big brute along the north shore. A monster! Hanno says we ought to go get him. You should come!'

He gave Ascha a huge wink and was gone.

Ascha went out to the yard. Outside it was cold and still. The air smelled clean, rain washed, the music muffled, as if wrapped in a blanket. Moonlight glinted in the elms. He patted his belly and belched contentedly. His homecoming was going better than he had hoped and the clan, even Hroc, had welcomed him with open arms. He smiled and ran his hand over the back of his head. Perhaps he would grow his hair long again. Braid and coil it in a topknot, like a true Theod. He smiled and shook his head at his own foolishness.

He went to the paddock and clicked his tongue. Caba came immediately. She blew through her nostrils, pushed her nose into his palm and allowed herself to be stroked.

He heard a step and turned.

A young woman stood bundled against the chill. She pulled back her shawl and let it fall around her shoulders. In the moonlight, he saw a broad brow, eyes set wide apart in an open face, a snub nose and curly hair.

'Saefaru?' he said.

'How is tha, Ascha?' she said with a shy smile.

'I wouldn't have recognized tha,' he said. 'It's been a long time.'

He let his eyes wander over her. She was rounder in the face than he remembered, and plumper. No longer the skinny girl whose form he had whittled up in the tree. She wore a dark dress edged in some brighter colour, a metal brooch at each shoulder and at her wrists, copper sleeve-clasps. His mind went back to when she would slip from her cabin when her father was asleep, run with him through the meadows and lie beside him in the grass, their legs entwined like ivy on a barn roof.

'Tha's become a fine-looking young man, Ascha.'

There was a wistful note in her voice.

He opened his mouth to speak but she held up her hand.

'They told me tha wouldn't be coming back,' she said. 'They said tha was going to be a hostage!' She spat out the word as if it were something unclean. 'I thought I'd niver see tha again.'

'Is tha well?' he said, his voice husky.

She nodded but he could tell she was crying. 'I'm married,' she said. 'And I have a son!'

He should have guessed. Her hair was tied in a single braid and from her belt hung the iron key of a married woman.

'He's a good boy,' she went on quickly. 'He'll make a fine warrior.'

A deep sense of loss, bitter as ashes, passed through him. Saefaru married with a son? All those nights he had lain awake, thinking of her. She had been his hope and his comfort. He felt as if something precious that had belonged to him had been suddenly ripped away.

The door opened and a man appeared, edged by the yellow light. The man shouted into the darkness, his voice hard and insistent.

'It's my husband, I must go.'

She made no move to leave, standing there with her chin lifted as if waiting for something to happen.

Ascha peered at the man in the doorway.

'It's Wulfhere,' she said, seeing the direction of his gaze. 'I married Wulfhere.'

'Wulfhere?' he said, disbelieving.

'He's a good man, Ascha. He's not what he was.'

'Wulfhere!' he repeated with disgust. How on Tiw's earth could she have married Wulfhere?

The man in the doorway shouted again, punching her name into the darkness and then went inside. Saefaru went to move away. As she did so, she turned suddenly. Ascha stepped in close. He put one hand behind her neck and drew her to him. He paused and then he kissed her, hard on the mouth. He felt the dry pressure of her lips and the touch of her tongue as she leant into him, and then with a gasp she broke away.

At the door, she gave a little wave to where he stood in the darkness.

Sweet mother of Tiw! He thought, and then she went inside.

***

One winter, many years before, Ascha is hare-hunting with friends near a lake not far from the village. The lake is frozen, the air raw and damp, and snow hangs heavy in the trees. Lost in the thrill of the hunt, Ascha has no idea anybody is behind him until a stone strikes him on the side of the head. He picks it up and turns, blood running down his cheek, and his heart sinks. Wulfhere and two cronies are standing loose-limbed and grinning, the ill-will hanging out of them.

Wulfhere is the youngest son of a poor freeman farmer and has been Ascha's enemy for as long as he can remember. He is older and stronger than Ascha, with thick arms and a mess of dirty blond hair falling over small and pig-like eyes. Wulfhere loathes Ascha and all slave-born and once beat an old slave woman until the blood flowed.

Sensing trouble, Ascha's friends slip away. Wulfhere and his friends jostle Ascha, slap his face, spit on him and accuse of him using a weapon.

'Weapons are permitted for hunting,' he says, his tone defiant.

Wulfhere leans his face into his. 'Only free born have the right to bear arms. And tha's not free born, is tha, *mischling*?'

Mischling, the half-breed.

Ascha clenches the stone in his hand. Face burning with shame, he swallows and says, 'I'm no *mischling.*'

'Na,' Wulfhere snarls. 'Tha's a slave-whelp and thi mother's a slave whoor who's been with half the men in the village.'

Ascha flings the stone into Wulfhere's face. A sharp yell of pain. Wulfhere coughs, his hand flies up and comes away all bloody.

'He's broken my fucken nose,' he spits.

For a moment, they stare at Ascha in blank astonishment and then they lay into him, fists swinging. Ascha punches one boy in the teeth. He turns, kicks another between the legs and then he runs. They chase him through the woods and along the lake-side. They are bigger and stronger, and he knows he cannot escape. Desperate, he steps onto the ice. It holds. Carefully, he takes another step, moving further out onto the frozen lake.

Wulfhere and his friends stop. Ascha sees that they are too heavy to follow him. He keeps on going and then turns. He waves his arms and jeers, taunting them. They stare at him with loathing and then bend and pick up stones. A rock comes skittering and sliding across the ice towards him. Another bounces, throwing up a hail of shards. Ascha feels a sharp burst of pain as a rock raps him on the shin. He goes on, trying to get beyond their reach. Grey water slowly moving beneath him.

The ice gives way, and Ascha goes under. The shock punches the breath from his lungs. Teeth trembling in their sockets, he kicks and takes a deep gulp of air. He hears a distant cheer and then the water closes over him, thick and cold and murky. More stones come slithering over the ice towards him. Overwhelming pain pounds through his head. He feels the cold sapping his strength. Somewhere he can hear shouts. He is sinking. No strength to kick, all feeling going in his legs.

Someone grabs his hair and pulls him up, lifting him out of the dirty water. He feels strong arms haul him ashore and then darkness closes over him.

When he comes round he is lying with one cheek pressed into the frozen mud, and Hanno is kneeling beside him thumping foul water from his lungs. A ring of villagers are pointing at him and whispering. But what he remembers is Wulfhere, his nose pulped and bleeding, and his eyes murderous.

***

The day after the feast, Ascha was returning from his morning ride. He rode the mare through the village and down to the river. As they neared the water's edge, ducks quacked, geese honked and the mare quickened her pace. It had rained heavily in recent weeks, and the river was swollen. Caba hesitated. Ascha patted her neck, whispered and walked her in until the water was over her fetlocks. He slid off her back and with his cupped hands scooped up water and washed the mud off her legs and belly. The mare turned her head and watched him. He was surprised at how warm the water was. He took a handful of twisted straw, scraped the water off her flanks and then mounted and rode back to the farm.

Rounding an alley corner, he saw a man at the jetty, cloaked and booted, stepping into a boat. The man turned suddenly and seemed to stare right at him. He hastily pulled the mare back into the shadows and watched as the boat pulled away and sailed upriver. Where, he wondered, was that bastard Wulfhere going to at this time of day?

'I saw Wulfhere at the jetty,' Ascha said later. 'He was dressed for travelling.'

'Sometimes he goes across the river to see his cousin,' his mother said.

'His cousin?'

'Yes.'

'How long will he be away?'

His mother stopped what she was doing and studied him. He ate and pretended not to notice, thinking no more questions.

'Two, maybe three days,' she said.

He nodded and carried on eating.

Since his return, his mother seemed reluctant to let him out of her sight. Sometimes he caught her staring at him as if she could not believe he was really there. She would reach across to brush the hair away from his face or lay a hand against his cheek. One day they went to the beach. They sat on an old sea-washed tree and watched the sea come in, wave after wave, sloshing over their feet. She told him how the year after he left there had been a storm surge. The river broke its banks and the meadows flooded. The sea ditches could not cope with the torrent, roots were stripped bare and houses washed away. The livestock had drowned before the Theodi could get to them and the crops were ruined. The starving time his mother called it. The poor had eaten cats and dogs, rats, birds, even tree bark. Their bellies had swollen and they had grown too weak to work. Some left the village. They went overseas, joined warbands and looked for new land.

A few, she said, had sold their children to buy food.

He stared at her, thunderstruck. 'How could they do that?'

'People have to eat,' she said as if that was the answer to everything.

She told him that without the Franks' silver, more would have died.

Ascha understood. Life among the Franks had not been easy, but he had not gone hungry. He picked up a pebble and hurled it into the sea, picked up another and then dropped it. They sat without speaking and then his mother glanced at him and said, 'Ascha, why did you come back?'

'I came to see you.' He saw the doubt on her face. 'You don't believe me?'

'Maybe.'

'Maybe?'

'You've changed. You're different.'

He laughed bitterly, his chest tight. 'How am I different? I was the son of a slave before and I'm the son of a slave now.'

She flinched as if he had slapped her across the face and then said, 'You are not what you were. There's something about you. Something you're not telling me.'

He said, 'There's nothing, Ma, nothing at all.'

Neither of them spoke. And then she said, 'Was it hard for you among those people?'

'Hard enough.'

'Tell me.'

He saw her tears falling and hardened his heart. 'You don't want to know, Ma.'

She stopped crying. She breathed in and said firmly, 'I think you should go.'

Sweet Tiw! What was all this about? 'Go where, Ma?' he said. 'I've only just arrived.'

'Go back to Frankland. Go to Pritannia. There's nothing for you here. Nothing has changed. You think it has, but it hasn't.'

He sensed the fear coming off her in waves, and then it dawned on him. 'You think the Cheruskkii will move against us? Is that it?' He reached over and took her hand. 'Radhalla won't go to war against us, Ma. He has bigger fish to fry.'

For a moment he almost believed himself.

His mother pulled a wry face. 'Did you know Radhalla has every smith on the northshore making weapons?'

He looked at her, aghast. 'Does Hroc know?'

'Hroc thinks he has everything under control,' his mother said spitefully. 'He says we have nothing to fear from the Cheruskkii. The Cheruskkii are our friends.'

He looked down at his feet and then back up at her. 'I'll take you away from here just as soon as I can, Ma, but I can't go yet. There are things I have to do.'

She nodded and he heard her sigh. 'I know,' she said.

The next morning when he was washing in the yard, he caught his mother staring at a weapon scar that skittered pale and ugly across his ribs. She squeezed his arm and said nothing, but he had seen the look in her eyes.

That night, Ascha went to the cabin where Saefaru and Wulfhere lived. He stopped outside the door and then turned and walked away. He stopped again, turned his head to one side, swore and then went back to the door and knocked softly. He was about to go when the door suddenly opened and Saefaru was there. She studied him, her hair blowing, saying nothing.

'I thought tha might like company,' he said.

He moved towards her and opened her dress and put a hand on her breast, cautiously caressing it. She watched him, doing nothing to stop him, and then looked both ways along the lane and held open the door.

'Tha'd better come in,' she said.

They sat and talked until the early hours, thigh leaning against thigh, their faces lit by a smoking lamp. He put his arm around her and they kissed, gently at first, laughing all the while, and then harder, his mouth mashing against hers. He moved his hand down her back and pulled her to him and felt his body stir as she responded. They kissed again and then she was pulling him towards the bed, the two of them slipping beneath the blankets as if it were the most natural thing in the world.

The next morning, as a pale dawn tiptoed through the rafters, they lay listening to the sparrows chattering in the thatch. Saefaru's head rested on Ascha's arm, her broad rump pushed into his groin. His arm was numb but pleasantly so and he felt no need to move.

'Tha must go,' Saefaru whispered over her bare shoulder, smiling.

He leaned over, kissed her and then pushed back the sheepskin and slipped naked from the bed, gasping as the cold hit him. Winter was coming, he could smell it in the air. They'd be bringing in the cattle soon lest they froze.

He padded across the earth floor, hugging his elbows, the chill seeping into his bones. The fire was out and smoking. He squatted down on his haunches and scratched at the hearth with a stick, grunting when a thin flame flickered. He got to his feet and went to the small cot pushed up against the wall. He pulled back the linen cloth that Saefaru had stretched over the crib to catch insects falling from the thatch and took a quick peek. Saefaru's son lay on his back, fat fingers making patterns in the air, kicking his legs and gurgling. The little face tilted and examined Ascha with cold, blue eyes.

Wulfhere's eyes.

He let the cloth fall and felt a stab of regret. If things had turned out different, that would have been his child.

He shivered and dressed quickly.

Saefaru lifted the latch and held the door open for him. Her eyes were half-closed with sleep and her shift clung damply to her hips. Outside, the sun was cold and watery. Three crows were pulling at something in the long grass. The elms loomed in the mist like ghosts on the moor.

He bent and gave her a deep kiss. She hugged him, and he felt her warm ripeness envelop him like an old cloak and then he was slipping down the alley, head hunched low, his breath fogging the air.

The next two nights he did the same, waiting until dark and then making his way to Wulfhere's cabin. A gentle tap and the door opened. Stupid! Anyone could have seen them. But deep down he felt he was owed and that somehow Saefaru still belonged to him. But it also felt good to plough another man's field, especially when that man was Wulfhere.

The morning of the third day, when he strolled back into the hall, Besso was waiting for him.

'Where's tha been, lad?'

'Out,' he said, all chirpy.

'Just out?'

'Out walking.'

'Tha wouldn't have been with that old sweetheart of yours would tha?'

'Why does tha say that?'

'Tha's playing with fire, boy.'

Ascha shrugged. What did he care? He felt alive to the tips of his fingers. How could someone like Besso understand that?

'Mess with his woman, and Wulfhere will kill tha soon as look at tha.' Besso said.

Ascha had a sudden picture of Saefaru's plump white limbs spread-eagled beneath him and stifled a grin. Half the fun lay in not knowing whether you would get caught. And he and Wulfhere had an old bone to pick.

'He can try,' he said with casual bravado.

Besso took another bite of apple and tossed the core over his shoulder.

'Hroc wants to go hog-hunting. He says there's a big boar on the north shore.'

Ascha's eyes widened. 'When?'

'Tomorrow. We'll be away two days.'

'Is it safe?'

'Hanno says he'll mind the village. Bring Tchenguiz. And bring bows.'

'Tha's going to give a weapon to a half-slave?' Ascha said with a wry grin.

Besso wiped his hands down his breeches. He got to his feet and headed for the door.

'A bow is a hunting tool not a weapon, as tha well knows.'

Ascha laughed out loud. He could still taste Saefaru's kisses on his lips and tomorrow he was going hunting. He kicked the core of Besso's apple and watched it bounce down the hall.

The journey to the lands of the Cheruskkii could wait.

11

Ascha overslept. He threw some water over his face, dressed and left the hall at a run, careering down alleyways to the river. Hroc and the other hunters had already loaded two marsh boats and were about to go. He waved to Hanno who had come to see them off, greeted the other hunters and then climbed down into a boat and took up a paddle. Tchenguiz was there with Besso's slave to carry the kill, carrying two bows and arrows for himself and Ascha.

Ascha looked back to the jetty and was stunned to see Wulfhere striding down the riverbank, swinging a boar spear. Wulfhere said a few words to Hanno and then turned to the boats. He saw Ascha and his expression darkened.

'Keep downwind, *mischling*, if tha knows what's good for tha!' he spat.

'Likewise,' Ascha snarled back.

Wulfhere had changed little. He was taller, his nose bent from where Ascha had broken it. Wulfhere climbed into the second boat, and the hunters pushed off.

Ascha dug the paddle in the water and pulled. He wondered with the faintest tremor of guilt if Wulfhere suspected anything, secrets didn't last long in the village, and then put the thought aside.

The boats slid through the water and turned north.

They paddled out towards the estuary. Half a day later they ran the boats aground on a muddy strand covered with animal bones, fish carcases and driftwood. A fisherman sat outside his cabin knotting nets while a dog crouched and bared its fangs. Slack-jawed children dressed in rags watched as the hunters hauled the boats up on the beach. One of the girls had purple blotches on her skin, a lazy eye and drooled.

'That's what tha gets when tha tups thi own kin,' Besso muttered.

They found a trail and followed it deep into the forest. There was a smell of mould and decay. Mid-afternoon they came across two young sows rooting for acorns and speared them in a frenzy of thrusts and stabs. A big boar trotting out of the trees took them all by surprise, a huge brute with massive legs and bones, a scarred snout and a bristled mane. Someone flung a spear, but it hit no vitals. Squealing in rage, the beast shook the spear free and plunged into the brush.

The wind stiffened, the clouds opened and the rain came down in torrents. The hunters formed a rough line, like two hands with fingers outstretched, and began working their way through the forest.

Ascha rested his bow against a tree and wiped his face. They were dog-tired, hungry and drenched to the bone. Sodden jerkins chafed at raw flesh. The rain had stopped but it was cold and growing colder. Somewhere off to his right, Hroc was yelling at them to close up. He could hear the fury and frustration in his brother's voice.

The trail grew steeper, Hroc leading them up a ridge where the ground was drier. Ascha frowned into the gloom. The boar was probably hiding in a thicket right now watching them make fools of themselves. He closed his eyes and thought of Saefaru and then thought of the girl at the river crossing. He tried to recall her face, thick dark hair and a chin like bird bone. He smiled, remembering the sunlight dappling on the river, the girl leaning back with her throat bare, one hand trailing in the water.

A vicious whisper, hot in his ear. 'What is it, little brother? Is tha lost or just asleep?'

The warmth rose to Ascha's face. On the leaf mould, Hroc's approach had been soundless.

'This is not the way to go, Hroc,' he said.

Silence.

'And where should we be going, little brother?'

There was an edge to Hroc's words that he had not heard before. The men heard it too. They stopped and turned their heads.

'The hog's not up there,' Ascha said, jerking his chin towards the ridge.

Hroc's eyebrows lifted. 'The hog's not up there? Then, by Tiw's holy bollocks, where is it then?'

Ascha felt their eyes upon him, Wulfhere leering at him over Hroc's shoulder. Ascha glanced around, swearing under his breath. The rain had turned everything into a boggy morass. How could he tell which tracks were fresh? The hunters leaned on their spears and waited. Behind them, he saw Tchenguiz moving to where a steep-sided gully, shrouded in thick undergrowth, ran off the edge of the ridge.

He walked back through the trees scanning the ground, looking for broken twigs, torn leaves. Anything. Boars were shy. Night-roamers. They would seek shelter in deep forest, close to fresh water.

Tchenguiz turned at the gully edge. He caught Ascha's eye, scratched the side of his face, looked down at the gully and back to Ascha.

'Come on, man! We're losing the light.' Hroc said.

Ascha breathed in deep. He pointed to the gully and said, 'I think he's down there!'

Wulfhere snorted, his hair plastered in rat-tails to the side of his head. 'No boar would go down there. Break its legs before it reached the bottom.'

Hroc nodded. 'Wulfhere's right. We'll go up on the ridge.'

He turned to go.

Wulfhere gave Ascha a greasy smirk. Ascha tried to resist the urge to punch him. The old hatred came flooding back. Stay calm. Don't rise to it. But he couldn't help himself.

'The boar's old and injured,' Ascha said carelessly. 'He knows better than to follow a trail to nowhere.'

A thick silence settled over them.

Hroc turned and exchanged glances with Wulfhere. Besso caught Ascha's eye and slowly shook his head. Tchenguiz was peering over the rim of the gully. No sound but the tapping of rain on leaves. Hroc's face darkened, and Ascha saw the anger in his eyes.

'Tha speaks of things tha doesn't know, little brother,' he rasped. 'I lead here and I say where we will hunt.' He stepped closer. 'Does tha understand?' He put his face close to Ascha. 'Does tha?'

Ascha could smell his brother's sweat. His chest was tight and thumping, and he struggled to control himself. One day he would have his revenge on Hroc, and Wulfhere too, but right now he wasn't ready. He had a job to do and he wasn't going to risk everything he'd worked for.

'Nothing to say?' Hroc snapped.

'Nothing,' Ascha said, the word dropping leadenly from his tongue.

The hunters sniggered. Beyond them, he could see Tchenguiz peering over the rim of the gully.

Hroc smiled coldly. 'Them Franks has given tha ideas, little brother. Does tha thinks tha knows better than free men? Get back with the other slaves and in future leave the thinking to us.'

Hroc's voice held such contempt that Ascha closed his eyes.

'That's what happens when the slave-born get above themselves,' Wulfhere smiled.

A couple of the hunters checked the lashings on their boar spears, but the rest snickered and shook their heads. Besso seemed about to say something and then was silent.

Ascha burned with shame, too stunned to reply. His Ma was right. He had expected life to change in some bold way. And yet nothing had changed at all. To Hroc and the Theodi, he was still the half-slave. He had always known they looked down on him, but it still hurt. He ground his teeth together and felt his eyes well with tears of rage.

There was a high-pitched yell.

A wood pigeon rose in a hollow tumult of clapping wings. The men swivelled. Tchenguiz was crouching at the lip of the gully, his dark face opened in a shout, one arm raised, the other jabbing at the gully.

'Fresh tracks! The pig is here!'

The men whooped and ran. Ascha breathed out. He turned to Hroc, but his brother was already striding away.

The boar was found lurking against an earth wall at the back of the gully. Ascha stepped forward with his bow, but Hroc laid a hand on his chest.

'Not tha, him,' he said, and snapped his fingers at Tchenguiz.

Tchenguiz raised his bow as the boar, its hair stiff with dried mud, came crashing through the brush. A difficult shot with the boar quartering towards them, but they all knew the Hun could do it. The bowstring thrummed and Ascha heard a meaty thud as the shaft struck home. The boar squealed and scrabbled to a stop. It stood wheezing heavily, black pebble eyes glinting with rage. It snorted and then lowered its head and charged, tusks angled to slash and rip.

Hroc shouted, 'My kill!'

The hunters leapt out of the way. The beast moved fast despite the arrow flapping in its shoulder. Hroc waited until the boar was almost upon him and then sidestepped and rammed his spear into the animal's side. The thrust went in low behind the shoulder plate, through the boar's thick hide, smashing deep into heart and lungs.

The legs buckled, and the boar was dead.

They gathered to marvel at what they had destroyed. A monster, bigger than any of them and twice as heavy. Food for a long hard winter.

Hroc pushed his hands deep into the hog's side and withdrew them wet with gore. He licked his fingers and then went to each of the freemen, drawing his fingertips across their cheeks, badging them with blood. .

Besso took a long knife and cut out the boar's heart. He held it up, said a prayer and buried the heart, a gift to Tiw. While Ascha, Tchenguiz and Besso's slave built a fire to keep away the wolves, the freemen settled down to enjoy the fruits of the hunt. Liver, hot and smoking, smeared with the salty juice of gall bladders. Fresh bone marrow, brains eaten raw from the cracked skull. They ate greedily, licking their fingers and grunting with pleasure, ignoring the rain that fell about their heads and shoulders. When they were stuffed with rich red meat, they rolled themselves in their blankets and lay down before the fire.

Ascha and the two slaves threw a rope over a thick branch and hauled the pigs up high. Working by firelight, they slit open the pig's bellies and gutted them, grey intestines looping down into the mud. It was hard, filthy work and took a long time. They cleaned the carcases, wrapped them in sacking and loaded them on poles ready to be carried to the boats.

When they were done, Ascha looked over at the sleeping Theodi. He watched them with murder in his heart, and then he lay down, rammed his gutting knife into the earth, pulled his cloak around him and slept.

12

The next day they paddled downriver. Ascha brooded. He was disgusted with himself for giving way to Hroc and swore it would not happen again. He might be a half-slave, but he was determined not to live like one.

They were almost home when they saw the ships. Three ocean-going long boats dragging at anchor not a stone's throw from the village, their sails hanging limp and oars stowed. A bank of mist was rolling in from the marshes, shrouding the tops of the masts and chilling the air. The hunters let the boats drift. They rested on their oars and peered into the milky-whiteness. Ascha saw the flicker of flames in the village and smelt burning. Armed men moved among the trees. He felt his pulse quicken.

'Raiders!' Besso bellowed. 'Turn back.'

'No!' shouted Hroc, 'Press on. Get to shore.'

Sluggish under the weight of men and pigmeat, the boats turned slowly. The hull rasped over mud and gravel and came to a stop. Ascha jumped out. He splashed through the shallows and clambered up the riverbank, chest heaving. He looked back and saw that the others had landed and were strung out along the riverbank.

He looked toward the warboats.

A man stood in the bow of the lead boat, his cheeks tattooed with tight whorls, a huge red shield covering him from shoulder to thigh.

'They're Cheruskkii!' Besso shouted.

'Cheruskkii?' Hroc said. 'It can't be!'

Ascha saw the raider put a hand to the side of his mouth. A moment later the Cheruskkii war cry swirled about their ears. He saw the Cheruskkii turn and scan the beach, looking for the source of the threat. Then they were running down the *terp*, fanning out toward them.

'They're coming,' Wado's boy, Morcar shouted. 'What are we going to do?'

'I'll speak with Radhalla,' Hroc said, moving towards the village. 'He'll listen to me.'

Besso barred Hroc's way. 'No,' he said. 'They'll kill tha.'

'But we're not at war!' Hroc shouted.

Besso said, 'Maybe not, but our village is burning, and those Cheruskkii haven't come as friends.'

They turned towards Hroc, silent accusation in their eyes. Hroc, the Cheruskkii's friend. A riverside cabin burst into flame with a dull *whoompf,* spewing out a black plume of smoke that climbed and flattened over the river.

'Then we'll fight here, and if needs be, we'll die here,' Hroc snarled.

Besso shook his head, 'There are too many of them. We'd be better off taking our chances in the marshes. We've got to stick together.'

'But we have to know what's happening,' Wada said.

They looked at each other, their faces pale with anxiety. Ascha could hear Morcar's teeth rattling in his head. Wulfhere alone seemed calm. He stood to one side, leaning on a spear, watching them, waiting while they decided what to do.

To his amazement, Ascha heard himself say, 'I'll go into the village. I'll go find out what's happening.'

Hroc turned to him. 'Tha?' he almost laughed and then grew serious. 'What if they catch tha?'

'They won't!' he said with a bitter laugh, 'I'm an unweaponed half-slave. What threat am I to them?'

Hroc looked at him with a frown, as if roused from sleep. He nodded slowly. 'Very well,' he said. 'Tha shall be our eyes, little brother.'

Tchenguiz called out, 'Cher'skkii come-lah!'

A dozen Cheruskers had reached the bottom of the *terp* and were running along the firm wet sand at the water's edge towards them. More were coming through the trees. They heard feet grinding on the gravel, the yells drawing closer.

'Now! We must go now,' screamed Wado.

Hroc turned to Ascha. 'Where shall we meet?'

Ascha thought quickly. 'Go to the pool, I'll meet you there.'

The pool was sacred, a shadowy place where ash and aspen whispered like hags in a coven. Once, a warband of Engli had come to thank Tiw for a successful raid. He remembered warships lined up on the strand like teeth on a comb, grim-faced men tramping through the reeds, the flash of blades as they hurled weapons stripped from their enemies into the murky water.

Hroc flung his arms around Ascha. 'I'll not forget this,' he said.

And they were gone.

Ascha took off, running deep into the trackless marshes, gathering pace as he went. He skirted the lake and dived into the woods, pounding down to the brook and sailing over it with a huge leap. He stopped to listen and then took off again, hitting the beaten path, ducking under the branches and pelting through the trees. When he could no longer hear the shouts of the Cheruskkii, he doubled back, circled to the far side of the village and slipped like a shadow into the warren of alleys on the village-mound.

The alleys were a mess. Baskets, clothing, pots and broken food jars lay on the ground. He heard the crackle of burning timber and could smell smoke and the sweet stench of burnt flesh. Some huts were burning, others were already charred and blackened ruins, open to the sky.

He was furious with Hroc for leaving the village undefended but even angrier with himself. He should have expected this. While he'd been fooling with Saefaru, the Cheruskkii had been preparing for war. He scrunched his eyes and ran on, fearful of what he might find, anxious for his mother and Budrum. He had to make sure they were safe.

He ran through the dark lanes. Wherever he looked bodies lay in the alleys, dark wounds under their chins and gashes on their heads and faces. A man lay spear-gored in a doorway, another slumped against a wall with his chin on his chest. Fear dried his throat.

Sweet Tiw! Let them not be hurt.

He crossed an alleyway, put his head round a corner and took a quick look. A band of Cheruskkii were looting Theodi huts, piling carts high with sheepskins, bed linen and all the ironware they could find. They were flushed with victory and spoke loudly with over-excited voices. He could see more Cheruskkii at the other end of the alley driving cattle and pigs down toward the boats.

He pulled his head in, stepped back and stumbled.

His hand reached out and met the cold clamminess of human flesh. A thick-set bearded man wearing a leather apron lay face down in the mud. It was Totta the smith. Totta's arm had been hacked off at the elbow and a cheek smashed by a shield boss. Ascha looked up and saw Totta's sons sprawled in the yard, their throats clogged with blood.

Ascha kneeled in the dirt, put back his head and let out a silent howl. Totta had made him his first chisels, his forge a tangle of black iron and gleaming copper, which Ascha had loved to visit. He could see him now, his burly arms pitted with burns, hammering leaf blades out of iron.

Ascha jerked his head up as two Cheruskkii came round the corner, their arms filled with skins. There was a hoarse shout, and the Cheruskers dropped the skins and drew their knives.

Ascha took to his heels, twisting through the alleyways and wattle-fenced yards, turning left, right, left until he lost them. He shot down an alley, crossed the street and paused to get his breath, heart thumping. A door opened and a Cherusker stepped out followed by a warm rush of laughter and voices. The Cherusker was very drunk and looked at Ascha with bleary eyes.

'Wha' tha' looking at?' he said. 'Can't a man take a piss around here?'

Ascha hit him as hard as he could, knocking the Cherusker down like a tree. He straddled him, shoved his arm against the man's throat, and pushed down hard, his throat burning with sudden anger. The Cherusker's feet flailed and his fingers scrabbled in the mud. There was a wheezing noise, a leg twitched and he went limp.

Ascha looked around.

Nobody had heard. He grabbed the man by the heels and dragged him, head bumping, down the yard to the latrine. He lifted the wattle hurdle that covered the pit, grimacing as the warm breath of human waste rose to greet him. He heaved the Cherusker to the edge and pushed. The man's tunic snagged. He cursed and heaved again. He could hear voices. Someone was coming. Ascha braced his feet and shoved. Two Cheruskkii appeared at the door, calling for their friend.

Ascha froze.

The men muttered something, laughed and then went back inside. Ascha pushed again, digging in his heels and pushing with his shoulder. There was a tearing sound as the tunic ripped and a soft groan as the Cherusker fell head first into the muck.

That'll teach tha to stay in thi own backyard, Ascha thought.

He replaced the wattle hurdle, checked that it was all quiet, and left.

The gate to the palisade was open. He slipped inside, paused and then ran and threw himself down behind the woodstack. Slowly, he raised his head. Goats watched him with baleful eyes. Scrawny hens scrabbled at his feet, red heads hammering the ground. Across the other side of the yard, he could hear a gang of Cheruskers talking. Heavy jawed men with hungry faces.

There was the slap of running feet and a youth ran into the yard calling out a name. The door of the hall opened and a well-dressed Cherusker came out. He was a few years older than Ascha with fine straight hair and a round pink face, like a boiled ham. The youth spoke fast, pointing urgently back towards the river. The Cherusker listened attentively and then issued a volley of commands. The men shouldered their spears and moved off.

Ascha waited until it was clear and then sprinted across the yard to the hall. Pressing his ear against the mud-chinked boards, he listened. He could hear men inside, Cheruskkii. But where were Budrum and his mother? He ran back, ducked beneath the raised floor of the granary and squatted down in the shadows.

'*Hssst!*'

He stiffened, eyes flickering around the yard. Again, he heard the sound. He turned and saw Budrum's face at the door of the weaving hut. He ran over with shoulders hunched. Budrum grabbed him by the sleeve and dragged him inside.

The hut was squalid and cold, the dirt floor littered with loom weights. No fire. His mother was sitting on an upturned cask, an old sheepskin around her shoulders. She looked up, saw Ascha standing before her and went rigid.

'Sweet Mother of God,' she murmured in her own language.

Budrum put a finger to her lips and shook her head.

Ascha lifted his mother to her feet and folded her in his arms. She stroked his cheek with the back of her hand and kissed his eyes.

'What are you doing here?' she whispered. 'It's not safe. And there is blood on your cheek. Are you hurt?'

He touched the side of his face. 'It's nothing. Hog's blood.'

'But where are the others?'

'They're in the marshes, by the pool. They're safe,' he said, switching to the dialect of the northshore so Budrum would understand.

'And Hroc?'

'Hroc's with them.' He squatted by her side. 'Ma, what happened here?'

Budrum and his mother exchanged glances.

His mother drew breath. 'The Cheruskers came yesterday, just before sunset,' she said. 'They said they were going on a raid and wanted to berth here overnight. We thought little of it. Outlanders often sleep here.' She smoothed the blanket over her knees and glanced at Budrum. 'They attacked early this morning. There was no warning. The first we knew of it was when we heard the screams. Some of the men fought back, but it was hopeless. They knew who they wanted and they killed anybody who resisted. It was horrible.'

He felt a dull and impotent fury. 'Go on, Ma,' he said.

'We were frightened. The children were terrified. The Cheruskkii gathered us all together. They told us we were traitors and they were going to kill us all.'

Budrum began to wail softly, her face buried in her hands.

His mother frowned at her and clicked her tongue. 'Come on, Budrum,' she said with irritation.

He put his hand on his mother's arm. 'Ma, what did you mean when you said they knew who they wanted?'

She turned to face him. 'They were looking for Hroc's sworn-men, those who had sworn to serve your brother after your father died. They went from house to house looking for them.' She clenched her mouth and paused to compose herself. 'They knew who they wanted. A few hid in Dodda's house and barred the door, but the Cheruskkii fired the roof and forced them out.'

He listened, mouth open. 'What happened?'

'They took them to the north field, by the hedge,' she said, stifling a sob. 'And then they killed them. Killed them all, bludgeoned them to death with hammers and iron bars.' A tear slid down her cheek onto her neck. 'One or two might have escaped into the marshes, but the rest are dead.'

Ascha sat back on his haunches and licked his lips. He felt sick. He got to his feet and walked up and down, closing his eyes and rapping his head with his knuckle. The Theodi had been sleep-walking, refusing to believe they were in danger. He should have persuaded them. He should have known! The Franks had warned him. Octha had warned him. They had all warned him. And the Cheruskkii had timed their raid well. A cold morning to keep the villagers abed, and the Theodi *hetman* away hunting. *Three keels!* Nearly two hundred men, more than enough to deal with a clan chief too proud to acknowledge Cheruskkii power. He pictured the rush of feet on frost-hardened soil, doors bursting open, men pleading for their lives. And then the screams as the axes fell. He pushed his nails deep into his palm, the rage rising.

He was struck by a sudden thought.

'Hanno, Ma,' he said, turning suddenly. 'What of him?'

His mother looked at him with a puzzled expression.

'Hanno?' she said. 'It was your brother Hanno who pointed out Hroc's men to the Cheruskers. It was Hanno who betrayed us.'

Ascha closed his eyes and opened his mouth. He felt breathless, as if he were choking. No, say this was not happening. Hanno would not have betrayed them. Not Hanno.

'Are you sure?'

His mother snorted. 'Of course, I'm sure! Hanno sold us to our enemies. He's a traitor and will rot for all time.'

Ascha leaned back against the roof post. He felt as if a knife was twisting his innards. He could see it clearly now. Hanno had left after Aelfric had made Hroc *hetman,* and then came back. And all those visits upriver. Hanno had been plotting with Radhalla all the time. He cursed himself, riddled with feelings of anger and guilt. The blame was all his. The Theodi had been hit by a storm that he could have prevented.

'Why did they not kill everybody?' he said when he'd had time to think. He meant, why did they spare you?

'They can't afford to make slaughter here,' his mother said. 'They need our young men and our tribute. They don't want us dead. They want us to work for them and fight for them. Now, the Theodi are free in name only. The Cheruskkii own them. The Theodi are little more than slaves.'

She laughed at that, a hard and bitter laugh.

'I saw them taking our cattle and sheep,' he said, remembering the oxen's sleepy march to the boats.

His mother scowled. 'Radhalla is a snake but he's not stupid. They've taken enough to teach us a lesson. The Cheruskkii need us. We are the People of the Pool, a holy tribe. We will suffer this winter, but we won't starve.'

He wasn't so sure. The Cheruskkii hadn't looked as if they needed the Theodi.

'I must go,' he said, rising to his feet.

'No,' said his mother firmly. 'It's far too dangerous. Wait until dark.'

Ascha slumped down, unwilling to argue. He would sleep a little and then go. From across the yard the aroma of roast meat clogged the air. He could hear laughter and singing, Cheruskkii warriors feasting in his father's hall.

Suddenly, everything was going wrong.

He slept fitfully. Some time later, his mother woke him, whispering urgently that it was time. Shaking his head, he looked about him, remembered where he was and quickly scrambled to his feet. He listened but heard nothing. It was cold and dark and the Cheruskkii were all asleep, heavy-bellied with food and ale.

'Come with me,' he said.

His mother shook her head. 'No, but you go. Tell Hroc to get far away from here. Tell him, if the Cheruskkii catch him, they will kill him.'

He nodded, full of misgivings.

They gave him what food they had. A few barley loaves, a little cheese, some watery milk. The Cheruskkii had looted everything of value. They would have stolen more, but his mother had taken down his father's blue-waved sword and boar-crested helmet and buried them in the pit beneath the floor before the Cheruskkii came.

'She's no fool, thi mother,' Budrum said.

He had to laugh. No Cherusker would think of sifting through the rat-shit, still-born babies and dead dogs under the floor of the hall to find Aelfric's sword and helmet.

He kissed them both, wrapping his arms around them in a fierce hug and then slipped out the way he had come.

'You mean that arse-wipe has betrayed us?'

The hunters stood around him in a ring. The trees sighed and the wind gusted across the sacred pool. Gone midnight and almost pitch-black, but he could just make the hunters out against the sky and hear their laboured breathing.

'They timed the raid for when you were away,' Ascha said. 'Hanno told them everything. He went from house to house pointing out your sworn-men. The Cheruskkii killed them. Agilbert and Tiba, Gyrth, Oswald, Ludeca, Oelf, and more. They're all dead.'

The men looked at each other, unable to take it in.

Young Morcar slumped down and began to weep. Hroc raised both fists and beat them against his head. He got to his feet and stumped away. He began punching a tree, pummelling it with his bare knuckles until his hands bled. Ascha watched him, knowing how he felt, your own flesh and blood, a traitor.

He handed out the loaves in silence. The hunters took the bread, tore off a chunk and chewed morosely, each man adrift in his thoughts.

It was Besso who spoke first.

'We have three roads. We fight, knowing they will destroy us. Or we ask for terms and accept your brother's lordship. Or we flee. Travel north and join an outlander warlord as his sworn-men.'

Nobody said anything.

They were poor choices. To die in your own village after it had been taken by an enemy was not an honourable death. Hroc would never ask Hanno for terms. And to flee meant exile – the living death.

Hroc sat with his head in hands, saying nothing. From time to time, he shook his head as if unable to grasp what had happened.

'We're all exhausted,' Ascha said quietly. 'Let's sleep and decide what to do in the morning.'

Hroc looked at him and nodded. Ascha agreed to take the first watch. Hroc took the second. Wulfhere said he would take the watch before dawn.

In the night Ascha was awakened by the patter of rain. He looked up and saw the dark outline of Wulfhere standing guard under the tree. Wulfhere turned and looked back at him, and Ascha thought he saw him smile.

When Ascha awoke again it was to harsh shouts, spears at their throats and Cheruskkii boots hammering at their ribs.

'Up! Up! You Theodi bastards!'

The Cheruskkii kicked them to their feet and drove them back to the village with blows and guttural shouts. Ascha saw that the river had risen during the night, lifting the Cheruskkii warboats and turning them. In the village, there were armed Cheruskkii on every corner. He was glad his father was not alive to see this.

The clan came out, lined the road and watched in silent agony as the hunters passed. No sound but the chill wind sighing across the marshes and the shuffle of weary feet.

The Cheruskkii drove them to Aelfric's hall. A barked command and the Theodi were shoved into the yard, hemmed in by Cheruskkii warriors. They looked about them and shivered nervously. The rain grew heavier, pouring down their faces in long ropy coils. The villagers began to gather as if drawn by a thread.

They looked beaten and downcast. Ascha heard them murmuring, like rollers on a distant beach.

He shuddered, not knowing what to do. What would happen now? He hunched his head into his collar and looked over his shoulder for the others. He saw Besso, Wado and Morcar, Ecga, Tchenguiz and Besso's slave.

But where was Hroc?

His mother and Budrum came running, their mouths tight with anxiety. Saefaru was among the women, a dark shawl over her head. She gave him a pinched little smile and bit her lip. She held her young son in her arms. The boy was swaddled in a blanket, looking out with big and solemn eyes.

The rain eased leaving the yard glinting with puddles. More Cheruskkii gathered. Ascha looked them over. He saw other tribes among them: Jutes, Danes and Engli from the Almost-Island, Saxons from the interior, Frisians from the west, Eastern tribes he didn't know. Hard-looking men, weaned on blood. All laughing and grinning fit to bust.

Silence fell.

They waited.

Ascha lifted his head. The crowd opened like a flower and Hanno came out. A new blue tunic, his hair swept up and tied in a knot, a jawline Ascha could have carved from stone. Hanno was accompanied by the baby-faced Cherusker Ascha had seen the day before. They were laughing at some private joke. Ascha shook his head. His mother always said Hanno could strike up a conversation with a rock and leave it thinking it had found a friend for life.

Behind them came Wulfhere.

Ascha folded his brow. What was Wulfhere doing with Hanno? Wulfhere looked up and caught his eye. He gave Ascha a wolfish grin and traced a slow and lazy forefinger across his throat.

And then Ascha knew.

Wulfhere had left his watch during the night. Wulfhere had told the Cheruskkii where Hroc and the hunters were hiding. Wulfhere had betrayed them! He saw Wulfhere turn and speak to Hanno, saw Hanno's smiling response. Wulfhere must have been working for Hanno all along. While he was bedding Saefaru, Wulfhere was not visiting his cousin, he was taking Hanno's messages to the Cheruskkii.

Ascha swore. How could he have been so blind?

There was a long delay and then Radhalla appeared followed by a bodyguard of Cheruskkii warriors.

Radhalla of the Cheruskkii was a powerfully-built man dressed in a winter tunic of white fox, a mail-coat sand-scrubbed until it gleamed and a black woollen cloak. Ascha took in a thick neck roped with muscle, a whirlpool tattoo in the middle of a low brow, like a third eye, and a head too large for his body. Radhalla walked heavily, like a brown bear dragging its feet, and was followed by the biggest bodyguard Ascha had ever seen. A huge brute with thighs like tree trunks, a heavy brow and a tassle of dirty yellow hair.

Nobody spoke.

Radhalla walked over to the Theodi hunters, and Ascha heard him ask Besso his name. He did the same to Wado and Ecga. As Ascha watched, the Theodi filled their chests and squared their shoulders almost as if, without realizing it, they wished to impress the Cherusker warlord.

Then Radhalla was before him, and he was staring into eyes as cold as snow.

'What's your name, boy?'

Ascha glared at him with hatred. 'Ascha, son of Aelfric,' he said.

Radhalla's eyes narrowed, scrunching the tattoo on his brow.

'Aelfric's son?'

'Yes.'

He felt the Cherusker assess him coolly.

'You the hostage who escaped from the Franks and travelled home overland?'

Radhalla's voice was low and gravelly, as if dug from a dark and ancient pit.

He considered not replying and then curled his lip and said, 'I am.'

'It was well done.'

'It was nothing,' Ascha spat. 'I doubt they missed me.'

'Maybe.' Radhalla said, inclining his big head. 'But if a hostage of mine had escaped I would hang the man responsible. And you should not make light of what you did. It was boldly done. Few northerners have travelled so far without the sea road beneath them.'

Ascha was taken aback. He frowned, uncertain how to respond. He hadn't expected honeyed words from Radhalla. He had the strangest feeling that the warlord of the Cheruskkii knew more of him than he would have wished.

There was the sound of a scuffle and a group of Cheruskkii burst into the yard. They were dragging a man behind them, pulling him by a strip of rawhide around his neck.

Hroc!

Ascha saw that his brother's arms were bound tight. He was dirty and smeared in mud. One eye was puffed and almost closed. Hroc's top lip was split open like a sausage and blood flowed from the side of his mouth.

A moan swept the Theodi, like the lowing of a great ox. The Cheruskkii fingered their weapons and looked about them edgily. Hroc was dragged to the middle of the yard. He stood there, swaying, his chin raised towards the sky. Beneath the bruises, Ascha saw his brother's face was the colour of ashes.

Radhalla acted as if he had not seen him. He put his hands on his hips, head jutting forward, and addressed the crowd.

'My name is Radhalla,' he said. 'And I am *hetman* of the Cheruskkii nation.'

He paused and looked about him. 'Let us consider why we are here.' He held up a stubby finger. 'You are a small clan, remote in your marshes. Your only hope of survival was to become part of our confederation. But what did you do?' He raised his eyebrows. 'You formed an alliance with the Franks, that's what you did. You sold your souls for Frankish silver.' He swung his head from side to side as if what the Theodi had done was beyond understanding. 'Couldn't you see what an insult that was?'

They waited in silence.

'Tiw be thanked, you came to your senses. Hanno invited us in to restore order, and we were happy to do so. Now that Hanno – Aelfric's true heir – is your rightful lord once more, we can welcome you back to the fold.'

There was a shout and a teeth-jarring clash of weapons from the Cheruskkii.

'I am a generous man and I will give you a chance,' Radhalla said and his mouth creased in what could have passed for a smile. 'For too long the Romans and the Franks have grown fat on the blood of others. Now, that is going to change. You will join us as we drive south. We will crush them and make their land ours. We will – '

'Lies! Lies! Don't listen to him, my people!' Hroc yelled.

A Cherusker stepped forward and smashed Hroc in the mouth, bending him to his knees.

Radhalla clenched his jaw. He closed his eyes and shook his head. 'That was stupid,' he said quietly. 'Very stupid! You have no power here, Hroc. You do not rule any longer. You are a nothing!'

Hroc worked at something in his mouth and then spat out a nugget of bone. 'You were my father's friend,' he said, his words slurring. 'He trusted you.'

Radhalla looked at him, his face expressionless.

'I'm a patient man, Hroc,' he said, so quiet that Ascha strained to hear. 'You could have joined us after your father's death but you wouldn't listen. Stubborn, that's what you were. I've got no time for people like that. Hanno here showed more sense.' He waved his hand in Hanno's direction. 'He's a clever lad is Hanno, has the interests of your clan at heart. It's thanks to him that your people survive today.'

Hanno moved forward and bent low over his brother. 'It needn't be like this, Hroc,' he said, his voice silken and assured. 'Accept me as your oath-lord and tha'll have all the honour and riches tha deserves.' He reached out his hand. 'Come, I am the elder after all, and I was our father's first choice. What does tha say, Hroc? Will tha swear for me?'

Hroc rose to his feet, wincing as he did. He stood unsteadily, his weight on one leg. The Cheruskii moved in, alert for any sudden move. Hroc looked around. He seemed calm and unbowed as if he had resolved his uncertainties of the night before and knew now what he must do.

He spat once, clearing his mouth of blood and muck.

'I am Hroc, son of Aelfric, *hetman* of the Theodi people,' he said with a thick voice. 'You all know me as a man of honour. I have ridden the wave-road and cut my way to glory in a thousand battles. I have made more slaughter than any man here.'

The Cheruskkii watched him carefully, fingering their weapons.

Hroc turned to Hanno and the pink-faced Cherusker.

'Hanno, tha's my brother and I love you before all others. Tha swore to serve me loyally, but tha's a traitor to thi clan and an oathbreaker.'

'I don't have to listen to this,' Hanno snapped. He went to move away but Radhalla and Sigisberht remained where they were, their eyes fixed firmly on Hroc. Hanno scowled and stayed put.

'And Sigisberht,' Hroc said softly. 'You were my friend. I trusted you'

Sigisberht smiled a cold smile, his face blank of all emotion.

The Theodi held their breath. The Cheruskkii waited, impassive. Ascha closed his eyes, counting the moments going past.

Hroc drew himself up.

'I will give you an oath,' he said and spat blood. 'I swear by Tiw and on my father's memory, let me live, and I will come for you. And when I do, I promise you, I will destroy you all.'

There was a stunned silence.

Radhalla moved his big head slowly up and down. He turned to Hanno and Sigisberht and raised his shoulders, palms uppermost as if saying, what do you expect after that?

Ascha could not take his eyes off them. Sigisberht looked bored. Ascha saw that Hanno had gone as pale as parchment. He had been made to look small and was struggling to control himself. The tip of Hanno's tongue slid across his lips and there were white spots on his cheeks.

He turned to Radhalla. 'Do as you will,' he snarled.

There was a long pause and then Radhalla said softly. 'Very well, take him to the pool.'

The Cheruskkii took Hroc back down the track to the sacred pool. The rest of the hunters were driven along behind him, herded by Cheruskkii spears and followed by a crowd of wailing onlookers. They gathered at the pool, ankle deep in muddy water. Hroc stood alone, his arms bound behind his back and his head bowed. Ascha got as close as he could until the Cheruskkii shoved him back. He gazed at the scene in horror.

Silence, save for the breeze blowing through the aspens and rippling the surface of the water.

Hanno stepped forward. He took the sacred bundle of the Theodi from a Cherusker and held it above his head. In a clear rich voice, unblemished by doubt or uncertainty, Hanno offered up a prayer to Tiw, asking him to look kindly on this sacrifice. When he'd finished he nodded.

'Do it!'

The Cheruskkii pushed Hroc forward.

Ascha felt as if time had stopped. A cold chill ran down his back. There were screams and wails from the Theodi women.

'Wait!'

He looked up to see his mother pushing her slight form between two burly Cheruskkii. She was breathless and her face was flushed as if she had been running. Her shawl trailed over one shoulder and the hem of her skirt was smeared with mud.

She glanced at Hroc and then turned to face Radhalla. She held up a small green flask, held it high so that all might see it.

'The potion!' she said to Radhalla, her voice thick with contempt.

The crowd murmured. Ascha saw Radhalla staring at his mother as if he had seen a ghost. She stood small and defiant, dark eyes flashing. Lost in the moment, Ascha was confused and then he remembered. Transgressors and malefactors were always drugged before execution. It dulled their senses and made their journey to the other life easier.

The Theodi held their breath.

Radhalla slowly shook his head, not taking his eyes off the woman.

'I want him to know what is happening here,' he said.

He gestured with one hand, and the Cheruskkii stepped forward and pushed Ascha's mother back.

Ascha's mouth opened in horror. He screamed Hroc's name and lurched forward. A Cherusker hit him in the belly with the butt of his spear and another punched him on the side of the head. He fell in the mud. Two Cheruskkii grabbed his upper arms and lifted him to his knees and held him tight. He wanted to cry out but his tongue was too thick for his mouth. He shook his head, struggled and looked down at the ground in despair. Then he watched as a rope was thrown over the limb of a birch and noosed around Hroc's neck. Five Cheruskkii formed a short line. They wrapped the rope once around their forearms and took up the slack. Ascha craned his neck, his breath coming in short pants. There was a strange look on Hroc's face, as if only now did he realize what he had done. He stood chin tilted high, his wrists bound behind his back, his mouth open, and his chest rising and falling in great breaths. When he saw Ascha, his lips curved in a faint smile and one eye closed in a painful wink.

He and Hroc had never been friends, but Hroc was his own flesh and blood. He turned and cried out to Hanno. Hanno, tall and fair, his hair blowing softly, glanced at Ascha and then looked away. Radhalla gave a signal, no more than a flick of his fingers and with a shout, the Cheruskkii ran, their legs splashing and squelching through the muddy water, dragging Hroc up by the neck.

An anguished moan from the Theodi as Hroc swung, dark against a cold grey sky.

The crowd fell silent. They watched Hroc dangle, legs thrashing and listened as the rope squeaked against the bark of the limb. Hroc stopped kicking, the rope was released and Hroc dropped like wet sand.

Two Cheruskkii picked up Hroc's body and threw him face down into the pool. A wicker hurdle was tossed over him and a young Cherusker, grinning at his friends, jumped into the water and climbed on top, pressing Hroc's body down into the mud, forcing him into the limbo between earth and water, between this world and the next.

The wicker creaked and the water boiled.

The hurdle rose and like a sea monster from the deep, Hroc's head and shoulders reared from the water, rivulets coursing down his face, his mouth stretched in a grisly yawn.

The Cherusker rolled off the hurdle with a dull splash.

The Theodi surged forward. The Cheruskkii laid about them with their lance-butts, beating them back.

Ascha forgot who he was. He dropped to his knees and howled as he watched the agony of his brother's death. He had heard that condemned criminals sometimes found the strength to heave the death weight from their backs and snatch a lungful of air before they finally succumbed, but never did he think it would happen to his own kin.

More Cheruskers waded into the pool.

To the jeers and catcalls of their friends, they threw the hurdle back over the body and flung themselves upon it, pressing Hroc down into the mud. Others scrambled on, kicking and splashing in the water, laughing like children on a raft.

There was a final twitch of the hurdle and then no more.

13

The hunters were thrown into a hut along with some of the villagers the Cheruskkii had rounded up in the marshes. The hut was small and dark, the floor slimy with piss and goat shit. The hunters peered anxiously at each other as they shuffled their feet. That night, a great cold fell upon the village. Ascha and the others stood for as long as they could, packed together under the thatch, until weariness forced them to lie down in the freezing filth and try, with muttered groans and curses, to sleep.

The villagers were taken away the next morning. The hunters waited. Some time later the Cheruskkii came for Besso, then Wado and Ecga. The following day, they came for Morcar. The boy pleaded and sobbed. He wrapped his arms round a roof post, dug in his heels and refused to move. The guards kicked him and beat his hands. Ascha and Tchenguiz held on to the boy's arms but, with spear-points at their throats, there was nothing they could do. They boy was dragged away, wailing.

He and Tchenguiz were the only ones left.

'What does tha think will happen?' Tchenguiz said.

Ascha squatted with his hands folded into a fist against his brow, his eyes closed. 'I don't know,' he said.

'Will they kill us?'

'Maybe,' he said.

Tchenguiz slept. Ascha leaned back against a hut post, listening to the rhythm of the Hun's snores and went from one part of his life to another, trying to make sense of it all. The shock of Hroc's death could not have been greater, but he knew he had to move on. He felt both uneasy and relieved. Uneasy, because he had no idea what would happen or what he should do. Relieved, because the waiting was over. What did he care if the Theodi were overrun? He was a Frank now and owed them nothing.

But he also knew it wasn't that simple. The game had turned and he was going to have to choose whose side he was on. To choose Hanno and Radhalla stuck in his craw – Radhalla had murdered Hroc and possibly his father too – but to choose Hroc meant death.

Ascha screwed up his eyes and saw Hroc rising from the water. He shook his head and shivered. Whatever his faults, Hroc had not deserved such dishonour. If he survived, he would have his revenge. Of that he was certain.

Outside, even the dogs were silent.

Late afternoon and they heard voices. The door opened with a kick of a stranger's boot and his mother came in, ducking under the wattle. She was carrying a basket draped with a red cloth. She stood in the doorway wrapped in her shawl, allowing her eyes to adjust to the gloom. She put down the basket, embraced Ascha and gave Tchenguiz the briefest smile before handing them the food she had brought. Two loaves, a piece of cheese and a few scraps of cold meat and sausage, wrapped in a knapkin. The bread was still warm, and the smell of it filled the hut.

They fell on the food while his mother sat back on her heels and watched. When they had eaten enough to think straight she looked at Ascha and spoke.

'Hanno has held an oath-swearing,' she said briskly in Latin. 'He has promised his protection and gifts to any freeman who swears to serve him.'

His first thought was relief that his friends still lived. 'And if they do not?'

She shrugged. 'They have all sworn: Tila, Ulfila, Wilfred, Taki, Putta, Tota, Mucca, Wado, Ecga, Duduc, even Besso. What else could they do? Hroc is dead and they are lordless. Hanno is *hetman,* and the Cheruskkii hold the town. We are in their pocket.'

It took him a moment to grasp what she had said. His brother's body was not yet cold and already Hroc's friends had gone over to the Cheruskkii.

'I'll never swear,' he said, shaking his head. 'I want *faida.* Vengeance!'

She looked at him and then took his hand and leaned forward, her face close to his. 'Listen to me,' she hissed under her breath. 'Don't be a fool. Save yourself! Give them what they want and they'll soon lose interest. Your precious *faida* can come later.'

'You want me to forget what they did here?' he shouted.

She put a finger across his lips. 'Forget, no.'

'What then?' he said more quietly.

'Harbour it. Use it. Make it work for you. Wait until the time is right.'

'And then?
Then do what you have to do.'
'Which is?'
'You will know when the time comes.'
'You always told me that only dead fish swim with the tide,' he said sourly.
She put a hand against his cheek. 'Let them think you swim with the tide. Let them think it, and you will survive. Otherwise, they will kill you as easily as they drink water.'
He looked at her but said nothing. She folded the cloth neatly and put it back in the basket and got to her feet.
'Ma, you want me to tell you why I came back?'
She shook her head. 'No. It is better if you do not.' She thought for a moment and then said, 'Does the Hun know?'
'No.'
His mother leant forward. 'Then tell him, tell him everything,' she hissed. 'He is your only friend here. The only one you can trust.'
Ascha frowned. He looked at her and then at Tchenguiz. The Hun sat patiently, not understanding a word. What had he come to when a slave was his only friend, he thought bitterly. But he knew she was right. She always was.
At the door, his mother hesitated. 'One thing more,' she whispered. 'The Cheruskkii are building a fleet. I have heard them talking.'
'A fleet?' he breathed. He knew it! He smacked his fist hard into his palm. So they would come by sea. He held her shoulders tight and looked into her eyes, 'Where, Ma?'
'I don't know.'
He breathed in deep and blew it out. Maybe, he thought, just maybe, there was a way he could have his revenge and give the Franks what they wanted.
If he lived that is.

That night, Ascha made up his mind. He hunched down on his heels with his hands wrapped around his knees and said, 'Tchenguiz, there is something I have to tell tha.'
Ten years before Ascha was born, Khan Aetla's Huns had erupted from the east like a flail across a child's face. Tchenguiz had been young then, little more than a boy, but he had ridden before he could walk and was proud to ride knee to knee with the Hunnic horde. When Ascha was a child, Tchenguiz would give him rides

on his back and tell him stories that set the blood pumping through his veins. He would talk of riders in their thousands wheeling across the plains, the clang of iron on iron, arrow-storms darkening the sky.

Aetla's Huns had torched cities from the Rhine to the western ocean and left the wheatfields of Gallia a desert of charred stubble. Eventually, the Roman general Aetius and his barbarian allies brought the Huns to battle. The fighting was vast and savage and raged all day. By sunset Aetla was defeated. Amidst the carnage, Tchenguiz was taken captive by Saxons loyal to Aetius and given to Osric, *hetman* of the Theodi and father of Aelfric. He began the long walk north to the Theodi homeland.

Life on the northshore had been hard. Unused to Hunnic features, the Theodi had looked on Osric's new slave with horror. Children threw stones, and women covered their faces as he went by. But, in time, the Theodi grew accustomed to him and he was left alone. He became our Hun and, if still strange, was at least no stranger.

Now, slowly, Ascha began to talk of his time with the Franks. He began with the day when Clovis chose him as a hostage. Once he started, the words poured from him like water. He went through it all. He spoke of his life as an exile and how the Franks had given him weapons and trained him and used him as a messenger and a spy even though he was a Saxon and a half-slave. And he explained how Clovis, the Great Khan of the Franks, had sent him back to his own people, to spy on the confederation and give the Franks warning of the uprising that was coming.

Tchenguiz listened in silence. When he had finished Ascha waited for him to speak, needing the approval of the man who had been his father's friend.

'Well, say something,' he snapped.

'What will tha do?' Tchenguiz said.

'If I live?' Ascha said.

'If tha lives.'

'I gave the Franks my word.'

'Then tha will find out the Cheruskkii war plans?'

'Yes.'

'And kill Radhalla?'

Ascha looked at him for a long time and then nodded. 'Yes,' he said quietly. 'I will kill Radhalla.'

The broad face of Tchenguiz opened in a huge grin.

'Wah! Ascha!' he said, 'Tha is warrior now. Like me!'

Ascha gave him a quick grin and squeezed his shoulder. He got to his feet and hammered on the door. When the guard came he said, 'Tell my brother I want to see him.'

They came for him the next morning. Tchenguiz got up too but the Cheruskkii shook their heads. 'Just the Theod. The Hun stays.'

He gave Tchenguiz a tight smile and stepped out.

He emerged into a grey wilderness. After the stench of the hut the air was clean and raw. The cold seared his lungs. Snowflakes swirled around his head, settling on his cheek and eyelids like icy butterflies. His wrists were wrenched behind his back and bound. Two strong hands gripped his upper arms and a stinking cloth was wrapped around his eyes. He was aware of Cheruskkii falling in either side of him and then he was marched away.

'Where are we going?' he said:

They made no reply.

He felt gravel under his feet and frozen mud. Somewhere a pig was grunting. They took him through the village and up the village-mound, and he guessed that they were going to his father's hall. They stopped and a Cherusker banged on a door. A voice said, 'Come!'

The door opened and he was shoved inside.

The rag was pulled from his eyes and the rope untied. He felt himself pushed forward with a hand in his back.

There was an odour of wood smoke and warm bodies. A fat log was smouldering in the sandbox and he could feel its warmth pricking his face. A dozen Cheruskkii lazed on benches, drinking beer, scratching and belching companiably. He could hear the click of dice. They looked up as he entered and then resumed their game. In one corner, under a blanket of pelts, a man and a woman were moving, their bodies joined in a rhythm as old as time. In another corner a group of young women from the village sat together. When they saw him they lowered their gaze and looked away.

Hanno sat at the table, his long body folded into Aelfric's great chair, picking his teeth with a bone toothpick. He looked relaxed, his pale skin slightly flushed. Behind him stood the big hulking Cherusker he had seen with Radhalla wearing two deep-bladed *seaxes* shoved crossways under his belt. On the table were the remains of a roast goose, a joint of beef, fresh loaves and a soft white cheese.

'Ascha! Come in, come in!' Hanno said. He pushed back his chair back with a loud scrape and came out from behind the table. He put one long arm around Ascha's neck and patted his face and ruffled his hair.

'I am sorry tha was held so long. An oversight while we ensured the village was secure. Come and sit. Has tha eaten? Have some beef. No? Well then, some beer perhaps?'

Ascha took the beaker Hanno offered him. He drank the beer in one long gulp and then in one sudden movement flung the beaker away and pounded the table with both fists. The dishes jumped and clattered.

'Hanno, he was our brother!'

The big Cherusker lunged around the table, firelight glinting on the iron edge of his *seaxe*. Hanno looked startled. The Cheruskkii looked up from their game, dice poised. There was a long silence, like waiting for the pebble to hit the bottom of a deep well. The log shifted in the hearth, and Ascha heard the crackle and popping of burning wood.

The big Cherusker's eyes flicked to Hanno. Do I kill him now?

Hanno flapped the thug away. The Cherusker shoved the knife back into his belt and leant against the hall post with arms folded and watched Ascha. The Cheruskkii resumed their game but continued to cast dark glances at him, muttering under their breath.

Hanno sighed and said: 'Ah, Ascha what am I going to do with tha?'

'Why did tha kill him, Hanno?' Ascha said softly.

Hanno looked weary. 'I didn't want Hroc's death,' he said. 'If he had acknowledged me it wouldn't have happened. I mourn his passing, as does tha. He was my brother after all. But sometimes these things are necessary, and they can turn out for the best. Tiw appreciates it when we serve him with honest men and not the criminals and thieves he is usually offered.'

Ascha closed his eyes and opened them again.

'Tell me, why did he have to die?'

'He stole my birthright, that's why,' Hanno said in a peevish tone. 'I was the first-born. It was my right. All I did was reclaim what was mine.'

There was no remorse in Hanno's eyes. It was as if he had reworked the ugliness of Hroc's death lest it spoil the idea of his own piety.

'Father chose Hroc to lead us, not tha.'

Hanno's face twisted in a snarl.

'Father was stupid. We're a northern nation, part of the Saxon family. Our future lies with the confederation.'

'Under Cheruskkii leadership? They are not even blood-linked, Hanno. Look at them!' He swept his arm towards the dice-players. 'They're not a nation. They're scum! The gutter sweepings of the north.'

There was a low warning growl from the Cheruskkii.

'Radhalla dreams of uniting the Saxon tribes,' Hanno said. He spoke in a dull flat tone, as if explaining things to a child. 'We could be part of that. Hroc would have kept us small and powerless. The Cheruskkii are the rising tide, Ascha. If we join Radhalla, we rise with them. It's what Tiw would wish.'

'You think Tiw wants this?'

Hanno closed his eyes. He sat down again and laid both hands on the table. 'I know the Cheruskkii are rough,' he said, dropping his voice. 'A little primitive, maybe. They do not have our traditions and customs, but we can work with them. We can become – '

'This is all shite, Hanno,' he shouted. 'What does tha want of me?'

Hanno looked at him with a pained expression on his face, 'I want to talk.'

'Tha wants my loyalty-oath?'

Hanno gave an apologetic smile, 'There's no need,' he said levelly. 'Tha's only an unweaponed half-slave and tha cannot take up arms against me. I would prefer to have thi support, but if not it doesn't matter.'

Ascha flinched. Maybe he had always known, but it was painful to hear all the same. He remembered his mother's words. He would have to choose. Right now, Hanno and the Cheruskkii had all the power, and he couldn't be sure Hanno wouldn't kill him too. If he was to survive, he would have to tread carefully.

The door opened with a gust of cold air, and the blonde Cherusker with the pink face came in. He walked briskly to the fire, rubbing his hands together.

Hanno turned and smiled. 'Ascha, this is Sigisberht, the nephew of *hetman* Radhalla of the Cheruskkii people. Sigisberht, my half-brother, Ascha.'

The Cherusker held out a plump hand and smiled a professional smile. Ascha hesitated and then took it. The hand was cold and soft. Sigisberht wore a cowhide cloak over his tunic with the edges thrown back to reveal a lining of lambskin. There was the glint of a finely worked gold brooch at the shoulder.

'My uncle has spoken of you,' Sigisberht said.

He unpinned the cloak and let it fall.

'Yes?' Ascha said, unable to hide his surprise that Radhalla had spoken of him to Sigisberht.

The Cherusker dragged up a bench and sat. 'You came home overland?'

His voice was precise and neat, every word in its place but the tone was soft, as if he sweetened his breath in honey.

'I did.'

Sigisberht picked up a beaker and dipped it into the beer bucket and looked at Ascha with an appraising eye. 'Impressive,' he said. 'But one thing puzzles me.' He took a little sip of beer and wiped the corner of his mouth with a knuckle. A frown appeared between his eyes. 'I do not understand how a half-slave hostage could escape from a Frankish military camp? Perhaps you would explain?'

'I can't.'

'You can't explain?'

'One day I just walked out and kept on walking.'

A cold stare. 'And they did not think to pursue you?'

'I think they thought I would go north to get a boat home. Or south to Roman territory. They may have thought I would make my way west to Armorica to find refuge among the *Bacaudae.*'

'The Bacaudae?' Sigisberht frowned, clearly uncomfortable with what he didn't know.

'Renegade slaves.'

'Ah!' Sigisberht said, tapping his lips with his forefinger. 'But you are going to tell me that you did none of those things?'

'No.'

'What did you do?'

'I went east. I crossed the Rhine at Colonia and then travelled up the Lupia and then over the top until I found the Wisurg and headed north.'

Sigisberht gave Ascha a long and thoughtful look.

'One of my people thinks he may have seen you before. In Gesoriac or Parisi maybe? Is that possible?'

There was something in Sigisberht's tone that dropped ice in Ascha's belly. His tongue worked a dry mouth. Could the Cheruskkii really have spies in those cities? Or was he bluffing?

'It's possible,' he said carefully. 'Sometimes I took messages to the Roman towns. I ride well and I speak Latin. I was an obvious choice.' He looked down as if ashamed at having done the Franks' work.

'You speak Latin?'

'My mother taught me,' he said and immediately felt the blood rise on the back of his neck. Among Saxons, a mother who spoke Latin was always slave-born.

Hanno jumped in, bored with where the talk was going. 'Sigisberht, did you know that our Ascha is a carver? Perhaps you saw the gable panel over the door as you came in? He has the gift, a true artist.'

Sigisberht gave Ascha a long and thoughtful look. 'A woodcarver?' he said, rolling his bottom lip to reveal a pink wetness. 'There is always a need for good woodcarvers.'

There was a sudden whoop of laughter followed by a long drawn out groan from the dice-players. Someone had won, someone lost.

Ascha looked Sigisberht full in the eye. 'I would like the chance to prove to you what I can do,' he said.

Hanno waved one arm in the air and said, 'It's just as I told you, Sigisberht. My brother Ascha is not like Hroc.'

Ascha could hear the relief in Hanno's voice. It wouldn't do for the Cheruskkii to suspect Ascha's loyalty just after they had hanged Hroc.

Sigisberht ignored him. 'What can you do?'

'Most anything. I'm a skilled timberer and I know shipbuilding.'

'Who says we need shipbuilders?' Sigisberht said, suddenly suspicious.

'Nobody,' Ascha smiled. 'But if you were to need help in building boats, I'm your man.'

Sigisberht thought it over. 'You might be able to help us,' he conceded. 'We are building warships, many warships. We could use your skills.'

'I would be happy to help in any way I can,' Ascha said softly. 'Where are the boats being built?'

'At Radhallaburh.'

'Radhallaburh?'

'My uncle's new fortress in the forest.'

It was as if a lamp had been lit in his head. A new fortress would explain why he had seen no ships being built along the river. Radhalla was building a war fleet far from prying eyes. He would have to go there. See the fleet at first hand. He thought of the woods, cold and gloomy, and shivered. The Cheruskkii were not called the *waldingas*, the forest people, for nothing. But this was his chance. The Franks would want to know how many ships Radhalla was building. When they would sail? How many fighters they carried?

And Radhalla would be there.

'How long would you need me?'

'Until next summer.'

'And then?'

'And then we raid Gallia.' Sigisberht said, with a matter of fact smile.

'Ascha, under Radhalla's leadership, we expect great things,' Hanno chipped in eagerly. 'We will strike the Romans a heavy blow and come back laden with wealth. We will be rich.'

Ascha looked at them.

'But what if you fail?'

Sigisberht frowned. 'Why would we fail?' he said.

Ascha breathed out. He had to overcome Sigisberht's suspicions without arising them further. 'Forgive me, I am no warrior, but I know that although the Romans and the Franks are allies, it is the Franks who lead. They are powerful, and it would be a mistake to underestimate them.'

The Cherusker frowned, clearly disliking the idea that he had underestimated an enemy. He made a little rolling gesture with his forefinger. 'Go on'.

'The Franks fight like us but they are better armed, well trained and there are many of them. They have learnt much from the Romans. Six weeks ago the Frankish army, the *scara*, trapped three boatloads of Heruli against the ocean and destroyed them in half a day.'

Neither of them had any idea what it would be like when Roman horse troopers caught the Cheruskkii on the flank, when the sky darkened before the javelin-storm and their shields shattered under the Franks' *franciskas.*

There was an exasperated sigh from Hanno. 'Ascha, the Heruli are chased away wherever they go. Stick to the woodcarving. Stick to what tha knows.'

Stick to being a half-slave, is what tha means, Ascha thought, but he smiled and shrugged helplessly and said, 'Tha's right, Hanno. What do I know of these things?'

What he knew was that the Heruli were tough because they'd been chased out of every land they tried to settle. For the Herul there had been no going back.

He was conscious of Sigisberht watching him, a sly smile at the corner of the Cherusker's mouth.

'You know, I like the way you think,' Sigisberht said slowly. 'You could be useful to us. You have lived among the Romans and seen what few of us have seen. You know how they fight.' He seemed to come to a sudden decision. 'You must come to Radhallaburh. Come and help us build our warships.'

Ascha swallowed with relief. 'Of course, may I bring Tchenguiz? He is a good worker and knows wood.'

Sigisberht turned to Hanno, eyebrows raised.

'The Hun-slave,' Hanno explained.

'Bring whoever you please,' Sigisberht said and turned away.

As he reached the door, he turned back. 'One other thing!'

Ascha waited.

'You did well to come home after so many years away,' Sigisberht said. 'But you must remember that you are a Saxon now, one of us.' Radhalla's nephew smiled an efficient and bloodless smile. 'Just make sure you don't ever forget it!'

14

Winter, the coldest he had ever known. Water froze in the pitcher overnight and birds lay dead on the ground. Ascha said goodbye to his mother, told her where he was going and that if anyone were to ask for him she knew where he could be found. He kissed her and then he and Tchenguiz boarded the Cherusker warboat that would take them south.

It took two days to travel to the lands of the Cheruskkii, and it was dark when they arrived. As the long ship grated over the gravel, the two of them vaulted over the side and waded through the icy shallows and up a ramp of coarse grey sand.

They stood, stamping their feet and looked about them.

Radhalla's fortress was impressive. A stout wooden stockade ran along a wide turf rampart overlooking a ditch piled high with thorn bushes. Guards patrolled the walkways with smoky torches. The gates were open and a line of ragged slave-workers were shuffling in, heads low against the wind. They had been felling timber in the forest and seemed faint from hunger and exhaustion. Many were barefoot, and their beards were iced hard. Ascha watched them pass in silence. Sometimes, he thought, the only solace for being a half slave, was that he was not a slave. Behind the slaves came teams of oxen, drawing huge logs on sleds. The oxen loomed large in the darkness, the sled runners squeaking on the packed snow.

He picked up his tool sack and went towards the gate.

The fort was crammed with shabby cabins built end to end along narrow lanes that ran out from the middle of the fortress like the spokes of a giant wheel. A Cherusker led them down a dark alley, the light of his torch sending shadows leaping and cavorting across the snow.

Somewhere a dog howled.

They came to an area of levelled ground overlooked by a huge timber hall. A bonfire was burning off to one side and, by its thick light, Ascha saw oaken beams, a steeply shingled roof and thick plank walls. The gable ends, doorways and roof ridge of the hall were carved and freshly painted.

'What is this place, brother?' he said, tapping the Cherusker on the shoulder.

'That is Radhalla's hall, and this is the *mara,*' the Cherusker grunted. It was here, he said, that Radhalla addressed his warriors and held religious ceremonies and oath-takings. Ascha looked around. Along one side of the *mara* stood a line of tall poles, each topped with a clean, crow-picked skull, capped with snow.

'And those?' he said.

'War trophies from the tribes the Lord Radhalla has conquered,' the Cherusker said with pride.

Ascha peered up into the swirling whiteness. He could make out the skulls of ox, horse, badger and beaver. The last pole carried the skull of a boar. A recent kill, blackening flesh still sticking to the bone.

Hroc's boar, Ascha thought bitterly.

The Cherusker took them to a cabin and left them. Ascha opened the door and stepped inside. The ceiling was not much higher than his head, the interior cast in shadow, broken by the thin light of a few scattered oil lamps. A raw table, bunks from floor to ceiling and a window the size of a child's body. Men sat on their bunks or squatted on the floor. The air was dense with the stench of unwashed bodies and piss from the brimming bucket standing in the corner. Damp clothes and skins drying on a line added to the fug. The men looked up and stared at him with hard and suspicious eyes.

'We be of one blood,' he muttered.

Someone yelled at him to shut the door. Didn't he know a gale was blowing?

A Cherusker with a scruffy beard and heavy jowls came over. He wore baggy britches and layers of woollen coarseweave and scratched at his belly with a grimy fingernail. The Cherusker studied him, chewing slowly.

'I am Heafoc, hut-leader,' he said. 'And you?'

'Ascha of the Theodi.'

'What do you do, Theod?'

'Woodcarver.'

'Another timberer?' Heafoc said in disgust. 'And what's that?' he said gesturing to Tchenguiz.

'My Hun slave.'

'Ugly turd, ain't he?'

Ascha said nothing.

'He'll have to sleep with the other slave-workers.'

'He stays with me.'

Heafoc looked at him. He was about to say more and then thought better of it. He licked his lips and shrugged his shoulders. 'Please yourself,' he said. Pointing to a bunk in the corner, he threw Ascha a couple of thin blankets and a muddy pallet of straw. 'You sleep over there. The Hun sleeps on the floor.'

That night there was a storm. The wind howled through the rafters, the cabin shook as if punched and the fire went out. Ascha and Tchenguiz awoke to the harsh clangour of iron on iron. Snow lay thick as sheepskin, nudging into every nook and corner, smooth drifts piling up against the stockade wall.

Ascha and Tchenguiz pulled on their cloaks and boots and fell out of the cabin. They scooped up handfuls of snow, stuffed them into their mouths and looked about them. Ascha recognized a group of craftsmen by their tools. He motioned with his jaw to Tchenguiz, and they wrapped their arms around their shoulders, buried their fists in their armpits and followed the craftsmen along an alley and into a broader lane, their breath clouding the air.

They came out at the river and stopped in amazement. During the night, ice had formed at the water's edge and the trees hung heavy with snow. All along the riverbank men and women swarmed dark against the snow's whiteness. The air echoed to the zip of saws and the hollow *tchock* of axe and adze on timber.

Along the shore a dozen ocean-going long-boats were drawn up on cradles. More were hauled up on the riverbank. The riverside was a jumble of sheds and awnings, crude workshops springing up everywhere, like fungus under a wet log. He saw ironsmiths and metalworkers, ropemakers, leathermakers and bone-workers. Shipwrights trimmed planks, cut ribs and shaped bows and sternposts. Carpenters made tubs and wooden nails. Cheruskkii women in black skirts and bright headscarves sat in long open-sided sheds weaving sailcloth while others greased sails in huge tubs of oil and animal fat. His nostrils flinched from the stink of hot pitch and the urine barrels of the leatherworkers.

'*Wah!*' Tchenguiz murmured. 'Radhalla build many ships.'

Ascha asked for the master of woodcarvers and was directed to a bearded man with a red face.

The man looked him up and down. 'What's your trade, lad?'

'Carver.'

'Thought so!' the master said. 'Then stay close to me. Do as I do and you'll be all right.'

The master was a half-Dane called Eanmund. He was short and balding and had travelled south to join Radhalla, leaving a wife and six children in the Almost-Island. Eanmund told Ascha what his duties were and what he should expect. Every morning, the fighting men trained for war on the *mara*, the woodcarvers and shipbuilders headed for the riverside, and the slave gangs drove into the woods to fell and haul timber. The carvers shared the boats between them, vying with each other to produce the finest and most life-like carving of strake and prow. Open-jawed dragons, snarling sea gods, hell-fiends with curving necks and twisted collars.

Eanmund took Ascha to meet the other timberers. They raised a hand and welcomed him with a warmth they showed only to those who shared their craft. Eanmund took Ascha to where the bone white ribs of a long boat rose like the crow-picked carcase of a long dead whale.

'This is *Swanneck*,' Eanmund said. 'She's a fine ship. See what you can do with her.'

Ascha dropped his tool sack and began work.

In the days that followed, Ascha fell into a well-worn routine. Every day, he walked along the riverbank with sleeves pulled down over his knuckles and teeth clenched against the cold. He counted the new keels laid down on the mud and he counted the ships that were half-built and those that were almost finished. He peered into the boatsheds, committing to memory everything he saw. He spoke to the other carvers and asked them about the vessels they were working on, the size of the boat and the number of oars each boat carried. He kept a tally of what he saw, cutting the numbers on a stick which he hid deep in the straw on his bunk.

As the weeks passed and the notches grew, Ascha felt a growing rip tide of excitement. Radhalla's fleet would darken the ocean from shore to shore. The biggest war fleet he had ever seen.

Ascha and Tchenguiz were walking from the cabin to the riverbank when a shout rang out, 'Ho! *Mischling*!'

Ascha turned and his heart sank. Wulfhere leaned against a cabin wall, surrounded by a gang of swaggering toughs, all armed and glittering with belts and cloak brooches. Wulfhere dropped his head to the side, thrust out his tongue and made a choking sound, his eyes rolling, in a crude likeness of a hanging man.

The others giggled and sniggered. Wulfhere smiled and said, 'Does tha know who tha father is yet, *mischling*?'

'My father was Aelfric, *hetman* of the Theodi,' Ascha growled, 'as tha well knows.'

'If that's what tha thinks, slave-born, tha can think again!' Wulfhere said to more laughter.

A choking anger welled inside Ascha. He bunched his fists and slammed Wulfhere against the wall in a hot and sudden fury. Wulfhere grinned and put up his chin, doing nothing to defend himself, while his friends smirked. Ascha was about to strike Wulfhere in the face when he felt a powerful hand close about his wrist.

'Na,' Tchenguiz hissed, his eyes flat. 'Not here.'

Something about the way Tchenguiz spoke cut through Ascha's rage. He allowed the Hun to pull him away, and they left with Wulfhere's mocking laughter echoing in his ears.

'That Wulfhere is dangerous,' Eanmund grunted later. 'Stay out of his way or Radhalla will have your hide.'

'What's it to do with Radhalla?' Ascha snarled.

'Plenty,' Eanmund said. 'Radhalla will allow nothing to weaken the unity of the confederation and punishes anyone caught fighting within the fortress walls. Some time ago, a Chaussi picked a fight with a Jute over a woman. Radhalla had the man stripped and thrown into a cauldron of boiling water. When they pulled him out, he was bawling like a calf at the slaughter and his skin hung from his back like a torn sail.'

Ascha caught Tchenguiz' eye and nodded his thanks. That toad-spawn Wulfhere had provoked him, hoping he'd be put in Radhalla's pot. He'd been lucky, very lucky.

Although he had the occasional feeling that he was being watched, he saw no more of Wulfhere. He worked hard and the days went. To the other carpenters he was friendly, but he kept his distance. As time passed his anger went from fury to cold determination. Someday, he resolved, he would have his vengeance.

More Theodi arrived. They were thin and downbeat, dressed in rags. Ascha asked them for news of his mother, of Saefaru and

Budrum. The Theodi were reluctant to talk. Life in the village was hard, they said. The men had been taken away by the Cheruskkii and, with no-one working the land, the farms had suffered. The Cheruskkii were brutal and treated the village as their own. Women were abused, and the villagers lived in fear of their lives. Clanfolk who crossed the Cheruskkii disappeared and were found days later floating face down in the river.

Ascha listened carefully. He hoped his mother and Budrum were well. Life could be hard for a slave-woman with no-one to protect her. He asked the villagers about Hanno. They said that Hanno ruled in name only. The real *hetman* was Sigisberht who took pleasure in finding new miseries to inflict upon the Theodi.

'He came to our door and asked about you,' one of the villagers said quietly.

'Who?'

'Sigisberht, Radhalla's nephew.'

'What did he want?'

'Wanted to know whether you could be trusted.'

'What did you tell him?'

'That you were a half-slave. You were no threat to anyone.'

He looked at them and nodded. 'Thank you,' he said gravely. And then as an afterthought he added quietly, 'Did anyone else come? A Frisian trader perhaps?'

But they had seen no-one.

One night Ascha was awakened by the thump of a booted foot against the end of the bunk. Two hulking shapes stood over him with a burning torch that sent grey shadows jumping across the cabin's walls. One was the big Cherusker he had seen with Radhalla in his father's yard. The other was shorter and had a broken nose and a face spattered with moles.

'On your feet, Theod,' mole-face said. 'Radhalla wants you.'

The night was bitter cold and the dark sky studded with stars. They took him down narrow alleys and across the *mara* to where a buttery light spilled from Radhalla's hall.

Inside, the hall looked like a wheat field after a thunderstorm. Bodies lay everywhere, limbs snarled in drunken sleep. Men slouched over tables cradling their heads on their forearms. One man was on the table, toes up, head back and mouth agape, like a corpse. The room was warm and smoky, rank with the stench of spilled beer, greasy food and ripe bodies. Radhalla's *gesith*, his close companions, had feasted well.

Radhalla was standing before the fire wearing a long black bearskin robe which he lifted to warm the backs of his legs. A few Cheruskers sat staring into the flames. A shaggy coated hound lay asleep on the floor. Radhalla looked up and gave him what could have passed for a smile.

'Ah, the Theod,' he said, never blinking. 'Give him a beer!'

A Cherusker got up, poured him a beaker of sour beer and handed it to him. Uncertain, Ascha took it. Radhalla waved him towards a bench while he sat in a high-backed chair. He stretched out his legs, wrapped his robe around him, cracked his knuckles and smiled. Ascha watched him, waiting. What in Tiw's name did Radhalla want? He could sense the two Cheruskkii standing behind him where he couldn't see them.

'I don't sleep well,' Radhalla said, patting his belly. 'I have gases and dreams. I am afraid to sleep.'

Up close Radhalla had small dark eyes, like a pig, a neck that was thick and fleshy and jaws that looked as if they could shatter stones.

Silence between them, broken only by the crackling of the fire and the snores of the sleeping men.

Ascha bent and tasted the beer, never taking his eyes off Radhalla.

'You were with the Franks a long time.' Radhalla said.

'Yes.'

Radhalla belched an odour of garlic and onions. He jerked his head and one of the Cheruskkii walked over to the fire and turned the log with an iron. The fire flamed and spat, and Ascha felt the heat rise like a blow in the face. A gout of pale smoke rose and flattened under the rafters. The man dropped the iron with a ringing clatter and came back to stand behind Ascha.

'And you are what age?'

'Nineteen, maybe twenty.'

'You are young,' Radhalla said, pressing his lips together.

'I'm old enough.'

'And you are a carver?'

'You know I am.'

Radhalla smiled, eyes locked. 'You hate me, don't you, boy?' Radhalla said.

He made no answer. He scanned the room, as if casually. He should kill the beast now. Pull a knife from one of the sleeping men and slash the Cherusker's throat before the two brutes behind him cut him to pieces. This was the closest he would ever get. He would die, of course, which made it all pointless. He wanted revenge but he also wanted to live and enjoy everything Clovis had promised him. Oh, he would kill Radhalla, of that he was certain, but he would do it in his own way and in his own time. He would do it when it was right.

'Why would I hate you?' he said evenly.

'Because I killed that brother of yours,' Radhalla said, smiling.

'He was my half-brother,' Ascha whispered.

'He was a fool, whoever he was. But your father was a good man.'

'Yes,' Ascha said. 'He was.'

'You know we were friends once, Aelfric and I.'

Ascha looked at him. 'So I heard.'

'Friends for many years, I loved that man.'

'What happened?'

'We quarreled.'

'What about?'

Radhalla gave a hard little laugh. 'I forget,' he said and stretched, his fists tightly bunched.

'Is that why you killed him?' Ascha spat.

Radhalla paused, arms outstretched.

'I never killed your father,' he said, surprised. 'Why do you think that?'

'Soon after he visited you, his horse was hit by a slingshot. He was thrown and died two weeks later.'

Radhalla pushed back his chair and got to his feet. He walked round the table towards Ascha. 'You think I did that, you little prick?' he shouted in Ascha's face. He jerked a scarred thumb at his chest. 'You think I would do that to Aelfric?'

When he spoke his whole body moved, as if his head had been hammered into his trunk.

Ascha breathed heavily. He licked his lips, conscious of the Cheruskkii at his shoulders.

'He had opposed you, and you knew he was afraid of horses.'

'*Tcha!*' Radhalla said and waved an angry hand. 'Everybody knew Aelfric couldn't sit a horse to save his life. He was stubborn and refused to join us, but I didn't kill him.' He thought for a moment. 'Wronged him, maybe, but he was still my friend.'

'Then who threw the slingshot?'

Radhalla shrugged. 'It could a been anybody. Probably Hroc. Or Hanno.

Ascha swallowed. Hanno or Hroc? Sweet Tiw! Not his brothers. He shook his head. 'I don't believe you.'

Radhalla shrugged. 'Then again, it might have been the Franks, but it wasn't me.'

Ascha's lip curled. He looked up at Radhalla and said, 'You're lying, you dirty sack of shit.'

A Cherusker hit him in the face with his fist.

The room spun, and he found himself on the floor. Mole-face kicked him in the belly and the breath exploded from his lungs. He rolled in the straw, his nose filled with the stench of rotting food and stale grasses. The Cheruskkii picked him up and dropped him on the bench. He sat, hands cradling his belly, doubled up with pain. He wheezed for air and wiped his mouth with the back of hand, blinking.

Radhalla gave him a grim smile.

'You've got balls, boy, I'll give you that.' He waved the two Cheruskkii away and gave what might almost have been a sigh. 'Listen, I didn't kill your father.' He sat and leaned back and put one foot on top of the other. 'Tiw knows, he was not a great leader, but he was a brave man and he knew who he was. Aelfric always put his people first and they loved him for it.'

Ascha felt a prickle of doubt. He had been so blind with wanting revenge it hadn't occurred to him to question whether there were others who might have wanted Aelfric dead. But could Hanno or Hroc really have killed Aelfric?

'This rabble don't love me.' Radhalla went on, looking around the hall. He drew back a foot and kicked the table leg. The sound exploded like a dog's bark. Heads lifted in anger, saw Radhalla and thought better of it. Mumbling they went back to sleep. 'They hate me but they'll fight for me and, if needs be, the bastards will die for me.'

Radhalla rubbed his belly and let out a rippling belch. He grimaced and then leaned forward and beckoned Ascha with a thick finger.

'Let me tell you a story.' Radhalla said, scratching his beard. 'Your father and I used to go raiding together. One summer we were in Pritannia. We found a rich estate and burnt the village and plundered the house. Some women were captured, a few children. There was a girl that Aelfric took a shine to. She was a strange little thing, not pretty, but lots of spirit. She kept her head covered, but you could see her eyes burning with anger. I'd a taken her myself, but Aelfric was war leader and had first claim. On the boat back the crew pleasured themselves with the Pritanni women, but Aelfric forbade any man to touch his girl. On pain of death, mind you. She was his and his alone.'

Radhalla looked at Ascha and frowned. 'I didn't like that. Didn't like it at all. We were friends and we'd always shared our women. But that was your father all over. She might have been no more than a slave, but Aelfric loved her from the day he clapped eyes on her.'

Ascha closed his eyes.

At the mention of his mother, his throat tightened and he felt tears in his eyes. He could imagine her, out of her mind with terror, trying so hard to be brave.

Radhalla scratched his chin and watched him, smiling all the while. 'Sigisberht said you are good at what you do. Said there was more to you than meets the eye. Said that although you were low-born and no warrior, you were very – what was it, ah yes – resourceful.'

Ascha said nothing.

Radhalla looked down at his beer. 'What do you think of my fleet?' he grunted suddenly.

'I've never seen anything more beautiful,' Ascha said hoarsely and to his surprise he realized he meant every word.

Radhalla grinned. 'Do the Romans or the Franks have anything like it?'

Ascha shook his head. 'No,' he said. 'They don't.'

One of the dogs stretched and yawned. It got to its feet, swinging its head back and forth, and moved closer to the fire, flopped down and went back to sleep.

'And the new young Overlord, what do you think of him?'

'Clovis?' Ascha said warily. 'He's shrewd and he's ruthless.'

'Then he's like his fucken father,' Radhalla said with a burst of anger. He breathed in heavily and then blew it out. 'You know he's sent men to spy on me?'

Ascha lifted his head, jaw dropping. 'No.'

'I found them and killed them,' Radhalla chuckled. 'Dumped their bodies in the woods. The last one I pinned to a tree by his tongue. I think the wolves got 'im in the end.'

He laughed.

How many men, Ascha wondered, had Clovis sent before he thought to send his Saxon half-slave? And why was Radhalla telling him this? Was this supposed to be a warning?

Radhalla blew his nose into a stained rag and stuffed it into his tunic. 'I'm tired of raiding. I hate the travelling. I get sea-sick!' He glanced at Ascha. 'There's got to be a better way. All this work every summer for a few boatloads of loot.' He smacked a meaty fist into his palm. 'I want more, much more.'

'What more is there? You have it all.'

'I'll tell you what more there is.' He grimaced and rubbed his belly. 'My brother, Ergul, lives in Pritannia. He says we should do what he did.'

Ascha tried to sit up, 'Which is?' he said.

'Settle. Colonize the land.'

Ascha looked at Radhalla in astonishment, 'You're going to settle in Pritannia?'

Pritannia lay across the ocean at the outer edge of the world. All too easy when the fog lay thick as milk to lose your way and disappear in a sea without end.

'Naaaa, Ergil and I, we fight all the time.' Radhalla said. He banged his fists together and let out a rich laugh. 'Ergil can stay in Pritannia and rot for all I care.'

'What then?'

Radhalla paused. He leaned forward and stared into Ascha's eyes. For a moment, the brutal mask fell away and Ascha saw warmth and a twinkling humour, the man who was once his father's closest friend.

'I've had enough of boggy swamps and damp forests. I want to see fields rippling with golden wheat,' Radhalla said. 'I want to get up in the morning to the sound of birdsong and feel sunshine on my face.'

'So?'

'So, this time there's no in-and-out-and-home-again. We're going to carve ourselves a fat slice of Gallia, that's what we're going to do. We're going to take the Romans' land from them,' he laughed richly and slapped Ascha on the shoulder. 'What do you say to that, my boy, eh? What do you say to that?'

15

After that, Ascha saw no more of Radhalla. He was not sorry. He was starting to feel a glimmer of respect for the Cherusker and this unsettled him.

It was the time of *Tiwfest*. The men gathered on the *mara* wearing their finest clothes, their hair combed and braided according to the custom of their nation. Prayers were said and a slave led out for sacrifice. The slave walked slowly, arms and legs bare despite the cold, eyes rolling up into his head. Drugged, Ascha thought. The slave was pressed to his knees, a burly Cherusker clubbed him on the head and the slave collapsed in a heap.

Radhalla appeared.

The warlord of the Cheruskkii wore a wolfskin cape over a tunic the colour of sunset and was accompanied by a file of Gesith carrying ancient rust-spotted helmets and breastplates, trophies from some long-forgotten war against Rome.

A line of Cheruskkii girls and young women followed, dressed in white and wearing crowns of woven leaves. Behind them came Radhalla's guests. Ascha surveyed them. They were high-born, mostly from the northern tribes, men who Radhalla had a mind to impress. He knew them all, no surprises there. And then his eyes were drawn to a man at the back, half-hidden behind the others. He squinted and moved for a better view, but the man's face was lost in the shadow.

The girls hitched their dresses above the muck and sang a song to Tiw, their voices pure and clear in the chilly air. The men leaned on their spears and listened, blinking back tears at the sweet sadness of it all.

When they were done Radhalla raised his arms.

'A great time is upon us, my brothers,' he cried. 'In a few short weeks the festival of *Eostre* will be here, and we shall embark on a great venture. Our aim is the destruction of the Roman war beast. Your task will not be easy but the eyes of the north are upon you. Your enemy is well-trained and battle hardened. He will fight savagely. You will need strong stomachs and an iron will. But the tide has turned and the days of Roman tyranny are over. We have assembled a vast fleet. The journey across the ocean will be long and hard but, with Tiw's blessing, we will crush the Romans and their Frankish allies and drive them into the sea. My brave wolves, I trust in your courage, your devotion and your skill in battle. There will be land and plunder and glory for all and if you have to die, let it be a hero's death.'

A silence and then the *mara* erupted.

Thoughts whirled through Ascha's head. If Radhalla meant what he said, the Saxon uprising would be a greater threat than even Clovis had feared. A raid was one thing, conquest was another. And now Radhalla had moved the sailing date forward. The Cheruskkii weren't waiting for the summer. They would sail in the spring.

He felt a flutter of alarm. He'd hoped the Franks' Frisian agent would get his information back to Frankland, but he'd heard nothing. If the Frisian didn't show up soon, it would be down to him to warn the Franks. And that would mean leaving Radhallaburh and making his way back to Frankland before the fleet sailed.

He groaned inwardly at the thought of the journey back to the Rhine, but he had no choice.

On the *mara* men cheered until their lungs were raw.

'*Radhallaaa!*' they bellowed. '*Rad-hall-aaa! Radhallaaaaaaa!*'

'Tchenguiz, I have to get away. I have to warn the Franks.'

The Hun looked at him. They were in the forest, selecting timber for felling. It was cold and crisp, the snow as deep as their knees and they were walking side by side, bending forward to resist the wind. Some way off, they could hear axes banging on the frozen wood as if it were iron.

'They will never let tha go.'

'I will have to find a way. The Franks have no idea what is about to hit them.'

'I come with you,' Tchenguiz said.

Ascha looked at him. Since opening up to Tchenguiz he had noticed that the Hun had become more direct in his remarks, as if the gulf between them was narrowing.

'Na, I'll send tha back to the village. It's not safe for tha here with Wulfhere about. Tha can take care of my mother and Budrum until I come for them.'

'It's tha Wulfhere wants to hurt, not me.' Tchenguiz said with a grin. 'Tha lie with his wife.'

Ascha's jaw dropped. 'How by Tiw's bollocks does tha know that?' And then another thought. 'Does Wulfhere know?'

Tchenguiz gave him a crafty smile. He put both forefingers side by side and slowly rubbed them together. 'The whole village knows.'

Ascha swore. He'd thought he'd kept his tumbles with Saefaru a secret, but it seemed everybody had known all along.

'Tha still think like a young boy,' Tchenguiz said. 'Them Franks teach tha nothing. Here, tha must grow up fast or that Wulfhere will kill tha.'

Ascha shook his head. 'I never wanted an enemy.'

Tchenguiz hawked and spat. 'Then tha's a fool. In this world, tha cannot live without enemies.'

They heard a thunder of hooves and turned to see Radhalla ride by on a huge black stallion. It was a fine sight, the horse blowing plumes of warm breath and kicking up a cloud of snow, the Cherusker's cloak dark against the winter landscape. Radhalla was a keen horseman who rode every morning, rain or shine. They had got into the habit of looking out for him. When they heard the crump of hooves, they would stop what they were doing and watched Radhalla gallop past, his big horse crunching through the sleet. Tchenguiz would shake his head and click his tongue admiringly and then they'd go back to their work.

Today, Radhalla was not alone. A stranger rode with him, mounted on a chestnut, his face hidden by a hooded cloak. Ascha knew immediately it was the man he had seen two days before on the *mara*.

'Stay here!' he said to Tchenguiz.

He knew there was a long stretch on the return leg where the Cherusker liked to gallop. If he waited there, he would see the stranger as he rode past. He went off at a crouching run, running between the trees where the snow was still firm and crisp. He ducked beneath the snow-laden branches, leaping over ditches and wallowing through the drifts. When he reached the spot he had in mind, he dropped down behind a felled trunk, pulled branches over his head and shoulders and waited, fingers raw, limbs aching with cold. He peered down the trail, the whiteness dazzling his eyes. At first, he saw nothing and then he spied two riders emerging from the trees, black smudges against the snow.

One rider spurred his horse into a trot and then broke into a gallop. The other did the same. Ascha dipped his head as he heard them coming. There was a thunder of muffled hooves and he saw Radhalla thunder past, the black cloak billowing behind him like night after day. The other rider was bent low over his horse's neck. He had thrown back his hood and his dark hair streamed like water. Ascha saw a thin hook of a nose and a savage grin.

Fara. Ragnachar's man. The thoughts soon came spinning. What was Fara doing at Radhallaburh? Was he linked in some way with Radhalla? And did the Overlord of the Franks know that his uncle's agent was visiting his enemy?

Ascha went to Eanmund and asked him where Radhalla lodged his guests.

'Why you want to know?'

'No reason.'

'They stay with Radhalla in his hall.'

'And if not there?'

Eanmund frowned. 'There's a lodge along the north road where he sometimes puts those who want to keep themselves to themselves.' He pointed upriver.

Ascha thanked him. Eanmund said he should think nothing of it.

Ascha and Tchenguiz left the fort and took the north road. The thaw had started, and the snow was melting and beginning to turn to slush. They came to a mud track and followed it down into a hollow in which stood a large cabin at the bottom of a steep bank, all but hidden by ivy and overhung by trees.

The drifts were melting revealing the green beneath but, in the hollow and on the cabin roof, snow still lay thick as turf. The cabin was no more than two rooms with a rough porch, outhouses and a workshop at the side. A well lay half-hidden in the trees.

They waited and listened. Nothing moved.

'Stay close,' Ascha said.

'What are we going to do if we find him?' Tchenguiz grumbled.

'I don't know,' Ascha said. He'd given no thought to what they would do. He climbed the steps, crossed the porch, opened the door and went in. The door swung open on leather hinges, their feet leaving a wet trail on the boards. The cabin was empty. There was a rough table in one room with a hard crust of bread on a plate and a jug rank with soured milk. In the corner was a wooden bed with a straw pallet and a couple of old and threadbare blankets. He picked up a blanket and then dropped it back on the bed. In the other room was a pile of old straw.

Tchenguiz knelt on the floor before the hearth and pushed his hand into the ashes.

'Still warm,' he said.

Ascha put up his nose and sniffed the air. A trace, no more than that, of an exotic but strangely familiar smell. He turned to go when his eye caught sight of something on the floor, half-hidden under the bed. He bent and picked it up, a small clay bottle, no bigger than his thumb. He pulled the stopper and put it to his nose. A powerful scent of musky spices hit him. He thought for a moment, replaced the stopper, pushed the bottle into his tunic and left.

Outside they found tracks in the yard leading to the road.

'Three iron-shod riders and two mules,' Tchenguiz said, kneeling. 'They left today, probably just after dawn.'

'Which way?'

Tchenguiz looked up at him. 'Southwards,' he said. 'Towards the Rhine.'

'Someone were looking for you,' Eanmund said when they got back.

'Who?'

'Trader. Cheese-head. Said his name were Dagobert.'

Ascha blinked. *Cheese-head.* A Frisian?

'What did he want?'

Eanmund raised his shoulders. 'Said you owed him for a bronze kettle.'

Ascha felt his mouth dry. He owed nobody for a bronze kettle. Was this the Frankish agent Clovis had promised?

Eanmund saw the look on his face and mistook it for something else. 'You don't escape traders that easily. Them bastards will always find you.'

'Why doesn't he come here?'

'Traders are not allowed to enter the fortress. He'll be in the village.' Eanmund made a vague nod to the world beyond the fortress walls.

Ascha felt as if a rock had been lifted from his shoulders. If this was the Frisian agent then he could fulfil his promise to warn Clovis of the uprising and still have time to deal with Radhalla.

He decided to wait. He shouldn't be seen to be in too much of a hurry to settle a debt.

Ascha and Tchenguiz left the fort, passing by a clump of Cheruskkii gate guards who stood around a small fire, stamping their feet and banging their hands together. Ascha pulled his cloak over his head and gave them a wave. The guards looked up and then went back to their fire.

The two of them moved into the forest, ducking under trees and wading through knee-high snowdrifts. As they brushed against branches, snow fell down their necks. Somewhere they heard a dog bark. They stopped and waited until all was quiet, and then went on.

Ascha was nervous. This was his first contact with the Franks since he had left Tornacum. How could he be sure this man was a Frankish agent? How would he recognize him and, if he was who he said he was, how much should he tell him? He wished he had remembered to ask Flavinius for the man's description.

They came to a jumble of broken-backed cabins on the riverbank, all overlain with snow. Ascha laid his cheek against the cold bark of a tree and studied the village.

Three boats moored at the jetty. Two were river traders who brought grain and took away furs to trade downriver. The third, a black-sailed, heavy-looking vessel, was a slaver that visited the fort from time to time, replenishing stock. A smaller boat was moored further up the riverbank and he assumed this belonged to the Frisian trader. The boats seemed empty, the crews probably drinking in the inn.

'Stay here and watch the road,' he said to Tchenguiz. 'Warn me if anyone comes.'

He went on, his feet crunching the snow. A light spilled from one of the cabins and he heard the hum of voices. He went towards the sound, climbing steps slippery with ice. He pushed at the door which yielded with an ancient groan, and stepped inside.

Eyes flicked at him and then away.

'One blood. . . ' he said half-heartedly, peering into the gloom.

There was a strong smell of hot food and damp clothes. By the brown and soupy light of oil lamps he saw a woman with frizzy hair stirring a black pot over a fire. Men with leathery faces sat at tables and talked. He wondered if one of them was the Frisian?

He felt a tug at his sleeve and looked down to see a scrap of a girl dressed in rags holding out her hand.

'What you got f'the pot?' she said.

He must have looked puzzled because the child shrugged and said, 'Don't give, don't eat.'

Then he understood. The woman cooked whatever was brought in. Those who gave got a share of the pot, and the woman and her daughter ate whatever was left.

He looked up as a man shouldered his way towards him.

'You the Theod?' the man muttered. He had a sharp face, a weak chin and dirty hair. Dressed like a trader, but with a *seaxe* and a long-shafted hatchet stuffed in his belt. He spoke in a Frisian dialect, his breath fouled by beer and onions.

He nodded. 'You Dagobert?'

The man scowled. 'Not here!' He dragged a cloak around his shoulders and left without another word.

Ascha followed him outside. He saw the Frisian disappear down an alley and followed warily. The alley stank of rotting food and pigshit, the snow filthy and trampled to slush. Just when Ascha thought he had lost him, the man stepped out from the shadows.

'How did you find me?' Ascha said.

'I asked around,' the Frisian said. 'One of the drinkers said he knew you, said he'd pass on the message if I gave him a beer.' He flapped a hand towards the inn

'You were supposed to be here a month ago,' Ascha said.

The Frisian wet his lips and looked over his shoulder. 'Well, I'm here now,' he said. 'What have you got f'me?'

A dog appeared around a corner and looked at them and then went on its way.

'What do you want?' Ascha stalled.

Dagobert squeezed his arm. 'Listen, Theodling,' he hissed. 'You know what I want.'

Ascha thought it over. If the Cheruskkii discovered he'd given information to a Frankish spy, he would die slowly and horribly.

'How do I know I can trust you?' he said.

'You don't!' Dagobert grunted. He hesitated and then said grudgingly, 'Before I left, that fat poof Flavinius said you owed him a beer.'

Ascha allowed himself a thin smile. He missed Flavinius.

The alley was quiet but for the sound of water dripping from the eaves. Ascha looked about him. If the Frisian was going to betray him he would know soon enough. He was in and had to go all the way. Throw the dice, see what happened.

He breathed in and blew it out.

'There's going to be an uprising of the Saxon and northern tribes against the west. It will come by sea and will be lead by Radhalla of the Cheruskkii. The Cheruskkii are building a warfleet here in Radhallaburh.'

Quickly, he went over what he knew of Radhalla's plans, running through the names of the tribes involved and the numbers of ships and men.

'Tiw's blood!' Dagobert breathed. 'It'll be like wolves to the slaughter.'

Ascha nodded. It would.

'When do they sail?'

'In two weeks time, after Eostre.'

Dagobert gaped. 'So soon?'

'Yes.'

The Frisian gave a low whistle. He seemed taken aback by the size and speed of the uprising. 'Where will they strike?'

'I don't know.'

Ascha felt a knot of anxiety in his chest. It was the only thing he had not been able to discover. Only Radhalla knew where the Saxon host would land.

Dagobert swore viciously. 'Listen, you Theod bog-trotter, we have to know where they will land. Whether it's above or below Gesoriac, otherwise they could lay waste to half the province and be out before the army moves up.'

'They won't be leaving.'

'What do you mean?' Dagobert said.

'It's not a raid. It's an invasion. They aim to seize land and hold it.' He remembered Radhalla's words, 'Radhalla wants a slice of Gallia.'

'The fuck they do,' the Frisian said. 'Saxons are raiders, not settlers.'

'Not anymore,' Ascha said. 'They want the land.'

Dagobert stepped in close and peered at him. 'Are you sure?' he said.

'I'm sure.'

Dagobert scratched his chest. 'I have to get this to the Franks,' he muttered, 'but first we have to deal with Radhalla.'

'We have to do what?'

'Kill Radhalla and Clovis will give us anything we want,' Dagobert said. 'All the gold we can dream of.'

Ascha shoved his hands deep inside his tunic and gave the Frisian a grim smile. 'Easier said than done. You might as well stop a rabid dog.'

'But you could do it,' Dagobert said, grabbing his arm. 'They don't know you are war trained. They don't suspect you. You could get close.'

Ascha angrily shook the Frisian off. 'Radhalla is always surrounded by his hall-troop. The *gesith* would never let an assassin get close enough to touch him.'

He remembered Radhalla by the fire and felt a pang of regret. He'd had his chance and might not get another. But he was not going to throw his life away for nothing. He'd come too far for that.

'Then kill him while he sleeps,' Dagobert said. 'I'll meet you and we'll get away on my boat.'

Ascha felt a shiver of alarm. The Frisian was too wild and too greedy to be trusted. If he wasn't careful, he would get them both killed. He laughed. 'You're crazy. I wouldn't live long enough to set foot on your boat.'

'They say he killed your brother,' Dagobert said.

'He did.'

The Frisian's lip lifted in a sneer. 'I didn't have you pegged as a coward.'

'I'll revenge my brother's death when I'm good and ready,' Ascha snarled. 'In the meantime, you stay away from Radhalla. I'm not going to boil in a pot for you.'

There was a sudden high pitched animal wail from the forest, like a child screaming. Ascha felt the hair on the back of his neck rise. He pushed Dagobert away and turned.

In the half-light, the grey of the snow and the grey of the sky merged into a single blur. A rustle of snow fell from the branches with a heavy plop. He heard a scrape at the end of the alley which may or may not have been a boot.

'I have to go,' he said urgently.

Dagobert rubbed his throat and rolled his head. 'Meet me again tomorrow night,' he said hoarsely. 'And think again about what I said. Kill that monster and we're made for life.'

Ascha ran down the alley. He paused to look around and then left the village, plunging deep into the forest. He was creeping past a tree stump, the darkness swirling around him, when the ground shifted and a figure rose at his side.

'Blast! I never saw tha.'

Tchenguiz threw back his cloak and shook off the snow.

'There was someone moving in the village.'

'Following me?'

'Maybe, yes.'

'Did tha see who it was?'

The Hun shook his head.

'Does tha think he saw me?'

Tchenguiz waggled his head. 'I don't know.'

At the edge of the village, they paused and checked behind them. There was no sign of Dagobert. The forest was quiet, blanketed by snow.

They waited a long time listening to the water dripping from the trees.

Then they went back to the fort.

16

He was working on the prow of a big war boat when they came for him. Eanmund saw them first. 'Hold up!' he said in his flat twang. 'Something's wrong.'

Ascha looked up and saw spearmen coming out of the fortress at the run. He watched as the men loped down the riverbank towards them. A bell began to clang, and the shipbuilders stopped working and turned their heads. Ascha felt a prickle of apprehension and looked about him nervously. This was not usual. Fighting men did not bother themselves with boat building.

The spearmen were *gesith*, Radhalla's chosen men. They quickly surrounded the boat and a Cherusker with red spiky hair stepped forward.

'Ascha the Theod, you are to come with us.'

Ascha dropped his tools and ran.

He sprinted the length of the boat, jumping from bench to bench, and leaped to the ground and was off. He heard shouts, a whistle, the sound of running feet. He vaulted a wicker fence and then he was through a dirty yard, into a shed and out the other side and down an alley. Men looked at him curiously. He slowed and pulled up his hood and then dived down another alley. He ran to the far end and came out at the fortress wall.

He stopped and caught his breath. Nobody about, but hens pecking the dirt and pigs grunting.

He breathed more easily.

There was the sound of a boot on gravel.

He turned and saw a line of armed Cheruskii slowly filing out from a lane. Half a dozen spear points swept towards him. He whirled only to see more Cheruskii behind him.

He felt his belly churn. The red-haired Cherusker barked an order. The Cheruskkii seized him. They hurled him against the wall and slapped his face. They punched him in the stomach and threw him to the ground. Then they picked him up and bundled him back the way they had come. Craftsmen and boat-builders put down their tools and came to see what was going on.

As they neared the river, Eanmund stepped from the crowd and barred their way. 'What's this about?' he shouted. 'Where are you taking this man?'

The Cheruskkii pushed him aside without a word.

'Stay out of it, Eanmund,' Ascha called over his shoulder. 'I'll be fine.'

He saw that Tchenguiz had also been seized. The two of them were driven into the fortress and towards the *mara* in a confusion of shouts and excited voices. A crowd had gathered. He saw Radhalla sitting on a low stool, ringed by *gesith* with weapons drawn and teeth bared, screaming at the crowd to get back.

Something had happened, he had no idea what, but he suspected he would find out soon enough.

He was pushed to his knees, spears hovering before his eyes.

He looked up.

Radhalla was bareheaded. Across one cheek, a weapon-slash had laid the Cherusker's face open from mouth to ear. Blood poured down Radhalla's cheek in thin rivulets and dripped onto his shoulder. His shirt was ripped and spattered with blood. A woman in a black kerchief held a bowl of water while another stood at Radhalla's elbow laboriously threading a bone needle with fishing line.

Radhalla's skin was grey and drawn. He smiled at Ascha with cold, unfathomable eyes and, as he did, Ascha saw the wound in his cheek gape a little like a second mouth. The woman held the edges of the wound together with finger and thumb and began to sew.

He noticed Sigisberht standing at Radhalla's side, rocking back on his heels, both thumbs thrust into his belt. In the cold air, Sibisberht's face seemed pink and newly-scrubbed. He watched Ascha with an air of satisfaction, like a cat that has just caught a mouse.

Ascha remembered the stories he had heard of Radhalla's cruelty. He closed his eyes and willed himself to be calm. You can do it, he thought. You can get through this.

There was a bustle of bodies, and the crowd parted.

Fighters came running onto the *mara,* carrying the body of a man shoulder high. The man was dead. No doubt about that. The body was hacked and battered, the skin yellow and purple, and the head lolled obscenely. The *gesith* threw the body to the ground; the corpse rolled and came to rest face up. A weak chin shrouded in bristles, cold dead eyes and a cheek smeared with blood.

Dagobert.

Ascha felt as if he had been kicked in the teeth. His heart pounded and his breath came in pants.

Sigisberht walked over to Dagobert's body. He lifted the chin with his toe and then let it fall.

The *mara* fell silent.

Sigisberht bowed to Radhalla and then faced the crowd.

'Brothers!' he said in his prissy voice. 'I am sorry to have to tell you that there has been a vicious and brutal attempt on Lord Radhalla's life. This...thing tried to murder our war leader.'

Sigisberht brought his foot back and kicked Dagobert in the face.

Ascha heard the sharp crack of bone.

'This man is an outsider,' Sigisberht said, stepping over Dagobert's lifeless body. 'A Frisian agent sent here to murder our leader. And with the cunning typical of his kind, he chose his moment well. He attempted to kill Lord Radhalla as he was coming back from his morning ride.' Sigisberht paused as angry shouts rang out. 'Radhalla, thanks be to Tiw, was unharmed. With his bare hands, he was able to hold off the attacker until help arrived.' He turned to Radhalla's bodyguard and bowed his head formally. 'We are grateful to the *gesith*, most loyal of Radhalla's followers, for their zeal and devotion.'

The snarling hulks behind Sigisberht looked out with unrelenting eyes.

Radhalla's morning ride! The one time when Radhalla was alone and undefended. Dagobert had nearly succeeded. Beneath Sigisberht's smooth words Ascha could detect the Cherusker's fury that the *gesith* had killed the Frisian before he could be made to talk.

'But there is more to this treachery!' Sigisberht said. 'There is a man here who has something to say.'

He turned and beckoned.

Wulfhere stepped forward, a pinched little smile on his face.

Ascha slowly got to his feet, his stomach turning.

Wulfhere dipped his head to Radhalla and cleared his throat.

'I am Wulfhere of the Theodi and I am proud to be part of the confederation's struggle against the Roman degenerates and their allies.'

He paused, taking his time, and then pointed to Ascha.

'Last night that man met secretly with the assassin. I saw them talking together.' He paused again. 'Ascha of the Theodi is as guilty of trying to kill Radhalla as if his own hand were on the knife.'

Ascha's heart stopped.

A hush and then the crowd erupted with howls of rage. All eyes on him, the Theodi traitor. Radhalla wincing as the needle went in.

'What do you say to that?' Sigisberht said coldly. He gestured to Dagobert's ripped corpse. 'Do you know this man?

Ascha felt his blood freeze. Futile to deny it. Too many knew the Frisian was looking for him. Have to tell the truth, or as much of it as he dared.

He took a deep breath, his mouth dry as sand. 'Of course, I know him,' he said, all matter-of-fact. 'He's a trader. A cheese-head.'

He was conscious of Sigisberht staring at him. Radhalla glanced at Sigisberht, one eyebrow raised, the needle pulling the tattered flesh together.

Wulfhere jabbed his finger at Ascha.

'That little shit spent five years with the Franks and he works for them now,' he said, spitting out the words. 'I tell you, I saw them together. He's a spy.'

'Did you meet with the Frisian?' Sigisberht said to Ascha.

'It's as I told you, he's a trader,' Ascha said coolly. 'I owed him for a bronze kettle. I met him and paid him. Gave him six rabbits for it. Eanmund will speak for me.'

Eanmund's broad vowels, right on the nail.

'What the boy says is true. I, Eanmund the half-Dane, swear it.'

Ascha heaved a small sigh of relief.

'He says you're a spy,' murmured Sigisberht. 'He says you were discussing Radhalla's murder.'

'He lies as often as he breathes,' Ascha shouted. 'He heard nothing.'

'Why would he lie?' Sigisberht said.

Ascha thought fast. He hoped with every bone in his body that Wulfhere hadn't heard what he had said to Dagobert, but if he had he was as good as dead. Either way, it wouldn't take Sigisberht long to unravel his story. That was what Sigisberht did, rooting out spies and assassins. They would search his belongings and they would find the tally-stick. It wouldn't take long for Sigisberht to work out that Ascha was a spy and to connect him to the Franks. He had to damage Wulfhere, quickly, before Sigisberht got any closer.

'There's always been bad blood between us,' he said. 'He betrayed my brother and now he's out to destroy me.'

Radhalla looked up, suddenly interested. 'Why should he want to destroy you?' he said, his voice muddied as he tried to speak without moving his jaw.

'He's jealous.'

'Jealous? Of what?'

Desperately, Ascha tried to think. He had put himself into this position and the only thing to do now was carry it off. 'Saefaru, Wulfhere's wife ...' He let the words tail away.

The crowd smelled a rat.

Sigisberht smiled pleasantly. 'What about her?'

The *mara* fell silent. Everyone looking and waiting, a small cleft of uncertainty had appeared between Wulfhere's eyes.

Ascha shrugged and tried to appear calmer than he felt. 'I think she's sweet on me.'

'You're a liar,' Wulfhere snarled.

But Ascha had seen the shadow of doubt cross Wulfhere's face. He had to make them think Wulfhere was acting out of a grudge. He turned and looked for Radhalla's eyes, held them. 'Saefaru and I were lovers before I went away,' he said. 'Since I returned from exile, we have been seeing each other again.' He gave a loud sigh. 'I think it's humiliating for Wulfhere and that's why he says these things.'

The *mara* held its breath.

Someone began to laugh, a rich and dirty cackle. The joke caught like the plague. Others joined in. Soon everyone on the *mara* was sniggering and tittering. The Theod was no Frankish assassin: he was just porking the other Theod's wife. Hilarious!

Wulfhere stood rooted to the spot. He had gone white and his mouth worked noiselessly. He bore a look of stunned disbelief. Ascha closed his eyes. Sweet mother of Tiw, he thought. Wulfhere hadn't known about him and Saefaru, and I just told him. He'd shamed Wulfhere in front of the tribes. Wulfhere would never let it go.

Wulfhere wiped the back of his hand against his mouth. He swallowed, his face pale with anger, and then turned to Radhalla.

'Lord! This half-slave has dishonoured me,' he said. 'I ask leave to kill him.'

Ascha ran his tongue over chapped lips and dug his nails into the palm of his hand. He hadn't expected this. He hated Wulfhere, but a Theod did not fight Theod. At least not like this. He looked at Wulfhere and then at Radhalla. For a brief moment he thought

Radhalla might deny Wulfhere. And then he realized that Radhalla had no choice. A lord could not refuse a freeman who had been insulted by a half-slave.

There was a long pause and then Radhalla gave a faint and almost unnoticeable nod of his big head.

Ascha's mouth dried.

The crowd went wild, baying for blood. They rushed to form a ring.

Wulfhere was quivering, his eyes popping with hatred. He drew his long-knife and swung his shield across his body and came shuffling on, weight on the back foot, shield forward.

'Give me a weapon!' Ascha screamed at Sigisberht. 'Anything!'

Sigisberht folded his arms and shook his head.

And then it dawned on him. Nobody was going to give him a weapon. He was a weaponless and shieldless half-slave, and this man was going to kill him.

He backed away, his nerves on full alert.

He pulled off his neck cloth and wrapped it tight around his left forearm and caught the loose end in his fist and turned and dropped into a crouch, arms wide. They circled crabwise. Wulfhere made a sudden slashing cut that would have disembowelled Ascha if he had not jumped back, nearly slipping in the mud and slush. The crowd cheered and whooped. Wulfhere came on, slashing and cutting. Ascha retreated. He stepped aside to avoid a blow and staggered and nearly stumbled. Wulfhere slashed again, and Ascha felt a hot slice of pain rip across his upper arm. He backed away and blundered into the crowd, hot breath on his neck and rough hands shoving him forward. Wulfhere came on, face half-hidden by the shield, dark eyes following Ascha's every move. Ascha twisted to avoid a shallow knife thrust and felt a hammer blow from Wulfhere's shield on his left side. He staggered, his head pounding. He looked into Wulfhere's smiling eyes and saw his past.

Wulfhere changed the grip on his long-knife and suddenly slashed at Ascha's belly. He flicked back his hips with arms outstretched but felt the sting as Wulfhere's blade passed across his ribs. He touched his side and his hand came up wet with blood. No pain. That would come later.

Wulfhere lowered his shield fractionally.

'I've waited a long time for this, *mischling*,' he said.

Ascha saved his breath, knowing that Wulfhere would take his time, happy to cut him to shreds before he killed him. Wulfhere was enjoying himself.

The crowd had become a yelling mob. He glimpsed Heafoc and his hut-companions shouting themselves hoarse, Tchenguiz and Eanmund and a knot of woodcarvers, their faces racked with concern. He saw Tchenguiz waving with both arms and pointing to Dagobert's dead body, shouting something, the words lost in the tumult.

Wulfhere came on, crowding him, blocking his escape, biding his time.

The Frisian!

Ascha took a step back and then whirled around and sprinted to where Dagobert lay in the slush. Lifting up one dead shoulder, he tugged at Dagobert's tunic. The belly-knife was gone, robbed by the *gesith*.

He howled with despair.

And then he remembered Dagobert's hatchet. Breathless, he struggled to lift Dagobert's dead weight. The crowd saw what he was doing and roared their excitement. He could sense Wulfhere moving in fast. Dagobert flopped over, one dead hand smacking the mud. Ascha fumbled through his clothes. There! Dagobert's hatchet was under his belt, hidden in the folds of his cloak.

Wulfhere guessed what he was doing and ran forward. Heart banging against the wall of his chest, Ascha drew the axe. He heard Wulfhere's feet slapping the slush and turned. Wulfhere came on. Ascha swung the hatchet and struck Wulfhere's shield, angling the blade to strike along the grain. The metal shield rim flew off and, with a loud crack, the shield split in two. The blow knocked Wulfhere off balance. He staggered and almost fell and then hurled the broken shards of his shield aside and came on again, slashing with his knife, trying to finish it.

Ascha swung at Wulfhere's face and, as Wulfhere jerked his head back, he dived and rolled and came up on his opponent's left, swinging the blade with a vicious backward cut at Wulfhere's leg. A sharp scream of pain as the hatchet bit deep and Wulfhere's knee gave way.

Grasping the hatchet with both hands, Ascha spun on his heel and chopped savagely at Wulfhere's side. There was a grunt, and Ascha heard a loud crack as the ribs gave way.

He leapt back, hatchet raised, and watched as Wulfhere slowly pulled himself to his feet, resting his weight on his undamaged leg. Wulfhere grimaced at Ascha, arms by his side, his face twisted with pain and loathing.

Ascha waited, his chest heaving, as the crowd watched in silence. Wulfhere's eyes were wide and his mouth was working.

'Once a *mischling*, always a *mischling*, huh?' he said, smiling with hate-filled eyes.

Ascha reached back and swung.

The blade struck Wulfhere between shoulder and neck and drove down through muscle and bone into the chest, shattering the heart. For a fleeting moment, Wulfhere stood, and then the long knife slipped from his fingers, his hands gripped the air and he pitched forward as dead as a stone.

Sigisberht raised a hand no higher than his waist and flicked his fingers. The Cheruskkii ran forward, spears levelled.

'Drop the axe,' one said.

Ascha looked at the hatchet in his hand and allowed it to slip from his fingers into the mud. A Cherusker kicked it away. The *gesith* formed a horseshoe around him and prodded him forwards. Ascha took a careful step and then walked towards Radhalla, his hand clutching his belly, blood oozing between his fingers.

He was worn out and his legs were trembling. He had killed his childhood enemy but he felt nothing. Radhalla watched him thoughtfully. The Cherusker dabbed at his cheek with a dirty rag, blood dripping into the slush. Dagobert's cut was long and deep, and Ascha knew that Radhalla would carry the scar for the rest of his life.

'Where did you learn to fight like that, boy?' Radhalla said.

Ascha held his gaze. 'My father was Aelfric of the Theodi,' he said, his breathing harsh and ragged. 'I carry his blood. Wulfhere would have killed me. It was him or me.'

He felt faint and was starting to feel the wound in his belly.

'You're right, of course,' Sigisberht said with a smirk. 'Nevertheless, you used a weapon which is forbidden by law, and you killed a freeman. For that the penalty is death.'

'I broke no law,' Ascha said evenly, not caring what they did to him. He paused and then said, 'The death-weapon was Tiw's gift.'

Radhalla looked at him, his head on one side, 'How so?'

'Tiw did not want me to die. He sent me the Frisian's axe.'

'You're saying the axe was a gift from Tiw?'

'Yes. He took Wulfhere's life instead.'

'A gift from Tiw?' Radhalla repeated.

The crowd picked it up and passed it on, the sound swelling as more joined in. They began to chant, stamping their feet and banging their shields.

'Tiw's gift! *Tiw's gift!*'

Ascha listened in amazement.

Radhalla turned, wincing as his jerkin rubbed his lacerated cheek. He swung his head from side to side, watching the crowd, trying to gauge which way the wind was blowing and then he turned to the men whose spears lingered at Ascha's throat.

'You!' he said to one of them. 'Do you think this weapon was sent by Tiw?'

The man grinned nervously. 'Ay, Lord,' he said. 'How else could an unarmed half-slave have killed Wulfhere?'

Radhalla rolled his bottom lip. He held Ascha's eyes, a half-smile playing at the edge of his mouth. 'How, indeed,' he said.

He frowned and slowly nodded his big head and then he said, 'The Theod lives, but he cannot stay here. He has killed within the boundary of the fortress. Send him and his slave back to his own people!'

It took a while before Ascha realized what Radhalla had said. As if in a trance, he stared at Radhalla. Sigisberht opened his mouth to speak but was silenced by a cold stare from Radhalla. Sigisberht scowled and jerked his head. Spearmen surrounded Ascha and escorted him towards the gate. The crowd surged, sweeping him along, slapping him on the back and cheering as if they had known all along he would triumph.

The leaden clouds parted, and blue skies appeared. At the gate they paused while Sigisberht spoke hurriedly to the captain of *gesith* and then the captain led them through the gate and out of the fortress. At first Ascha couldn't believe it and then as he realized he was really leaving Radhallaburh, he turned to Tchenguiz and grinned. He would see his mother, sit in his father's hall, and eat home-cooked food. He put back his head and let the sunlight wash over his face.

They were going home.

The *gesith* took them out of the fortress and down the path. A dank chill lay about the woods, the ground still patched with rags of snow. They came to the fork and took the grail to the village, moving now at a brisk pace. Ascha frowned. He looked back over his shoulder and then turned to his neighbour.

'Where we going, brother?' he said. 'This isn't the way.'

The Cherusker turned and punched Ascha hard in the mouth.

Ascha stumbled and nearly fell. Spears and blows spurred him on. He tasted blood and his jaw throbbed. The slash in his side stung ferociously.

He saw Sigisberht up ahead talking to the captain of *gesith*, the captain laughing politely. Ascha exchanged anxious glances with Tchenguiz. Something wasn't right. He felt a grim foreboding. Sigisberht looked up and held Ascha's eyes and smiled.

They went through the woods, sunlight flickering through the trees, to the village. A single vessel stood by the jetty. A black sail, black as death, blotting out the sun. Men stood in the bows, heavy-set, cold-faced beasts. A human cargo of men and women squatted in the well of the boat with their necks bound and their heads held in a hard and wooden embrace.

And then he knew.

No. Not that!

He shoulder charged the nearest Cherusker and knocked him flying and then took to his heels, running as fast as he could.

He heard yells behind him and Tchenguiz' desperate shout, 'Run, boss, run!'

He ran, blundering through the bushes and nettles, branches and brambles slashing at his face. He tripped and almost fell before he found his feet and plunged on. He felt a sharp pain in his side and heard the shouts of men behind him. Branches reached out and grabbed his legs, tree roots snaked across his feet. Gasping, he jumped down into a ditch and pushed through old bracken. He clambered out, feet sliding on the mud and then his knees gave way and he tumbled, rolling down the bank. He lay stunned for a moment and then he heard the shouts and yells drawing closer. He went to get up when a boot struck him on the side of the head. Another crashed into his ribs. He wanted to cry out but it was if his mouth was full of sand. There was a hard crack on the back of his skull.

And then everything went dark.

17

He awoke in the middle of the night and lay without moving, letting the pain roll over him. He was lying in the belly of a boat with his wrists and elbows bound and a wooden pole yoked to his neck. He ached all over and the cut in his belly was stiff and sore. He could feel the boat moving beneath him. Dirty streaks of cloud scudded across a waning moon and a chill wind pummelled the ship's black sail. The stench of shit and bilge water was overpowering.

He went to rise and felt a hand on his arm.

'Don't move or they will come,' a voice said from out of the darkness.

'Tchenguiz!' he said. 'Is it tha?'

'Wah!'

'Where are we?'

'We're on a slaver. The Cheruskkii sold us.'

'A slaver?'

It was a moment before he understood and then his stomach lurched and he retched, splashing his tunic and breeches with his own filth.

Sweet Tiw! Say it wasn't happening, not a slave!

'Where are we going?' he moaned.

'Downriver. We will reach river mouth maybe midday tomorrow.'

There was a hardness in the Hun's voice and he wondered if Tchenguiz blamed him for what had happened. Ascha closed his eyes and sank into a void of bottomless despair. After all he'd been through, to be taken by slavers? The thought was too much to bear.

There was a shout from the bow.

One of the slavers swaggered down the boat and began laying about him with a cudgel. Ascha heard the smack of wood on flesh and whimpers from the other slaves. Instinctively, he drew into the shadows and waited until the slaver had gone back and everything was silent again.

The realization came to him slowly. 'We'll sail past our own village?' he said.

'Ha,' said Tchenguiz. 'We will.'

He lifted his head and looked about him. In the soft gloom, he could see men, women and children pressed together, all roped and yoked like himself.

'How many in this boat?'

'Eighteen,' Tchenguiz said.

Ascha looked at him. 'And crew?'

'Five, maybe six.'

Too many to overcome. What could he do? Throw himself overboard? He would drown. Shout to the village as they went past? No likelihood he would be heard and, trussed to the yoke, the slavers would gut him like a pig as soon as he opened his mouth.

Anger, fear and despair came together in a rush. It was as if he'd been dropped into some dark tomb and a stone slab laid over the hole. He slumped down against the side of the boat, closed his eyes and wished the Cheruskkii had killed him for death would have been kinder than this.

The hours of darkness were a nightmare without end. The slaves suffered horribly from thirst and were desperate for a handful of water, but the slavers paid no heed. Ascha was wet and cold and hungry. He shivered and his teeth chattered. Unable to sleep, he dozed fitfully, drifting in a fog of pain and misery.

Dawn came with a cold sun shining as they slid into the estuary.

He saw his village on the terp, wood smoke uncoiling like a dirty rag over shingled roofs. Above the marsh flats, the sky was thick with crows. He could smell the familiar stench of peat and sedge and brine. He looked towards shore. A dark line of trees streaked with silver, the river black as pitch.

'Na, Ascha,' Tchenguiz said gently. 'There is nothing we can do.'

'But I shouldn't be here,' he said, the panic rising. 'I have to warn the Franks. I have to get away!'

'Nothing we can do,' Tchenguiz said firmly.

He turned back and stared until his eyes misted, unable to let go. His mother would be in the garden, tending her vegetables, Saefaru in her cabin by the moor. Would she be thinking of him, he wondered, or of Wulfhere lying cold in the mud at Radhallaburh?

He watched until the village blurred into the horizon.

Tchenguiz was right, nothing he could do. He felt all out of breath, overcome by a feeling more desolate than he'd ever known.

He thought of the times he'd seen boatloads of slaves driven to a nameless future. Now he was one of them, an exile once again.

Two days later and they were struggling to make headway against a stiff onshore wind. The crew had rigged up an awning to shield themselves from the rain and spray, but the slaves had nothing. They sat with knees hunched and water streaming down their faces. The wind blew the rain sideways until they were blue with cold and drenched to the bone.

The slavers cast their eyes skywards and muttered among themselves. They sent a boy back down the boat, a skinny youth with a rat-like face and long hair slicked behind his ears. The boy stood over Ascha, and a knife came from his clothing.

Ascha flinched.

The boy bared his teeth in a grin and then cut the tree fork from his neck with two deep passes of the knife. Another slash and he had severed the ropes binding Ascha's wrists.

Ascha kicked the yoke away. He rubbed the back of his neck and stretched and heaved a small sigh of relief.

'Row and you eat,' the boy said. 'If not . . .' He jerked his thumb over the side to where the grey waves rolled.

Tchenguiz wrenched himself round. 'And me,' he said, offering his ropes.

The boy hesitated and then cut the bonds. Tchenguiz licked his raw and bleeding skin and then looked at Ascha and gave him a quick grin. The boy passed among the slaves cutting their bonds.

Ascha got to his feet and went to a bench and grasped an oar. One of the slaves took the other. He was tall and slim and wore a tattered shirt that flapped from bony shoulders. He nodded at Ascha with grave politeness and then the two of them stretched their feet against the rowing board and began to pull, their sweeps flowing together like returning geese.

After the squall had died away and the oars were taken in and stowed, they spoke. The slave was a Gaul named Lucullus and spoke a mongrel dialect, a mix of Frisian, Frankish and Saxon. Ascha could understand him but found the Gaul's speech curiously exotic, like an overpatched blanket.

'Where are you from?' Ascha said.

'Burdigala,' the Gaul said, squeezing the words from the side of his mouth like porridge from a bag.

Ascha knew Burdigala, but didn't let on. 'How long have you been a slave?'

The Gaul thought for a moment and then said, 'Three years.'

Three years? Ascha thought with dismay, a lifetime.

'And how were you taken?'

'We were sailing to Rotiagus with a cargo of wine when Saxon pirates saw us and gave chase. We tried to outrun them, but it was no use.'

'Your family must be rich?'

'My father is a senator,' the Gaul said. 'We own 400 slaves.'

Ascha glanced at him. Beneath the grime that shadowed his cheeks, he saw the Gaul was good-looking with dark eyes, long black hair curling over his shoulders, and a full and sensuous mouth. Probably charming too, Ascha thought enviously, in that slightly menacing way women deplored but secretly found attractive.

They talked some more. After he was taken, Lucullus had been passed from one master to another. The last had been a Cherusker who sold him to the slavers to pay a gambling debt.

'And them?' Ascha motioned with his jaw to the other slaves.

Lucullus shrugged. 'Easterners,' he said, his tone brandishing disdain.

The other slaves sat with their eyes closed, rocking gently, resigned to their fate. A young girl had her arms around the shoulders of two boys who, Ascha guessed, were her brothers. The boys were asleep, beyond weeping. She caught him looking at her and twitched her head away.

'And the big feller?'

Ascha gestured to a weather-burned giant who looked as if he had fought his own war and lost. His bearded face was misshapen and swollen with sores. He had a large leaking bruise on his forehead, one eye was filled with blood and the nose sliced open.

'Gydda the Jute,' Lucullus said. 'He was sold at Noricum. They caught him trying to escape and...'

He put one long finger up to his nose and flicked it away.

The Jute looked up as if he'd guessed they were talking about him. He repeated the gesture Lucullus had made, putting one thick finger by the side of his nose and yanking it sideways and laughed loudly revealing a mouthful of blackened teeth.

'One blood,' he said to Ascha, his voice deep.

'We be of one blood,' Ascha replied.

'You're no Cherusker,' the Jute said. He spoke slowly with the flattened speech of the Almost-Island peoples. Like pigs farting, his father used to say.

Ascha shook his head. 'Theod,' he said.

'Gydda knew a Theod once,' Gydda said.

'What was his name?'

The big man paused and frowned. 'Aelfric,' he said. 'Aelfric Osricson.'

Ascha jerked his head and looked at him, eyes narrowing. He saw Tchenguiz glance up. 'How do you know Aelfric?'

'You know him?' the Jute said. He slapped a massive hand against his thigh and laughed delightedly. 'He is still your war leader perhaps?'

'No, he died almost a year ago.'

A shadow crossed the Jute's face. 'Ah, that is a sadness. He were a good man, Aelfric'

'He was more than that. He was my father.'

Gydda's lips curved in a gentle smile. He wiped a huge hand against his shirt and thrust it towards Ascha. 'Gydda is honoured to meet the son of the great Aelfric.'

Ascha winced as Gydda's fist crushed his hand, but he was aware of Lucullus looking at him with new interest. It had been a while since he'd thought of his father. He felt a tinge of sadness and gave Gydda a short smile. Men always had fond memories of Aelfric.

He turned back to Lucullus. 'Where are they taking us?'

'Levefanum, which you northerners call Thraelsted.'

Thraelsted, the slave-town. But Levefanum sounded vaguely familiar. 'Is it far?'

'The mouth of the Rhine. The slavers think they'll get a better price for us there.'

Ascha looked at him. The Gaul spoke about the price of slaves as merchants might discuss the price of wine.

'The slavers,' Ascha said, nodding towards the crew. 'What are they?'

'The scum of the earth,' Lucullus said. 'The slavemaster is Kral, and the boy who cut your bonds is his son.

Kral was a big bellied man with fish coloured skin. Ascha watched him, filled with fear and disgust. Kral now owned him as he owned every slave on board. Kral would decide whether they lived or died. He was Kral's property, and Ascha loathed him with every muscle in his body.

Kral looked up suddenly and caught Ascha staring.

'What you lookin' at?' he shouted, raising his fist. 'They warned me about you. You're the Frankish spy. You want to kill me? I know you do. I can see it in your eyes. Well I'll tell you something, I will kill you first. Mess with me and I will kill you, like that.'

He snapped his fingers, the sound of a dry branch breaking.

Ascha looked away.

He was a slave, a tool with the power of speech, to be bought and sold like cattle.

He breathed in deep and held it, closed his eyes and waited for the panic to subside. He must control the fear. Not give in. He was the son of Aelfric Osricson. He would survive.

Kral's boy came down the boat carrying a sack which he threw at them. The sack burst open spilling onions and turnips across the deck. The slaves had not eaten since Radhallaburh. They jumped up and scrabbled for the food while the slavers laughed and jeered. Gydda picked up a turnip in one huge hand and smashed it against the side, breaking it into chunks.

'You have to eat,' he said gnawing the white flesh. 'Eat to live.'

Ascha followed his lead, picking up a turnip and pounding it to fragments. The turnip was hard and fibrous and difficult to chew. Lucullus held an onion in his fingers and bit into it, delicately as a squirrel might a nut. Ascha saw the girl trying to break a turnip against the strake. He took it from her, hammered it into chunks and handed them back. She took them without a word and offered them to her brothers.

Kral's son watched them. He kicked an onion towards Gydda and laughed when Gydda snatched it and shoved it into his mouth. He kicked another, laughing all the while. There was a warning shout from Kral. The boy turned to say something, and Gydda sprang.

In one easy movement Gydda had grabbed the boy with one hand, pulled the boy's belly knife with the other and laid it against his throat. Kral's son screamed in terror. Kral roared and came running, shoving the other slavers aside, his face dark with fury. The slaves drew back and watched fearfully as the slavers circled Gydda, weapons drawn. Gydda gave them all a grin, his open mouth full of turnip, and backed away, eyes flicking from side to side, taking the boy with him. The boy hung from Gydda's arms like a rag doll, feet jerking wildly and blubbering.

Ascha went to rise.

Lucullus laid a hand on his arm. 'It's not your business,' he hissed out of the side of his mouth.

'I know,' Ascha said. He shook his arm free and got to his feet and pushed his way through the slavers. He wasn't sure why. He just knew that killing the boy was not right. The boy should not have to suffer for his father's deeds.

He shouted at Gydda. 'Put the boy down, Gydda.'

Gydda looked at him and shook his head, sweat flying from his brow. 'Gydda will not,' the Jute said. He backed away, taking the boy with him, one thick arm tight around the boy's throat. The boy wailed, long green ropes of snot sliding down his cheek.

Ascha moved towards Gydda, one hand outstretched. 'Let the boy go, Gydda. Let him go or they will kill us all.'

Nobody moved.

Gydda began to laugh.

He stopped laughing and blinked uncertainly. The boat rolled and the wind flicked whitecaps off the waves. Gydda looked to Kral and the slavers and then to Ascha. He leaned to the side and spat and then slowly lowered the knife. Ascha took the blade from Gydda with one hand and grabbed the boy with the other and dragged him away.

There was the sound of escaping breath from slaves and slavers. The boy erupted in choking sobs. Ascha pushed him toward Kral without a word.

Gydda slapped his thighs and threw back his head and roared with laughter.

He never knew why Gydda had done as he asked. Maybe it was because Gydda saw something of his father in him. Maybe he realized that if he did not let the boy go they would all die.

Maybe it was none of those things.

Kral carried the boy off to the stern while the slavers laid into Gydda. They hurt him bad, stopping only when they realized that if they killed him they would have nothing to sell at Thraelsted. But Kral returned determined to make the Jute pay. The slavers held Gydda down while Kral straddled him and took his seaxe and ran it down both sides of Gydda's head, taking off his ears.

Gydda screamed once each time and then was silent. The slavers left him lying on his side with his blood leaking onto the deck in a slowly widening pool.

Tchenguiz and Ascha sluiced sea water over the Jute and cleaned him up as best they could while Gydda lay with his hand to his mouth, moaning like a sick animal.

The slavers returned and drove them down the boat. This time Ascha did not resist. He was only thankful the yokes were not brought out again. A slaver came with shears and sheared them one by one, the women and children first and then the men. They watched in silence as their hair fluttered like small birds onto the deck, leaving their heads raw and naked and bleeding. When it was done, they couldn't look at one another. Each found their own bit of horizon and stared at it with empty eyes, silently calculating their chances of survival.

Now, Ascha thought, we look like what we are.

The boat sailed west and then turned south-west. Kral took them inshore, slipping between the sandy coastline and an offshore bracelet of islands where the sea was less choppy. Ascha recognized where they were. The Raiders' Road, his father had called it, the sea-path to Gallia and Pritannia.

The rain eased and the sun feathered their faces. Ascha sat back and watched the ocean roll past. The last time he had sailed this road, he had been with his father and brothers, heading for Samarobriva. He had been a different person then, he thought bitterly, full of hope.

Later, while Gydda sang dull Jutish songs in a tuneless voice, Ascha and Lucullus spoke together.

'How do you know Gallia?' Lucullus said. 'Did you raid there?'

Ascha guessed that the Gaul was curious, trying to make him out. 'I was a hostage of the Franks for five years,' he said quietly. 'I served in the Frankish *scara,* under Bauto. We campaigned against the Heruli near Andecavus.'

'You served with Butcher Bauto?' Lucullus said, incredulous.

Gydda stopped singing and a giant grin appeared on his face.

'Gydda knew it!' he said and rose to slap Ascha on the shoulder. 'You are the son of Aelfric. You had to be a fighter.'

Lucullus gave him a sardonic smile and said no more.

Ascha felt a quiet satisfaction. Slave or no slave, now they knew who he was.

After that a change came over Gydda. The big Jute stuck close to Ascha like a burr. Gydda would not speak unless Ascha spoke to him first and slept at Ascha' feet, like some huge wolfhound.

Lucullus saw it too.

He rubbed the side of his cheek with the back of his hand and said, 'Damned if Gydda hasn't taken a liking to you. The big lunk seems to think he's your bodyguard.'

Ascha looked round and saw Gydda, his earless face streaked with mud and blood, winking and grinning.

Ascha felt the wind shift on his cheek as they entered the Rhine mouth. The Rhine here was huge, he thought, as wide as an ocean.

'What land is this?' he said to Lucullus.

The Gaul waved a long arm towards the north bank of the river mouth. 'That is Friesland,' he said. 'The other side belongs to the Franks, the Salt-People.'

Ascha surveyed the muddy smear to the south.

Clovis' kingdom.

He breathed in a lungful of sea air and allowed himself the tiniest tremor of hope.

Thraelsted lay on a fork of the Rhine close to a small harbour. It had once been a Roman naval base, so Lucullus said, and the broken ruins of the *castellum* that had guarded the harbour still stood on a low promontory behind the village. Ascha saw boats coming and going, slavers and traders, warships sharking through the waves. Green pasture ran to the river under a thin cover of birch. At the water's edge, there was a squalor of cabins, dominated by a ramshackle hall with a bowed roof.

'I was here before.' Lucullus said. 'That shed is where they will sell us.'

Kral got them on their feet. They were driven off the boat and onto a landing and then pushed down a walkway of rough planks that had been layed across the mud from the harbour to the settlement. Guards stood with legs akimbo and watched them pass, lashing out occasionally with sticks and whips. The slaves hurried by with arms raised, shielding their faces. One older man delayed too long and was knocked to the ground with a single blow.

At the end of the walkway they came to a muddy yard packed with people. Hawkers and traders milled and bargained, taking each other by the elbow to whisper a deal or share a confidence. Raiders from the warboats in the harbour weaved through the throng, drunk and flushed with booty. Women in headscarves sold milk, cheese, eggs and chickens from makeshift stalls. Ascha saw a fair-headed

Dane in a green woollen cap empty a sack of silver and broken jewellery into a woman's lap and grab armfuls of food to take away.

Kral's guards drove them across the yard to a timber stockade, guarded by Frisians. Behind the stockade, he could see an obscure mass of slaves. He was shocked by their appearance. They looked haggard and filthy, their heads shaved, dressed in rags and covered with grime. He heard the murmur of many voices and the occasional anguished wail.

We're to be kept in a holding pen, he thought. Like sheep.

The gate was drawn up by a mud stained rope and they were pushed inside.

By the end of the day the stockade had been churned into a muddy soup, a place stripped of all colour but shades of brown. Wherever Ascha looked, slaves squatted against the wall or sat gazing into nothingness with never ending stares. Some lay in the mud, their heads wrapped in their arms, asleep or dead.

The stench was overwhelming. It filled Ascha's nostrils and clogged his throat. Tchenguiz hunkered down on his heels and, Gydda went and sat beside him. Neither of them spoke, but they cradled their heads in their arms and slept. Lucullus was leaning on the stockade wall, looking out.

Ascha wanted to talk, but was unsure how far he could trust the Gaul. The fog that had clouded his thoughts since Radhallaburh had lifted and he could think more clearly. He was ashamed at how far he had sunk. He had overcome abandonment and exile and he knew he could overcome this. You've got a job to do, he reminded himself. Maybe the slavers had done him a favour, bringing him so close to Frankland. If he could get across the Rhine, he would be in Frankland and could warn the Franks. But he couldn't do it alone. He needed help and the only one who could help him was the aloof and aristocratic Gaul.

Ascha joined Lucullus. The Gaul made room for him and they stood side by side without speaking. A young woman went by. She wore a mud stained robe and had an anguished look about her, like a startled bird. A child walked by her side, her hand to her mouth, holding onto her mother's dress.

'They're not going to survive,' Lucullus muttered.

'Lucullus, I need to get out of here,' Ascha said bluntly.

The Gaul looked at him. 'You can't! Do you want to lose your ears like Gydda?'

'I won't be a slave.'

'You'll get used to it,' Lucullus snorted.

'I will not be a slave,' Ascha repeated. 'I must escape.'

'Where would you go? The slave-hunters would find you before the day was out.'

'Then help me.'

'Why should I help you?'

'Because I have news that is vital to the military high command of Frankland and Roman Gallia,' Ascha snapped, breaking into Latin. 'And you would do better to help me rather than ask damn fool questions I cannot answer.'

The Gaul's jaw dropped.

He studied Ascha as if seeing him for the first time. He stroked his chin and rolled his tongue around his teeth and looked over his shoulder at the Frisian guards and then nodded and said, 'Very well, I will help you. But you'll only have one chance. If they catch you, they'll mark you for life.'

He tapped the side of his nose.

'And Tchenguiz?'

'What about him?'

'He's coming with me.'

Lucullus rolled his eyes. 'You'll stand a better chance alone. The Hun stands out like a daisy on a dung heap, but you're Saxon, one of their own.'

'That's it?'

'No,' said Lucullus. 'There's anger in your eyes and that's dangerous. You are a slave now and must act like one. If they see anger in you, the good masters will move on, but the brutes will buy you just to whip the devil out of you. If you value your life, look away.'

'I'm not a slave,' Ascha said through clenched teeth. 'I'll die first.'

'Die, if you must,' Lucullus said calmly. 'But you're not taking us with you. Slavery is a curse, not a choice.'

He wondered about that. He had chosen to spy on the Saxons when he could have stayed in Gallia. He had chosen to go to Radhallaburh when he could have remained in his village, and he had chosen to let Radhalla live when he had the chance to kill him.

His problem was he'd had too many choices.

There was a sudden bustle and the gate opened and a knot of armed men moved into the stockade, shouting and whipping back the slaves.

'What's happening?' Ascha said in alarm.

'It seems we are about to be sold,' Lucullus said.

The slaves were driven in from a side door. They found themselves in a large hall with a broken roof and a floor streaming with water. The shutters were thrown back and a crowd of women and children gathered to gawp. Slave dealers assembled at one end of the hall while Ascha and the others were driven in at the other. The slaves huddled together and waited. The buyers moved forward and began to inspect them, pulling at their mouths, pinching their upper arms and prodding their ribs, making them walk up and down as if they were horses.

First to be sold were the children and young adults. The young, Ascha assumed, were soft and easy to train. A trader grabbed a young boy by the ears, pushed back his head and used his thumbs to roll back the boy's lips, exposing his teeth. The boy grimaced with pain, the trader grunted, waved his hand and walked away.

'What is she doing?' Ascha said, pointing to a middle aged woman in a red shawl holding two children by the hand.

'She's selling them,' Lucullus said. 'In Levefanum it's good business. People buy young children and sell them at a profit when they're older,'

And then Ascha remembered where he had heard of Levefanum.

'Lucullus,' he gasped. 'I know a merchant here. We met on the Rhine. I think he would help me.'

Lucullus looked at him, his eyes glittering. 'What was his name?'

Ascha struggled to remember. 'Octha! His name was Octha. He said to call him if ever I needed help.'

Lucullus rolled his bottom lip and put his head on one side, thinking it through. 'Would he buy you?'

Ascha thought for a moment. 'I saved his life. I think he would.'

'Kral will want a good price, and slaves are not cheap.'

It all came back to him. Octha's booming laugh, the chests being lowered onto the *Clotsinda,* Herrad's soft smile. 'He's rich, rich enough.'

Lucullus nodded. 'Then we must move quickly. I'll speak to Kral. No, on second thoughts, the boy is better. He owes you. Leave it to me.'

Ascha watched as Lucullus sidled over and spoke to Kral's son, bending his head. The boy listened, looking up at the lofty Gaul. He turned suddenly, and Ascha saw him shake his head.

Lucullus came back. 'I am sorry. The boy knows of no Octha.'

'Go back and ask him again,' Ascha said. 'Tell him it's important. Tell him I will make it worth his while.'

Lucullus turned.

'Wait!' Ascha said. He pulled off the burnstone that Octha had given him, thankful that the slavers had not taken it, and handed it to Lucullus. 'Give him this.'

Lucullus glanced at the burnstone. He went and spoke to the boy again. Ascha saw Kral's son shrug his shoulders in a gesture that could have been regret, and then moved away.

Lucullus sloped back with his hands stuffed in his tunic and an apologetic look.

Suddenly everything felt like dirt.

The Frisian woman sold the two children to a Danish merchant. She brushed the dust from their shoulders, gave them a quick hug and a kiss and left, happy with her sale. The girl and her two brothers were traded to a red-faced farmer and his wife. The wife clapped her hands, tapped the girl on the shoulder and led her away, the boys following like new-born lambs.

Some buyers tried to buy Ascha and Lucullus, but Kral refused.

'He'll get a better price if he sells us all together,' Lucullus muttered out of the side of his mouth. 'Otherwise he'll never shift the Jute or your Hun.'

By late afternoon, they were the only slaves left in the hall. Kral paced up and down, slapping his cudgel against his thigh. The doors opened suddenly and Ascha looked up hoping it was Octha, but instead a woman came in accompanied by a thin-faced foreman and several men.

Ascha's face fell.

The woman was Frisian, tall and solid with a round-hipped body and a heavy jaw. She wore silver wire rings on her fingers and carried a heavy iron key on her girdle. She strode into the middle of the hall and looked about her as if she owned the place. When she saw that most of the slaves had been sold she shouted angrily at the foreman and then stumped over to Kral. She nodded towards Ascha and Lucullus.

'How much for those two?'

'I'm selling them as a bundle,' Kral said with a greasy grin. 'Four strong men, all trained for farm work. Good workers. Reliable.'

'Reliable!' the woman sniffed. She took Kral to one side and they began to talk, heads low. Kral's son stood by his father's side, drinking in every word. From time to time, he turned and glanced at Ascha, but said nothing.

The woman was taller than Kral and used it to her advantage. She stood close to the slave-master, forcing him to look up at her. Ascha saw her look at Gydda, touch her nose and ear, and shake her head. Nobody wanted a slave who had been cut. But Kral wouldn't budge. It was all or nothing.

The deal was done.

They shook hands. Ascha looked to the door, hoping against hope the merchant would suddenly appear. Kral gave the woman an oily smile. She crooked her finger and the armed men unwound themselves from the door and strolled over. One of them was a big man with long but thinning hair, tied back. He held up a set of iron fetters and shook them in Ascha's face. Ascha struggled but two men gripped him by the arms while another bent and fastened the fetters to his wrists and ankles. An iron collar was clamped to his neck, and a chain looped through the shackles and the collar locked with a pin. The fetters were heavy and pinched cruelly.

Ascha held his manacled arms up to the foreman's face. 'Is this necessary,' he snarled.

The man shrugged. 'Orders are orders,' he said.

Ascha told him what he could do with his orders.

The foreman smiled and took a good swing and punched Ascha in the face. Ascha staggered. His chains were yanked, and he was dragged away. Shuffling out of the door, fetters clanking around his ankles, Ascha looked back.

Kral's boy stood at the end of the hall, staring after him.

18

They walked all day through a flat country that had no end, sunlight streaming over green fields. It was late when they left the road and took a dirt track which led to a farm. In the fields, slaves leaned on their spades and watched them with dark and sullen eyes.

That night they slept on straw with their feet fettered, and the barn door chained and locked. They were tired and hungry, and their feet were raw where the chains had rubbed.

The farm slaves told them that the woman who owned them was a widow who had lost her man on a raid. The widow was a hard mistress, they said. Labour on the farm was back-breaking, mostly felling and lugging logs, dunging fields and digging sea-ditches.

Ascha half-listened and lay in the dark imagining white sails off the Gallic coast, keels grinding over the gravel, Radhalla's raiders storming ashore. He had to warn the Franks that the Saxons were coming, but first he had to get away.

The next day the four of them were taken out of the barn and their shackles removed. The foreman and two guards led them to a field that squelched underfoot, gave them each a mattock and traced a line in the dirt with his heel.

'Each man digs his own height and three times his length,' he barked.

They looked at the mud and at each other and then the whips began to fall.

Ascha thought about what he should do. He was determined that he was not going to spend the rest of his life as a slave on the widow's farm. The slaves were chained at night, but were unchained to work. During the day they were supposed to be guarded but the guard usually went back to the farm where it was warm. He decided he would make his escape soon, after the foreman had taken them to the fields. If he was lucky he would not be missed until the evening roll-call. He would go south and try to get across the Rhine to Frankland. He would hide during the day and travel at night.

Steal some clothes, a cap to hide his slave-cropped hair, a cloak. Make for the Rhine and see if he could work his passage over. They would hunt him down, of course. The slavecatchers would mount patrols on the roads and waterways. Use dogs probably. And the foreman would take great delight in punishing him if they found him. But they would expect him to travel east towards the Saxon homeland, not south to the Rhine. The plan depended on his ability to evade capture until he got to Frankland. Once there he would have to persuade the Antrustions that he was a Frankish spy and not a runaway.

He flexed his toes, remembering Bauto's words.

Would the other slaves betray him? He'd given them no inkling of his plans but he could never be sure. The real worry was Lucullus. If the Gaul decided to give him away, he was lost.

That night he took Tchenguiz aside and told him.

'It'll be dangerous,' Tchenguiz said.

He nodded. It would.

'Tha'll need food,' Tchenguiz said. 'I'll save some of mine.'

Ascha nodded his thanks. He had already saved a piece of cheese and a chunk of bread and hidden them, wrapped in a cloth, under his blanket.

A sudden thought struck him. 'Tchenguiz, does tha ever think of my father?'

'Ha!' Tchenguiz said. 'Thi father was my friend. I miss him every day.'

Ascha smiled and then the guards came, banging their cudgels against the barn door, to chain them in for the night.

Two days later, Ascha made his move. The guard had escorted them to the field and left them. They stood in a trench, knee deep in brown and scummy water and exchanged glances. Ascha shook hands with Gydda, Lucullus and Tchenguiz and patted the food bag he had hidden under his tunic. They gave him a tight smile and wished him luck. He clambered out, head flicking to and fro, took a deep breath and then ran at a half-crouch across the field. The earth was heavy and glutinous and stuck to his feet in thick lumps. He squatted down and breathed again. He wouldn't have long, maybe half a day, before they realized he was gone. He turned and saw Gydda, Tchenguiz and Lucullus, heads bobbing, swinging their shovels. He ran heavy-footed to the hedge and went to ground again.

He was about to move on when he heard the coughing bark of a vixen. He froze. Something was wrong. He turned and saw Tchenguiz waving and pointing frantically towards the farm. He swivelled and saw the foreman and several guards coming back down the track.

He swore and ran his fingers over his shorn head in an agony of indecision. What should he do? Make a run for it? But it was too early. They'd catch him in no time. He would have to go back and hope they hadn't seen him. He upped and ran across the field. A quick sideways glance told him the foreman was already at the field's gate. He saw guards and could hear dogs. He floundered on, his feet as heavy as lead. He came to the trench and with a shout leapt in. He collapsed at the bottom, covered in mud and his chest heaving, hoping he hadn't been seen.

'Take this and dig,' Tchenguiz said, shoving a spade into his hand.

He took the spade and furiously began to dig.

The guards surrounded the trench. A curt command and the four slaves were ordered out. They climbed up and stood in a line. The foreman inspected the ditch, slapping his club against his boot and then walked along the line of slaves. Ascha stood, his breath coming in long juddering bursts and waited. His ribs ached and he guessed that the wound had opened again. The foreman came to Ascha and paused, looking him up and down, and then poked him in the chest.

'The widow wants to see you,' he snarled. 'Look lively.'

Ascha spat to clear his mouth of grit. He wiped his hands down his breeches and handed the spade to Tchenguiz and then went with the foreman to the farm.

The widow's house was stone-built and whitewashed, the yard paved and freshly swept. By the door, an ancient mule with a stiff mane and a white belly stood in the traces of a two-wheeled cart. The foreman rapped on the door and pushed Ascha inside.

The house was clean, the floor strewn with fresh rushes, the room almost bare save for benches, a table and a bed built into the wall. The shutters were half-closed and the room was dark and subdued.

He could smell cabbage and musty linen.

The widow was sitting on a bench by a fire, talking to a man who sat with his back to the door. The stranger wore a mud-spattered cloak that steamed gently in the fire's warmth. An old sword propped against the wall. No shield.

'You wanted to see me,' he said.

The widow looked up.

The man turned and put back his hood, a swathe of curly grey hair hanging over his neck and ears, a big smile in a whiskery face.

Octha.

Ascha filled his chest with air and slowly let it out. 'You took your fucken time,' he muttered.

Octha surveyed Lucullus, Tchenguiz and Gydda with a sour expression. 'All of them?'

'All of them,' Ascha said.

'I owe you a life,' Octha grumbled. 'I owe them nothing.'

'Don't worry, old man, I'll see you paid.'

The widow struck a hard bargain, unwilling to lose her labour when all the young men were away raiding. Octha haggled, but eventually he and the widow agreed a price.

The widow put Octha's silver on the scales, adjusted the weights, and beamed.

'How did you find me?' Ascha said.

Ascha and Octha were riding in the cart, bouncing down the thickly rutted road towards Thraelsted. Gydda and Tchenguiz sat on the cart's tail, swinging their feet and staring out at the country. Lucullus slept, draped widthways across the cart, his head wrapped in his thin arms.

'The slaver's boy came looking for me,' Octha said. 'I sent him away but he kept coming back. He was very persistent. He told me the widow had bought you and showed me the burnstone I'd given you.'

Octha put his hand in his tunic, pulled out the burnstone on its cord and gave it to Ascha. 'The widow's husband used to be a friend of mine. The rest was easy.'

'I am grateful, to the boy and to you,' Ascha said. He took the burnstone and put it around his neck.

Octha glanced at him, not unkindly. 'Get some sleep,' he said. 'We have a long way to go and you look as if you need it. Herrad will be waiting for us when we arrive.'

Ascha felt overwhelmed with relief. He looked up at the wide sky and then out at the slowly unwinding landscape. He thought of

Herrad and smiled. He was looking forward to seeing her again. And then he rested his head on his arms and slept.

A fine rain, almost a mist, was falling when they clattered through a stone arch and into the courtyard of the *castellum*. A parcel of labourers watched them with idle eyes, and a dog that had been sleeping in the dirt got to its feet and barked.

Ascha gazed about him.

In one corner of the courtyard, a broken and wind-bitten tower stood like a fat thumb. The courtyard was hemmed in by a wall that was broken in places and open to the fields beyond. Octha's house was a large two-storied building, built from ragstone robbed from the *castellum*. One wall of the *castellum* had collapsed and stones lay tumbled in the field. He saw sheds and workshops and another stone-built building with a shingled roof and iron-bound doors which he thought must be the merchant's warehouse. Stacks of barrels and crates and large two-handled wine storage jars stood in one corner, and a wood pile served as a hovel for pigs. A thin track pushed through a gap in the wall and ran to the water's edge. He caught sight of a jetty with a boat moored alongside. The tide was out and water glinted on the mud flats. He could smell the sour odour of sun-dried sea-weed.

The door opened, and Herrad came out. She wore a dress of homespun in green, open at the sides, over a linen undergarment. Her hair had grown and fell to her shoulders in a dark and shimmering mass. She put her hands to her eyes against the sun and watched them approach. He was struck by how calm she seemed. The cart rolled to a halt and he climbed down.

'It's good to see you again, Carver.' she said, more polite than warm. She offered him a cool hand and he took it. He stared at her, painting her face with his eyes, and then he saw himself as she might, smeared with mud and filth, dressed in stained rags, his hair cropped close. He felt his face flush and dropped his head in shame.

Gydda and Tchenguiz stood shuffling their feet and looking about them, bewildered by the sudden shift in fortune. Lucullus half-lifted a hand in greeting and smiled, his gaze frank and open.

'These are my friends,' Ascha said roughly.

Herrad smiled. 'You had better come inside,' she said and turned to lead the way.

'After you,' Lucullus said to Ascha and bent from the waist with a little Gallic flourish. Ascha scowled and pushed past him. Octha whipped the horse and drove off to the stable

The house was dark and warm with the smell of dogs and cooking. At the far end he glimpsed a bed pushed up against the wall and partly hidden by a leather curtain. There were two chests and a cupboard. An iron cauldron hung on chains over a low fire. An old woman in black was gutting a chicken at a long wooden table. She looked up as the men came in, her elbows wet with entrails. Herrad said something to her, and the woman wiped her hands and left.

'Femke will bring you water to wash,' Herrad said. 'And food.'

The woman came back with a ewer of water and a copper bowl. She took some leaves from a bag and crushed them and stirred them in the water and then stood back. The men mumbled their thanks and took it in turns to wash, throwing the water over their faces and rubbing their hands together. The table was laid and the girl gestured for them to sit.

'A blessing on this house,' Lucullus said, giving Herrad an easy grin.

She smiled at him, and Ascha felt a splinter of envy work its way under his rib. The old woman returned with eels, cold fish, hard yellow cheese, round wheels of soft white cheese, ham, a block of butter, a loaf of grey bread and a red-glazed bowl of boiled eggs. She went away and came back with a pitcher of cold thick milk. The men gazed at the food, wide-eyed.

Octha returned.

He pulled up a stool, stepped over it and sat. Leaning forward with his elbows on the table he gestured for them to eat. Herrad went and sat by the fire and bent to her sewing. The men ate greedily, shoving the food in their mouths and running their fingers around the wooden plates and licking them clean. Octha passed the food along and watched silently. When they finished what was before them, Octha signalled to the old woman and she brought more.

Afterwards, they pushed back the bench and sighed with contentment.

'I'll show you where you will sleep tonight,' Octha said.

Ascha felt impossibly weary. He got to his feet, but Octha motioned for him to stay. 'You and I have too much to talk about,' he said.

Octha left with Tchenguiz, Lucullus and Gydd, while Ascha and Herrad sat by the fire, listening as the footsteps receded across the yard. He wanted to speak but couldn't think of the words. He could see the line of her throat against the fire, her skin the colour of dark honey. In the dancing firelight he saw what he had not seen before, that her cheeks were pitted with tiny pocks, lingering scars of some childhood fever. He was struck again by her calmness, so much more than he remembered. Once she looked up from her sewing and he thought she was going to speak but she only smiled and went back to her work.

The door swung open with a crash and Octha entered. He laughed suddenly for no reason, pulled up a bench, stirred the fire with an iron poker, smacked his palms together and called the old woman to bring more beer. He poured for Ascha and tipped his beaker and drank heavily, slurping down the beer. He rubbed the back of his hand across his mouth and beamed at Ascha.

'It's good to see you again, my boy,' he said, slapping Ascha's knee like a hearty uncle.

'Good to see you too, old man.'

'Last time we met you were travelling to Thuringia. How in Tiw's name did you come to be a slave and who are those men you made me buy?' Octha said, jerking his thumb towards the door.

Ascha hesitated. His mind urged caution but he had lost time and he desperately needed the merchant's help. 'How do I know I can trust you?' he whispered.

The merchant looked at him and smiled. 'You saved our lives, lad. You can trust me.'

Ascha breathed in deep and let it out very slowly. 'First, I am not Thuringian, nor Frankish.'

The merchant smiled uncertainly. 'What then?'

'I am Saxon.'

The girl gave a little shudder of revulsion. She gasped and went to rise and then sat down again. Octha knitted his brows. Ascha took a quick sip of beer and began to talk. He spoke for a long while. He told them of his upbringing, how he had been born a half-slave, how he came to be a hostage for the Franks, how he was trained and sent home to spy. He told them of the occupation of his village by Radhalla's Cheruskers and the dead bodies of his friends lying in the muddy alleyways of his village. He spoke of his brother's death and the long boats drawn up on the gravel at Radhallaburh.

Finally, he spoke of the danger that the west was in, of the destruction that Radhalla would bring, and how he had to get word of Radhalla's fleet to Clovis.

Octha listened in silence, picking at his teeth with a birch twig. Now and again he gave a strange little grunt, as if something Ascha had said confirmed own thoughts.

Ascha's eyes flicked to the girl. She sat further back, her face partly hidden in the shadows. At first she had busied herself with her sewing but after a while she put her work down and sat with both hands in her lap, listening. When he talked of how his mother was taken as a slave, he felt her eyes upon him, the firelight washing her cheeks, her mouth parted slightly. Outside, he could hear rain pattering on the shingles. There was a storm brewing in the Rhine mouth.

He told them more than he thought he would, probably more, he thought later, than he should have done. Afterwards, for the first time in months, he felt a sense of peace, as if a cold slab had lifted momentarily from his grave allowing a narrow bar of sunlight to drop into the darkness.

There was silence.

Octha threw away the twig. He blew out his cheeks and exhaled. Both he and Herrad looked subdued and thoughtful.

'This is serious,' he said. 'If that many northerners are let loose in the west it will sow panic from here to Ravenna. Tiw's breath! Think of the slaughter.'

He muttered something to the girl and she rose and fetched more beer. As she passed, Octha touched her hip and gave her a little smile.

Ascha flushed and felt as if a stone had dropped to the pit of his belly.

'They'll devastate the country,' Octha went on. 'They'll burn and rape and murder. Trade will collapse all along the Rhine and it will be like when the Huns came.'

The three of them looked at each other without a word. Octha raised his hands in the air and let them drop and gave Ascha a rueful smile. 'I knew you were more than you seemed.'

'Can I ask you something?'

'Of course.'

'Why did they try to kill you on the boat?'

Octha shrugged his shoulders. 'They thought we were carrying silver.'

'But Wacho knew there was no silver.'

'Then someone wanted me dead.'

'Why would they want to kill you? You're just a trader?'

Octha seemed distracted, his mind elsewhere. Thinking about what a Saxon uprising would do to business, Ascha suspected.

Octha brought himself back and gave Ascha a faint smile. 'Oh, I have my uses,' he said.

'And what would they be?'

The merchant pushed both hands deep into the sides of his gown. 'The barbarian warlords like to live like Roman senators. I get them the things they want, Roman jewellery, glassware, wine, silks.'

'And?'

Octha hesitated. 'And while I'm about it I keep the Franks informed on what's happening beyond their frontier.'

'You spy for the Franks?' Ascha said.

Octha squirmed. He looked down and stroked one hand across the other as if his palm was dusty. 'Let us say I help them from time to time.'

'You help them?'

'Yes.'

'And what do they do for you?' Ascha asked, thinking as he asked the question that neither of them were what they seemed.

'They pay me and I get access to their towns for trade.'

'Then why were you attacked?'

'Perhaps not everybody is happy with the way I do things,' Octha said. 'Or perhaps someone thought I should be taught a lesson.'

'Radhalla?'

Octha shook his head. 'His power is in the north not here, and Radhalla has no grudge against me.'

'What do you know of a man called Fara?'

Octha stiffened. 'Fara? Dark-haired Frank, face like a ferret, with a scar here?' He drew a finger across his left eye.

'That's the one.'

The merchant picked up his beer. 'Why do you ask?'

'I think he followed me from Tornacum. And I saw him again at Radhalla's fortress.'

Octha paused, the beer midway to his mouth, and looked at Ascha. 'Fara was at Radhallaburh?' he breathed.

'Yes.'

Octha put down his beer, and Ascha saw his hand was trembling.

'Fara works for Ragnachar, the Overlord's uncle,' Octha said. 'He's a dog and does whatever his master bids.'

'You don't like him much do you?'

'When Childeric died, Ragnachar expected to be made Overlord. He thought Clovis was too young to rule. He considered himself to be more throne-worthy.'

'And was he?'

'Clovis is young but he's shrewd and he has ambition whereas Ragnachar is an unprincipled brute.' Octha leant forward and put a hand to the side of his mouth. 'You know it's rumoured he has relations with members of his own family.'

Ascha clicked his tongue but said nothing. Among the northern clans, relations between kin were not unknown. On cold winters' nights people sought warmth and comfort wherever they could find it.

'What happened?'

'Clovis won the throne with his mother's help, and Ragnachar has harboured a grudge ever since.'

'Could Ragnachar be plotting with Radhalla to attack Clovis?'

'Maybe?'

'It would suit Ragnachar to have Saxons raiding in Clovis' rear,' Octha said, tugging his beard. 'It would destabilize Frankland and give him a chance to take over.' Octha leaned forward with his elbows on the table and laced his fingers together. 'Can you prove Fara was at Radhallaburh?'

He thought of the perfume flask and then grunted and said, 'No.' For the briefest of moments he thought he saw relief pass across the merchant's brow.

'Then say nothing,' Octha said. 'The Overlord distrusts his uncle but he will never go against him. For Clovis, royal blood is everything and it will do you no good to accuse Ragnachar of treachery without proof.'

They sat in silence. Ascha's mind went back to Hanno's betrayal. If my kinsman planned to betray me, I would want to know, he thought.

'What will you do now?' Octha said.

'I must go to Tornacum. I have to warn the Franks.'

'Of course. Is there anything you need?'

'A horse.'

Octha nodded. 'You can have the gelding. When does the fleet sail?'

'The first day of Eostre.'

Octha gazed at him in horror. 'But the festival of Eostre began three days ago.'

Ascha felt his stomach turn. The journey had taken longer than he thought. The fleet was already on its way. 'Then I must go now,' he said, getting to his feet.

Octha laid a hand across his chest. 'It will soon be dark and the roads are treacherous. Go tomorrow.'

Ascha hesitated, torn between wanting to ride to Tornacum and the realization that if he stayed he would see more of Herrad. 'I'll leave at first light,' he said.

19

He wrapped a cloak around him and went into the yard. Some of the merchant's men were sitting in the yard and Ascha nodded to them as he passed. They nodded back curtly. At the *castellum* wall he stood at the gap where the path ran down to the river and looked out at the rippled mud flats and watched the blood red orb of the sun drop into the dark and distant sea. He heard the door open and saw the girl come out of the house with a bowl of water which she emptied into the yard. She turned and was about to go back in when she saw him. She put down the bowl and walked over, her arms folded against the evening chill.

'How is your wound?' she asked.

'Better. Thank you.'

He touched his side with his fingertips. The wound had festered, but Tchenguiz had cleaned the cut and stuffed it with hair, mud and spittle and bound it. It was sore but healing slowly.

'You should rest and not walk too far.'

He shrugged. 'I have to ride tomorrow to Tornacum. I will rest then.'

She took the news in silence. After a while they turned and walked alongside the wall.

'Do you remember when you carved the prow dragon on the river ship?' she said.

'I remember it well.'

'It was beautiful. You made the dragon come alive.'

He shook his head. 'A prow dragon is supposed to bring luck.'

'And it didn't?'

'The boat master died – and Baculo. When I got home my father was dead, my brother...' His voice tailed away.

'It was not your fault.'

'Maybe not.'

'The story you told us. Was it true?'

'Every word.'

'Your mother is a slave from Pritannia and your father is a Saxon warlord?'

'Yes.'

He watched as she tried to come to terms with what he had told her.

'Then why are you doing this?' she said softly. 'You're not a Frank.'

'I don't know.'

'You don't know what you want?'

He shrugged. 'I want what everybody wants: gold and glory.'

'So it was the gold?' she said with a little sniff.

'It was never just the gold!' he said, louder than he intended.

'What then?'

He hesitated and then said, 'I promised the Franks I would do it if they would make me a free man. If they would make me whole.'

'Is that why you agreed to work for them? For your freedom?'

He nodded. 'I owe them. They said they would give me what my own people would not.'

'They're using you. You just can't see it.'

'Maybe,' he said, tightening his lip. 'But I gave my word.'

She leaned against the wall and studied him. Behind her, the sun had slid almost beneath the sea.

'And now?'

He looked down at his feet in shame. 'Now the Cheruskkii own the Theodi and I have become this,' he said, running a hand over his slave-cropped hair.

'You want revenge on those who've wronged you?'

'I think about it every waking moment,' he said forcefully.

'But revenge will not make you free nor give you back what you have lost.'

'I know,' he said.

He looked at her, she looked at him and there was silence between them. And then he said, 'You and the merchant...are you married?'

'No, we are not married.'

'But you are his woman?'

She said nothing.

'You are so young, and he is so very old,' he said. 'Old enough to be your father.'

She sighed, the faintest hiss of escaping breath. Her hand reached out and pulled at a weed from a dense patch that grew as high as her waist. She held the plant in one hand and plucked at the leaves with the other, watching the seedheads drift away.

'I am from Armorica, but my family is originally from the island of Pritannia. We owned land in the east. Good farming land. When

I was a child a Saxon war band came to our village. Their warlord told us that they ruled now, and we could either accept their rule or go. Most people stayed, but my father and some others decided to leave. He had dealt with Saxons before.'

She shrugged, her father's decision, not necessarily a wise one. 'My father brought us and a few followers over the water to Gallia, to Armorica in the west. A lot of people did what we did at that time. We came with no more than the clothes on our backs. It was a catastrophe.'

She paused again he saw there were tears in her eyes. 'Life in the new land was hard. We had lost everything. One day we were attacked by raiders and my sister was taken. I never saw her again.' She stopped, and he saw the effort it took to talk. 'My father knew Octha. He had traded with him in the old country, and they had known each other for many years. Octha was good to us. He said he would help find my sister.' She shivered and then went on. 'I knew he liked me. I had seen him looking at me, his eyes following me around the room. When I was fourteen he went to my father and offered to take me away. To care for me as if I was his own.'

He looked at her and then looked across the river. The mudflats and the sand dunes bristled with grasses, the birches by the water's edge swayed in the breeze.

'I was flattered. Octha was rich. He traded all along the Rhine and as far south as Parisi, all those wonderful places. Did you know he has been to Rome?'

'He bought you,' he said hoarsely.

She shook her head, and he saw the hurt in her eyes. 'It's not like that. His wife is dead, and his son drowned years ago. He took me from a bad place. He protects me, and I care for him. We are friends as much as... anything else.' She looked away, gazing at something he couldn't see.

He saw the truth of it, how the decision had been made for her; a tidy arrangement with gold and furs for the father, silks and jewels for the mother, and a beautiful girl for the merchant. Her father kept his followers and the trappings of rank for another year or two, and Octha had a young girl to keep him warm on winter nights. Perhaps she thought she was in love. More likely she had done what her father wanted. He imagined her and the merchant together, the old man touching her gently, as if she were a flower whose petals might tear.

'But your name is Frisian.'

'Octha didn't like my old name, so he changed it. He said Herrad was a new name for a new life.'

'He owns you,' he whispered.

She shook her head. 'Nobody owns me,' she said defiantly. 'Octha takes care of me. It's just the way it is.'

'And you,' he said. 'What do you do for him?'

She flushed, the red seeping up from her neck and colouring her cheek. Gathering her skirts, she went to leave and then changed her mind. She stood for a moment, clasping her elbows and then turned to face him.

'I did what I had to do and have no regrets,' she said, the anger blazing. 'But who are you to say what is right and what is not? You are a half-slave and you are a spy. You work for the Franks against your own people. Tell me, Saxon, who are you to judge me?'

That night he couldn't sleep. He lay in the straw, listened to the men snore and went over what the girl had said.

He lay there for a long time.

In the middle of the night, he awoke with a start, feeling a prickle on the back of the neck where the fine hairs rose. He got up, shivering, his arms thrown about his shoulders and went to the window only to find it barred and shuttered.

There were bales of hay on the loft floor. He dragged one over to the window and stood on it to open the shutters. They were stiff, and he needed all his strength. He heaved as hard as he could and the shutters opened with a loud crash against the side of the barn. A cold night with a hard white moon standing over the sea, black clouds sailing before a freshening wind. He breathed in the odour of pine and a faint trace of wood smoke.

He blinked and looked again.

The sea was dotted with lean dark shapes, like basking sharks to the feeding ground.

The Saxon fleet had come.

20

He hammered on the door of Octha's house until until the old man was there, blinking and rubbing his eyes. A servant came up behind him with a blanket thrown over a tousled head.

'What is it?'

'The fleet has come, and I need weapons for my men.'

'The fleet? Weapons?' he said sleepily. 'How can I give them weapons? They're slaves.'

'There are Saxons in the harbour and you have a warehouse filled with goods. Give my friends arms and they will guard you and the girl while I am away.'

'I have my own men,'

'You trust them with a Saxon fleet in the river mouth?'

Octha thought it over and then nodded. 'I'll give you arms, but no one must know,' he growled. 'Even Frisians draw the line at arming slaves.'

Octha went back into the bowels of the house and returned moments later carrying several old shields which he threw down in the yard. He went away again and reappeared with an armful of spears and a few rusty long-knives which he dropped with a clatter. The spears were black and shiny with age, the shields warped and their bosses heavy and cumbersome. But they would do.

Ascha picked up a spear and ran a thick thumb along the edge of the leaf-shaped blade.

Finally, he thought ruefully, he had his spear giving.

Ascha led Octha's gelding down the bank to the boat. Octha bustled up and thrust a woollen cap into his hand.

'Here, wear this and, with luck, they'll think you're a Frankish colonist,' he said.

Ascha pulled on the cap, hiding his cropped hair, and took the *seaxe* Tchenguiz handed him, but refused the spear and shield. He wanted to travel light.

Tchenguiz blindfolded the horse and walked it with much clucking and soft whispers up the board onto the boat. Ascha followed. The girl cast off. Ascha waved once to the merchant, Gydda and Lucullus, and then the girl took him and the horse across the Rhine. Tchenguiz stood by the horse's head throughout the journey, while Ascha and the girl sat in the stern. Neither of them spoke.

On the other side, Tchenguiz led the horse off the boat and removed the blindfold. Ascha mounted. He nodded his thanks and then he walked the horse up the riverbank. At the top, he touched the gelding's flanks with his heels and broke into a trot. He looked back and saw the girl standing by the boat, the tail of her kerchief fluttering in the breeze. He gave her the barest wave. She made no move, but he could feel her eyes upon him.

Then he saw her no more.

He rode all that day and well into the night. When it was too dark to see, he dismounted, rolled himself in his blanket and slept, the horse roped to his wrist. He awoke before dawn and travelled on. He crossed the Roman road that came down from Colonia, the road he had walked the year before, and turned west. The sun was high in the sky when he reached Tornacum, the air full of the rumble of carts, the shouts of cattle drivers and street vendors crying their wares. He saw women with live fowls under their arms making their way to market, alleys thronged with pedlars and hawkers. The narrow streets were packed. Toss a grain of corn and it would never touch the ground, he thought.

He made his way to the Basilica, tied the horse to a post and climbed the steps. A shaven-skulled Antrustion stepped from the shade, barring his way. He saw more Antrustions lurking in the shadows and his stomach tightened.

'Out of the way, Antrustion. I must see the Overlord.'

'The Overlord?'

'Yes.'

'And who might you be,' the Antrustion said, leering at his companions. 'The Emperor of Rome?'

'It's urgent,' Ascha said.

The guard shook his head, the smile fading. 'Nobody sees the Overlord.'

'You don't understand,' Ascha said, 'I must see him.'

The Antrustion put his face close to Ascha's. 'And I said you can't!'

A captain walked over. 'What's going on?'

The Antrustion stiffened. 'Says he wants to see the Overlord.'
The captain ran his eyes over Ascha. 'Kick him out!' he snarled.
'If he resists, give him a thrashing.'
The Antrustion grabbed Ascha by the elbow. Ascha lost it. His
knife flashed. He whirled and had the man's arm up behind his
back and the blade hard against his throat before the Antrustion
knew what was happening. He heard shouts. The captain swore and
pulled his *seaxe*. Men came running, spears levelled.
Ascha spoke fast, 'Captain, my name is Ascha Aelfricson. I am a
royal hostage and I am here on the Overlord's business. I need to
see the Overlord urgently. If you do not believe me, go and fetch
Flavinius but do it quickly before I tire of keeping this man alive.'
Without taking his eyes off Ascha, the captain raised a hand and
flicked his fingers. An Antrustion stepped forward. 'My
compliments to Secretary Flavinius,' the captain said. 'Tell him he
is needed at the main door. Now!'

'Dear God! You look rough,' Flavinius wheezed. He was
breathless and sweating from running. He took Ascha's hand in
both of his and looked him up and down. 'I would never have
recognized you. How have things been?'
'Later, Flavinius. I need to see the Overlord urgently.'
'Of course, dear boy, I'm sure you do. The Overlord meets today
in Council. It's a busy day, but we'll see what we can do. Come
along with me! Thank you, Captain. It was well done.'
The Antrustions scowled and reluctantly stood back to let them
pass. Ascha followed Flavinius through the great doors and into the
hall, their footsteps echoing on the stone flags. Antrustions lined the
walls but made no move to stop them. Torches burned sootily in
ancient wall brackets, throwing a dim yellow light across the floor.
At the end of the hall was a ring of high-backed chairs filled with
Frankish and Roman dignitaries, Roman and allied nations on one
side, the Franks on the other.
Flavinius touched Ascha's elbow. 'The Grand Council!' he said
panting.
Clovis sat in the middle in a high-backed chair, his legs bent and
his chin cupped in his hand. He wore a blue woollen cloak, pulled
tight against the cold. Next to him sat Basinia wearing a red silk
dress and a short cape in some light coloured fur. Her hair was
tightly braided and covered with a white linen cap.

On the Overlord's left sat the Romans, mostly aristocrats and landowners dressed in togas or a mix of Roman and Frankish dress. Their leader seemed to be a man with curling grey hair and a beard like a goat's chin tuft.

'Syragrius,' Flavinius said. 'The Franks call him the King of the Romans. He rules over Roman territory in Gallia, or what's left of it.' Ascha listened intently as Flavinius named the other Romans.

The Franks were stocky, thick shouldered men with coarse faces, their heads shaven to the crown. They sat with legs splayed and their knees bare, scratching and talking. Behind every Frank stood a slave stood holding his lord's spear and shield. More slaves in white tunics padded between the chairs bringing food and drink. In the shadows, Ascha could see servants and hangers-on, lawyers, priests, musicians and clerks.

He saw Bauto, his face as brown and gnarled as oak, and others he recognized. He was startled to see the hawkish features of Fara among the Franks. Fara was leaning forward, whispering into the ear of a Frankish lord.

'Who is Fara talking to?' Ascha said, and pointed.

'That's Ragnachar, the Overlord's uncle,' Flavinius said.

Ragnachar was a fleshy man with a long horse face and dull eyes set far apart. He wore his hair long, as if determined to show the world he was of royal blood, and sat with his knees spread wide and his belly hanging down like an empty sack. He was listening with an air of bored indifference to a small Roman with a head as bald as stone who was addressing the Council. The speaker seemed nervous and spoke rapidly, moving his hands in the air to make his point, while a Roman holy man in a black robe translated his words into clunky Frankish.

'Stay here,' said Flavinius.

He approached Clovis, and Ascha saw him bend and speak into the Overlord's ear. Clovis looked up suddenly, and Ascha saw his eyes flit across the hall, searching for him. Clovis got to his feet and left the debate. Flavinius followed, waving frantically to Ascha to come forward. Clovis swept up. He took Ascha's hand and squeezed it and kissed him on the cheek.

'My little Saxon,' he said. 'So you have not forgotten me?'

'No, Lord,' Ascha said. 'I have not forgotten you.'

'What news do you have?' Clovis said, placing a skinny arm around Ascha's neck. 'Something interesting I hope. I'm so bored of all of this stuff.'

Ascha spoke fast, the words falling out of him, leaving nothing out. When he had finished, he felt as if a great weight had slid from his shoulders. He had kept his word and done what he had promised.

Clovis bit down on his thumb. 'Are you certain of this?'

Ascha saw the tension in the Overlord's face. 'On my life,' he said.

Flavinius went as if to speak, but Clovis held up his hand. 'Shut up, Flavinius,' he said abruptly. 'Let me think.'

They waited while Clovis deliberated, gnawing his thumb. After a while the Overlord threw a glance at Ascha and nodded. 'Very well,' he said, with an air of finality. 'I think you're going to have to address the Council.'

Ascha felt his skin crawl.

He heard the words but could not believe them. Address the Council.

Clovis passed his eyes over Ascha in a long slow stare, for the first time taking in Ascha's tattered and filthy clothes. He pulled off Ascha's cap and winced when he saw his cropped head. 'You look dreadful,' he murmured without irony. 'What have you been up to?'

He turned and snapped his fingers and at once an Antrustion stepped forward. The Overlord pulled off the man's helmet and gave it to Ascha. 'Put this on,' he said. 'If a terror raider is going to address the Great Council he should look the part.' He drew the Antrustion's *franciska* and stuffed it into Ascha's belt. Then he stood back and looked Ascha up and down. 'Should stir them up nicely,' he said. 'Now, come along.'

Heart hammering, Ascha exchanged a quick look with Flavinius and then followed Clovis onto to the Council floor. There was a loud clash of cymbals as Clovis entered. The little Roman who had been speaking stopped in mid-flow and stepped aside with obvious irritation. Clovis held up his skinny arms for silence. A curious murmur rippled round the hall. Ascha stood before the Council, all eyes upon him, elves dancing in his belly. Despite the helmet and the *franciska* in his belt he knew he looked out of place, his clothes filthy and travel-stained. He saw Basinia studying him closely, Bauto was impassive, and on Fara's face a frown of dark puzzlement.

The Overlord spoke.

'My brothers! Noble allies! One of my agents has just returned from the field and his news is so startling that I have asked him to address you directly. Forgive the intrusion, but I was sure you would want to hear what he has to say.'

He turned and winked at Ascha. 'The floor is yours.'

Ascha surveyed the ring of faces. He saw expressions of curiosity and distaste and indifference. Nobody liked spies. He touched Octha's burnstone round his neck, breathed in and held it, slowly breathed out.

'My name is Ascha, and I am the son of Aelfric, *hetman* of the Theodi clan, of the north-shore Saxons.'

After the initial uproar had died down, they let him speak. He cleared his throat, licked his lips and then began. He spoke slowly and deliberately, knowing that what he said in the next few moments might forever change his life. He told the Council he had just returned from deepest Germania and he had come to report a serious threat to Frankland and Roman Gallia. The northern tribes were uniting into a powerful confederation led by Radhalla, warchief of the Cheruskkii nation. The alliance was made up of the inland and north-shore Saxons, the forest people, the marsh folk and the between-the-rivers tribes. He listed them: the Cheruskkii, Drusi, Tecali, Susudatii, Taifali, Chaussi and Mersovii, together with the Chalusi, Warni and the Ascalangii. And the Theodi, he added with a heavy heart. The confederation, he told them, was allied to other northern nations: the Jutes, Danes and Engli from the Almost-Island, as well as some Frisian tribes. When Radhalla sent the war-arrow out, it was likely that even more would join.

He spoke in Frankish, Flavinius' Latin translation following a beat later, the hall silent enough to hear a toothpick drop. They listened to every word, their mouths open and their eyes widening in horror. He saw Bishop Remigius sink into his chair as if anxious to put as much distance as possible between himself and the Saxon fiend. Abbess Genovefa passed a hand from brow to chest and then across her body, her lips moving silently. Bauto hunched forward, his elbows on his knees, and his chin in his hands. Basinia's face was a mask of contempt, while Fara stared at Ascha with cold and murderous eyes.

Even the clerks stopped what they were doing to hear what he had to say.

Clovis steepled his fingers and crossed one ankle over another and listened with a sly smile.

The Council, it seemed, had suddenly become interesting.

Ascha detailed the Cheruskkii war aims. He told them how the Cheruskkii had planned the uprising for a long time and had built a war fleet at Radhalla's fortress on the Wisurg. How they had built ocean-going ships with tall masts for themselves and the other inland tribes who had no access to sea-bound rivers. He told them that the fleet was the biggest that he or anybody in the north had ever seen.

And finally, he told them that the fleet had sailed and was already in the Rhine mouth.

'If weather permits,' he said, 'they will be here within the week.'

After he had spoken, there was a stunned silence, and then an angry murmur, like a nest of wasps disturbed. The delegates yelled, waved their arms and tried to shout each other down. Others shook their heads in shocked silence or sat with open mouths, frozen to their seats.

The questions flew like slingshot.

'How many ships. How many men?'

'The alliance has forty five keels. About half are big beasts. Sixty-oars. The rest are forty-oars or smaller. The other northern nations will supply more boats.' He paused. 'There are about seventy ships in total.' He made a swift count. 'Say three thousand fighting men.'

They stared at him and he knew they were thinking of the horror that three thousand terror-raiders could unleash on the west.

'How sure are you of this?' A big-shouldered Frank shouted.

'I saw the fleet myself in the Rhine-mouth two days ago,' he said.

The Bishop began to wail. 'Dear mother of God, what will become of us?'

Ascha could hear their thoughts; saw them weighing the odds, thinking of their own skins.

'Syagrius!' Clovis said.

Syagrius rose slowly to his feet. He adjusted the folds of his toga and waited until the crowd were quiet and then asked whether the Saxon spy thought the Saxon fleet might not be planning to invade Pritannia rather than Gallia.

'No, Radhalla has no plans to invade Pritannia,' Ascha said firmly. 'His brother is there, and they would fight. Radhalla wants Gallia.'

'Then would you be so kind as to inform the Council where in your view the confederation fleet will make landfall?' Syagrius

212

said. He spoke with a crisp patrician accent, a voice veined with authority.

Ascha hesitated. The one thing he hadn't discovered. The fleet could land anywhere in Roman or Frankish territory.'

'I don't know.'

'But where do you think?' Syagrius gently persisted.

Ascha thought for a moment. 'My belief is he will land south of Gesoriac and strike at Lutetia Parisi, the heart of Roman territory. That's what I would do.'

The Council was silent. Syagrius bit his lip and sat down.

'Ragnachar of the River Franks,' said Clovis.

Ragnachar got to his feet. He dragged his britches up over his belly and looked around at the Council and then he spoke. He began by questioning whether Ascha's report was serious and reminded them that there had been similar reports of a Saxon uprising before. To believe these rumours now would play into the hands of their enemies. Even if there was a confederation of the northern tribes, it was unlikely to last. Everybody knew there was no unity among thieves and murderers. Saxons were opportunists who liked to raid and loot and then go home again. He spoke well in a smooth and confident tone, and Ascha could see the Council quietly listening. Lastly, Ragnachar cast doubt on whether the Saxon was telling the truth. By his own admission, he was himself a terror-raider. There was no proof such a fleet existed and the Saxon's evidence was tainted.

Ragnachar blew his nose into his hand and wiped it on his tunic. 'And if there is a barbarian fleet over the horizon then we should pay the Saxon raiders off and stay out of their way until they have gone. They will go home as soon as they have got what they came for.'

'You would negotiate with these beasts?' Syagrius asked.

'It buys us time,' Ragnachar said with a bored shrug. 'And we – or at least our Roman allies – can afford it.'

He gave a little smirk and then sat down. There was a murmur of approval from those who felt that paying the raiders off was preferable to fighting them.

Ascha quickly stepped forward. Delay, he knew, would be fatal and was exactly what Ragnachar and Radhalla wanted. The fleet would be upon them in a matter of days.

'My Lord, send men to the Rhine mouth and you will discover soon enough whether I am telling the truth,' he said. 'But you have missed the point. This is not a raid. Radhalla has had a bellyful of raiding. He hasn't assembled this Saxon host for loot and plunder.' He gave a dry little laugh. 'He's coming here to settle. He wants your land!'

Every man and woman in the hall looked at him in horror.

'Sweet mother of God!' he heard the Bishop Remigius mutter. 'If they're planning to settle, that's the end. They will disembowel us. Gallia will smoke on its own funeral pyre.'

'Is this right?' he heard Bauto growl.

'On my mother's eyes,' Ascha said. 'They want Gallia for themselves.'

There was uproar.

Clovis had been sitting with his fingertips on his lips. Now he pushed back his chair and got to his feet. He raised his hands and appealed for calm. When the din had subsided, Clovis spoke. He summarized the Saxon threat with a few well-chosen words and then went on, speaking forcefully and fluently, to remind the Great Council how the Romans and Franks had always feared the stealth and speed of the Saxons, their ability to move at will around the shores of Gallia. But now is our chance, he told them. Against individual raiders, they had no defence but if, as the spy reported, the Saxons had assembled a fleet – and this, Clovis said with a sly nod to his uncle, could easily be proved – then the allies only needed to discover where the Saxons planned to make landfall, and they could smash them before they moved inland.

'Act now, my brothers and allies,' Clovis said, 'and we can ensure that these ravening wolves will never again threaten our shores. Never again will we have to pay them off. If we unite, we can destroy the Saxon terror-raiders once and for all.'

There was a long pause and then Ascha saw heads nodding in agreement. One by one the delegates, Frank and Roman, raised their arms.

'Always better to put out the fire in a neighbour's house than wait for your own to burn,' Syagrius said, lifting a languid arm.

Ragnachar saw that he had been outmanoeuvred and scowled. Reluctantly, he put up a pale plump hand.

Ascha watched, awestruck by how quickly Clovis had used his information to change the Council's mood.

The Overlord turned to Bauto and ordered him to post scouts and beacons, to raise the levy, and to mobilize the army with all speed. He spoke crisply and to the point and it occurred to Ascha that the

Overlord had already given a great deal of thought to how to defend his land.

Bauto bent his grizzled head. 'Lord, the *scara* will be ready, and with the help of our Roman allies we will destroy the Saxons the moment they come ashore.'

'Praise God!' said Remigius. 'We must smite them hard.'

'Smite them we shall, Bishop,' Clovis said, 'although I fear the Saxons will do all they can to smite us first.'

'You've done well, Theodling,' Clovis said later when the Council had broken up. 'Better than I ever thought possible, we owe you a great debt. My father had spies across the Rhine for years but you've told us what we needed to know. Your report was terrifying, but it was worth it to see the looks on their faces.'

He squeezed Ascha's arm and gave a harsh and unpleasant laugh.

Ascha grinned, the relief pouring from him like water from a pail. He smiled at Clovis unable to believe what had just happened. He had done what he promised. He had warned the Franks of the Saxon uprising. Maybe now he could take it easy? He felt drained but exhilarated. A week ago he was a slave with a wretched future and now here he was addressing the Great Council.

'Your promise, Lord?' he said. 'You promised you would make me free.'

Clovis sucked his teeth and took him by the arm and led him to one side.

'And so I shall, all in good time. But I need you to do one thing more for me.' He lowered his voice and spoke urgently. 'I want you to go back to the Rhine-mouth and keep watch on your Saxon friends. We must know where and when they will land. Find that out, Theodling, and you shall have everything you could possibly want, and more besides.'

Ascha's face fell. He'd been foolish to think it was all over. There was always more to be done.

'Of course,' he murmured dejectedly. 'I'll take care of it. I'll go straightaway.'

'No, stay here tonight. You can leave tomorrow. Bauto will arrange an escort and Flavinius will find you a bed. And clean clothes,' Clovis added with a little sniff.

He paused and then seeing Ascha's expression, suddenly pulled off his ring and handed it to Ascha. 'Here, take this,' he said. 'I want you to have it.'

Ascha hesitated. The ring was heavy and gold with a King's head etched on the face. He slipped it on.

'Lord, your uncle Ragnachar...?' he blurted.

Clovis scowled. 'I will deal with my uncle when the time comes.'

'But...'

Clovis slapped a hand across Ascha's mouth and put his face close to Ascha's. 'Just remember who you are,' he hissed, 'and never, ever, mention my uncle again, unless you want to remain a half-slave for the rest of your life.'

Ascha swallowed. Octha had been right. He nodded and took a deep breath. 'I would ask a favour. A merchant, Octha the Frisian, rescued me from slavers. I would like to pay him back.'

'From slavers!' Clovis whispered, gazing at Ascha. A little shudder of revulsion seemed to pass through him. 'You poor boy! Flavinius will give you gold and anything else you need. Did you say Octha the merchant? Strange, I thought he died years ago.' He suddenly gripped Ascha by the upper arm. 'We are almost there, Theodling. Now get some rest. You look worn out and you have a busy week ahead of you.'

He patted Ascha's cheek, gave him a quick smile and was gone.

Ascha looked at Flavinius and then at the floor. He had the uncomfortable feeling that he had been used, that Clovis had steered him, as he had steered the Great Council, in the direction that Clovis wanted him to go.

He sighed and studied the ring. He rubbed it against his shirt and then looked at it again. It was, he thought, a very fine ring.

Outside, Ascha put back his head and breathed in deep. There was the sound of footsteps and he saw Ragnachar and Fara hurrying by. Ragnachar walked with his feet splayed, leaning on a slave's arm for support. A cart drew up at the foot of the steps, and Ragnachar's slaves shouldered him in.

Fara looked up and saw Ascha. He gave a cold smile, full of menace.

'What is it,' Flavinius said.

'Stay here,' Ascha said.

He went down the steps two at a time. Fara came to meet him.

'We've met before I think.' Fara said.

'On the road to Colonia, a year ago.'

Fara thought for a moment and then his face cleared. 'You're the woodcarver!'

'Yes.'

'Do you know who I am?'

'I know who you are.' Ascha pulled out the small clay bottle from his tunic and tossed it to him.

Fara caught it with one hand. He pulled out the stopper and put it to his nose and breathed in. 'It's very pretty,' he said. 'Where did you find it?'

'At Radhallaburh.'

'The Saxons' fortress.'

'Yes.'

'You believe it is mine. It is not.'

'No?'

'No.'

They watched each other.

'You think that if I had been to Radhallaburh, I would have left something like this?' Fara said.

'I don't know.'

'But that's what you think.'

Ascha said nothing.

'What are you going to do with this?'

'I haven't decided.'

Fara pursed his lips. 'He hasn't decided.' He dropped the bottle to the ground and put his boot on it and crushed it, twisting his heel savagely until the bottle was powder.

'Well, my young friend, when you've decided, let me know.'

'It's your word against that of Ragnachar and Fara,' Flavinius said sadly. 'The Overlord distrusts Ragnachar, but his uncle brought him up and he will never take the word of a Saxon half-slave against that of his own kin.'

'What should I do?'

'For now, nothing. But you should be careful. These are dangerous people and I'm sure they're watching you. Yes, they're watching.'

That evening there was a knock at the door. Flavinius came in and said, 'It's a messenger from Basinia. She wants to see you.'

'When?'

Flavinius shrugged. The question was idiotic. Immediately!

The servant led Ascha through the winding streets to a solitary stone house set in a yard on the eastern side of town near the river. There was little to suggest it was a royal dwelling but the bored

Antrustion standing guard at the door. Inside was dark and sparsely furnished. A large canopied bed set on a stone floor, a table and benches. Rich hangings in silk and tapestry hung from the walls. The house was cold and gloomy, and the fire and scattered oil lamps did little to take the chill off the stone.

Basinia was propped up in bed wrapped in sheepskins like an invalid. She held a wooden bowl on her lap and was nibbling the flesh of a rabbit leg. Without her veil or headdress she looked older. Her face was pale and drawn, and he saw her hair was turning grey.

As he entered, the queen looked up, tore off a last piece of mauve flesh with her teeth, dropped the bone into the bowl and wiped her hand across her mouth.

'You spoke well today,' she said.

'Thank you, Lady.'

The servant who had brought him leaned against the wall, one foot propped against the stone, whistling tunelessly under his breath.

'You have given us a great service.'

'I said I would.'

'Yes,' she said. 'You did.'

He waited. Basinia picked up another rabbit leg and chewed at it.

'My son seems to have become attached to you,' she said. 'At first I was not sure but now I begin to think that you could be very useful to us.'

'How, Lady?'

She put her head on one side as if thinking how to answer. 'Not many have what it takes to do what you do. To spy on your own people takes courage and boldness. And few could have addressed the Council in the way you did. We could use your talents.' She looked up at him. 'Would you be willing?'

Once he would have jumped at the opportunity. Now he was not so sure. 'I am always happy to help,' he said. The reply was no more than a courtesy but something in the way he said it seemed to satisfy her. She nodded without taking her eyes off him.

'Where do you sleep tonight?'

The question took him by surprise. 'At the house of Flavinius.'

'Then tell Flavinius to take himself elsewhere. *Eleri!*'

There was a rustle and a flicker of movement in the corner and a young slave-woman, half-lost in the shadows stepped into the light. She stood with her eyes downcast and her hands by her side.

'This is Eleri, of my household.' Basinia said without looking at her. 'Does she please you?'

He ran his eyes up and down the girl. She was young and pretty with a hard face and reddish brown hair that hung down her neck. There was something familiar about the line of her cheek and the shape of her mouth. She looked at him sharply and then looked away.

'Very,' he said, turning back to the queen.

Basinia gave a short mannish laugh. 'Good!' she said. 'She is yours for tonight.'

He looked at her, thunderstruck. 'I don't understand.'

'Bring her back before you go,' the queen said, handing the bowl to the girl. 'And do not abuse her, Saxon, or you will answer to me.'

It seemed as if he barely had time to explain to Flavinius and bundle him into the street when there was a tap on the door. He opened it and saw Eleri, her head covered with a dark shawl and her feet pale and bare.

He stared, lost for words.

She raised an eyebrow.

'You'd better come inside,' he said huskily.

Eleri stepped past him, her skirt brushing softly against his leg. She pushed back her hood and slowly ran her eyes round the room, taking it all in. Then she looked at him, waiting.

He closed the door and took a step towards her. He could smell her hair, clean and faintly scented. Outside, he heard women's voices in the street, the scrape of a dog's bark.

Ascha felt his throat thicken, not knowing what to say. 'Is Eleri your real name or a slave name?' he said awkwardly.

She gave a hard little laugh. 'What do you care,' she murmured.

He took her by the elbows and kissed her lightly on the lips. She smiled and kissed him back. He helped her take off her cloak and then he touched her hand and led her inside.

Later, he lay with his arm around her, one hand cupping her breast, listening to her breathe.

'Are you awake?' he said into her hair.

'Mmmm,' she said.

She pushed herself up on her elbow, turning her head to look at him. Her hair was dark and loose and fell around her shoulders in a thick wave.

'I've met you before,' he said softly.

'A year ago,' she said her voice lazy with sleep. 'You were with the Lord Clovis. I served you wine.'

Then it came to him, Clovis standing before the fire explaining his plans for a greater Francia, the two women, one old and the other young, the ruby rich taste of the wine on his lips.

'Do you remember me?' he said.

'I remember you, but you have changed,' she said, smoothing his hair with the tips of her fingers. 'Your face is thinner and you seem much older. The last year has not been kind to you.'

There was the trace of an accent. Neither Gaul nor Frank. Something else.

'Where are you from?'

'From?'

'How did you come to be here?' he said, a little exasperated.

He felt her shrug. 'I have been here a long time. I was a gift to Lord Clovis.'

'A gift?'

She sighed, bored with the drift of the conversation. 'And you, Saxon? Do you have a girl you like?'

'No,' he said.

She looked at him and then said, 'I don't believe you.' She pulled the blanket up so that it covered their shoulders and gave him a soft and knowing smile. 'Tell me, what is she like, your sweetheart?'

He leaned back on his elbows and smiled and then said, 'She is beautiful, just like you, with green eyes, just like you, but a little taller with chestnut hair, and maybe a year or so younger.'

The smile slipped from her face. 'I must go,' she said, her voice suddenly clipped, but in a way that left him uncertain whether she was telling him or asking him.

'Go?'

'The queen will be expecting me.'

He leant across and ran one finger down the side of her cheek, under her chin and down into the little dip at the base of her throat.

She shivered, her cheek warm against his.

'Not just yet,' he said.

21

W hen he awoke he was dismayed to find Eleri had gone. It was still dark, the sky only just beginning to lighten and he had hot sandy eyes and a head full of wool. He dragged on his boots, pulled his cloak around him and left. It was chilly, and he shivered as he hurried through the streets, nobody about but a few peddlers driving their pack animals. He came to the bridge and quickly crossed to the western part of town, his feet thumping hollow on the wooden boards.

At the other side, a man stepped from the shadows and plucked at his sleeve.

'My master would like a word? Will you come?'

'That depends on who your master is.'

The man looked at him with surprise. 'I serve Syagrius. The Governor of Roman Gallia,' he said.

The Antrustions who were to escort him back to Thraelsted would be waiting at the stables, but he was curious to meet Syagrius.

The Governor's servant led him to a pretty two storied house with a tiled roof and a small garden overlooking the river. He was shown up to the first floor. Syagrius was standing by a large window, dressed in a woollen gown, a blanket thrown his shoulders against the chill.

Syagrius turned when he heard his feet crackling on the straw and came towards him, putting out a hand. Ascha took it. The skin was dry and papery to the touch. In the fresh light of morning, the governor seemed smaller. His round and serious face was shrunken, his eyes had pouches under them and his beard was tinged with grey. It was, Ascha thought, the face of a man who has fought hard and knows he has lost.

Syagrius smiled slightly. 'Thank you for coming,' he said in Latin. 'Will you take something? Some warm milk and cake perhaps?'

Ascha accepted but refused the offer of a seat. He couldn't stay long. He had to get back to the Rhine-mouth and the Antrustions wouldn't want to be kept waiting. It occurred to him that Syagrius had known he was leaving and his servant had waylaid Ascha at the bridge which meant he knew where he was staying. Probably knew about the girl too. Did everyone know his business in this town? He sipped the milk and broke off a piece of cake to eat. He was hungrier than he thought.

'I wanted to tell you how grateful I am,' Syagrius said. 'Your report on the Saxon threat was alarming, but most helpful.'

Ascha bowed slightly. Yesterday, he had addressed the Grand Council, today he was taking breakfast with a Roman Governor. Hard to believe just a few days ago he was a slave.

'It was my duty,' he said, feeling that he ought to try his hand at modesty.

'Your duty? Well, yes. I suppose it was,' Syagrius said. 'Your Latin is excellent, by the way. Old fashioned and with an accent I cannot place, but very good. From where did you acquire it?'

Ascha felt the warmth rise on the back of his neck. 'My mother,' he mumbled. 'She was from a high-born family in Pritannia.'

'Ah, that would explain it,' Syagrius said mildly.

A woman walked lightly across the room carrying a bundle of linen. She smiled at Ascha and withdrew. Outside, he heard the sound of carts trundling down the alley, a man shouting at his wife. The servant who had brought him came and sat on a bench by the door.

Syagrius sipped his milk while Ascha waited, chafing with impatience.

Syagrius said, 'You realize that if the Saxons take over Roman Gallia, it will mean the end of Roman rule in this province?'

Not something he'd thought about, but probably true. The Romans had lost so much territory to the northern tribes they couldn't afford any more setbacks.

'They can still be stopped,' he said.

Syagrius gave him a keen look. 'Do you think so? You are Saxon-born and you know them. There was a time when I thought we could defeat the barbarians. Play them off against one another. But now...I am not so sure.'

'Rome is still powerful.'

'Dear boy, Rome is unravelling as we speak. We used to be feared, but now the barbarians take our land and make us pay for the very light of day.'

Ascha shook his head. 'Roman power has faded, but Roman life continues.'

Syagrius looked at him. 'What do you mean?'

222

'Northerners don't want to destroy Rome. They want a share of Rome.'

Syagrius stroked his beard, lifted it up and let it drop.

'You think we can live together? Is that it? Does the leopard lie down with the lion? Can Rome do business with *barbari*?' He spat out the word.

Ascha bridled. 'Barbarians have defended the empire for years,' he said more politely than he felt. 'My father fought with Aetius against the Huns. A barbarian sits on the imperial throne and barbarian warlords control Roman provinces. Working with barbarians is nothing new.'

Syagrius pursed his lips doubtfully. 'I know many who speak as you do. My friend Sidonius says that the barbarians are strong and vigorous. He says that we should come to an accommodation with them. That way, the best of Rome will survive.'

'You don't believe it?'

'Do I think that learning Frankish, shaving my head and dressing in animal skins will ensure the survival of Imperial Rome?' Syagrius snapped.

'That's not what I meant.'

Syagrius sighed. 'Maybe you are right. Maybe we must learn to share our lands and our rents – even our women – with pagans. Treat the barbarians as honoured guests and maybe they will protect us and allow us to live.'

'Barbarians are not so different from Romans.'

Syagrius looked at him. 'You think not?

'They want a roof over their head and a land they can call their own.' And to feel sunshine on their faces, he thought.

'Even Saxons? Do Saxons want that too?'

'Even Saxons.'

Syagrius thought for a moment and then shook his head. 'No,' he said. 'Not the Saxons. We have educated the Franks. They share our values and want what we want. But the terror raiders are brutal savages who want only to destroy us and drive us into the sea. If they seize control of this province, *Romanitas* will disappear. It will mean the end of civilization.'

'Nothing ends. Every death leads to decay and then a rebirth,' Ascha said, surprised at his own conviction. 'Rome will go on – not in the same way maybe – but Rome will survive,'

Syagrius' gaze shifted. 'You are young and can afford to believe that, but I have winter in my blood and do not. For me, life is a short sojourn in an alien land and, when we are gone, there is nothing but oblivion.' Syagrius smiled. 'And that's as it should be. All I ask is a little more time, just a few more years – that and the destruction of the Saxons.'

Syagrius got to his feet. Ascha took this as a signal to leave and rose also. He had enjoyed the talk more than he had expected. Syagrius smiled and squeezed Ascha's hand.

'Good luck, my boy. Live each day as though it were your last.'

Ascha followed the servant out. At the foot of the stairs, he paused. 'Why did your master want to see me?'

The servant looked puzzled. He thought for a moment and then said, 'He admires you. He sees you as an example of how Romans and barbarians might live together.'

When Ascha looked back he saw Syagrius watching him from the balcony. Ascha lifted his hand and waved.

The Governor waved once and then went inside.

At the stables, he found half a score Antrustions saddling their horses and loading a cart. He made himself known to their captain, a hard-bitten blue-eyed Frank with a shock of corn-coloured hair, shaved high at the back.

'Sorry to have kept you,' Ascha muttered.

'It's not you we were waiting for,' the captain scowled and nodded towards a high-born Frank who was walking towards them accompanied by a manservant. The Frank was young and richly dressed in a red tunic and a blue woollen cloak held at the shoulder by a golden cross-brooch.

'Who is he?'

'The younger son of Lord Dagric,' the captain said. 'We've been ordered to take him to Thraelsted to buy slaves. It was a last moment change of plan,' he added

The young man gave the captain a superior smile and offered him his hand. 'And who are you?' he said turning to Ascha.

Ascha told him.

'Ah, the Saxon half-slave,' the young Frank said with a sneer. 'I have heard of you but I don't approve of low-born gutter rats with ideas above their station. Make sure you stay downwind of me.'

Ascha seethed inwardly but choked it back. 'Of course, Lord,' he murmured, while the captain raised his eyebrows and grinned.

They left Tornacum to the clatter of hooves and the trundle of cartwheels and took the road north to Noviomagus. A day's hard riding and the stone road gave way to cordwood and then to a dirt track. They crossed a flat landscape of birch woods and grasses as high as a man's waist, their faces and clothes spattered with mud. Early evening, as the light began to fade, the captain called a halt.

While the Antrustions unloaded the carts, erected the tents and tethered and watered the horses, Ascha and the captain talked. The captain was in his late thirties and came from Cambarac. He was aloof, like all Antrustions, but Ascha no longer cared. The captain had served under Bauto, and they had friends in common. That night Ascha ate roast lamb, sizzling hot from the fire, and listened to the rasping double-call of the corncrakes in the marshes.

The young nobleman ate alone in his tent, attended only by his servant.

'Got his nose so far up his own arse, he thinks he's Roman,' the captain grumbled.

Ascha awoke to the roll of thunder, a distant rumble, coming closer. With a jolt, he recognized the sound of hooves, of horsemen riding at the gallop. He heard shouts and cries of alarm. Rolling to the end of the tent, he stuck his head out into a swirl of noise. Antrustions were spilling from the tents, barefoot and bareheaded. He saw the captain, sword drawn, bellowing orders.

'Quickly! Form up on me!'

The attackers were darkly bearded and carried lances and curved bows. They galloped through the camp, shrieking strange and high-pitched cries. As he watched, an Antrustion pitched forward with an arrow in his chest, buried almost to the fletching. The riders came in fast, twisting in the saddle to fire their bows and leaning out to slash and thrust. The Franks grabbed spears and shields and ran to meet them. A rider thrust a lance into an Antrustion's belly and rode on while the Frank screamed and writhed. Another Frank stumbled. Immediately, one of the strangers dragged his pony to a stop, bent on a bow, and shot the Frank where he lay.

Ascha ducked back inside the tent. He picked up his *seaxe,* stuffed it into his belt and scrambled out the back. He heard the drumming of hooves behind him. One of the riders had seen him and was coming for him. No time to hide. He ran at a crouch through the long grass. Glancing back, he saw the rider looming over him, heard the pony's juddering breath, and threw himself to the side as a lance rammed into the turf by his ear. He rolled into a ditch and quickly scrambled away. Far off he could hear shouts and yells, the crash of iron on iron. The Antrustions were trying to form a shield wall and he could hear their excited cries.

'They're coming in again!'

'Stay close. Keep those shields up!'

'They're trying to get behind us

'On your left, Edgar! Watch that bastard!'

He poked his head up and saw the rider probing for him in the long grass with a tufted lance, dragging the horse round in its own length, his feet held by strange leather straps. He waited until the man's back was turned and then climbed out of the ditch and crawled through the grass towards the rider.

The stranger had a squat build and wore a quilted coat, belted at the waist, a short hareskin cloak and a pointed cap with a fur rim. He could smell his sweat. Ascha drew his long knife. He took another quick look and then got to his feet, reached up and seized the man's belt and heaved. With a grunt of surprise, the rider crashed to the ground, one foot still held by a strap of twisted leather. Ascha grabbed a fistful of greasy hair, pulled back the head and stroked his blade through the man's throat.

He looked up, panting.

No-one had seen him.

He checked the rider's weapons. Apart from the lance, the man had a belly knife, an axe and a small leather-covered shield. A powerfully-curved and horn-tipped bow stood in a holster behind the saddle with a quiver of arrows. Grabbing the bow, Ascha yanked at the thongs holding the quiver and raced towards the camp.

The riders were milling, preparing to come in again. He could see the Franks standing shoulder to shoulder in a tight knot of overlapping shields, those with shields holding them over those without, spears flickering like an adder's tongue. The captain stood in the front rank, shouting commands. Ascha glanced around. Already more than half the Franks were dead or badly injured.

He knelt and notched an arrow. He aimed for a rider on the edge of the group and pulled. The bow required all his strength to draw. Gritting his teeth, he released too soon and saw the arrow fly over the man's head.

Slow down, damn you! The rider had heard the whisper of the passing arrow and was looking over his shoulder, squinting into the

226

trees. Ascha fitted another shaft, drew, held his breath – and released. The arrow thudded into the man's lower back. He threw up both arms and slid to the ground. Ascha saw the riders turn and their eyes lift.

Quick now! Heart pounding, he notched another arrow.

One of the riders pointed at him with his lance.

A storm of high-pitched yipping and then they spurred and came for him.

He pulled the bowstring to his ear.

A dull *thrummm* as the bowstring thwacked against his arm. The shaft caught the lead rider under the chin, angling up under the base of the skull. The man's head exploded in a welter of blood and bone. He rose from the saddle, both arms spread wide, and hit the ground with a loud thump.

Two riders peeled off. The third kept coming. Ascha drew another arrow. It's him or me, he thought. He heard the drumming of hooves and saw the pony's flared nostrils, the point of the lance floating towards him. He waited until he was sure, and fired.

The man ducked and Ascha saw his shaft disappear into the trees.

Cursing, he threw aside the bow and ran for the Franks' shield hedge. He heard the riders yipping and spurring their mounts to try and cut him off. The Franks were cheering, waving him on. He heard the captain's bellow, 'C'mon man, C'mon!'

A quick look back, they were gaining, closing the distance. Panic squeezed his insides. He ran faster, crashing through the dew-soaked grass, feeling the sawing rasp of his own breath and the fluttery tickle between his shoulder blades where at any moment he expected to feel the bite of the horseman's lance. He yelled with fear and anger and then willing hands were grabbing his shirt and hair and dragging him bodily through the shield wall.

He tripped and fell headlong, a pony almost on top of him. The pony refused the Franks' spears and shied. An Antrustion rammed a lance in its chest and it screamed, throwing its rider. The captain's sword swept and the man's face was a crimson mask.

'Don't think that bastard will try that again,' the captain said.

'Look!' someone shouted. 'Over there.'

They looked round, and Ascha held his breath. The riders had found the young nobleman. Alone in his tent, the boy had been cut off and was trying to hide beneath a wagon, but the riders had seen him and were circling, yipping their strange cries. The youth was plainly terrified and scrabbled backwards, trying to worm his way into cover.

Two riders leapt from their ponies, grabbed him by the ankles and dragged him out, bawling like a calf. The young Frank got to his feet and tried to run. A rider tossed a lance that pierced the boy's thigh and he fell. The riders gathered like wolves around a lamb. The Frank knew what was coming and his wail was piteous. The riders let him sob and then they killed him, thrusting down with their lances as the boy wriggled and screamed in the grass.

The Franks watched in silence as one of the riders dismounted and with a single downcut took the young Frank's head and held it up for all to see. The rider leapt back onto his pony. He rode over the boy's headless body and then with a final whoop, the riders thundered off, taking their wounded and the boy's head with them.

There was a quaking silence.

The Franks turned and looked at each other.

'Close enough?' said an Antrustion with a grin.

'Close enough,' Ascha agreed.

Afterwards the Antrustions went among the enemy dead, cutting off the ears of those they had killed. They mutilated the bodies, disembowelling and slashing them to ribbons, and then rolled them into a ditch and left them to rot. They gathered up their dead, including the young Frank, wrapped them in blankets and laid their bodies on the grass. While some of the Franks dug a shallow pit, the others went into the trees to cut timber. They came out dragging logs of oak and ash and stacked them in the pit until they were shoulder-high, filling the spaces with brushwood and dead branches.

When the pyre was ready the Antrustions spread a blanket and sat cross-legged, dividing up their friends' weapons and personal things, and the ears of their dead enemies. Then they got to their feet, lifted the bodies and laid them on the pyre. One of their number approached Ascha, knuckling his forehead and clearing his throat.

'What is it?'

'Lord, me and the lads was wonderin' if you was a Tiw-believer.'

'Why?'

'We'd like you to say a few words for our brothers,' the Antrustion jerked his head toward the dead Antrustions lying face up on the logs.

The captain turned away with a scowl on his face, angry he'd not been asked.

Ascha gave it a moment's thought. His mother believed in the Christian Tree-God and his father was a Tiw-believer. In exile he'd learnt not to rely on the gods; his life would only change if he changed it for himself, but now he nodded and said, 'I would be happy to.'

He spoke as Hanno would have spoken. He said the prayer for the dead and expressed the hope that Tiw would accept these brave men into the afterlife. They were true friends and loyal to their Overlord. They had fought well and died with honour. When he was finished, the Antrustions were subdued. They bowed their heads, nodded their thanks and turned away. The captain threw a blanket over the bodies to spare the Antrustions the sight of their friends burning and then took a fire tool from his belt-pouch, struck a flame and lit some dry moss which he stuffed deep into the pyre's underbelly. The men watched in silence as the flames roared through the dry brushwood, pushing gouts of thick black smoke into the sky.

'We should go,' the captain said. He picked up the young nobleman's blue cloak, unpinned the gold brooch and slipped it into his tunic. 'I'll keep this for the boy's father,' he said.

Ascha said not a word. None of his business what the Franks did with their dead.

'Who were they?' he said. The pyre was burning strongly and they both stepped back from the heat.

The captain shrugged. 'I don't know. They looked like Easterners, probably Alani.'

Alani? Apart from Tchenguiz he knew no Easterners, but then he remembered Fara's man, Gibuld. Was he an Alan?

He was mulling this over when the captain said, 'You know it was you they were after.'

Ascha looked at him. 'Why would they want to kill me?'

'They assumed you would be a young well-dressed nobleman. They killed the boy thinking he was you.'

Ascha creased his brow. 'I don't understand.'

'Someone suspected you might be murdered on the road and sent that lad along as a decoy.'

'He was killed for me?'

'I'm sure of it.'

The wind gusted and the leaves blew high, swirled and fell and rose again. The funeral fire burnt steadily, the logs charring and gently collapsing. As the Franks turned away and made ready to leave, Ascha went over what had happened. Who would attack a troop of Antrustions to kill him? And who could have sent the young nobleman as a decoy? He rubbed his face and shook his head, unable to make sense of it all.

'Thank you, Captain,' he said soberly. 'If I had been travelling alone, I would not have survived. It's a pleasure to be under your command.'

The captain gave him a strange look. 'Under my command? I have orders to escort you to Thraelsted to confirm the Saxon fleet and then we are at your disposal until the fleet leaves.'

'You mean you are under my command?'

The captain waggled his head. 'You seem to have become a valuable property, Saxon,' the Frank said with a wolfish smile. 'And the Overlord doesn't want you dead. At least, not yet.'

22

They reached the *castellum* on the evening of the following day as the sun set behind the town. A fresh breeze swirled about, and they could smell the tang of the sea.

Octha came to meet them, hurrying down the steps as soon as he heard the horses clattering into the courtyard. Ascha slid off his horse and ran to the wall. He sighed with relief when he saw that the Saxon fleet was still there, scores of them dotting the bay and the inner roads of the river mouth. The wounded Franks he had sent back to Tornacum in the cart, but he had pressed the rest hard, determined to get to Thraelsted before the fleet sailed. He knew that only by seeing the Saxon long ships would the Franks be convinced the fleet existed.

'What happened?' Octha said.

'We were attacked on the road,' Ascha said.

'Attacked, who by?'

Ascha shrugged. 'I don't know, but the Captain thinks they were Alani.'

'But there are no Alani this side of the Rhine. And how could they have known where you would be?'

Ascha looked at him. 'You knew, old man,' he said.

'You think I had something to do with this?' Octha shouted. 'I had nothing to do with it.'

Ascha led his horse off towards the stables. He had to admit it was unlikely the merchant was involved. To take him out of slavery and then arrange for him to be killed didn't make sense, but someone had wanted him dead. Ascha handed Tchenguiz the horse's reins and gave him the bow and quiver. The Hun ran a loving hand over the bow's bellied curves. He drew a red-hackled arrow from the quiver and then pushed it back and grunted his thanks.

The Franks climbed the steps and went inside the house, filling the room with their big bodies and loud voices. Slaves scurried to bring beer and prepare food. Octha bustled, clapping backs and pumping hands, welcoming the Franks to his home. Every so often he looked up and glared at Ascha.

Ascha sighed. Maybe, he'd spoken too harshly.

Lucullus appeared at his side. 'So you're back then?' he said with a sly grin. His eyes dropped to the ring Clovis had given him and the leather purse on Ascha's belt.

Ascha wasn't in the mood for the Gaul's clever remarks. He looked for the girl. At first he couldn't see her, and then she was there and he realized how much he had missed her. She seemed surprised to see so many men. She brushed a heavy fall of hair from her face and greeted them warmly. Ascha looked at her, and she at him and he thought he saw in her eyes, if not on her lips, the suggestion of a smile, but he could not be sure.

The old woman, Femke, came with an armful of bread and a big pot of herb relish and laid them on the table. Two slaves entered carrying a cask of beer. The Franks dragged benches to the table, took spoons from their boots and began to eat, using the bread to scoop up relish and cramming it down their throats with blind-eyed pleasure.

Octha sat beside Ascha and the captain. He smiled as if wanting to put aside their recent spat and said, 'The Overlord believed you?'

Ascha nodded. 'The Franks have raised the levy,' he said, and felt a thrill of excitement just saying the words. Briefly, he recapped for the merchant what had happened at the Council meeting.

'It sounds as if it went well,' Octha said.

Ascha was pleased at what he thought was a new respect in the merchant's voice. 'It did,' he said, 'and I can pay you what I owe you.' He tapped the purse so the coins clinked.

Octha bent his head. 'Praise be to Tiw!' he said with the slightest hint of irony.

'But what of the fleet?' Ascha said.

'Growing bigger by the hour.'

'When do you think they'll sail?'

Octha gave it some thought. 'Probably tomorrow, maybe the day after. They've been making repairs, taking on food and water, training for war,' he said. 'Radhalla works his people hard.'

'We have orders to watch them,' Ascha said. 'And warn the Franks the moment they leave. The Franks and the Romans plan to destroy them as soon as they land.'

'Good! We all hope you will succeed,' Octha said fervently.

'A pity more Frisians aren't as hostile to sea-raiders as you,' the captain growled.

'We have plenty of reason to fear them,' Octha said carefully.

'But you trade with the raiders?' the captain insisted.

The merchant squirmed. 'We sell them a little food and beer. And we buy the loot and slaves they have taken,' he said. 'Sometimes our young men go with them on raids. The trade is good, but Saxons are uncomfortable bedfellows and we're always glad to see the back of them.'

Ascha was curious to see how the captain would respond, but the Frank carried on eating. Frisian lack of scruples about trading with the Saxon sea-wolves was well known.

The merchant moved away. Ascha sipped his beer. He saw Herrad talking to one of the Frisian women and watched her, his eyes following her every gesture. He saw the way she touched the woman's arm to make a point and saw the woman's answering smile.

There was a dry chuckle at his side.

'She's a fine girl,' the captain said. 'I can see why you're sweet on her.'

Ascha jerked as if stung. 'I'm not sweet on her,' he snapped angrily.

'I can see it in your eyes, boy,' the captain said with a hint of a smile, 'but you have a rival.'

He pointed with his beaker, and Ascha saw Lucullus lean in and whisper something in the girl's ear, one hand resting lightly on her shoulder. There was a smile on the Gaul's lips, and his hair was thick and glossy on his neck. Herrad looked up suddenly and caught Ascha watching her. She smiled and Lucullus turned to see who she was smiling at. He lifted his hand in a casual half wave at Ascha and then his eyes slid back to the girl.

'He's just a slave,' Ascha scowled, but the envy washed through him like bile.

'If he was my slave, I'd teach him to mind his place,' the captain said.

Ascha brooded. The Gaul was like a cat, always landing on his feet. He remembered Lucullus telling him with a grin how he'd been sold because his master's daughter had developed a fondness for the good-looking Gaul. He thought about that and then he got to his feet, picked up his cloak and went over to Lucullus. He bent low to the his ear. 'A word, now, outside.'

Lucullus followed him out.

The weather had changed. The wind was squally although the air was warm and heavy.

'Ascha, what is it?'

'It's nothing. Let's walk.' He put his hand on the back of Lucullus' neck. 'I think we landed on our feet, meeting Octha. It could have been worse.'

'Much worse,' the Gaul agreed.

There was silence.

'This thing between you and Herrad.'

'What thing? There is nothing between us.'

'All the same, I want it to stop. I want you to leave her alone.'

He spoke too loudly, as if he were driving a mule.

'But we are friends,' Lucullus said. 'And besides, who else can she talk to.'

Ascha stopped and turned to face Lucullus, 'What do you mean?'

'We share a faith. It is only natural she would want to talk to me.'

Ascha felt a quiver of sudden fury. 'You saying she would sooner talk to you than anybody else?'

'That's not what I said.'

'You mean the rest of us are barbarians?'

Lucullus gave him an easy smile. 'Franks, Frisians, Saxons. To those of us born under Rome's rule, you are all barbarians.'

Ascha hit Lucullus a wild punch on the side of the head. Lucullus staggered and recovered. Ascha saw a flash of anger in the Gaul's eyes and hit him again. Lucullus fell sprawling in the mud.

'Get up!' Ascha shouted. 'Get up!'

Lucullus went to rise. He seemed to have second thoughts and slumped back.

Ascha bent over him. 'I am no barbarian,' he yelled. 'Do you understand?'

Lucullus looked up, his face showing anger and resentment, while his hand went to his jaw and slowly rubbed it. He did not appear frightened but made no move to rise. Ascha walked away and then suddenly ran back and kicked Lucullus in the ribs.

'If you value your life, don't ever call me that again.'

When he looked back, Lucullus was stumbling towards the house holding his jaw.

It began to rain, slow at first and then without mercy. Rain drops rilled on the roof and splashed in the mud. Ascha dragged his cloak over his head and climbed up the bank to the gap in the wall. He stood under the parapet and sheltered under the wall's lee with the cattle and stared into the grey wetness. Earlier, Octha's servants had lit a fire in the yard and the pale smoke of the wet timber rose thick and heavy. Through the driving rain, he could see the roofs of Thraelsted and beyond, the faint outlines of the anchored warfleet. He peered into the greyness.

Somewhere out there was his brother and his clan.

He wiped the rain from his face and felt a pang of loneliness, a numb pain like tooth-ache. He wondered if he was doing the right thing. For the first time, he began to realize that when the Saxons hit the beaches of Gallia, the Theodi would be with them and when the Franks and the Romans attacked the invaders, as they were bound to do, his own people would die alongside the Saxons. The realization came as a shock. He swallowed and blinked, oblivious to the rain streaming down and soaking him to the bone

The rain eased and the wind was not so strong. There was silence broken only by the rustle of the trees and the steady dripping from overhanging rafters.

The door of the house opened and some Franks appeared. They were drinking beer and talking in loud voices. He watched them go to the fire, draw up crates and barrels, stretch their legs and drink some more.

A woman came out of the darkness.

She jumped a rivulet of running water, lightly as a young woman would, and walked towards the fire, lifting her skirts clear of the mud. He peered into the thick ambush of shadows. He could not see her face but, by the cast of her shoulders and the slimness of her hips, he knew it was her. He felt his heart start to thump. Pushing himself away from the wall, he ran quickly down the bank.

'Herrad?'

She stopped and smiled uncertainly. One of the Franks threw a log onto the fire and the flames crackled and leapt. There was a burst of laughter and a few sly remarks which may or may not have been directed at them.

'Walk with me?' he said.

She hesitated, alarmed perhaps by his intensity. She looked over her shoulder at the house and then went with him, moving away from the noise and the people into the shadows.

The rain stopped and the mist lifted, driven by a fresh sea breeze that rolled over the *castellum* wall. She walked with him across the yard, stepping over the puddles with an easy stride. He glanced at her. She seemed composed. His thigh brushed hers and she moved away as if scalded. They went up the bank to the gap in the wall of the *castellum*. He had not thought about what he would say and now that they were alone he felt only relief that she had come.

He stood by her side as she held her elbows and looked down at the Saxon fleet. Her face was a pale smudge in the darkness.

'So many ships,' she said after a while, and he could hear the hard edge to her tone.

'You hate them don't you?'

'Who?'

'Saxons. Barbarians!'

'They drove us out of Pritannia. And they took my sister. They are cruel and vicious and without mercy.'

He wanted to ask her about her sister, but held back, unwilling to pursue a matter that neither of them could handle. He hesitated and then said, 'Does that mean you hate me?'

She thought for a moment. 'You are a Theod, not a Saxon.'

'They are the same thing, no?'

'Not for me.'

She turned and gave him a faint smile. He was aware of her arm by his side and the warm smell of her. She was close enough to touch.

'Are your people out there?' she said looking to the bay.

'Yes, they're out there,' he said and felt the fear curdle in his belly. Franks and Romans were getting ready to slaughter Saxons. They would not distinguish between Theod and Cherusker. The thought depressed him.

No sound but the drip of water under the timbers.

'What happened between you and Lucullus?' she said eventually.

'Nothing.'

'Were you fighting over me?'

He could sense the disapproval coming off her in waves.

'Lucullus got a little above himself.'

She rolled her eyes to the sky. 'Lucullus is a friend,' she said. 'No more.'

He couldn't reply. His tongue was dry in his throat.

'Perhaps you envy him?' she said quietly.

'I do not,' he burst out, but knew she had put her finger on the truth. He had envied the lanky Gaul since they had first met.

'Lucullus did not deserve what you did.'

'He is my property,' he said moodily. 'I can do with him as I like.'

He noticed a look of cold scorn appear on her face and felt ashamed and stupid. This wasn't what he had wanted. With Basinia's slave girl it had all been so easy, so straightforward. How could two girls who seemed so alike, be so different?

'I should go,' she said.

'No, don't go,' he said. He put one hand up against her cheek and held it. Delicately, he touched her hair. The slightest twinge went through her and then she closed her eyes. He slipped an arm around her waist and drew her to him, pressing his hands against the small of her back. He kissed her full on the mouth. Her lips were soft and he could smell her body, warm and natural, enveloping him, pulling him in.

She broke away, 'I can't do this,' she said sweeping the hair from her face.

He felt the tight cramp of desire at the pit of his stomach and leaned in close to kiss her again.

She shoved him hard, both hands punching against his chest. 'I said no!' she shouted.

He was overwhelmed by sudden fury. He grabbed her wrist, pulled her towards him and raised his other hand. She stood for a moment with her chin uplifted, glaring at him, as if defying him to strike her and then she ripped her arm free and was gone.

Ascha closed his eyes. He clenched and unclenched his fists and tried to work out what had just happened. He had been clumsy and ham-fisted. A barbarian! He let out a sound that was somewhere between a snarl and a sob and then swivelled, punching the stone again and again in a sudden explosion of rage.

Around the fire, heads lifted and watched him curiously.

He slid down the wall and sat in the mud with his back against the cold stone and his head on his chest, licking his knuckles.

Everything had turned as bitter as wormwood.

By the fire, he could hear people laughing.

He pushed his way past the men and women at the door and made his way into the house. The Franks had been drinking all evening and most were drunk. Had they already forgotten their dead friends, or did it just seem that way? Lucullus was sitting with the girl and Gydda and Tchenguiz. There was a smear of dried blood on the Gaul's cheek, and one eye looked as if it were beginning to close. Herrad sat next to him, a comforting arm around his neck. Lucullus looked up as Ascha entered and then looked away.

The captain came over, red-faced and cheerful. 'Your man seems to have picked a fight with a stone wall,' he said with a grin.

Ascha swore but said nothing.

A babble of noise in the room, people laughing and shouting to one another. He watched Herrad lift her hair off her neck and then drop it. She knew he was there, but she wouldn't look at him.

He felt close to breaking, a branch blown down in a storm. Herrad despised him as a barbarian, and the price for buying his freedom was the destruction of his own people. Even Radhalla had not wanted that. He felt his heart thudding. There was a strange roaring in his ears, and his mouth was dry. The hall was spinning. Somewhere, far away, he could hear a distant voice saying his name.

He looked up to see Octha standing in front of him with a pitcher of beer. Octha put down the beer and drew up a bench and sat down. 'You look rough,' he growled. 'What's holding you together? Cobwebs?'

Ascha shook his head. He ran both hands over his face and blew out his cheeks. Right now, the merchant was the last person he wanted to talk to.

'Go away, old man. I have things on my mind.'

Octha put back his head and guffawed.

'We all have things on our mind, lad,' Octha said. He splashed beer into a beaker and handed it to Ascha. 'Y'know what? I think it's high time you and I got drunk.'

23

He must have passed out because when he came to his head was throbbing and there was a foul taste in his mouth. When he got to his feet, the walls spun and the floor seemed to tip. He went outside, ducked his head in the trough and immediately felt better.

He went to the gap in the wall and stared at the ships in the bay. He knew they would have to leave soon, Radhalla could not afford to wait much longer. He felt sick at the thought of the battle to come.

Herrad came out from a door to feed the hens. He watched her wipe her hands on her skirt and go inside. He breathed in to clear his head, crossed the yard and pushed at the door. He nodded politely to Octha and the captain and wished them a good morning. The captain didn't reply, but Octha looked up and agreed it was a fine morning. The old man looked as fresh as a daisy, Ascha thought ruefully.

The girl was grinding something in a clay bowl and didn't look up.

'I want to go out to the fleet,' Ascha said.

'Why would you want to do that?' the captain said suspiciously.

'Because I want to make a final count of the ships and to do that I need to get close,' he said, the lie springing easy to his lips.

'It's not safe,' Octha said. 'The Saxons have the town sewn up tighter than a pig's arse. Nobody gets in or out.'

'I'm still going.'

'Don't be a fool,' the captain said, raising his voice.

'They catch you, they'll kill you,' Octha said.

And then Ascha heard the girl say, 'I'll take you.'

Ascha gazed at her in wonderment and shook his head. 'No, it's too dangerous.'

'Safer than if you go on your own,' she said coolly. 'I take the boat out almost every day. The Cheruskkii know me. If you're well hidden, I don't think they'll stop us.'

'She's right,' Octha said. 'Herrad is up and down that river all the time.'

Ascha raised one quizzical eyebrow. 'You would do this?'

'When do you want to go?' she said.

'Now,' he said. 'I want to go now.'

He followed the girl out and watched while she pulled the rowboat out from the reeds. He waited while she gathered her skirts and stepped down into the boat. Her arms and feet were bare, her skin browned by the sun, her hair combed and folded, thick and dark, behind her ear. He got into the boat and lay down, finding that if he curled between her feet, his knees bunched under his chin, there was just enough room. She threw a sail cloth over him that stank of salt and fish and long days drying in the sun. He lay under the sailcloth and listened as the girl made ready.

There was the creak of oars and then the sensation of movement. It was hot under the sailcloth, and the motion and smell of fish made his stomach heave. He closed his eyes and gave himself up to the rhythm of the oars. After a while he lifted up a corner of the sailcloth to let in some air. He saw the *castellum*, Thraelsted, and the hulls of the Saxon fleet sliding past.

'Are you all right?' she whispered.

'Never better,' he growled and heard her snort with laughter.

Lying in the half-dark with his head between the girl's feet, covered by sailcloth, was a little like having her skirts thrown over his face, he thought, and once this idea had taken hold he couldn't let it go. He could just see Herrad's feet, small and neat, pressing against the side of the boat as she pulled on the oars. Her legs, bare and brown, disappeared into the soft shadow of her dress. He smiled to himself, aroused by the girl's closeness.

He was torn from his dreaming by a breathless voice. 'You must direct me,' he heard her say. 'Where do you want to go?'

'I want to find my clanship, the *SeaWulf.*'

Herrad went quiet. Now she knew he had not come to count warships. He waited, hoping she would help him. There was a long pause, and then he heard her say, 'Would you know her?'

He'd know the *SeaWulf* anywhere. He had carved her prow, sailed with her to Gallia. He knew his own work. 'Yes,' he said. 'She'll be further west on the landward side of the fleet, with the Cheruskkii boats.'

The tide was ebbing and some of the longboats were marooned on the mud. The rest were anchored out in the river, roped together like bundles of firewood. He took his time, his eyes resting on each ship before moving on. The confederation fleet was huge, no doubt about it, longboats from every clan and nation, a forest of masts.

Slowly, they worked their way across the bay. No sound but the girl's laboured breathing and the boat's gentle creaking.

Ascha raised his head, but the girl shushed him. 'You must stay under cover,' she said. 'We're almost within the fleet'

Ascha ducked down. He could hear the sounds of revelry, drunken singing, guffaws of laughter, muffled voices.

Someone shouted, 'Hello my pretty. Come aboard and you can stroke my oar.' Herrad laughed good-naturedly and, when the boat faltered suddenly, he imagined her taking a hand off the oar to wave.

'We're almost there,' she said. 'Tell me which is your ship?'

He lifted the sailcloth and, almost immediately, saw the *SeaWulf* on the far side of the inlet, her mast lowered and the prow monster rearing with snapping jaws and glaring eyes. He felt a thrill of excitement at the thought of seeing Hanno and Besso. The *SeaWulf* lay on the far side of the inlet with her mast lowered, the prow monster rearing with snapping jaws and glaring eyes. Not a big ship, but beautiful and his heart swelled with pride to see her.

He touched the girl's knee and pointed. 'Bring us alongside to landward so we can't be seen.

The boat turned, he saw familiar faces at the strake and felt his stomach flutter with excitement. Herrad ran the boat smoothly between the *SeaWulf* and the shore. Murmurings of delight when the crew saw the girl was coming towards them, and then the boat bumped, scraped and came to a stop.

'You can come out now,' the girl said and he could hear the nervousness in her voice. He threw back the sailcloth and stood up, blinking at the astonished faces lining the *SeaWulf*'s side.

'We be of one blood, my brothers,' he said. 'Can I come aboard?'

'Ascha! Is it really tha?' they said, grabbing his wrist and hauling him up. The Theodi crowded around, slapped his back and shook his hand. He felt his heart lift. He was back amongst his own.

Besso appeared, his meaty face jowled and stubbled with beard. 'Ascha, come here,' he boomed.

They embraced. Ascha pressed his face into Besso's shoulder and breathed in the smells of woodsmoke, sweat and the sea. The smells he had known all his life.

'We heard tha'd been taken by slavers,' Besso said. 'What happened? And how did tha get here.'

'It's a long story,' Ascha said, looking around. 'Are there any Cheruskkii aboard?'

'Na,' Besso grunted. 'They leave us well alone.'

There was a stir and the crowd parted. Hanno appeared. He looked thinner, his eyes dark-rimmed sockets and his hair dry as old rope. 'Hello, little brother,' he said, smiling softly.

They hugged and held each other and, for a moment, Ascha forgot why he was there. Hanno gently pinched his cheek and ruffled his hair and turned to grin at the crew. 'Look, who it is!' he said. 'Our own Ascha.'

Hanno called for food and beer and then there was a sudden stir. Hanno said, 'But Ascha, who is this?'

Herrad had climbed up the side. She stood holding on to a rigging line, her hair blowing in the breeze, more nervous than he'd ever seen her.

'She is with me,' he said. 'Her name is Herrad.'

Hanno welcomed the girl with a broad smile. 'It's the first time I've ever heard of a girl climbing onto our ship. Usually they're doing all they can to get off.'

They all laughed at that, even the girl.

Ascha asked after his mother and Budrum and was relieved to hear they were well. Theodi returning from Radhallaburh had told her that Ascha had been taken by slavers. His mother had grieved, but Besso had told her that Ascha was strong and determined and would come home, as he came home before. Ascha bit his lip. He thought of his mother alone with her grief and his eyes filled.

'Now tha's here, tha must join us,' Hanno beamed. 'We are engaged on a great adventure.' His arm swept wide across the fleet. 'With Tiw's help, the raiding will be glorious! There will be loot and slaves and wealth for all. We'll not go hungry this winter.'

Ascha searched his brother's face for a flicker of guilt or regret, but he saw nothing. Hanno seemed content to let bygones be bygones. Above them, the sea-ropes cracked against the mast and the boat rocked. The wind was stiffening, the tide turning. The girl stood watching, as if ready to flee at a moment's notice.

'I can't come with tha, Hanno,' he said quietly.

'Tha's sailed before. It's no matter if tha's unweaponed. We can use tha on the rowing benches.'

'No, tha doesn't understand. I came to tell tha. They know the fleet is coming. They're waiting for you.'

The smile fell from Hanno's face. 'What does tha mean?'

'The Romans and the Franks have raised their armies. The beacons are ready and the coast is watched night and day. They're already marching to meet you.'

'I don't believe tha,' Hanno said. He frowned and looked away.

'It's not a game, Hanno. Tha's sailing into a trap.'

'So tha says, little brother,' Hanno said coldly. 'But how does tha know all this?'

'It doesn't matter how I know. All that matters is that *tha* knows. The Franks say they will destroy the Saxon host to the last man. They say every village in the north will be in mourning.'

The crew muttered among themselves. They shifted from one foot to another and looked at each other anxiously. Ascha saw their long faces and sensed their disappointment, their hopes of glory and easy loot dissolving before their eyes.

'What does tha want, Ascha? What does tha expect of us?' Hanno said testily.

'Turn back! Go home! Raid Pritannia if you will, but tha must avoid Gallia.'

Hanno scratched his arm and shook his head. 'Na!' he said. 'It's not true. He got to his feet and began to pace up and down the deck, his cheeks flushed. 'I don't believe it. It's a trick, a filthy Frankish trick,' he shouted. 'Tha's trying to deceive us. Radhalla would never make such a mistake. He told us that we would land unopposed.'

'Hanno, it's Radhalla who has deceived tha,' Ascha said. 'If tha goes ahead with this, you will all die. And it will be death without honour.'

'Stop!' Hanno screamed, cupping his hands over his ears. 'Stop this right now!'

The *SeaWulf* fell silent.

Ascha gazed at Hanno with astonishment. He saw that he had blundered. He had assumed Hanno would be grateful for the warning and had given no thought to how his words would be received. He'd put his brother on the spot before the whole crew. He wished now he'd taken Hanno aside and spoken to him alone.

'Tha's right,' he said evenly. 'Radhalla would not bring you here if the raid was doomed.'

Hanno jerked his head from side to side, his eyes sparking with suppressed fury.

'Tha's changed, Ascha. Tha's not what tha were. I don't know who tha is anymore.'

'Tha knows, Hanno. I'm Ascha. I'm thi brother.'

'What did they do to tha when tha was away? Is tha working for the Franks now, or maybe the Romans? Has tha sold thi birthright to those shit-eating scum?'

He pointed an accusing finger at Herrad. 'Or is it her?' he said with a snarl. 'Has she turned thi brain to mush? Taught tha to sell thi people to those who would enslave us?'

The girl lifted her chin and stared back at Hanno, cool and unafraid.

'She has nothing to do with this, Hanno,' Ascha shouted. 'It's the Cheruskkii who have enslaved you, not the Franks. The Franks gave you silver and fed you during the starving time. What have the Cheruskkii ever done for us?'

'Tha's let me down, Ascha.' Hanno said. His shoulders suddenly slumped. He looked dejected.

Ascha appealed to Besso, hands spread wide. 'Besso, for Tiw's sake, tell him!'

Besso lifted his huge shoulders and pulled the corners of his mouth down but remained silent.

'Tha's not wanted on this boat, Ascha,' Hanno said. 'Tha'd better go!'

Hanno turned his back and with arms folded looked out to sea.

Ascha raised his hands and let them fall with a slap to his sides. There was a cool breeze on his cheek and he felt a little tug as the *SeaWulf* pulled at anchor. The tide was turning. He was vaguely aware of the girl standing by the side, watching him. He let out a little sigh and moved towards her and then turned suddenly to Besso.

'Does tha think I'm a traitor, Besso?'

'Na, lad,' Besso said. 'Tha's doing what thi father would have wanted tha to do.'

Ascha looked at him, grateful. 'You know the Franks and Romans are waiting for you?'

Besso rested his hand on Ascha's shoulder. 'I know, lad, but I gave Hanno my oath. We must all do what we have to do.'

'But what's wrong with him?' Ascha whispered, glancing at Hanno. 'He was always the gentlest of men.'

'He's not himself,' Besso said. 'Ever since Hroc's death, he's changed, in here,' and he tapped the side of his brow with a stubby finger.

Was that it, Ascha wondered? Was Hanno's mind bending with guilt for Hroc's death? Tha should a thought of that before tha hanged him, Ascha thought bitterly.

'When do you leave?' he said.

'When Radhalla decides,' Besso said, 'but it won't be long now.'

They both fell silent.

Ascha was downcast. How could he fight his own clan, men he had known and loved all his life?

'Do you know where Radhalla will make landfall in Gallia?' he whispered.

Besso shook his head, 'Radhalla is the only one who knows, and he's not telling anybody.'

Hanno stood by the prowhead staring out across the Rhine mouth. Even with his back turned, Hanno seemed lost, his dreams of leading the clan to glory unravelling before his eyes. Ascha jerked his chin at the girl and the two of them swung over the side and dropped into the boat.

He grabbed an oar, and the girl took the other. He stretched his legs and pulled hard, no longer caring who saw him. As they moved off, he looked back. Besso and a handful of Theodi were leaning over the side of the *SeaWulf* watching them go. Ascha lifted a hand in farewell and Besso waved back.

There was no sign of Hanno.

They rowed without speaking, no-one paying them any attention, a man and a woman of less interest than a girl on her own. Whatever happened, he knew now there was no going back.

Herrad said, 'You're different from your brother.'

'Am I?' He gave a sharp laugh. 'I used to worship the very ground he trod on. I wanted nothing so much as to be like him.'

'No, you are very different,' she said. She thought for a while and then said. 'You are stronger. And you do things for a reason.'

They rowed past a large double-stemmed warboat. He knew the boat by its prow, a black and gaping-jawed dragon with a twisting serpentine neck, Eanmund's work. It was quiet, the crew ashore or asleep. He could see a stocky middle aged man on the prow. The man unbuckled his belt and began to piss.

They rowed on.

He'd done what he could, he told himself, but it had not been enough.

A gurgle of water.

He looked at the man pissing and saw with a jolt that it was Radhalla. At the same moment Radhalla saw him. He held the dripping oar above the water and let the boat drift while he stared at Radhalla, and Radhalla stared at him. He wondered whether he should try to hide, or at least turn his face away, but he did neither. He was aware that Herrad had also stopped rowing. Radhalla acknowledged him with the faintest tilt of his head and then was gone.

'Do you know him?' the girl said in a small voice.

He gave her a sideways glance. The effort of rowing showed in the pink tinge to her cheeks, the rise and fall of her breast and the slight parting of her mouth.

'I know him,' he said.

He pulled, held his oar for a beat to adjust their direction, and pulled again.

'Are we in danger?'

Her face was expressionless, a tremor at the corner of one eye the only clue as to what she was feeling. They were moving faster through the water, although the tide was against them. Almost without realizing it, they had both picked up the pace.

He nodded. 'Great danger.'

Canoes and small boats passed between ships and shore but there was no sign of pursuit. Only a matter of time he thought.

They hauled the rowboat up the riverbank and pushed it into the reeds. 'We must be quick,' he said. 'We don't have much time.' He held out a hand and she allowed him to pull her up. Her hand felt warm and dry to the touch. He knew she must be frightened but she did not seem troubled, and he realized that he accepted her calmness now, accepted it as part of who she was.

When they entered the house, the captain and Octha were playing dice. Several Antrustions were asleep in one corner, and Lucullus and Tchenguiz were sitting with their backs against the wall. Ascha removed his weapons and poured some beer for himself and the girl. They both gulped it down and then he told them all what had happened. The girl went to Octha and laid a hand on his shoulder and he saw Octha gently pat her hand.

'Did he recognize you?' the captain said.

'I think he did.'

The captain shrugged. 'Why should Radhalla care? He has other things on his mind than one escaped slave?'

There was a coarseness to the Frank's tone that Ascha didn't like.

'He will know that I went to see my brother,' he said.

Octha squinted at him. 'What of it?'

He realized that Octha had guessed all along what he would do. 'I told him the Franks knew they were coming,' he said.

The captain's face darkened. 'You did what?' He got to his feet, knocking over the bench with a loud crash. Ascha tensed as the Frank's hand dropped to the long knife at his belt. There was a pause while everybody waited to see what would happen. The Frank scowled. He raised a hand in disgust, turned and walked out, slamming the door behind him.

'Why did you tell them?' the merchant asked when the captain had gone.

'They are my kinfolk. What was I supposed to do?'

'They'll track you down,' Octha said quietly. 'Herrad is well known in the village, and the Cheruskkii will link her to me. People will remember having seen Frankish troopers here. They'll find you soon enough.'

Ascha swore. He didn't regret warning Hanno, but he'd been foolish to allow himself to be seen. Now he'd put the girl's life in danger.

'We have to leave,' he said, getting to his feet.

The Antrustions gathered their kit and left. Tchenguiz and Gydda went to the door. Lucullus moved cat-like to Ascha's side.

'You're going?' Lucullus said.

Ascha nodded.

'Just you and the Franks?'

Ascha turned with a sudden spark of anger. 'They won't spare you, Lucullus. You've been seen with me and you could never pass for a Frisian. You're coming with us.'

'Worth a try,' Lucullus said with a grin, and made for the door.

Ascha picked up his cloak and threw it over one shoulder. He looked expectantly at Octha.

The merchant shook his head.

'I'm staying,' he said with a twisted smile. 'I'm too old to run away. You go.'

Ascha sighed. 'It's not safe, old man.'

'I'll tell them I bought you from the widow, and the Franks came and freed you. I will tell them you forced Herrad to take you out to your brother. I've traded with these people. They know me.'

'They also know you served in the legions.'

Octha laughed. 'Tiw's breath! Half of Frisia served Rome. Along this frontier, we were the Roman army.'

'I don't like it.'

'What's not to like. It's you they're after, not me.'

'And Herrad?'

Octha breathed in deep and let it out slow. 'She stays,' he said.

The room fell silent. Ascha felt his colour rise. The girl looked at him and then at the merchant.

'This is stupid,' Ascha shouted.

'Probably,' Octha said, 'all the same, she's staying.'

Ascha shook his head. 'You can endanger your own life, old man, but you're not risking hers. If the Cheruskkii discover you and I are linked, Radhalla will not spare either of you.'

The merchant gave him a long hard look. The girl moved across the room to the merchant's side and laid a hand on his arm.

'Go, Ascha,' she said. 'I will stay with Octha.'

'You're staying?' he said harshly.

'Yes,' she nodded. 'You go. I'll be fine.'

He saw the determination in her chin. So be it. He'd not been able to hide his feelings for her and the merchant, sly old dog, had seen what he had seen. She had made her choice. He jammed his *seaxe* and *franciska* into his belt and then turned and headed for the door.

'Where will you go,' Octha called after him.

'South,' Ascha said without looking back. 'We'll ride to Tornacum and wait for the Saxons there.'

And he stormed out, slamming the door.

24

They rode out of the gates and took the trackway south, the Franks riding in file behind the captain and Ascha, Tchenguiz on a horse that belonged to one of the Franks killed by the Alani. Gydda and Lucullus followed on foot. Ascha looked back once and saw the girl watching them from the doorway.

They rode in silence, Ascha lost in his own thoughts. The merchant had made it clear the girl belonged to him. Ascha was furious with the old man but even angrier with himself, he was to blame. He forced himself to think calmly. He had a job to do and was letting his feelings get in the way. He looked to the east where storm clouds stood high over the wetlands and then back to the west where the fleet lay. He pulled up and waited for the captain to draw abreast.

'Captain, we can't leave. We have to watch for when the fleet sails. And we still don't know where the Saxons will make landfall.'

The captain chewed it over and then nodded. Without another word, they turned their horses and rode back. Just short of the *castellum* they found a dirt track, light coloured against the grass, leading up a grassy rise. Ascha made a clicking noise and pulled the horse off the road, the captain and the Franks following. They came to a small stream and walked the horses across. On the hillside the trees were thick and leafy and hung low over the path. The Franks bent over their horses' necks, cursing and muttering as the boughs scratched their faces and snagged their clothes.

It was almost dark when they got to the top. Against a purpling sky, they could see the stone finger of the *castellum* and Thraelsted and the bay beyond. In the fading light, the freshly-hewn timber of the Saxon warboats stood pale against the dark water, like maggots on a lamb's carcass.

Ascha swung his foot over the saddle and dropped to the ground. The Franks dismounted, tethered the horses, laid out their bedrolls and began to prepare food.

Ascha touched Tchenguiz on the arm.

'Go up there and tell me if tha sees anything.'

Ascha and the Franks rested as night fell.

Some time later there was a yell. He saw Tchenguiz waving and went up the hill at a lope.

'Cher'skii come!' the Hun said, pointing.

At first he saw nothing.

He blinked and peered into the middle distance.

And then he saw them.

A long dark line of armed men, led by a man on a horse, moving slowly towards the *castellum*.

Herrad felt stifled. Once Ascha and the Franks had left, Octha had gone from window to window closing and barring the shutters. The room felt stuffy and airless. With a sudden cry of irritation, she got to her feet and took down the bar and threw back the shutters. A silvery light crept into the house from a pale moon swept by dark clouds. The night was quiet as sleep. She lifted her head and breathed in the damp scent of grass and pine.

She heard the creak of a door, and Octha came in. He glanced at her, rubbed his hands together and sat down. He seemed not to have noticed the open window.

'Do you want to eat?' she said, her voice strained in the stillness.

He didn't answer.

The silence spread like water, filling the room.

Herrad sighed, pulled the knife from her sleeve and reached up and sliced at the ham hanging from the rafters. She cut a few thick chunks and then filled a bowl with bread and meat and set it before him.

'Why did you send them away?' she said.

Octha looked up at her as you might look at someone who spoke suddenly in an unknown language. He opened his mouth to say something, and then closed it again. He looked down and tossed his head a few times, as he did when he was in the wrong.

She had not understood all that had gone on between Octha and Ascha, but she had recognized the look in Ascha's eye and guessed that it had to do with her. She was no longer sure what she felt for Octha, pity or nothing at all, but she knew it had been a mistake to stay. How could Octha have been so thoughtless? But then he was a man and could do anything he wanted, and she was a woman and could not.

She lit an oil lamp and carried it over to the table. She was working on a beaded necklace strung with rawhide and now she picked up the necklace, knowing she would not sleep anyway. She was frightened of what would happen if the Saxons came. Just thinking about it made the muscles in her stomach clench, but at the same time she felt listless and unable to move. She drew in her shoulders and shivered. She remembered when her sister was taken by raiders and tensed with sudden pain as she recalled her mother's anguished wails, and her father's slow and burning anger. Even now, she could see her sister's face, and missed her more than she could say.

You have to be strong, she had told herself then. Do what you must to live. And she had lived by that rule ever since.

She studied the necklace in the half-light and then dropped it in disgust. The work was poor, the beads badly matched. She would have to undo it and start again.

She smiled, a hard little smile, and bent to her work. Rummaging in a wooden box, her fingers settled on a fat bead which she held up between finger and thumb. In the warm glow of the lamp the blue glass glittered brightly, the colour of sea water on a summer's day. She pushed the bone needle into the bead and then angrily pulled it through.

Outside, there was a dry sound, like a boot scraping on cobbles. Herrad froze, her needle poised. She ran a hand through her hair and listened.

But it was only the wind gusting through the trees.

Ascha couldn't sleep. He got to his feet, walked up the rise and looked down over the Rhine. No lights. No movement. A feeling of dread crept over him like a winter mist, numbing his limbs and chilling his heart. Something was wrong, he just knew it.

He ran back and went from one sleeping man to another, kicking them awake.

'What is it?' the captain said, reaching for his weapon.

'Get your men up,' he said. 'We're going back.'

They left the horses tethered and went down on foot, the moon giving enough light to see the pale thread of track. They travelled fast, running in a pack over the twisty brook and down the lane. When they neared the *castellum* they went to ground and crept along in the darkness, stopping every few moments to listen.

They heard no sound but the whispering of the grass and the sighing in the trees. Insects rose in clouds, breaking on their faces and rain pattered lightly on the leaves. There was a strong smell of damp wood and animal dung. In the moonlight the wall was the colour of wet leather, covered in thick, bony ivy that rustled faintly each time the wind passed.

They went to where the wall had collapsed in a sprawling heap of rubble. Tchenguiz squeezed Ascha's arm and pointed. An armed man stood in the shadows. Ascha nodded and the Hun ran off at a snaking half-crouch along the wall. Ascha caught a glimpse of him crawling behind a fence and then he lost sight of him. When he saw him again he was a dark shadow behind the sentry.

The shadow rose. They heard a faint cry and the man fell.

They waited and then they got to their feet, moving forward at a run, jumping over the crumpled body of the Cherusker sentry and crossing the broken wall into the courtyard. The captain jabbed a finger at the warehouse and two Franks peeled off into the night. A third ran to the barn.

Clouds slid across the moon like silk across marble.

Ascha squatted on his heels and waited. He loosened his long-knife in its sheath, tightened his belt a notch, pulled a piece of bread from his tunic and began to chew.

Come on, come on, he thought, mindful of the time that had passed since he gave the order to go back.

A Frank came running silently across the courtyard. 'Workshops clear,' he mouthed.

They waited some more and then they saw another Frank flitting along the foot of the wall where the shadows were deepest.

'Four in the barn,' he whispered. 'The house-slaves are there as well. The warehouse has been looted but it's clear, didn't see the merchant or the girl.'

'The barn first,' Ascha hissed. 'Then the house. Come on!'

They moved off at a crouching run, heading toward the barn. Smashed barrels, crates and broken storage jars were strewn over the yard and the doors of the warehouse gaped. The Saxons had already cleared out Octha's warehouse and sent wagon loads of plunder back to the fleet. Ascha grunted, pleased there would be fewer Cheruskkii to deal with.

They listened and then they drew their weapons and slipped inside the barn. It was dark, but not so dark they couldn't see. He could make out several Cheruskers sprawled in the straw. One of Octha's servants was hanging by the neck from a beam. Huddled against the far wall was a group of women, Ochtha's slaves and servants. They were asleep save for one older woman who stared at the Franks with wide and terrified eyes. She was Femke, the woman who had fed them when they arrived.

Ascha laid a finger across his lips, shook his head and saw her nod with understanding.

The Franks took up positions around the sleeping Cheruskkii. One Cherusker raised a bleary head and blinked at the armed men standing over him. His mouth opened in a silent scream, and then the blades came down.

Ascha watched the butchery without feeling. They were Cheruskkii and deserved to die. One of the women awoke and would have squealed if Femke had not clapped a hand across her mouth and silenced her. The Franks grinned and held up bloody fists, thumbs uppermost, their eyes and teeth white in the darkness.

Ascha crossed the barn floor and knelt beside Femke.

He spoke urgently, 'Femke, where is Octha and the girl?'

Femke looked up at him and turned her head towards the house.

'Are there Saxons with them?'

She nodded again.

'How many?'

She thought for a moment and then held up five fingers.

He went to the door of the barn and looked towards the house. A faint puff of smoke issued from the roof, like breath on a cold morning. He felt the cold grip of anxiety grab him by the gut.

Somewhere a dog howled in the night.

Rain tapped on the roof, and a damp shroud of wind wrapped itself around the tower. He signalled to the captain and then beckoned Tchenguiz. There was a band of deep shadow to their right, and they used that for cover as they ran to the house, leaping over a low wicker fence and throwing themselves against the wall on either side of the door. The captain and the Franks waited until they were across and then followed, feet slapping in the mud. More Franks went around the back. The shutters were open. Inside, a lamp was burning and Ascha could see its yellow light fluttering in the draught.

He strained to hear the slightest sound, his throat tight, almost swelling.

Silence.

He breathed out, screwed his eyes shut and released them. Not allowing himself to think about it, he lifted the latch and pushed, hoping the door was well oiled. The door swung open and they slipped inside.

Ascha paused and allowed his eyes to adjust.

Three men sat at the table, he could hear them breathing. Stepping closer, he saw that they were asleep. One was Octha, the other two were Cheruskkii. There was no sign of the girl. Octha had been badly beaten. His head lolled and his face was bruised and bloody. Iron-grey chest hair curled over a shirt that was torn and spattered with blood. The merchant's wrists were bound to the arms of the chair. His hands a raw and bloody mess. One of the Cheruskkii lay with his head on his arm, like a child, the other was sprawled in a chair with his head back and mouth open.

Ascha scanned the room. There'd been a struggle. Benches upended, wall hangings pulled down. The bedding chest had been opened and blankets tossed on the floor. A woman's workbox had been overturned, scattering beads across the floor. There was a stench of stale beer and the musky smell of men who have spent too long in each other's company.

Ascha and Tchenguiz circled the table, carefully stepping over the loose beads. They waited and they listened and then at a nod from Ascha they each clamped a hand over a Cherusker's mouth and put a blade beneath his throat and pulled it towards them. There was a sigh of escaping air and blood flowing over the table in a dark and widening pool. One of the Cheruskkii, a young man, twitched as he died, as if his passing were no more than a dream.

Octha opened his eyes but showed no surprise to see them. He put his head back in an effort to smile but his teeth were punched out and his mouth was bloody. Ascha put a finger to his lips. They stared at each other for what seemed a long time. There was a look of unfathomable sadness on the merchant's face, as if he had seen things he never hoped to see. He began to sob, his body heaving uncontrollably.

Not now, Ascha thought. Not now.

He touched Octha's arm and mouthed the girl's name. The merchant's eyes swivelled towards the far end of the house and a soft moan slid from his lips.

Ascha drew his *franciska* and passed his *seaxe* to his left hand. He and Tchenguiz turned as one. The merchant's sleeping quarters were at the end of the house screened by a curtain of animal hides. They edged forward, nerves screaming, peering into the shadows. He was half way down the room when the shadows shifted and a man came at him from out of the darkness. Instinctively, Ascha jerked back from the slashing blow, feinted and then, as the man turned, he stepped forward and punched the *seaxe* in hard just below the ribs. He held the Cherusker close, feeling the sour warmth of the man's breath on his face, and then yanked the blade free.

The Cherusker fell without a sound.

Across the room, he saw Tchenguiz grappling with another Saxon. The Hun parried the Cherusker's blow, laid open the man's thigh and then hooked the man's knife arm away and killed him with a vicious chop to the head.

Breathing heavily, Ascha lifted the curtain and stepped inside.

A bed covered with sheepskins, a table and cupboards, more skins on the floor. Herrad was roped to a roof beam, her arms stretched above her head. She was barefoot, dressed only in her shift, and her mouth bound with a dirty rag.

Ascha reached up and sawed at her bonds. She let out a little gasp and leaned on his shoulder as her legs gave way. He helped her to the bed and was pulling at the rag in her mouth when he heard a faint sound.

Herrad looked up at him and then past him and her eyes went wide.

Ascha whirled.

He caught the glint of moonlight on an iron blade and then a pale figure cannoned into him, driving him back across the room. He saw a long knife thrusting up towards his groin and he twisted violently to avoid the blade, swinging the *franciska* in a savage downward slash.

A shrill scream ripped the night air and then Ascha crashed to the floor. He rolled and kicked himself free. Scrambling quickly to his feet, he stood, chest heaving and alert to every move. In the dirty grey light of approaching dawn he could see a man, writhing like a snake and clutching his arm.

It took him a moment before he saw it was Radhalla's nephew, Sigisberht.

Tchenguiz pushed past, his long knife raised.

'Don't kill him!' Ascha shouted. 'We need him.'

He kicked the bench out of the way and stepped in for a better look. Sigisberht was lying on his back, his shirt ripped open and his plump white belly spattered with blood. He saw that his blow had almost severed the Cherusker's arm at the elbow, the limb now hanging by a tattered scrap of flesh. Sigisberht gasped, his breath coming in little pants, and his face clammy with sweat.

He could hear the Franks shouting to each other outside as they went through the buildings searching for stray Saxons. Tchenguiz went from window to window, flinging open the shutters which crashed noisily against the side of the house.

Ascha turned to the girl.

She sat on the edge of the bed staring at the floor with her hands clasped in front of her and her face half-hidden by her hair. He saw that she was shaking. She had been beaten: there were bruises on her wrists and on her cheek. Blood soaked her shift.

He took a sheepskin from the bed and draped it across the girl's shoulders. The Frankish captain came up. He glanced at the girl and then looked at Ascha.

'Bastards cut off his fingers to make him talk,' he muttered.

He held up a hand and drew a thick finger across the knuckles.

The girl suddenly got to her feet and, with faltering steps, padded across the room to Octha. Ascha watched as she took the old man's grey head in her arms and held him against her breast while he sobbed bitterly and hot tears carved channels through the grime on his cheeks.

'I'm so sorry,' Ascha heard him say, over and over. 'I'm so sorry.'

The merchant had been wrong, his reputation worthless. Sigisberht would have wanted to know everything, and he had no doubt Octha would have told him. Not at first maybe, not when his manservant was taken out and hanged. Not even when the Cheruskkii turned their attention to him, first the beatings and then the knife, every step a fresh hill of pain until he could bear no more. But there was always more. And when the Cheruskkii laid hands on the girl, and Octha realized what they would do to her, he would have babbled like a babe.

Herrad went out and filled a pan with water from the cask. She took a wooden ladle and dipped it and held it to the merchant's lips. Octha's drank greedily, the water running down his chin. The girl soaked a cloth and began to clean the old man's face. She held

Octha's hand and gently trickled water over the mutilated stumps, talking softly as a mother would to a child.

There was a sharp cry as the captain and Tchenguiz lifted Sigisberht onto a bench. The Cherusker's hair was plastered to his brow and his face was as grey as death. He clasped his arm with fingers that were clogged and sticky with blood. He looked up at Ascha and smiled without mirth.

'Ah, the Theod,' he said.

'Yes.'

'I knew you were not what you seemed.' Sigisberht said and gave a short hard laugh. 'I tried to tell Radhalla I thought you were working for the Franks but he wouldn't have it.' He shook his head and closed his eyes as the pain rolled over him. 'He liked you too much. Thought you were a survivor, the half-slave who escaped Frankish exile and made his way home. But you'll burn for this, you traitor.'

Ascha slapped him across the face.

Sigisberht's head snapped back, and he gasped but his eyes were cold and blue and glared at Ascha with unveiled loathing.

'When does the fleet sail, you sack of shit? What's your landing point?'

Sigisberht smiled at him, through him and beyond him.

Ascha turned to find the girl standing beside him. She was silent, her face composed but for a faint and almost unnoticeable tremor at the corner of her jaw.

Sigisberht looked up and his lips drew back in a ghastly grin.

'You chose well, Theod. Best piece of tail I've had in a long while. No wonder the old man had her tucked away.'

There was a sudden blur of movement as the girl rammed her knife into Sigisberht's eye.

Sigisberht hurtled back and crashed to the floor. He lay with his legs splayed, and the bone handle of the girl's knife protruding from his face.

'Tiw's breath!' the captain said.

Herrad leaned forward. She hawked from deep in her throat and spat on Sigisberht's body. Mucus spattered the smooth curve of the Cherusker's belly and slid slowly towards his groin.

She had the knife all the time, Ascha realized, but must have known that if she used it against Sigisberht, the Cheruskers would kill them both.

Sigisberht's leg twitched and there was a dry whisper in his throat like the sound of windblown leaves. Ascha stepped forward and pulled the girl away. He drew his *seaxe* and placed the point of the blade in the hollow where Sigisberht's neck joined his shoulder.

He put his weight behind the blade and pushed in hard.

They put Octha on a mule with his arms strapped tight to his chest and led him away. Herrad walked beside him leading the mule by the bridle. She walked with a firm step but kept her head down, looking at no-one.

Ascha watched and grieved.

The women from the barn had been standing together in a clump like uprooted weeds, but when he looked again they had slipped away. The Franks would have left Octha's servant hanging from the beam, but the girl insisted he be buried.

The men looked to Ascha who nodded. 'Do as she says,' he said.

The Franks cut the servant down. They scraped a shallow grave outside the wall and tossed the body in. They cut the ears off the dead Cheruskkii, shared them out and then dragged the bodies out by their feet, heads cracking on the stone steps, and dropped them in the yard. All save Sigisberht who they left in Octha's house as bare-arsed naked as the day he was born with his ears hacked off, his nose cut with the slave-mark of a runaway and a girl's knife embedded in his eye.

Let Radhalla choke on that, Ascha thought.

Later, they sat on the rise and watched as the Saxons fired Thraelsted. The Saxons surrounded the town and then went in, slaughtering and burning as they went. Plumes of dark smoke belched into the sky and flattened over the roofs leaving the air bitter with the smell of burning. Tchenguiz and Gydda sat and took bets on which house would burn next. When the slave market caught fire, they threw up their arms and let out a wild whoop of joy.

They laid Octha on the grass under a tree and made a small awning out of blankets to keep off the wind and rain. Lucullus bound his hands with rags, and Herrad folded a cape and pushed it under his head. The merchant was in pain but there was little else they could do. After a while he slept, his face pasty with fatigue.

The girl sat apart with her arms crossed over her chest and her chin on her knees, her face hidden by her hair. The captain brusquely offered her water but she shook her head.

After that they let her be.

Ascha watched the girl for a long time. He picked up his cloak and went over and sat near her and considered the possibility of touching her. He didn't look at her or speak to her, and she did not smile or acknowledge him in any way. He noticed that she was trembling, quivering all over like a little animal, but whether this was from fear or cold or some other feeling he wasn't sure. He felt helpless, sick with guilt and rage, not knowing what to do.

'I'm so sorry,' he whispered clumsily and squeezed her shoulder, all out of words.

She turned, her face crumpling. 'It was not your doing,' she said. 'I chose to stay.'

He placed a careful arm around her and gently drew her to him. She was wrong: this was all down to him. He should have known what the Cheruskkii would do, should have insisted that the old man and the girl leave. He had failed to protect her and he would carry the shame of it for the rest of his days.

They remained like that with her head on his shoulder watching the town burn.

'Those poor people,' she said after a while. 'Is there nothing we can do?'

He shook his head. 'Radhalla's making the Frisians pay for Sigisberht's death.'

'But they are not responsible.'

'He knows that, but it's the only way he can get back at me.'

He felt a sudden chill, as if a dark and furtive foreboding had crept into his mind.

'He will kill you for this,' she said.

'Yes,' he said. 'If he can, he will.'

A Frank came running down the rise. He gave a passable Roman salute, his hand slapping his chest, and then said, 'The Captain said you are to come, Lord,'

The captain was lying arse uppermost staring out over the bay. He turned and beckoned Ascha with a wild, long-armed wave. 'Thought you should see this,' he said.

Ascha threw himself down. The Rhine was thick and brown, shifting slowly beneath a sky overhung with ramparts of billowing white cloud.

Ascha squinted.

The fleet was on the move. White sails unfurling and the flash of sunlight as the long boats oars rose and dipped. Slender shapes slowly turning to slip downriver. Faint cheers as the two-headed war drums called to each other across the water.

'Tiw's breath!' the captain said. 'That's a pretty sight.'

Ascha felt uneasy. Sigisberht's death would change everything. He was no longer just an escaped slave. Radhalla would know he was a Frankish agent and would guess that Ascha had warned the Franks and Romans that the fleet was on its way.

He stood. 'Radhalla knows we're watching him,' he said. 'He could be moving the fleet downriver where we can't see them.'

'You think he'd move the whole fleet to avoid you?'

'I think he might.'

'For a Saxon half-slave you have a high opinion of yourself.'

Ascha leaned to one side and spat. 'For your sake, Captain,' he said with a snarl, 'you'd better hope I didn't hear that.'

The captain opened his mouth and then closed it again.

Ascha looked back down the rise.

The merchant was awake. He lay with his hands crossed on his chest talking to Herrad, the girl kneeling on the grass beside him. Ascha watched as she took a flask and poured a little water into the old man's mouth and then wiped his lips with the edge of her skirt and sat back on her heels.

The captain said, 'We have to warn the Overlord.'

Ascha shook his head. 'We can't leave until we know for sure where they'll land.'

'The coast watchers will tell us where he makes landfall.'

'It's not enough! Radhalla could still trick us. Give me until this afternoon to see what I can find and then we'll go.'

'My orders were to stay with you until the fleet sails,' the captain said, choosing his words with care. 'I'm not waiting. I'm going back to Tornacum.'

'What is this? You can't go.'

The captain looked at Ascha with pale blue eyes. 'I've given twenty years of my life to the Overlord's service, worked my way up. It's not been easy but I did it. And then you come along and in no time you're top of the shit-pile, bosom-friends with Bauto, hobknobbing with the Overlord.' The Frank's lip lifted in a sneer. 'How could someone like you do what you have done?' he said, his voice dripping with scorn. 'You're a half-slave, not even a Frank. You stay if you want, but we're leaving.'

Ascha swore.

He couldn't leave without knowing the Saxon landing point. It was not enough to know the fleet had sailed. Was Radhalla going for Roman Gallia or Frankland? Know that and you could catch the Saxons on the back foot. Drive them into the sea. But how could he manage without the Franks' help?

'Do whatever you have to do,' he said coldly. 'Tell the Overlord the fleet is on its way. He will want to know.'

He watched as the Franks saddled their horses, mounted up and rode out. He felt a weight of disappointment but pushed it away. It's all a game, he thought. He shook his head and went to join Herrad and the merchant, squatting down beside them.

'How are you, old man?' he said, his eyes directed at the girl.

'I've been better,' Octha said. Herrad put a hand on his shoulder and Octha patted it. She had bandaged her wrists with cloth torn from her dress and had wound up her hair and tied it. 'Those Saxon bastards have burnt my home,' Octha murmured. He looked up at Ascha. 'Why did the Franks leave?'

'The fleet has put to sea and the Franks are going back to Tornacum'

Ascha saw Octha and Herrad exchange worried glances.

'What will you do now?' she said. Her voice was calm but sombre.

He rubbed his chin and got to his feet. 'I'm going to take a look around. See if I can find some food. Stay here and whatever you do, don't move or show yourselves.'

'Will you be coming back?' she said, and he saw the alarm in her eyes.

He looked at her and gave her a quick smile. 'Yes,' he said. 'I'll be coming back.'

25

He left Gydda and Lucullus with the old man and the girl while he and Tchenguiz mounted and rode down to Thraelsted. The track was thronged with people who had fled when the Saxons came and were now making their way back. They came out of the forest in small and furtive groups, pushing handcarts and carrying bedding. When they heard the riders, they ran off the road and Ascha saw them skulking in the trees, waiting for them to pass.

The *castellum* was a burnt and roofless shell, the floor a mess of charred and broken beams. Octha's sheds had been looted, and his animals lay dead in the field. Ascha and Tchenguiz dismounted and went through the outbuildings looking for food. Ashes drifted over their feet. On a shelf at the back of the house, Ascha found two blackened pots of beans covered with ashes. He blew off the ash and took the pots away. A couple of hens had survived the flames and were pecking in the yard. Tchenguiz chased and caught them. Wrenching off their heads, he tied them by the legs to his saddle.

They rode on toward Thraelsted.

Villagers stood in the smoking ruins of their homes and silently watched them go by. They walked their horses to a low bluff and shivered in the cold salt wind that came roaring off the river. They heard the slow smack of water and the cries of the gulls hanging in the air. The fleet was in full sail, heading towards the open sea, oars dipping as the longships struggled to make headway against the wind.

They rode down to the harbour where, a lifetime ago, Kral had unloaded his slave cargo. The beach was a carnage of debris and discarded loot. Rigging, sailcloth and sodden driftwood hung sluggishly in the water while barrels, tubs and broken oars bobbed on the rising tide.

A knot of Frisians stood at the water's edge staring out to sea. When they saw Tchenguiz and Ascha they turned and watched them warily. A man and a boy were sitting on a rock, their eyes fixed on the retreating fleet. Ascha turned the horse's head and rode towards them.

He greeted them and said, 'Where's the fleet gone?'

The man looked at him and spat. 'They've gone to Gallia,' he said. 'Everyone knows that.'

'But where, man? Where in Gallia?'

The Frisian shrugged. The child hung on his father's elbow and stared.

Tchenguiz touched Ascha lightly on the arm, 'Boss?' he said and pointed.

There was a shadow in the water in the middle of the bay. At first he thought it was a rock, a thick grey fist of stone lying in the sand and mud over which waves broke and fell.

His horse shook its head. He pulled the reins to go when there was a shout from Tchenguiz. He looked back and saw Tchenguiz urging his horse down the bank and into the water. Ascha peered, and his mouth dropped.

The rock was a man and he was tied to a stake, up to his neck in water, and the waves already breaking over his head. Ascha kicked his horse and followed Tchenguiz, splashing through the shallows.

'You there! Who are you?' he cried.

The man's head turned, but it might have been the motion of the waves.

Ascha hesitated. Ever since Wulfhere had chased him onto the ice and he had fallen through, he had hated water. He dropped the reins and slid off the horse. The water was icy cold. He shuddered and began to wade towards the stake.

'Boss!' he heard Tchenguiz call.

'Stay back, Tchenguiz!'

The beach shelved gently, the tide rising, almost at the turn.

And then it struck him. The people on the shore hadn't been watching the fleet. They'd been waiting for the man at the stake to die. The man was slumped, struggling to raise his head above the waves. As Ascha watched, he stirred and coughed and gasped for air, letting out a low wail.

Ascha stiffened.

Hanno!

He dived headlong into the water.

Hanno's head was now under water. Please Tiw, let him not be chained, nothing he could do against chains. Half a dozen strokes, and he was there. He slid his hands down the stake's cold hardness, found the rope and fumbled in his tunic for his long-knife. With one pass he cut the coils, pulled Hanno away and grabbed him by the shoulders and kicked with all his strength.

A wave rolled him over. Salt water filled his throat and he felt himself going under. Panic enveloped him. He kicked wildly, dragging Hanno towards shore, he felt gravel rolling under his feet and then two strong hands lifted him by the shoulders and dragged him into the shallows.

Coughing and spewing water, he got to his hands and knees. Tchenguiz was kneeling over Hanno who lay face down on the sand. There were spoor marks in the sand where Tchenguiz had dragged him up the beach. Ascha stumbled and raised Hanno by the shoulder. His brother's skin was cold and clammy. He seemed lifeless.

A chill crept through Ascha's heart. 'Hanno, it's me, Ascha. Can you hear me?'

Hanno opened his eyes.

He coughed suddenly and sobbed clinging to Ascha, holding him as if he never wanted to let him go. Tchenguiz handed Ascha a horse blanket. Ascha wrapped Hanno and held him tight to stop the shivering.

'I misjudged tha,' Hanno slurred. 'Tha was right!' His teeth were chattering, and he was shivering uncontrollably.

Ascha stroked Hanno's head, the hair thick with salt and mud and then Hanno's eyes closed and he passed out.

Was this what it had come to? First one brother and now the other, a slow death, staked out on the mudflat and left to drown.

He gripped Hanno by the arm and shook him violently. 'Hanno, listen to me! The fleet! Where has Radhalla taken the fleet?'

Hanno opened his eyes and whispered.

Ascha bent and put his ear to Hanno's mouth.

'Gesoriac,' Hanno mumbled drowsily.

'*Gesoriac*? South or north?'

'South. They're making for Parisi.'

Ascha shook him again. His brother's head lolled and his eyes flickered sleepily.

'Tha's sure it's south of Gesoriac?'

Hanno rolled his head. 'Radhalla said it when he staked me.'

Ascha felt a wave of relief. At last! Now he knew where the fleet was heading. He had Radhalla exactly where he wanted him. He smacked his fist into the palm of his hand and got to his feet.

'Don't leave me!' Hanno suddenly screamed. He cast about, arms flailing, and found Ascha's legs and held them tight, his hands like claws.

Tchenguiz pulled Hanno back and looked up at Ascha. Ascha knew what he was thinking. Hanno would slow them down. But he couldn't leave him.

He bent and squeezed his brother's shoulder.

'On our father's memory,' he whispered. 'I promise!'

When they got back to the camp he jumped down, lifted Hanno off the horse, carried him over to the fire and laid him on the grass. Herrad and Lucullus came running up.

'Who is this?' Herrad said.

'My brother,' he gasped. 'Can you help him?'

She knelt and cupped her hand across Hanno's brow, and he heard her intake of breath.

'Get these wet clothes off him,' she said sharply. 'And you too or you'll catch your death.'

Lucullus and Tchenguiz peeled off Hanno's clothes. They wrapped him in the blanket, lifted him and laid him by the fire. Ascha watched as Lucullus felt Hanno's wrist and checked his eyes.

A tremor ran through him and his teeth began to chatter in his head. He turned away and undid his belt and quickly took off his clothes. He kicked off his boots and stood naked and shivering, fish white save for his face and arms. Tchenguiz grinned and threw him a blanket and he wrapped it around himself.

Gydda came with dry wood, got the fire going and, as the dry brush took hold, Ascha felt the fire's warmth work its way into his bones. He sat and shuddered while Lucullus and Herrad knelt beside Hanno and talked in muted tones. Octha lay some way off, saying nothing.

Sparks rose and floated and then fell to earth.

Herrad picked up Ascha's sodden clothes, twisted them to wring out the water and then shook them out and draped them over a bush.

'Get closer,' she said, speaking over her shoulder. 'You're too wet to burn.'

He shuffled towards the fire. 'We have to go,' he said through chattering teeth. 'We have to warn Bauto. Radhalla is sailing to Gesoriac and will march on Parisi.'

Octha woke up. 'Parisi?' Ascha heard him mutter. 'Why would Radhalla march on Parisi?'

They went down to the burnt-out *castellum*. They found Octha's boat untouched and sailed across the slow water, Octha and Herrad, Ascha and his companions, and Hanno. It was a rough crossing, the ship blown across the grey river, whitecaps scudding before the wind. They took an old waterproofed cloth and rigged it to keep the rain off their heads but the wind blew the rain in sideways and soaked them to the bone. Gydda and Tchenguiz huddled together. They gripped the sides and blinked salt-spray from their eyes, their faces sheened with greasy sweat. Ascha drew his knees up to his chin, pulled his cloak over his head and kept his eyes firmly on the distant shore. Herrad sat in the stern with her head bowed and her eyes closed. She rolled a strand of her hair around her fingers and seemed oblivious to the cold. Once she opened her eyes and saw him looking at her. He quickly looked away. It unsettled him, her coolness in the face of all she'd gone through.

They went back across the river and brought over the mule and the two horses. When they finished it was late in the afternoon and dusk was falling. He fretted that he was losing time. He thought of the Saxon fleet struggling to clear the Rhine mouth and hoped the wind had delayed them. He still had to warn Bauto and it was a long ride to Gesoriac. But he felt responsible for Octha, Herrad and Hanno and was reluctant to leave them.

Gydda built a fire. Lucullus spitted the chickens and roasted them. They ate the food and waited for nightfall. Gydda and Tchenguiz sat away from the fire and talked. Herrad covered Octha with a blanket and stayed with him until he fell asleep. Ascha laid his back against a tree and watched over Hanno. His brother slept fitfully, jerking, moaning and letting out strange little cries.

He saw the girl get to her feet and walk out through the trees towards the grassy sweep of the riverbank. On impulse, he rose and followed her. An old path ran along the riverbank. She turned, saw him and walked on. He fell into step beside her, pushing through knee-high grasses and weeds that rustled softly. They walked together in silence, no more than a hand's breadth between them, their shoulders hunched against the river wind, listening to the frogs croaking in the marshes. She did not look at him again but kept her eyes before her as if waiting for him to speak.

'How do you feel?'

'How do you think I feel,' she said, without malice.

He let it go.

'I'm leaving for Gesoriac tomorrow. I have to warn the Franks the Saxons are coming.'

'What will become of us?'

'You should go to Tornacum. You will be safer there.'

'Will you help us?'

'Yes,' he said, and paused. 'Can Lucullus be trusted?'

She thought before answering. 'Yes, you can trust him.'

'He wouldn't betray me?'

'No,' she said. 'Lucullus would never do that.' She thought for a moment and then said, 'Is there anyone you trust, Carver?'

He turned away, thinking she was laughing at him, but the idea that he had forgotten how to trust shocked him.

They were passing a small ruined building that stood back from the river, half buried in a grove of trees. Ascha glanced around. A stone altar covered with weeds and broken walls patched with red plaster. The pillars that had once supported a roof of baked tiles lay in the long grass like bones on a beach.

'What is that place?' he said, wanting to hear her talk.

She gave the ruin a fleeting look. 'It's a shrine,' she said. 'The Romans had many gods before they accepted the true faith.'

He gazed at her in surprise, 'Do you have a faith?'

'Yes,' she said. 'Don't you?'

He shrugged. 'I don't know what I believe.'

'You should have a faith,' she said. 'You are not God to decide your own destiny.'

He swept a hand like a scythe through the grass and breathed in deep. 'I've learned to carve my own destiny,' he said. 'It's better that way.'

'You can't find truth on your own,' she said.

Her hair had come loose. She took a comb and wound her hair in a coil and deftly tied it, her bracelets jangling faintly at her wrists.

'You believe your god protects you?'

'I believe it every moment of every day,' she said.

He shook his head, her quiet conviction suddenly irritating. 'Where was your god when my mother was taken as a slave?' he said, hearing the dry rasp in his voice. 'And where was he when Sigisberht came calling?'

He regretted the words as soon as they had left his mouth.

She turned and faced him. Her eyes glistened and her cheeks were flushed.

'You are right. God was not there to protect me!' she said. 'But God made sure that man paid for what he did to me.'

He pictured Sigisberht sprawled on his back with the girl's knife in his eye. No arguing with that, he thought.

A strand of hair had fallen, and she pushed it back behind her ear. And it was with that small gesture he felt something he had not felt before. He no longer cared about her life with Octha, or what had happened with Sigisberht. He loved her, and that was all there was to it. The realization came to him with no surprise, and it occurred to him that he had always known.

Chastened, he said, 'I didn't mean to hurt you.'

She glanced at him, and her face softened. 'You are a good man, Carver, but you want too much. It is not wise to reach so high.'

'You think I should stay a half-slave, digging shit-pits and waiting on tables for the rest of my life?' he said hoarsely. All he had ever wanted was to be the same as his brothers. To be free of the shame and the feeling of worthlessness that had dogged him as long as he could remember.

'No, but everything you could be is already within you. Work for the Franks if you must but none of this will bring you peace of mind. Only you can give yourself that.'

She picked up her skirts and left him, her small strong back driving her on.

He watched her go and wondered what his mother would have made of her.

The next morning, Ascha crawled out of his blanket as a pale cold light moved up from the east. He sat for a moment trying to open his eyes and then he pulled on his boots, picked up his long-knife and pushed it in his belt.

He shook Tchenguiz by the shoulder. 'C'mon! We have work to do.'

While Tchenguiz rolled their blankets and saddled their mounts, Ascha kicked Lucullus awake and took him aside.

'I want you to do something for me,' he said.

Lucullus said nothing.

Ascha hesitated. 'I want you and Gydda to take the old man, Hanno and Herrad to Tornacum. Cross the bridge at Ceuclum and take the stone road south. When you get there, go to the Basilica and ask for Flavinius. Tell him I sent you. Ask him to send the Greek physician to my brother and to Octha. There is a *mansio*, an inn, outside the town walls on the road to Lutetia Parisi. Put the old man there. Then go to Flavinius and stay there until I come for you.'

Ascha pulled out the leather bag of coins that Flavinius had given him and handed it to Lucullus. 'Take this. Buy whatever you need.'

Lucullus shook the bag and tapped out a few solidi into his palm, the gold gleaming brightly in the sunshine. He touched the tiny coins with his finger and looked at Ascha in astonishment.

Ascha gripped him by the arm.

'Do this for me and I will reward you, Lucullus. But if you abandon them or harm them in any way, I will come for you, I will find you and I will hang you from the highest tree.'

'I understand,' Lucullus said.

Ascha took the reins of his horse from Tchenguiz. He tightened the girth and then threw himself on its back.

Gydda grinned and raised a huge hand. 'Gydda will see you both in Tornacum,' he said. Lucullus weighed the bag of gold in his hand and gave Ascha a tight smile. Ascha and Tchenguiz wheeled their horses. They twisted in the saddle, waved goodbye to Octha and the girl and then they headed west.

26

Gesoriac. A walled town on the cliff top on the edge of the sea. Below the town, at the foot of the cliffs was a small harbour strewn with vessels and fringed by a cluster of tiny grey houses. The Frankish warcamp lay on the cliffs outside the town and was a shambling city of wagons, tents and makeshift huts.

They had ridden all day and through the night. They arrived sore and weary. In the camp Frankish troops repaired weapons, whetting blades and re-hafting spears. Horsemen rode up and down between the tents, harness jingling, yelling at men to get out of their way. There were shouts and cries and the harsh din of armourers beating iron. The wind brought the dry smell of dust and horse dung mingled with the tang of the sea.

Bauto's tent lay in the middle of the camp. Ascha pulled up and slid achingly to the ground. He handed the reins to Tchenguiz and approached the tent. This time there was no delay. As soon as he gave his name, he was admitted. His star was rising.

Inside, all was stir and bustle. Bauto sat on one side of a long plank table, talking to two high-born Franks. Armed Antrustions flanked his seat, a fighter watched the doorway, and a crowd of clerks armed with scrolls crowded the back of the tent.

'Ah, it's you, Saxon,' Bauto said when he saw him. 'I'd given you up for lost.' He gave him a big leathery smile and clasped Ascha's hand. He gestured to the Franks. 'You know Lords Charibald and Ingoald.'

Ascha gave them a stiff nod. 'We be of one blood,' he said courteously.

The Franks were tall men, heavy in build but without fat. Charibald wore the crushed nose of a fighter and a grizzled beard, while Ingoald had a thick moustache and an old war wound in the middle of his forehead deep enough to hold three fingers. They glanced at him casually as if he were dirt on their boot.

Still the half-slave.

Bauto placed both hands on his knees and leaned forward. 'What news?'

'We came here direct from the Rhinemouth. The Saxon fleet has sailed.'

The three of them stared at him open mouthed. 'When?'

'The day before yesterday.'

'Holy Tiw!' said Bauto. He lurched to his feet, looked around the room and slowly sat down again.

A long silence while they took it in.

'How long do we have?'

'One day, perhaps two,' Ascha said. 'They're sailing into a head wind which will have slowed them down some, but they can't be far behind us.'

Charibald flashed a glance at Bauto and leaned in.

'Which way are they heading?' he said.

'South of Gesoriac. Probably the mouth of the Samara. I think they're making for Parisi,' he said with conviction, quietly pleased he had the last piece of information.

'That's a long haul,' Ingoald said.

'Yes.'

'You sure of this?' Bauto burst out. 'Saxons can't be trusted. You of all people should know that.'

'Yes,' he said. 'I'm sure.'

He told them how he had discovered Hanno on the beach at Thraelsted and what Hanno had overheard.

Bauto scratched his chin and then grinned, showing big white teeth.

'There always was more to you than a half-slave,' he said with a sly smile. 'Think of what you could have done if you'd been born a free man?'

Bauto saw the look on Ascha's face and barked with sudden laughter. 'Na, you've done well,' he said. He slapped Ascha on the back and turned to speak to a slave. The slave went away and came back with bread, sausage and wine. Bauto sloshed the wine into beakers and handed them round. 'Here's to victory!' he said, holding up his beaker. 'And the slaughter of our enemies.'

'To Victory!' the Franks shouted, 'and the slaughter of our enemies.'

Charibald and Ingoald tipped their heads back and drank. They then smacked their lips, laughed and held out their beakers for more. Ascha, still smarting from Bauto's jibe, took a mouthful of wine and let it trickle down his throat. If he had been born free, he wondered, would his life have been different? And would he have grown up like his father, or like Hanno or Hroc?

He shook his head, with no way of knowing.

The sky was vastly blue and distant, swept with wisps of white cloud. Ascha sat on his horse looking out over an ocean that was wide, clean and empty. The wind gusted, nudging his cloak and bringing the smell of the sea, warm and thick.

That morning, he and Tchenguiz had watched Bauto lead the Frankish army out of Gesoriac, the column winding south like some vast iron-clawed serpent. They had sat on their horses by the side of the road and watched the wagons trundle by, listening to the rattle of harness, the scrape of iron on leather and the sullen tramp of booted feet.

Now the air was full of listless heat.

The sun beat down with all its aching power, flashing off helmets, prickling the men's eyes and flaming their pale northern skin.

A month earlier and all this would have been a sea of soft-swaying wheat, but now the fields were stubble and dry earth. The dust rose in clouds, working its way under their shoulder straps, rubbing their shoulders raw. Every man chewed the grit kicked up by the man in front.

He drew a flask from his belt and pulled out the stopper with his teeth. Dribbling water on his neckcloth, he rubbed it about his face and under his chin. He was beginning to feel uneasy. They'd seen nothing of the Saxon fleet, not a ripple. Even with the winds against them, the fleet should be in sight. Ascha sighed and wiped his brow. He drank from the flask, retied his neckscarf and then turned his horse to the south.

Mid-afternoon Ascha and Tchenguiz came upon Bauto and his captains. They were by the side of the road watching the *scara* go by. Ascha dismounted. The Franks had barely greeted him when there was the sound of drumming hooves and two scouts rode up and reined in. Their horses were covered in dust and sweat and looked worn out. The men slid off their horses and saluted wearily.

'What do you have?' said Bauto.

'Nothing, Lord. We have searched the coast in both directions but there's no sign of them.'

Bauto scowled and flashed Ascha an accusing look.

Ascha bit his lip. 'It's not possible,' he said. He had a sudden bile-sharp foretaste that something was wrong. Where was the fleet? How could they have been delayed this long?

'Maybe they went back to Frisia.' Bauto said.

'No, he has to make his move now or he'll lose his chance.'

'You're sure it was below Gesoriac?' Bauto said.

Ascha shook his head with irritation. They'd been over this. 'That's what Hanno heard Radhalla say before they staked him.'

He felt a sudden shudder of doubt. He and Bauto both looked at one another sharing the same thought.

'He's tricked you, you stupid prick!' Bauto said and gave an angry laugh.

Ascha clawed his fingers through his hair. If the information was wrong then either Radhalla had changed his mind or Radhalla had never planned to land south of Gesoriac. Which meant that Hanno had deliberately misled him or Radhalla had cold-bloodedly staked Hanno out on the mud and given him false information, knowing that if found alive he would pass it on.

Ascha felt sick to the pit of his stomach. Somehow, he'd been duped and his hopes of obtaining his freedom and taking revenge on Radhalla were drifting like summer mist.

'But if he's landed, where the fuck is he?' said Ingoald.

'Could be anywhere between the Rhine and Hispania,' Charibald muttered darkly.

'No,' Bauto said. 'He has to be further north, somewhere along this coast, or we would have seen them.'

Ascha swivelled in the saddle and looked back along the cliffs. And then it came to him. 'He's not raiding the coast. He's already broken out. He's driving inland.'

'Inland? But where to?'

'Tornacum. He's making for Tornacum,' he said and felt his stomach churn.

They looked at him blankly.

'He'll not do it,' Charibald breathed. 'He wouldn't dare.'

Bauto's face was set hard. 'He might. And if he succeeds in punching his way through to Tornacum...' He let his words drift.

The Franks looked at each other, and Ascha knew what they were thinking. The Overlord was in Tornacum, as was the treasure house of the Franks, and the grave of Childeric, father of the Frankish nation. Take Tornacum and you could go anywhere, Colonia, Cambarac, Parisi, the Rhine. The Franks would be headless and with the Frankish *scara* chasing their own tail in the south, there'd be nothing to stop you. You'd be master of northern Gallia in weeks, and the Overlord's dreams for Greater Francia would be no more than a fireside memory. Ascha swore viciously. But that wasn't all, was it? Because he'd sent Octha and the girl to Tornacum. And Hanno! He'd put his brother and his friends right in the path of the Saxon host. He'd been so sure of himself and now they were all in mortal danger.

'He might already be there,' Charibald said gloomily.

'No, not yet,' Bauto said. 'But he's got a head start. And it will take us time to turn the army around and send word to Syagrius and Ragnachar.' He leaned over and spat onto the half-bare ground. 'Our only chance now is to try and slow Radhalla down. If we can do that, we can buy time.'

'I'll go,' Ascha said.

Bauto gazed at him, unblinking. 'Don't you think you've done enough,' he growled.

Ascha felt his heart thump. 'I have to go,' he said. 'The report was mine, and it's only right that I take care of it.'

Bauto rolled his lower lip and then nodded. 'Ride to Tornacum. Get the Overlord and the queen away to safety before the Saxons get to them. Then find the Saxons and do what you can to delay them. I'll send word to Syagrius and Ragnachar to meet us at Tornacum.'

He grabbed Ascha by the wrist and pulled him close. 'We ain't always seen eye to eye, but I'm relying on you now. Delay Radhalla, or we're lost!'

27

It was late by the time Ascha and Tchenguiz rode through the gates of Tornacum. The town was on the edge of panic. News of the approaching Saxons had travelled, and the streets were jammed with people trying to get across the river before the northerners came.

We've let them down, Ascha thought. No-one thought Radhalla would penetrate this far inland. They rode through the winding alleyways, into the market square and pulled up outside the Basilica. He wished now he had left Herrad, the merchant and Hanno back in Thraelsted instead of sending them here. He would have to find them, but first he had to get Clovis away and do what he could to delay Radhalla. Ascha slid off his horse, gave the reins to a waiting boy and ran up the steps

'Tchenguiz! With me,' he called over his shoulder, and went through the doors.

Inside was chaos and confusion. Clerks scurried to and fro, carrying scrolls and books and storing them in chests which were stacked as high as a man ready to be carried away. At the far end of the hall, he could see clerks feeding documents into a blazing fire. Ascha and Tchenguiz passed quickly down the hall, their feet echoing on the flagstones. Hearing them approach, the clerks looked up in sudden alarm and then went back to their work.

They found the Overlord pacing up and down outside his chamber, biting his knuckle. Every so often he stopped and issued orders to servants who immediately scurried away. He had a sword strapped to his hip and was attended by a nervous posse of Antrustions who shouted and glared at the approaching intruders with hostile eyes.

Clovis turned to see what the din was about 'Ah, Theodling,' he said. He was dressed in a plain woollen tunic dyed green and edged in red, and a short fur-lined cape which he had pulled close around him and pinned with a heavy red metal brooch. He threw Tchenguiz a look of barely concealed distaste and then turned and led the way into his chamber gesturing for Ascha to close the door behind them. There was no fire in the hearth and the air was dank and chill.

Ascha shivered.

'Well?' Clovis snapped, and Ascha felt the Overlord's cold grey eyes fall upon him.

'Saxons, Lord! They're coming and you're in grave danger.'

'What do you mean, coming?' Clovis hissed. 'They're already here!' He jabbed a bony finger towards the window. Off to the west, the sky was lit with an orange glow. 'Those are Frankish farms and villages burning. You were supposed to keep them out. I was relying on you! How could you let this happen?'

'We lost the fleet,' Ascha said. 'Radhalla outwitted us. By the time we'd realized what had happened they'd already landed.'

It sounded lame, and he knew it.

Clovis closed his eyes and shook his head in disbelief. 'How on Tiw's fucking earth could you lose a whole fucking fleet?' he spat. 'How long do we have?'

'Two days, maybe less.'

'Two days? As long as that?' the Overlord said, with heavy sarcasm. 'You're telling me those murdering savages could be in Tornacum within a couple of days?'

'Yes.'

Clovis walked over to the fireplace. He leaned his forehead against the wall, breathed in deep and then he turned and pointed at Ascha, his eyes hard as stones. 'Listen! If the Saxons take this town, they will take Francia. And if we fall, it will mean the end of Rome in this province. I shall be killed and everything I have worked for since my father died will be finished. Everything! Do you understand?'

'I understand,' Ascha said, holding his gaze.

'No, I don't think you do,' Clovis said nastily. 'You see, if I die, you get nothing. You go back to being a Saxon half-slave. That's if Radhalla chooses to keep you alive, which I doubt. He turned suddenly and shouted to no-one in particular, 'And where is Bauto and my *scara*? Where are my warlords when I need them? The bastards will pay for abandoning me like this. They are traitors, all of them. Traitors!'

'Tell him he must leave,' Tchenguiz whispered, looking Clovis over, not trustfully.

'Bauto is coming,' Ascha said. 'So is Governor Syagrius with his Romans. And Bauto has sent for your uncle. But we have to get you away from here.'

He hesitated, doubting his words as soon as they'd left his mouth. Would Ragnachar come to his nephew's aid or would he choose this moment to seize power for himself?

'I'm not going anywhere,' Clovis said, jerking his eyes around as if the Saxon horde were already pouring through the door with axes raised. 'I'm the Overlord of the Franks and it's a question of honour.' He chewed his thumb, biting hard until the blood smeared his lip. 'I will send my mother away to Cambarac, but I'm staying.'

'You must leave!' Ascha burst out. 'We can't defend the city. The walls are broken and there are too many entrances. They would overrun us like rats.'

'If the Saxons want me they can come and get me,' Clovis said grimly. 'Tornacum is my city and is sacred to the Frankish people. I insist that we stay here and defend it.'

Ascha had half expected this but if the Overlord of the Franks chose to stay there was't much he could do about it. 'Very well, Lord,' he said. 'We will do what we can to defend the city.'

The Overlord would forget his honour soon enough once Radhalla had him hog-tied and burning over an open fire.

Clovis gave him a thin smile. 'I knew you wouldn't abandon me.' He put one hand up and gently patted Ascha's face. Ascha clenched his jaw and pulled away. Anger flared in the Overlord's eyes and then faded. He let out a long sigh and laid an arm around Ascha's neck, squeezing his shoulder and digging his nails into the skin until Ascha winced. 'Well, Theodling. It seems that once again my life is in your hands. What troops did you bring?'

'I have no troops, Lord. I came alone.'

Clovis stared in astonished disbelief. 'Well then, it's hopeless!' he whispered. He threw his hands in the air and gave a harsh and brittle laugh. 'We'll all die together!'

'Nothing is hopeless,' Ascha said. 'What horse troops do you have?'

Clovis rubbed his jaw. 'There's a few mounted Antrustions and a unit of Roman auxiliaries that Syagrius lent us. You can have those.'

'Auxiliaries? From which province,' Ascha asked. He wanted nothing more to do with the captain and his mounted Antrustions.

'Roman. They're Roman,' Clovis said testily.

'I know, but from which province?' Ascha said.

Clovis shrugged his shoulders. 'I think they're Pritanni. What difference does it make?'

Pritanni. His mother's people.

'Horse troops could find Radhalla and delay him until the army moves up,' Ascha murmured.

'You won't stop those Saxon murderers with a few horse soldiers.'

'We don't have to stop them. Just cut them off and chew them up a little.'

Clovis looked at him and then nodded. 'Horse troops could do that,' he said.

The Roman auxiliaries were camped in a field by the side of the road to Colonia, their horses hobbled in the shade of some nearby trees. Ascha reined in and looked them over. About fifty men, he thought. Rough-looking and unshaven with dirty hair tied back and kerchiefs knotted round grimy throats. Can't have been easy, he thought, fighting alongside the Franks, but they seemed well-armed and well-mounted.

The Pritanni watched him with dark and impenetrable eyes.

He nudged his horse forward.

As he did so, one of the Pritanni stepped forward. Youngish, mid-twenties, scrawny-thin with curly brown hair that hung to his shoulders. His woollen tunic was filthy but had once been pure white with blood-red edging. He had a shabby look about him, but Ascha saw that his wargear was clean and bright. He wore a mailcoat and carried a long sword at his hip.

Ascha addressed him in Latin. 'Do you command here?'

The man nodded. 'I am Rufus Basilius,' he said, speaking the same language. 'We are from the 5th *vexillatio* of the Legio II Britannica, responsible for defending the Saxon shore in this sector.'

'My name is Ascha Aelfricson. I am a royal hostage in the service of the Frankish Overlord.'

The other nodded politely. 'I have heard of you. You are the half-slave, no? The one they call the Carver?'

Ascha told the Pritanni that although he was born a half-slave, his mother was high-born and had grown up in their island. For as long as he could remember, she had refused to speak to him in the

278

language of pagans and barbarians and spoke instead in Latin, the language of heaven. He told them how his mother used to tell him stories of their island, speaking softly of cool woods and rolling hills, of fresh streams and slow rivers, bustling red-roofed towns and the seething green-grey ocean that girded the land of her birth.

He told them that he knew they had suffered at the hands of the northern pirates and knew too that they hated the Saxon terror-raiders more than any wild beast. He told them how the Cheruskkii had killed his brother, burnt his village and murdered his friends. Now was the time, he said, to avenge their people. Rome and Rome's allies needed them, and with their help they could strike a blow for God against the murdering dogs that had consumed half their land.

When he had finished, Rufus said quietly, 'What is it you want of us?'

'The Saxon wolf pack has already landed and is marching on Tornacum,' he said. 'The Franks want us to delay them until Bauto's army comes up. We will travel light and we will travel fast. You will take your weapons, water and a bedroll. If any man falls behind we will leave him.'

The auxiliaries looked at each other and then at Ascha. Rufus leaned over and spat in the dust. He seemed to think for a moment and then gave a slow nod.

When Ascha gave the order to mount up and move out, the Pritanni did so without a word.

Ascha led the Pritanni out of Tornacum, riding northwest across the grassy plains. He drove them hard, wanting to find the Saxons before they came close to Tornacum. The day was dry and sunny. Ascha looked up at a blue sky scuffed with clouds and felt the sun's heat on his neck. His shirt stuck to his back and the sweat ran down his spine. They came to a crossroads, and he turned and led them north, towards the sea. It was some time later when they came across a clear stream running through a shady copse of trees, and Ascha called a halt.

The Pritanni rode into the water, dropped their reins and slid off their horses' backs. The horses drank, sucking water in long draughts, and then the Prianni stretched their aching bodies and lay down in a mass of fern and bracken. They listened to the sound of running water and birdsong and let the sunlight caress their faces.

Rufus sank to the ground beside Ascha.

'Do you know this country?'

'Yes, I was here once before when I was a hostage.'

'Where are we going?'

'I know a place. It lies across the Saxons' path.'

'Is that where we will wait for them?'

'Yes.'

'How is it called?'

'Viroviac,' he said. 'It is called Viroviac.'

The auxiliaries drank their fill of water, filled their flasks and then mounted up and went on. They rode in silence through a landscape bursting with summer foliage, warm yellow light slanting through dappled leaves. It had rained only the day before and the grass was green and lush. The light was fading when they reached Viroviac. There was little to see. The remains of a Roman watch tower and a few mud-daubed cabins. The village was deserted, every house shuttered and barred. Hens cackled and scratched, goats bleated and pigs ran loose in the street.

The auxiliaries made camp. They killed a pig, roasted it and dipped into their food sacks for hunks of grey bread and cheese. Later, they cleaned their weapons and talked of the day to come. Some spent the night in the village, the rest slept under the trees. A few wandered off to sleep in the watchtower, but soon came back, fearful of the spirits.

Ascha and Rufus were on a ridge facing the sea, reins drawn in close. The day was blistering hot, the clouds thick and white like bundles of sun-dried linen. Ascha had sent Tchenguiz and the scouts prowling out to the west to find Radhalla. Now he and Rufus sat, resting their fists on their saddle pommels, waiting for them to return. Ascha turned and heard the saddle creak. The Roman troopers were strung out down the reverse slope of the ridge. Horses stood under the trees and stamped and shifted from leg to leg. They jerked their heads and whiffled in long shuddering sighs. The men chewed hard biscuit and spoke in subdued tones. Some poured water into their cupped hands for the animals to drink. One trooper had wrapped a scrawny arm around the neck of his mare and was crooning soft words into her ear, as a lover would.

'Rider coming!' a Roman called. 'I think it's the Hun.'

Ascha looked back and saw Tchenguiz riding towards them. He rode fast, jumping the field ditches and slipping effortlessly between the trees. They watched as he galloped up the ridge and came to a halt in a cloud of dust.

'Teach him to mind his manners!' Rufus scowled, blinking the grit from his eye.

'What is it?' Ascha said, grabbing the Hun's bridle.

'They're coming,' Tchenguiz said, drawing in great heaves of air. He pointed back the way he had come. 'Many men,' he gasped. 'Be here in half a day.'

Ascha felt his heart begin to race. 'Heading which way?'

'Tornacum,' Tchenguiz said. 'They're heading for Tornacum.'

28

Out on the plain it seemed as if the earth itself was alive and moving. A dark mass of men and wagons was flowing on an unturned course across the landscape, trailed by a roiling cloud of dust. He could see the shimmer of iron weapons and in his mind he could hear the rumble and squeak of scores of wagons.

Ascha moistened his lips and shifted his position slightly in the saddle. 'Get the men mounted and formed up, single column,' he said. 'We'll wait for them to get close and then hit them in the flank and rear. It's open ground. Good riding. Do it right and we can scatter them, maybe buy ourselves some time.'

Rufus breathed in deep. 'There's a lot of them.'

'Then we'll have to reduce their numbers,' Ascha shouted angrily. 'The one thing Saxons fear more than anything is horse soldiers. And we have the advantage of surprise.'

Rufus nodded and turned away. Ascha took his helmet from the pommel and pulled it on. He fastened the ties under his chin and then he gathered his rein, touched the horse with his heels and moved out.

Ascha led them over the rise and down the dusty slope. When they reached the bottom, they turned and trotted along the base of the ridge towards the Saxon rear. Off to his left, Ascha could hear the tramp of feet and the chink of iron on iron, the rumbling of wooden wheels and the rattle of harness. His heart was thumping with excitement and his mouth had gone dry, but he felt calmer than he had since Gesoriac. He plucked a leaf from a branch and chewed it. Do this right, he thought, and there was a skinny hope they could disrupt the Saxons enough to delay them.

Ascha gave the order, and the Romans wheeled and broke into a quickening trot, bridles jangling and horses snorting. Tchenguiz was at Ascha's side. A young Roman trumpeter rode with them, holding his long brass trumpet tightly in his fist as if it were a weapon. The trumpeter was nervous. He licked his lips and shifted in his seat, blinking constantly.

Iron scraped on leather as the Romans hoisted their shields and drew their swords. Ascha drew his own *spatha* from its scabbard and laid it against his shoulder.

Sweet Tiw! Let me not disgrace myself.

'Keep tight,' he called. 'Keep tight and hit them hard.'

They came out at the rear of the Saxon host, a ragged edge frayed with stragglers, the foot-sore and the hangers-on. As they heard the sound of drumming hooves, the hindmost Saxons looked back over their shoulders. They gaped in amazement and then in horror as they saw what was coming. They began to flee, running wildly with no thought of where they were going, no thought but the need to get away from the riders bearing down on them.

Ascha lifted his *spatha*. 'Sound the charge!' he yelled.

The trumpeter put his horn to his lips.

Nothing.

'Come on, man! You can do it,' Ascha shouted.

The trumpeter spat and put the trumpet again to his lips. A stuttering false note, and then he blew.

'*Jubilate in Christo!*' the Pritanni screamed. The troops kicked their horses from a trot into a canter and then into a gallop. The horses tossed their heads and laid back their ears. Ascha felt the blood coursing through his veins, every nerve in his body tingling. Crouched low over the gelding's neck, its nose almost on the ground, he called, 'Close up! Close up!'

There was a thunder of hooves, and the dust rose in eye-stinging clouds. The Saxons looked back with terror in their eyes and then the auxiliaries were upon them, hacking and slashing at a seething tide of bodies. Gripping his reins in his teeth, Ascha swung at a yellow-haired Cherusker. The blade slid off the helmet, sliced off the man's ear and bit deep into the shoulder. He stuck another man with the point, kicked his mount forward and swung again. Saxons fell screaming under the horses' hooves. The Romans swirled through, and the Saxon host disintegrated into numberless islands of jabbing spears.

Wherever he looked, he saw men running and horse soldiers riding them down. Above the tumult of screams and yells, he could hear the rasp of his own breathing. He yanked the reins and swung at a bearded Saxon, blinked as the man's skull exploded, spraying him with blood. He swung again and took off the face of a northerner.

He saw an auxiliary lean out and cut off the head of a golden haired Cherusker with a single sweep of his sword. Ascha pulled his horse around. A big man with a shaven head and long side-braids came at him with a spear. Ascha dug his heels into the horse's flanks and slashed down. The impact as he struck the man's head sent a jolt running up his arm and shoulder. A spearman thrust at his face. He made a short and vicious cut and the man fell. To his left, he saw Tchenguiz ram a lance with both hands into a man's belly and then kick the lance free with his bare foot and ride on.

Suddenly the field cleared and they were out the other side.

He waved to the young trumpeter. 'Another pass,' he shouted. 'Quickly! Sound regroup!'

The trumpet's blare shivered the air.

The Romans dragged their horses around and trotted back. Once more they kicked the horses into a gallop and rode the Saxons down, ruthlessly skewering bodies and smashing skulls with their *spathas*. Those caught in the open were cut down, the rest ran for their lives. Ascha hacked at a Cherusker cowering behind his shield. He hit the man just above the neck and heard the blade click on bone. He swung at another, cursing when the man stood his ground and caught the blow on his shield. He thrust again and again.

The third time they came, the Saxons were ready for them. They had turned and formed a wall of shields, rammed their spear butts in the ground and waited. Those out in the open gathered in tight knots of shields and prickling spears. Horns wailed and a trumpet blared and as Ascha ordered the charge, a hail of javelins arced through the air. A dozen Auxiliaries went down in a squall of arms and legs. The Romans rode up to the shield wall and hacked and slashed at the northerners, using their horses to break up the wall. Once cut off and out in the open, the Saxons were ruthlessly slaughtered.

Ascha lost all sense of what he was doing except the need to kill and kill again. He saw an auxiliary slide slowly off his horse with a spear buried in his side. Somewhere, above the crash and din of iron on shield boards, he could hear a horse screaming, tangled in its own entrails. A horse crashed into him knocking the air from his lungs and then careered off, its eyes mad with terror.

Ascha shouted the withdrawal and they rode away, riderless horses trotting alongside them, jerking and shaking their heads. He recognized one as the young trumpeter's, the saddle empty and the trumpet dangling from one of the pommels.

At the foot of the ridge, he reined in and waited. The Pritanni gathered. No sound but the pawing and snuffling of horses. Ascha pulled at his neck cloth. He swept his sword blade clean, sheathed it and rubbed a blistered palm over his face and looked around him. The men grinned at each other, their faces filthy with mud, sweat and speckled with blood. He saw Tchenguiz, and they exchanged huge smiles, delighted to see each other alive.

When the auxiliaries had assembled, he led them back up the ridge. At the top, he twisted in the saddle and looked back. A mess of dead and dying covered the plain like grass. He could hear the distant shouts of the Saxons and the cries of their wounded.

He allowed himself a thin smile of satisfaction and then he led them away.

That night, the Pritanni went back to where the Saxon campfires glowed. Riding without sound through the trees, they came to where they could hear the murmur of northern voices. The Pritanni had wrapped branches in rags and dipped them in buckets of pine pitch. They paused, their horses snorting and blowing softly, while men passed between them, and the torches flared.

The horse soldiers came out of the darkness like demons from hell. Whooping and hollering, they fired the Saxons' wagons and tossed their torches onto tents that were starched by the sun and dry as a bone. Men fled from their tents with their clothes and hair ablaze. Flames shot high, shadows leapt and capered, and there was a strong smell of burning. The glare of burning wagons threw a yellow glow across the night sky.

Afterwards, Ascha turned his horse away and led them out of the forest towards Tornacum.

They came to a field outside the city and pulled up. A high and grassy mound squatted on the landscape like an unlanced boil. On the other side of the mound, behind a dead wickerwork of trees, the moon hung fat and white.

'Wah!' said Tchenguiz. 'What is this place?'

'It's a grave,' Ascha said, coaxing his horse forward. 'Childeric, father of Clovis, was buried here a year ago with all his war horses.'

Tchenguiz shook his head in disgust at the waste of good horse-flesh.

Ascha pulled up, dismounted and dropped the reins. The auxiliaries slipped off their mounts, stood their lances against the boll of a tree, and flopped wearily to the ground. Ascha began to climb the mound. Tchenguiz and Rufus watched him and then followed. At the top, he turned and looked about him. This would do, he thought.

Childeric's death mound occupied one side of a small plateau bare of trees through which ran a shallow depression sloping up towards the east. On the far side, he could make out the tangled green mess of an old limestone quarry. Across the plateau ran the road to Viroviac, the road down which the Saxons would come.

Make a stand here and the troops would have the higher ground, anchored between Childeric's mound and the quarry. He ran back down the mound and walked to the edge of the quarry and looked over. In Roman times, he supposed, the quarry would have provided stone for the city's buildings, but it was now choked with bushes and weeds as high as a man. He stepped down from the edge, clambered through the bushes and weeds, allowing the germ of an idea to grow in his mind, and then climbed back up and went to join the others.

He told Rufus to leave some men to warn them of the Saxons' advance.

Then they mounted and rode down into Tornacum.

He left Tchenguiz with Rufus and his auxiliaries and rode on alone. He crossed the old bridge to the house of Flavinius on the east bank of the Schald. A light rain began to fall, and he pulled his cloak over his head. When he arrived, he dismounted and knocked on the door. The door opened, and he stepped inside.

They were all there: Lucullus, dark and aloof, Gydda, his head bumping the rafters, Flavinius, plump and smiling,

Flavinius was shocked by Ascha's appearance, and Ascha smiled to see himself as the Roman saw him: dirty and stinking, his clothes and hair filthy with blood and dust.

Hanno sat by the fire, staring into the flames. He did not look up when Ascha entered, but Ascha saw him cock his head on one side and listen like a bird to the sound of Ascha's voice.

'There was a message for you,' Flavinius said. 'The queen wants to see you before she leaves.'

He nodded. He was in no hurry to see the queen.

'Gydda, you know the Saxons are coming?' he said, slapping the big Jute on the arm. 'Tomorrow you will fight alongside us.'

Gydda gave him a slow smile. 'Gydda fight with Ascha,' he said and put his head back and laughed.

Ascha knelt by Hanno and said, 'How is tha, brother?'

Hanno bent his head, and Ascha could see his face working.

'Why did tha rescue me, Ascha?' Hanno mumbled. 'Tha should have left me to drown.'

'What's this? I did no more than tha did once for me,' Ascha said breezily. 'Does tha not remember the time tha rescued me from the ice?'

'That wasn't me,' Hanno muttered.

Ascha laughed. 'What's tha saying? Tha rescued me. I remember it well.'

'It was Hroc who went on the ice and pulled tha out,' Hanno murmured. 'Hroc saved thi life, not me. I cleaned you up. Tha saw me when tha came round and thought I'd saved tha and I let tha think it.' His tone was colourless and without emotion.

Ascha gazed at him. 'And all these years I thought it was tha.' He shook his head and sighed before turning to Lucullus. 'Come, a word,' he said, switching to Latin. They moved away from the fireside.

'How is my brother?'

Lucullus looked back at Hanno. Ascha waited. The Gaul's fingers, he noticed, were long and thin and the back of his hand was covered with fine black hair.

'Your brother is not well,' Lucullus said, pushing his words out of the side of his mouth. 'He rambles in his speech and he sees things. Up here.' Lucullus tapped his brow with a meaningful finger.

'What kind of things?'

'He says that he sees his brother.'

'He sees me?'

'No, his other brother, the one who died. And sometimes he calls out for his father.' Lucullus threw Ascha a questioning look.

He remembered what Radhalla had said. Could Hanno have had anything to do with his father's death? Was that why his mind was slipping?

'Will he recover?'

Lucullus waggled his hand in a maybe, maybe not kind of way.

Ascha gave Lucullus an appraising stare. 'I was wrong about you, Lucullus. I suspected you of…many things. I want you to know I am grateful for what you have done.'

The Gaul shrugged his bony shoulders.

'I owe you. If there is anything I can do for you.'

Lucullus threw him a crafty sidelong glance. 'I would like to buy my freedom,' he said. 'You could do that.'

'It will cost you,' Ascha said softly.

There was the faintest smile from Lucullus. 'I think my family can afford it.'

A servant brought him hot water and a linen towel. Ascha washed and scoured his body and then threw himself down on Flavinius' bed and slept. After a little while he awoke and dressed hurriedly. Flavinius had laid out a clean shirt and britches and taken his own mud-sodden clothes. Ascha sent Gydda off to find Tchenguiz. The manservant said that Lucullus had gone out earlier but didn't know where. Ascha chewed it over. He'd been a fool to talk to Lucullus about buying his freedom. It put ideas in his head and he had a premonition he would not see the Gaul again.

Hanno hadn't moved. He sat staring at the fire, lost in his own thoughts.

Ascha went back the way he came, crossing over the wooden bridge, hooves clopping on the boards. Two days ago the river had been lined with cargo vessels but now the boats were gone and the wharves deserted. On the other side of the bridge he turned and rode towards the south gate.

Passing the Basilica, he looked up at the huge windows and considered whether he should go and see Clovis, and then put the thought out of his mind. He had too little time and he was anxious to make sure the girl and Octha were safe.

The Overlord could wait.

The light was fading and the sun slipping fast when he reached the inn. The *mansio* was a crumbling stone house with a low bowed roof that lay on the side of a hill some way outside the city to the south. Only part of the inn was in use, the rest had long since been abandoned. He stabled the horse and went in. Men sat and looked at him and there was a smell of warm cabbage. He was aware that he cut a different figure now, bathed and dressed in clean clothes, a long sword on his hip. He could almost pass for a Frankish high-born. The mood in the inn was quiet. Hard to believe there was a Saxon army a day's march away.

He was excited about seeing Herrad again but he was nervous, unsure how she would receive him. Busy with his own thoughts, he was not prepared for the stooping figure in worn-looking robes who shuffled along, his twisted foot rasping on the stone floor, to greet him.

'It's good to see you, my boy,' Octha said with some warmth in his tone. He put his arms around Ascha and kissed him on both cheeks.

'How are you, old friend?' Ascha said, embracing him gently. Octha looked gaunt and haggard, his skin the texture of wax. The merchant held up his hands, thickly wrapped in stained bandages.

'Couldn't be better,' he said hoarsely.

'How is the inn?'

Octha pursed his lips and nodded. 'Your Lucullus took good care of us.'

The room was clean and dimly lit. A bed, smothered in goatskins, and a small table. A fire burned in the hearth. Octha called for beer and a servant brought a jug and two beakers and put them on a table and went away. Octha looked at Ascha, raised both hands and smiled helplessly.

Ascha leaned across, picked up a beaker and held it to the merchant's lips.

'Have you come to see me or Herrad?' Octha said, his words slurred. A trickle of beer ran down his chin.

'Both I hope.'

Octha looked at him and smiled a thin smile.

He knows, Ascha thought. He knows everything.

'And why did you come?'

'I came to warn you. The Saxons are coming. Their army is marching on Tornacum. We slowed them down but they'll be here soon enough.'

Octha passed a hand across his face, and Ascha saw the fear in his eyes.

'You should leave,' he said, and felt guilty that once again he'd put Octha in harm's way. He knew he should insist the old man leave, but he'd been down that road before.

'You knew all along the Saxons weren't going to land south of Gesoriac,' he said.

'I suspected it, yes, but I never imagined they would come here,' Octha said wearily. 'We thought we would be safe in Tornacum.'

'And you knew Radhalla's war was with Clovis, not the Romans?'

'I heard rumours, nothing more.'

'Radhalla tricked us,' Ascha said. 'I should have trusted you.'

Octha smiled gently, not disagreeing. 'What are you going to do?'

'Bauto is marching north with the *scara*. Syagrius and Ragnachar will join us here. Together we will stop the Saxons.'

'Ragnachar?'

'Bauto says he will come.'

Octha looked at him with scorn. 'You believe that?'

'I don't know. Maybe he will and maybe he won't.'

'There will be a great battle.'

'Yes.'

An uneasy silence fell between them.

'Ascha, you've done enough,' Octha said. 'Why don't you leave now?'

'Where would I go?'

'It doesn't matter. There's nothing for you here.'

People were always sending him away. 'Where can you go but where you come from?' he said with a trace of bitterness.'

Octha shook his head. 'That's not true. This is not your fight.'

'But I have made it my fight.'

'You have no idea what you're doing here. You think that Clovis or Syagrius are any different from Radhalla?'

Ascha raised both hands and let them fall. 'Clovis wants to build a new empire and Syagrius wants to rebuild the empire he has lost, but at least they believe in something. Radhalla is against life. He destroys everything he touches. If it wasn't for Radhalla my brother and perhaps my father would be alive, and you and Herrad and Hanno would not have been harmed.' He looked away. 'I have to stay and see this through?'

Octha gave him a crooked smile. 'And after Radhalla is dead, will you stop then?'

Ascha frowned. He'd given no thought to what happened after Radhalla's death.

'Kill Radhalla,' Octha added bluntly, 'and another warlord will take his place. It's the way of the world.'

'I just want to do what is right,' Ascha said hotly.

'And Herrad? What do you want for her?'

Ascha felt the blood rush to the back of his neck. He was suddenly confused and didn't know what to say.

Octha sighed.

He leant across and put his head close to Ascha's and laid his bandaged hands on Ascha's shoulders. His eyes were round and watery and Ascha saw that the skin across his cheekbones was mottled with tiny red veins. He looked at Ascha for what seemed like forever.

'I know you love Herrad,' he said softly. 'I have known it a long time. And there's nothing wrong with that. You are ambitious and want to overcome the hardship of your birth. She is beautiful and has her best years before her. But what can you give her, a young man who will go out and fight and perhaps die? And if not tomorrow then the day after? If you really loved her, you would let her be.'

Ascha ran his palms along his knees. The old man was right. He loved Herrad but what could he, a Saxon half-slave, offer her? He closed his eyes and opened them again. 'And is that what you want old man?' he said, tightening his jaw. 'That I let her be?'

A sad smile appeared on the merchant's face.

'What I want is to live out my days with Herrad and then leave her with someone who will care for her as much as I do.'

Ascha shook his head. 'I will not give her up,' he whispered fiercely.'

'Nor do I expect you to.'

'What then?'

'Ascha, I am not long for this life. Grant me what little time I have left'

Silence.

Ascha tossed the merchant's words around in his head. He reached down and picked up a piece of wood and threw it on the fire. A shower of sparks rose and drifted, and a yellow flame swept up the side of the branch. They both watched as the wood burned bright and then died and crumbled into ash.

There was the sound of feet, and Herrad walked into the room. He saw that she had changed how she looked. Her hair was tied up in an open-work cap of woollen yarn, she wore a long white linen dress, pinned at the shoulders, and her feet were bare. She carried a cape over one arm. She smiled at Ascha and kissed him on the cheek, as a friend would.

'It's good to see you,' she said. 'We were worried.'

'It's good to see you too,' he said, happy to be in the same room as her. 'I came to tell you the Saxons are coming.'

'So the rumours are true,' she murmured. 'I couldn't believe it.'

'Animals! They are all animals!' Octha said suddenly, and began to weep.

Herrad went to the merchant, patted his shoulder, unfolded a cape and laid it across his knees while Ascha watched them, feeling like a stranger.

The evening passed uncomfortably. The innkeeper brought fried pork and greens, and they picked at it without appetite. Octha sat in a chair, hardly eating, his head back and eyes lightly closed. After a while he seemed to doze. Ascha and Herrad talked in muted voices, not wanting to disturb the old man.

'What will you do?' she said after a while.

'I will stay and fight,' he said simply.

'You are heavily outnumbered.'

'Yes.'

'Then I will pray for your safety.'

He looked at her and she looked at him and they were silent for a long time. He had thought when he saw her he would know what to say, but he found he was without words. It occurred to him that this might be the last time he would see her and the thought filled him with an indescribable sadness.

The girl got to her feet and laid a hand on the back of the merchant's neck.

'I think Octha is tired,' she said. 'He needs to rest.'

It was his signal to go.

She walked with him into the courtyard and stood with her shoulders hunched, clasping her elbows. The sky was beginning to turn red with the coming of sunset, and he could smell rain in the air. Far off he heard shouts and singing in the town, the sounds of soldiers carousing, and at that moment he knew that if he lived nothing in the world would matter but her.

'I have to go,' he said.

'Yes,' was her reply.

'Come with me tonight? I don't want to be alone.'

'She looked at him for a long time while she thought it over. Then she nodded. 'Come back later,' she said. 'When Octha is asleep.'

29

Ascha left the horse in the stable and went back to the city on foot. Reaching Tornacum, he made his way to the queen's house. There was a line of wagons outside with sleepy-eyed oxen in head yokes chewing thoughtfully. He tapped at a side door. It opened and an Antrustion waved him in. He found himself in a room at the back of the house. A young woman stood by the window looking out at the street. In the shadowy interior he thought for a moment it was Herrad. A little shorter maybe, but a similar line of nose and chin. The woman turned and he saw it was the slave girl, Eleri.

'Ascha, is that you?' she said with surprise. 'I hadn't expected to see you here. Why did you come back?'

'I had to,' was all he said.

She rolled her eyes. 'Then you're a fool. Come with me. The queen is waiting.'

She led him into the main hall. Slaves scurried to and fro, their arms piled high with blankets, drapes and bed linens. Others were filling chests and panniers with bundles of clothes. There was an air of feverish urgency mingled with more than a whiff of fear.

'Stay here,' Eleri said. 'I will fetch the queen.'

A moment later he heard the hard rap of heels on the wooden floor, and Basinia entered. She was dressed for travelling. A loose fitting gown in some fine material with an overjacket in the same colour, a dark cap and veil, a waterproof overcape, and fur lined boots. She stood slender and erect. Heavy gold earrings hung almost to her shoulders, and her lips were painted red making her mouth look like an open wound. Perfume, rich and heavy, hung in the air about her. She could have been a girl of twenty-five.

The queen coolly surveyed him and then handed her wrap to Eleri.

'The Saxons will soon be here,' she said.

'Yes,' he said. 'But you know the Overlord intends to stay in Tornacum.'

He thought he saw a shadow pass across her eyes.

'My son can be very stupid at times,' she said. 'He doesn't always see the dangers that surround us.'

'I think he sees them, Lady, but he chooses to ignore them.'

'Then you know that you are both going to die?'

They stepped back to allow two slaves carrying an oaken chest to pass. The chest was black with age and heavy, and the strain on the mens' faces was plain. He wondered if Basinia had sent the young Frankish nobleman to Thraelsted as a decoy for him. He would have asked her outright but he had no wish to be in Basinia's debt.

The queen stared blankly at him. 'It would be a shame,' she said, 'after all you have done for us. You will lose everything you have worked for.'

'What are you trying to say, Lady?'

She scowled, unwilling to put her thoughts into words. 'You understand that if my son dies, you will have nothing. You will remain a half-slave for the rest of your life. Of course,' she added, 'if you die that will hardly matter.'

He understood well enough, the message plain. If the Overlord died, his promise to free Ascha would die with him. And if Ascha lived, and her son died, Basinia would make sure he suffered.

'If it is to happen, it will happen,' he said coldly.

Basinia raised a hand in disgust. 'Neither of you need die. It's unnecessary.' She went to the window and was silent for a long time. Then she turned and said, 'I want you to go to Radhalla and offer him the town in exchange for my son's life. And yours too,' she added as an afterthought.

'I doubt whether Radhalla will consider it a fair exchange,' he muttered.

'Nevertheless, you will go?'

'No, Lady.'

'I thought you might say that,' she said. 'Is there nothing I can offer you that will change your mind?'

'I'm not about to barter for my life with Radhalla.'

Basinia seemed to sag a little and then drew herself up and shook her head, her cheeks bloodless. 'Then it's goodbye, Saxon. I am leaving for Cambarac and my boat is waiting. I will see you on the other side, if not in this life then most certainly in the next.'

It took him a moment to work through the implication of what she said. Basinia had a boat? By tomorrow Tornacum would be a charnel house, but a boat offered the chance of escape.

He swallowed, knowing there would be a price for what he was about to ask.

'Would you be willing to take my brother and my friends to Cambarac?'

She looked into his eyes, and then nodded. 'Bring them and we will take them,' she said quietly.

Basinia lifted her hand.

Ascha hesitated, then bowed his head and brushed the back of her hand with his lips. The queen looked at Ascha, and her mouth moved jerkily. 'Take care of my son, Theod. He is all I have. There is a sharp bend on the river just south of the town. I will tell the boat to wait for you. We will wait until mid-morning tomorrow, no later.'

They exchanged glances, and he knew they'd made a deal. She would offer passage to Octha, Hanno and Herrad if he did everything he could to keep Clovis alive.

She swept past him and was gone without another word.

The Antrustion guards and the servants bustled to make ready. He could see slaves and servants loading the wagons outside. Eleri went to go and then paused and looked over her shoulder directly at him.

'Take care!' she whispered. 'Your life is in great danger.'

'I'm not afraid to die,' he said casually.

Her mouth twitched. 'Radhalla is not your only enemy. There are others who want you dead.'

He looked at her. 'Who wants me dead, Eleri?'

She closed her eyes, shook her head and turned to leave. Ascha grabbed her wrist, pulled her away from the door and closed it with his foot. Outside he could hear the queen shouting at the slaves and servants. There was the sound of a slap and a high pitched wail.

'What's going on, Eleri?'

'Nothing! Is this the thanks I get for trying to help you?'

'What do you know?'

'I cannot tell you. Let me be!' She struggled and tried to pull her arm away.

He stared at her, working it through. 'The morning after I spent the night with you I was attacked by the Alani. And a year ago I was followed on the road to Colonia by men who already knew that Clovis had sent a spy to the north. You served us, Eleri. You heard us talking. You knew where I was going. You told them.'

'Let me go, you're hurting me.'

'It had to be you. Who are you working for, Eleri?'

She threw a cape over her shoulders, looked at him and shook her head. 'I cannot. He would kill me.'

'Who will kill you?'

She said nothing, her thin lips pressed tight.

He thought for a moment. 'Was it Fara? Ragnachar's man?'

There was a pause and then a reluctant nod.

'You said you were a gift. Who gave you, Eleri? Who gave you to the Overlord?'

She turned away and then looked back. 'Ragnachar gave me to Clovis, and he passed me on to his mother. The Overlord has little interest in women,' she added with a brittle smile.

'And the queen used you, didn't she? Set you up as a royal whore. You slept with royal guests and whatever you learnt, you told Basinia?'

He remembered the night he had spent with Eleri, lying beside her, kissing her eyes, her throat. He put a hand to the side of his face. 'Sweet Tiw! You're working both sides. You've been passing information to Basinia and to Fara.'

'I had no choice. Fara said if I refused he would cut me,' she said with a shudder.

'Does the queen know?'

Eleri gasped and shook her head. 'No, and you must never tell her. If she discovers I have been disloyal she will punish me. She thinks I work for her and her alone.'

'And Fara?'

'You have no idea what you are getting into here. You have become a thorn in Ragnachar's side. Fara is a very dangerous man. If he finds you, he will kill you.'

'Does he know I'm here?'

'Yes, he knows.'

'Who told him, Eleri?'

'I don't know.'

'You don't know?'

'Fara has spies everywhere,' she said, pleading. 'There is nothing Clovis does that Ragnachar doesn't know about. Anyone could have told him.'

'Who then?'

She thought for a moment. 'Maybe Flavinius?'

Flavinius? He felt his jaw drop. Flavinius had said he should not tell Clovis he had seen Fara with Radhalla. But Octha had also told him to say nothing. Was there no-one he could trust?

There was the crack of a whip outside, the clop of hooves and with a groan of timber, he heard the wagons move off. He stepped in close. 'Eleri, I need to know. Will Fara harm Clovis?'

Eleri shook her head. 'No, he will leave that to Radhalla. But you are a threat, and he will hurt you as easily as breathing.'

'Eleri!'

The girl jumped like a scalded cat. They both turned. The queen stood in the doorway with her hands clasped before her and her face cold and wintry. She gave them a bleak smile. 'When you two are quite finished?' she said, a rasp in her voice like a stick through gravel.

Eleri bent her head and moved away. She stopped in the doorway, turned, ran back and kissed him hard on the mouth and then she was gone.

He went over in his mind what Eleri had said and tried to imagine what Fara would do. The house was quiet. The wind must have picked up because somewhere a door was banging and the shutters began to swing, squeaking on iron pins. He was sure he was being watched, he felt the eyes boring into the back of his head, but he saw no-one. He heard a sound behind him and turned with a start but it was only a rat scuttling along the foot of the wall. He thought of the girl, and Octha waiting at the *mansio*. They were safe for the moment. And then the fear hit him, his blood ran cold, and he had a sense that something was terribly wrong. He will hurt you, Eleri had said. No pleasure in killing his enemies when he could make them suffer.

He turned and ran.

Pricked by a gathering urgency, he cut down a narrow gravel alley and ran past the waterfront shacks of the rivermen. He stopped to listen, heart yammering and then he was off again. Somewhere on the river road he could hear horses clopping. He came to Flavinius's house and stopped and listened. Cats yowled in the night. He could see the door was open. He looked both ways up the dirt street.

Nothing.

He drew his *seaxe* and stepped inside. Mouth drying, he scanned the room. A body was slumped in a corner. He bent and lifted the man by the shoulder. It was the servant of Flavinius, dead. Ascha let the body fall. He listened and then went on. In the next room, propped up against a wall, he found Flavinius. No sign of Hanno. Ascha looked out of the window at the street and listened. When he was sure it was clear, he squatted down beside Flavinius. The Roman was still alive; his eyelids fluttered open and he looked up at Ascha with dark and mournful eyes. Ascha saw that his fingers were interlocked and bloody. Gently, he lifted his wrists. Two deep cuts had laid the belly open from ribcage to groin. Flavinius sat in a pool of his own gore, cradling his guts in his lap.

A cold chill crept through Ascha's bones and froze his heart. He wiped his mouth with a sleeve and tightened his lip.

Flavinius had not betrayed him.

'Flavinius,' he said urgently. 'Can you hear me?'

The Roman looked up at Ascha and tried to speak. 'They took Hanno.'

'And Lucullus?'

Flavinius shook his head. 'He never came back.'

His voice faded to a whisper and his head slumped to one side.

Ascha ran his palm over the Roman's face, closing his eyes. He said, 'I'm sorry I ever doubted you,' and then he shoved the *seaxe* in his belt and ran out into the street.

He ran at a steady lope through reeking alleys. It was dusk, and the rain had stopped. He turned a corner and saw the old bridge ahead. Across the river he could hear the sounds of drunken revelry. A chill wind blew in from the west, and the sun was dropping like a stone.

As he crossed the bridge four horsemen came out from behind a house on the far side. He stopped and looked back over his shoulder and then drew his *franciska*. The riders sat silently watching him. One of them carried a long and heavy bundle across his horse's neck. Like a sack of grain.

'Where are you going, Saxon?' they said.

He stood, watching them for some time with his feet slightly apart and the *franciska* held lightly by his side. Then the rider with the bundle detached himself and rode forward, hooves echoing on the wooden decking. He rode up to Ascha and halted the horse almost within spear-reach. It was Fara. Hanno was slumped head down across the horse's neck. His wrists and ankles were bound, and Ascha could see there was blood on his shirt and face. He could not tell whether he was alive or dead. Fara sat upright in the saddle and looked down at him, the moonlight gleaming on Ragnachar's seal around his neck. The horse pawed the timber decking and shifted its feet and sighed.

'You don't give up do you?' Fara said.

Ascha didn't answer.

'You have caused us many problems.'

'I know.'

'You believe you have the right to destroy what has been planned for years and then just walk away?'

'The right, no.'

'Then why?'

'It was what I had to do.'

'What you had to do?' Fara looked back at the others and laughed without humour. 'For a half-slave, you have big ideas, do you not?'

He said nothing. He looked behind him and moved to the edge of the bridge so the Franks could not surround him. He glanced over the parapet at the river darkly streaming down below and eyed the ground that separated them. Pointless, and they both knew it.

'You came here to kill me?' Fara said.

'I came here to kill Radhalla. I had no thought of killing you.'

'But you are here now?'

'Yes.'

'What is it you want from me?'

'I want my brother,' he whispered.

'He wants his brother,' Fara smiled. He slapped Hanno on the back. There was a faint groan. 'You want him alive or dead?'

'Go screw yourself.'

Fara almost smiled. He said, 'What will you give me to get him back alive.'

Ascha did not speak.

'Will you give me your solemn word as the son of a slave-whore that you will leave this city and never return?' Fara said.

'Go fuck yourself,' Ascha snarled. He made a sudden grab for the bridle reins but Fara knew what he would do and pulled the horse back. It reared. Ascha ducked the flailing hooves and sidestepped, but Fara turned the horse easily and rode back a little way and then turned again to face him. Ascha stood in the middle of the bridge, his eyes flickering and his chest heaving, judging the distance between them.

At the end of the bridge, the three Alani sat on their horses and watched in silence.

'I warned you,' Fara said.

'People have been warning me all my life.'

'You want your brother?'

'Yes.'

There was the flash of a long knife in the moonlight.

'Then take him.'

'No!' Ascha yelled.

Fara looked at Ascha, and a smile twisted across his face. He bent low over the horse's neck and then he made a single long pass with his knife, opening Hanno's throat from ear to ear. In one easy movement he scooped up Hanno's feet with the crook of his arm and flicked his body off the horse. Ascha heard his brother's skull crack against the parapet of the bridge and then with a deep splash Hanno fell into the river.

Fara turned his horse and rode back across the bridge to where the others were waiting. He said something which made them laugh, and they turned and rode off towards the north. Ascha sucked air into his lungs, ran to the edge of the bridge and peered into the depths. He leaned over the parapet and looked down, searching for his brother. The water was black and moved darkly, ripples glistening in the half light. He could see nothing of Hanno. Across the river he could hear horses trotting away.

Ascha leaned against the bridge and wrapped his arms across his chest and screwed his eyes tight shut. Some day, he would mourn his brother Hanno but right now he felt empty, drained of all feeling.

So numb he couldn't feel the sadness.

***

Half a lifetime ago, Ascha and his mother are sitting on the mossy door step of the long hut watching the cows being driven back for milking. The cows move lazily, their big bellies swaying from side to side, neck bells tinkling. Small boys walk beside them pushing the cows' flanks. The boys are barefoot and stripped to the waist, their skin the colour of mud.

'So you're going?' his mother says, her face tight.

'Yes,' he says, unable to hide his joy. With Hanno's encouragement, he has done a deal. He will carve the *SeaWulf's* new prow monster if Aelfric will let him go on the raid.

His mother picks at the stuff of her skirt. She looks up at him and then looks away. Lately he has noticed her spending more time in his company. He has caught her gazing at him, touching him, reaching across to brush the hair back from his brow. Her eyes are red-rimmed and swollen, and he wonders if she is suffering from the grass fever.

'When do you sail?'

'In three days,' he grins, unable to hide his joy.

'Your father has let you go?'

'He says I can go as an oarsman, unweaponed.'

'Good,' she says.

He gives her a keen look, 'You want me to go?'

'No, but I think you should.' She lays her hand along the side of his face. 'It's time.'

'Time?'

'You must travel. See the world. There is nothing for you in this wilderness.' She waves towards the green marshes, the water sparkling in the sun, the reeds lush, pricked with blue and yellow irises. 'Get away. Learn. It's your only chance to make something of yourself.'

The cows are almost past, the boys thwacking sticks on their rumps, shouting *Hup! Hup!*

'I can do it,' he says.

She gives him a sad look. 'I know, but you are still young. I worry.'

'I'm old enough.'

'Fourteen,' she says, miserable. 'And you think you're a man!'

'Hanno will look after me.'

'But will Hanno care for you as I do?' she says bitterly.

He notices for the first time that there are strands of grey in her hair.

'We'll be back by the autumn,' he says and flashes her a wicked grin. 'With more loot than you can shake a stick at!'

'There'll not be a day goes by that I'll not be thinking of you,' she says.

He nods, knowing it's true.

The breeze shifts, gusting the smell of ship's caulk and raw sewage towards them. He sees his mother's nose wrinkle and smiles.

He touches her arm. 'I must get back,' he says gently. 'They'll be wondering where I am.'

***

Ascha sat on his heels outside the *mansio* and waited. He sat there for a long time, watching as the lamps went out one by one. Finally, when the inn was dark, he crossed the yard and tapped lightly on the door with the back of his hand. The door opened and a slim shape appeared. Herrad took his arm in both of hers without a word and they walked toward the town, her shoulder pressed against his. It was warmer but not much, and the sky had cleared. Across the fields he could see the dark and brooding shape of the Basilica.

The *mansio* was situated on a hillside. Striding down the slope they lost control and as their feet ran away with them the girl laughed a little and clutched his arm tighter. He remained quiet, brooding. She looked at him, caught his mood and fell silent. Above them starlings rolled and swirled in a noisome and shifting cloud. They threw back their heads and watched them dive and swoop until the starlings seemed to come to some vast and collective decision and withdrew to their roosting place beyond the town.

It was the night before a battle, and the streets of Tornacum were deserted. Drawn by some instinct, the few people left had gathered by the river. They had broken into a warehouse, and men rolled winebarrels into the alley and smashed them open to get at the wine while women came running with jugs and pitchers. People lay sprawled in a stupor. Others lurched down alleys with their arms wrapped around each other singing at the top of their voices.

The town was lapsing into an orgy of drunkenness.

He put an arm around Herrad, and they went on. When his hand touched hers or brushed against the soft inside of her bare arm, he felt her shiver. They found a tavern in the shadow of the Basilica. Inside was hot and noisy, the air warm and thick with the smell of grilled meat and heavy bodies jammed tight. Frankish fighting men and a few girls, drinking and laughing, trying to forget what would happen tomorrow.

They found a bench in a corner and shared a beaker of wine while the innkeeper's surly daughter set out some bread and cold meat.

He saw men looking at Herrad with lust in their eye, but there was something about Ascha, a touch of madness, that made them think again.

He drank morosely while Herrad ate and looked about her. He had a sudden picture of his brother's body sinking through cold dark water, mud and weeds clogging Hanno's mouth. He shook his head and closed his eyes. His heart was thudding and there was a roaring in his ears.

He felt Herrad take his hand in hers and squeeze it. 'You look exhausted,' she said.

He smiled, shook his head and ran both hands over his face and blew out his cheeks. 'I'll be fine,' he said. The empty feeling had passed, and it occurred to him that Hanno had been dead to him since the day that Hroc was hanged.

A shift in the music caused them both to turn.

An old woman, sixty if she was a day, small-boned with a tiny round face moved onto the floor. A *tumba* struck up and she began to dance, slowly at first and then with gathering speed. She danced almost without effort, a fluid sinuous movement as intricate as a silken knot. Ascha watched her move, her feet flickering across the floor, her face composed, one arm raised above her head and the other trailing a white headcloth. The crowd drew back to give her room and then fell silent, their heads nodding to the rhythm as the old woman's feet rapped on the floor, and her thick body twisted gracefully through the steps of the dance.

The music came to an end, and the woman bowed and then held out a hand to Herrad. The girl shook her head, but the old woman gently insisted. The crowd murmured encouragement. Herrad looked to Ascha and smiled. She moved onto the floor and took the other end of the headcloth. The music struck up and the two women, one old and the other young, began to dance, their bodies linked in the gloom by the headcloth's dazzling whiteness.

Ascha leaned back and watched them. He saw that the girl danced as well as the old woman, but in a different, more youthful way, flicking her hips and throwing back her head, taking delight in showing off her skill. The crowd laughed and began to clap. Faster and faster, the two women danced, their bodies twirling and spinning, feet pricking out an intricate pattern on the floor.

Herrad closed her eyes and gave herself over to the music, her hair a swirling chestnut wave around her shoulders. Ascha watched mesmerised, his eyes drinking in every move of her body, the twist of her back, the stretch of her throat and the curve of her breasts. And as he watched, it was as if the grey shadow that had sat on her

303

brow since Thraelsted fell away and at that moment he knew he wanted her more than he had ever wanted a woman in his life.

The music stopped.

There was a beat of pure silence and then the two women fell laughing on each other's shoulders. The old woman pulled Herrad's head down and kissed her on the brow, and the crowd cheered with warm good humour. Herrad ran and sat beside him. She was flushed and panting, lips parted with effort. She looked at him and saw the admiration in his eyes and smiled.

He held her face and kissed her cheek and traced the line of her mouth with the tip of his finger. 'I want you,' he said.

'I know,' she said, laughing.

'Not like that. I want to be with you. Always!'

She looked away, sipped a little of the wine, ran a small pink tongue over her lips, looked at him again.

A roar like a blast of warm air made them both turn. A fist-fight had broken out and several Franks were laying into each other. Their friends formed a ring and whooped and cheered themselves hoarse. Someone emptied a flagon over the men, soaking them, and a girl shrieked with laughter and then covered her mouth with her hand. Someone hit the man who had poured the wine and soon half the inn was brawling, the fight spilling into the street.

A cheer went up outside and an Antrustion burst in, his face lit with excitement. 'It's Syagrius and his Romans!' he shouted. 'They're here!'

'Come on! Ascha said, grabbing her hand and making for the door.

The inn emptied.

Ascha and Herrad rose and pushed their way through the crowd. A column of Roman soldiers was winding into the market square, marching four abreast in regular order, eyes straight ahead, their oval shields overpainted with a red cross. At their head rode Syagrius on a white horse. He wore an old military *cuirass* that looked as if it had been made for someone else, and a cloak the colour of fresh blood. The Governor was plainly exhausted but did his best to hide it, smiling and waving to the crowd.

Ascha pulled at a soldier's arm. 'Is this all you have?' he said. 'Where are the rest?'

'That's all there are,' the man said. 'There are no more.'

Ascha knew it would not be enough. The Saxons still outnumbered them three to one.

When they reached the *mansio* everything was quiet save for the faintest rustling in the trees, the birches pale as bones against the darkness. They crossed the yard and went into the stable.

'Go on up,' she said. 'Give me a few moments.'

He climbed the ladder and lay in the dark of the loft and waited, his insides knotted so tight he could hardly breathe. There was a warm smell of dung and hay and the sound of wind blowing through the thatch. The horses snuffled, stamped and kicked the wooden stall. After a while he heard the door creak open and the girl in a low voice call his name,

'Are you there?'

'Yes,' he said. 'Come on up.'

He heard her step on the ladder and made out her figure in the half-light. 'Is he all right?' he said.

'He's asleep. I put a cape over him. It might get cold and I didn't want him to catch a chill.'

She felt for his hand in the dark, lacing her fingers into his.

'I can't stay long,' she said.

'I know,' he said.

She lay down in the hay beside him, not moving but staring up into the rafters. He could hear her breathing softly and smell the warmth of her skin.

'Do you remember when we met?' she asked him.

'Of course.'

'You looked lost and a little nervous. And the next day – on the boat – you were so fierce.'

'I loved you from the moment I saw you,' he said.

'I know,' she said. 'I saw it in your eyes. And again at Thraelsted, I saw it then.'

'Was I so obvious?' he said.

She said nothing but turned her face towards him. He felt the soft pressure as he pulled her to him and kissed her with cautious tenderness.

'Are you sure?' he said.

'Yes, I'm sure,' she said, smiling into the darkness.

He pulled his cloak over them, shifted and lay with his arms around her.

She turned to him, 'Ascha?' she said, her voice soft and furry.

'Mm-hmmm,' he murmured.

'Am I as you like?'

He brushed the hair from her cheek and whispered 'You are all that I or any man would ever want.'

'Yes,' she said. 'Truly?'

'Truly.'

'What is it? What's wrong?'

He touched the girl's face. 'Nothing.'

'Tell me,' she said.

'I can't.'

'Tell me.'

The stable was so quiet. 'They're dead,' he said.

'Who? Who are dead?' She supported herself on her elbow and looked down at him.

He shook his head. 'Flavinius. Hanno.'

'Both of them?' she whispered.

'Yes.'

'Why didn't you tell me?' She was crying.

He swallowed, looking at her with tears in his eyes. He ran his fingertips across her shoulders, over the bare nape of her neck and down the long smooth slide of her back. 'I would have. I wanted to.'

'Then why?'

'I thought it might come between us.'

She lay back beside him quietly sobbing. He could feel her shoulders moving and taste the tears running down her face.

'And Lucullus?'

'Not Lucullus,' he said. 'I think Lucullus has gone.'

He didn't blame the Gaul. He would have done the same in his place. And if Lucullus had stayed with Hanno, Fara would have killed him too.

'How did it happen?'

He shook his head. 'I don't know. It just happened.'

She cried and he felt her breath, hot with tears, and he held her tight and told her he loved her. And then he told her that in the morning he wanted her to take Octha and leave the *mansio*. She was to follow the river south of the town where she would find a boat which would take them to Cambarac.

'A boat? Whose boat?'

He thought for a moment and then he sighed. 'It doesn't matter whose boat, they are expecting you.' He hesitated. 'Ask for Eleri,' he said. 'She will help you. Give her my name and she will do the rest.'

And he told her to go to sleep.

'I will sleep if you sleep,' she said. She took his hand and kissed it, laid it over her breast, and he held her against him pale and naked under the cloak and then she slept.

It rained in the night and the wind blew and he listened to the rain tapping lightly on the thatch and the mice scampering through the straw and knew he would not be able to sleep without thinking about what had happened. Later, sometime before dawn, Herrad beside him breathing gently, he woke with a start, utterly convinced that Hanno was in the room, weeds trailing around his neck and dripping water.

But when he looked, nobody was there.

30

Eleri awoke and sat upright. The floor was moving slightly and it took her a moment to remember where she was. She slid from her mattress, picked up her cloak and went up on deck.

All was quiet, the queen and her servants still asleep. Mist shrouded the trees along the river and hung heavy over the water. Nobody about but a solitary Antrustion guard leaning against the stern-board with his ankles crossed, chewing a twig. The Antrustion looked her up and down, his eyes roaming over her body with casual indifference.

'Where you going?' he said, forcing a smile. She could see tiny flecks of wood stuck between his teeth.

'What's it to you?' she muttered. She gathered her cloak about her and went down the plank. On the riverbank she paused to look in both directions and then took the track to the left. She walked slowly with her arms clasped, listening to the breeze passing through the trees and the waking sounds of the riverbank. It was damp and cool and there was a rich smell of mould. She wound the cloak tighter around her, pulling her head into her shoulders like a waterfowl.

She went a little further down the track and then crept shivering down the grassy bank to the water's edge. She sat on her heels and watched the river flow. Insects danced, ducks trailed ripples and a pair of moorhens bobbed among the rushes. She stayed like that for a long while, breathing in the morning.

She wondered if Ascha the Saxon would make it out of Tornacum. She hoped so, but thought it unlikely. In her experience, men like Ascha did not last long. A pity, as she had grown fond of him. Yet perhaps she shouldn't have told him so much. She had let her heart rule her head and that was not wise. In future, she would be more careful.

She walked on.

She loved this time of morning when everything was clean and quiet. A murder of crows sat on a branch and watched her, ruffling their feathers and cawing softly. Somewhere in the village a cock began to crow. She heard ducks quacking and the sound of horses and looked to see who could be riding at this hour.

Four riders were coming down the riverside track, men on dark horses, their heads hooded by their cloaks. Antrustions, returning from some errand for the queen, she decided. But the horses were not Antrustion mounts and the riders did not look like Antrustions.

She looked back towards the boat. The guard was nowhere to be seen, everybody still asleep. She could cry out, but that might wake the queen. Silly girl, she chided herself, foolish to come out alone. Anything might happen. She heard the muffled chink of a bridle. She looked at the riders, and they turned their heads and seemed to look at her. Then they rode on.

She closed her eyes and let her breath go in one long shuddering sigh of relief. She slowly got to her feet, pushed her hair back from her brow and turned to go back to the boat.

She knew by the silence that the horses had stopped.

A cold wind blew through her heart, and her mouth opened and her hand rose to touch her face. There was a faintest sound behind her, the rustle and squeak of a leather boot on wet grass and, as she turned, she saw coming towards her the smiling face of Fara.

Ascha awoke with a sharp sense of loss. Herrad had slipped away, and he was alone. He pushed away the cloak and laid his palm over the warm hollow her body had left in the straw and then he dressed, pulled on his boots and went down the ladder to the stable. The sky was a dark grey washed in pink. He saddled the horse, stuffed his *seaxe* and *franciska* into his belt, picked up his shield from where it stood against the wall, shouldered it and mounted. He rode out of the yard, hooves clopping on the cobbles, turned the horse at the gate and took the road to Tornacum. As he went by the inn he had a strong sense that he was being watched. He looked up at the shuttered windows of Octha's room and imagined he saw a faint movement, a shadow behind the shutter, but could not be sure.

The skies were clearing and he knew it was going to be another hot and breathless day. He breathed in deep and let it go, remembering everything from the night before. The girl's dress, damp with sweat, clinging to her hips as she danced, the touch of her skin and the smell of her as she lay beside him in the straw. He thought of Flavinius and of Hanno and felt a cloud pass over him, and then he thought of Herrad and his heart lifted and he smiled and kicked the horse's flanks and cantered up the road.

He found Tchenguiz and Gydda waiting on the steps of the Basilica. When they saw him, they rose as one, their weatherbeaten faces creased in smiles. He dismounted, tied the horse and the three of them shared a breakfast of sour milk and hard bread.

He told them that Flavinius was dead, his brother too, and that Lucullus had gone. He spoke slowly, rolling out each word. They listened in silence, their eyes full of him.

'I misjudged them,' he said. 'I doubted Flavinius and Lucullus who were true, while the brother I loved most in the world betrayed me.'

Gydda and Tchenguiz looked at one another. Neither of them had known Flavinius, and Ascha knew that Tchenguiz, like his mother, had never cared for Hanno. Lucullus was already forgotten.

'Tell us who did it,' said Tchenguiz, 'and we will kill him for tha.'

Ascha said nothing. Fara was protected by his rank and by those he served. Maybe one day he would get his revenge, but for now he would have to let it go. Kill Fara and everything he had worked for would fall about his ears.

Ascha wiped the back of his fist across his mouth and got to his feet. He felt restless and was eager to be off. Across the square he could hear the dull tramp of marching feet. The Overlord's Franks and the Governor's Romans were marching out to face the Saxons. He watched the soldiers plod by with their heads down, feet shuffling in the dust, lugging their heavy shields.

Ascha noticed a dusty group of men, dressed in weather-beaten ponchos of leather and rabbit skin. They were sitting against a wall on the other side of the square in the shade of a timbered house. Outlanders, he guessed, by their hair. They took no notice of the marching men and seemed to be asleep.

Ascha went over to them, a half-smile pulling at his face. He paused, kicked one man's boot and demanded the name of their leader.

'Who wants to know?' growled a heavily-built man in thickly-accented Frankish. He was tattooed, pig-tailed, heavily-bearded and sat with his back against the wall, his legs stretched out and a stained neck-cloth over his face.

'I do,' Ascha said. 'Because if this bunch of dog shit were under my command I would have them flogged around the city walls until their backs bled.'

The man sighed. He pulled the cloth away with a blunt hand and looked up. His face opened, and he leapt to his feet.

'Ascha!'

'How are you, Gundovald?' Ascha said.

Gundovald put two huge arms around Ascha and hugged him. He turned and shouted to the other hostages, 'Ho! Look who's here. It's Ascha, our own little Ascha!'

They surrounded him, pumping his hand and hammering his back.

He was happy to see them. Friedegund the long-shanked Suebian, Atharid the Thuringian, Hortar the little Alaman, Hariulf and the others. It had been a long time. Gundovald held him at arms' length and looked him up and down. He took in the sword and the fine linen shirt and let out a low and languid whistle. 'So, you survived, Carver? And you seem to have done well for yourself. You anything to do with this war against the Saxons?'

Ascha shook his head, 'I run errands for Lord Bauto,' he said.

'Bauto? You should watch that old dog,' Hortar said sourly. 'One a these days, that bastard's going to get us all killed.'

They laughed, Hortar's bad-temper never changing.

Ascha felt a tug at his sleeve. 'We must go,' Tchenguiz said.

Gundovald reached deep under his poncho and withdrew a black and hairy flask. 'Bathe your throat for old times' sake before you go.'

Ascha took the goatskin. He pulled the stopper with his teeth, lifted the flask and drank deep. The wine was rank and foetid, but he didn't care. He wiped his mouth with the back of his hand and grinned.

At a nest of roads outside the town, Ascha found Syagrius and a group of Roman officers sitting on their horses gloomily watching the swaying ranks of Roman and Frankish troops go by. In the shade of the trees beyond, Ascha saw Rufus and his Pritanni, their horses shaking their heads and flicking their tails. Rufus lifted a lazy arm in greeting, and Ascha did the same.

Ascha wished the Governor a fine morning and Syagrius agreed it was a fine morning. He asked if the Governor had news of Bauto, and Syagrius shook his head. Ascha told Syagrius what he had seen on the road from Viroviac, and Syagrius smiled and nodded.

'You did well. Although whether it will be enough...' he left the rest hanging.

They talked some more, of the Frankish Overlord's decision to stay in Tornacum, of the Saxon line of march, but mostly of what the Saxon army might do when they found the small force of Franks and Roman waiting for them.

On the road, the men trudged by in silence, each man lost in his thoughts. Ascha was surprised to see the Frankish captain who had left him at Thraelsted, marching with his men. The captain looked up and saw Ascha sitting calmly on his horse, passing the time of day with the Governor of the Romans, and his jaw dropped. He scowled, shook his head and marched on. Ascha watched him go with mixed feelings. He had liked the dour Frank, but he knew that for men like the captain, he would always be the Saxon half-slave.

Syagrius turned, struck by a sudden thought. 'When battle begins, I want you to pass my commands to the Franks,' he said crisply.

Ascha looked at him in confusion. 'Lord, it is not my place.'

Syagrius smiled. 'Probably not, but it is what I want. I need someone I can trust. It is important that Franks and Romans fight as one.'

The Governor touched his horse with his foot and moved out. Ascha blew the air from the cheeks. Rufus had heard the exchange because he caught his eye and gave him the ghost of a smile. Ascha swallowed. By asking him to translate the Governor's commands, Syagrius had put him in charge of the Overlord's Franks. He would command Antrustions in defence of a Frankish town.

The allied army took the road that he and the Pritanni had taken three days earlier. Ascha caught up with Syagrius, and they rode together. When they came to the grass-covered mound of Childeric's grave, Ascha pulled up.

'This is the place I spoke of,' he said.

Syagrius called a halt. He turned to Ascha and said, 'Then let us take a look.'

They rode down the dip and up the other side. They reached the edge of the forest, turned in the saddle and looked back up the rise to where the Romans and Franks stood silently watching. This was what Radhalla would see when he came out of the forest.

They rode on across to the quarry on the right flank and looked over and then they rode back across the front of the waiting troops to Childeric's mound on the left. Syagrius took his time. He looked around him, calculating distances, measuring angles, working it all through.

When he was done he stroked his chin, pursed his lips, looked at Ascha and nodded.

'You are right. This will do very well,' he said. 'Dispose the men across the road. Franks and Antrustions on the left, Romans on the right. Put archers and slingmen on that mound and on the flanks. The ground is too rough to use the horses so we'll have to dismount. One man in five to hold the horses in the rear. Post lookouts. Tell them to keep their eyes open for dust clouds tomorrow morning.'

'There is more,' Ascha said.

He explained how a small and determined group of fighting men, hidden in the upper reaches of the quarry, could strike the Saxon host unawares.

'As the host comes past, we'll rise up and strike them in the rear, like so!' Ascha said, and he swung an imaginary sword at the back of the Governor's head.

They rode back to the quarry and looked over.

'It might work,' Syagrius said. 'God knows we need something. Who would you use? You can't hide that many men down there.'

'Give me the royal hostages and what's left of the Pritanni,' he said. 'They fight like dogs. And they'll follow me.'

Syagrius thought it over. 'Very well,' he said. 'Take them and do what you can.'

That night the men lit fires and spread their blankets on the ground. Nobody could sleep. They sat on the packed earth cowed and glum, sharpening their blades with whetstones and talking. The Franks combed their hair, braided it and shaved the backs of their heads. The Romans played board games. Ascha heard the murmur of voices, the grating of iron scraping on stone and the click of dice. All over the plateau men knew that by the next day most of them would be dead.

Ascha found Rufus and his Pritanni and then went in search of the hostages. The night was warm and the air was thick. He found the hostages sitting round a fire, talking softly and cooking. Friedegund lay on his blanket singing softly in his own language. Further off, he could hear Hortar and Atharid arguing over some trifle. He breathed in the aroma of fried bacon and was filled with a sudden yearning for his past. All those years he had spent with these men, marching and fighting.

He shook his head and then tapped Gundovald on the shoulder.

'I need you!' he said, addressing them all. 'We have work to do.'

Ascha led the hostages and the Pritanni towards the rear. They circled around and then entered the quarry, climbing over rough ground littered with boulders and overgrown with weeds. They went down a rocky path and up toward a bluff of stone. After a while the quarry narrowed and the opposing walls grew closer.

'This way,' Ascha grunted, and began to climb.

They followed him, clambering up over the rocks, straddling boulders and leaping from one slab to another. The going became steeper and they clutched at bushes and grass roots to haul themselves up. Near the top, just below the lip of the quarry and hidden by bushes and wiry stunted trees, they came up on a small grass clearing. Ascha stood on a boulder and looked around, checking on their position. He was slightly out of breath, but he was also excited by what he had in mind.

He climbed further and peered through the foliage.

He had a good view across the plateau. Off to his left and slightly in front of the quarry was the right flank of the allied army. In the distance he could see the fringe of forest and the road down which the Saxons would come.

Here, he thought, is where we will fight.

He took Rufus and Gundovald aside, spoke quietly to them and then made his way back to the allied lines.

The next day before dawn, Ascha awoke. He kicked Tchenguiz to his feet, and they both went down the slope toward the woods. Ascha squatted and studied the country to the north. The sky changed from slate grey to a crisp blue washed with pink. He thought he could hear a rolling sound far off, like approaching thunder.

Tchenguiz looked at him. 'What is it, boss?'

'Listen!'

For a while they heard nothing and then they heard the faint and distant thump of war drums followed by the melancholy wail of horns. Ascha looked back up the slope. The allied camp was stirring, the troops slowly getting to their feet. Men stood looking out to where the road disappeared into the horizon. Nobody spoke, but the air was heavy, like before a storm.

They waited.

A flash of colour and two riders came galloping out of the trees, shouting and waving their arms, Rufus's men. Ascha held his breath, eyes squinting into the distance. And then he felt a quivering in the pit of his belly, like a nest of spiders, as the first of the Saxons slowly emerged from the trees.

Lifting Octha's burnstone to his lips, Ascha kissed it and muttered a quick prayer. Sweet Tiw! If today is the day that death taps me on the shoulder, do not let me shame my father's memory.

He turned and bellowed the call to arms.

31

Herrad and Octha left the *mansio* with Octha riding on the mule and Herrad leading. They went down a dirt path and across several fields and through a small wood. Dogs barked and the air was smoky. When they came to the road they turned south. They found many people all going the same way, bearded peasants and barefoot women and children, carrying their bedding and belongings in trundling wagons and squeaking carts. Townsfolk with baskets on their backs pushed handcarts, their feet kicking up dust that slowly drifted.

Herrad was surprised to see fighters with spears sloped over their shoulders moving away from the town. Deserters, she thought, fleeing the coming battle to go home to their farms and families. Some had made a bonfire by the side of the road and were cooking food they had looted. She smelled the aroma of roasting meat and her mouth watered.

When the road curved in towards the river, she stopped and checked on Octha. He was slumped low over the mule's neck and breathing heavily, his face tight with pain and tiredness. His hands, which she had wrapped in rags that morning, were bleeding again.

'Do you want to stop?' she said.

Octha raised his head and gave her a wan smile. She bit her lip. He wouldn't be able to travel much further. She hoped the boat would still be there, hoped that Eleri had waited.

They went on, moving into open country, following the road through the woods. Behind the trees she caught occasional glimpses of the river, and when the road curved she saw, far off, the murky outline of the Basilica through a haze of smoke.

A group of men sitting by the side of the road glanced up and followed her with their eyes. She looked away, not wanting to provoke them. One of them called out to her and offered water, but she pretended she hadn't heard and whipped the mule to make it go faster. Down the road she looked back over her shoulder and saw the men were still watching her.

When the road began to swing away from the river, she turned off and led them down a bare dirt track, wanting to stay in sight of the river. They walked more slowly, Octha swaying from side to side. She was concerned in case he fell. Buried in the trees, she saw cabins and clay-daubed hovels and peasants working their yards. A woman with a grubby-faced child on her hip came to her doorway and looked at her.

'Can we get to the river from here?' Herrad called.

The woman chewed something and then spat into the dust. 'Keep going and you'll come across the river path,' she said. 'Ain't much but it's enough.'

'Is there a boat?'

The woman shook her head. 'No boats,' she said. 'Boats all gone.'

Herrad made a sound that might have been a sigh. She glanced at Octha and then back at the woman.

'Do you know Eleri?' she asked, trying one last time.

The woman put her head on one side and then said, 'Nobody that name round here.'

They rode on.

She could see the River Schald through the trees, the water sparkling in the sun. She was weary now, and her feet ached. She found the river path, overgrown with weeds as high as her shoulder, and followed it. The sun flashed through the branches and then, where the river turned sharply to the left, she saw a large square white sail and a boat almost hidden beneath the trees.

She heaved an enormous sigh of relief and gave Octha a smile. Octha sat bowed in the saddle, past caring. She gave the mule's rump a mighty slap and they broke into a trot, long grass whipping at her legs. As they came closer, she saw figures moving on the boat, mostly women with a single Frankish Antrustion and a couple of male slaves. They stood in a huddle looking down at the deck.

She called out and saw them look up. Herrad pulled the mule to a halt and approached the foot of the gang plank.

'I am a friend of Ascha the Carver,' she said. 'Which of you is Eleri?'

The people on the boat glanced at one another and then at a tall woman in a fur cape. The woman looked Herrad up and down haughtily and then summoned her with a brisk flick of her fingers.

'Who are you?' the woman said, her voice grating.

Herrad felt uncomfortable. The woman was high-born, but why was she staring at her so intently? 'I am Herrad,' she said. 'And this is Octha the merchant. Are you Eleri?'

The tall woman frowned, and her lips twitched.

'No, I am not Eleri,' she said, her voice grating. She snapped her fingers and the servants drew back. On the deck lay a slight form covered by a woollen cloak. The bare legs of a young girl emerged from under the cloak. Herrad saw that the girl's feet were black with mud and flecked with blades of grass. On the deck beneath the body a puddle of blood had pooled.

'There's your Eleri,' the tall woman said. 'Now, come aboard. We are about to leave.'

Trumpets brayed and captains yelled commands. Men hefted their shields and grabbed their lances and ran to take their positions. The Franks rattled their weapons against their shields and shouted defiance. The Romans made no move, their faces still as stone. Ascha glanced over his shoulder. Saxons were pouring out of the trees like a thick and angry swarm of hornets, weapons glinting.

'More a them bastards than there are fleas on a dog,' Ascha heard a Frank mutter.

Ascha pulled his helmet over his head and tied the laces beneath his chin. Ripping the leather cover from his shield, he pushed his arm through the strap, gripped the handle and lifted it. He breathed in deep. The number of northerners was terrifying, sunlight glittering on the edge of their spears. He bent, scooped up some dust and rubbed it over his hands. He drew his *seaxe* and heard the dry hiss as the blade slid over old leather.

The Franks raised their shields and screamed their war cries, shaking their spears and rattling their shields in a hollow clatter of wood and iron. The Romans followed, '*Jubilate in Christo!*' they yelled. '*Jubilate in Christo!*'

The sound echoed and died.

The drums and horns fell silent.

The two armies watched each other without moving. A light breeze came up from the plain, softly threshing the grass and cooling the skin.

Ascha peered at the row of brightly painted Saxon shields. Why don't they come, he wondered? Somewhere over there were the Theodi. The thought of fighting his own troubled him, and then the seed of an idea crept slowly through his mind.

He ordered Tchenguiz to go bring up his horse. When the Hun returned, he handed him his shield, sheathed his *seaxe* and jumped onto the horse's back.

'And where does tha think tha's going?' Tchenguiz said.

'To speak with Besso.'

'Them Cheruskkii will kill tha.'

'Maybe.'

'Tha want I come with tha?'

'No,' I'll do this alone.'

He kicked the horse's belly, trotted down the slope and cut diagonally up the other side. There were skylarks above him and the air was warm as breath. He heard catcalls and jeers as the Saxons saw the lone rider approaching, but then they grew quiet. He moistened his lips. The Saxons were ranged across the plateau, hairy-faced and filthy. Many were barefoot and bareheaded and they all stank. He could hear them whispering and the thought passed through his mind that they knew him. He was the Theod who had killed Wulfhere, the man who had left Radhalla's nephew with a dagger in his eye, the one who led the Roman horse soldiers against them at Viroviac.

He was pleased that they recognized him and, for the first time in a long while, he felt calm and untroubled. Reining in he shouted, 'Where are the Theodi?'

The cry passed down the line. Some way off, he saw a tall shambling man with a face the colour of baked earth step out.

Besso.

The Theodi were clustered around him. Not many, maybe sixty or seventy men, but Ascha knew them all. They stood behind their shields, waiting to hear what he had to say.

'We be of one blood,' he said.

'We be of one blood,' Besso agreed. 'You've been busy, boy. Wherever I go I hear thi name.'

'Besso, I want to speak to the clan.'

Besso looked at him, scratched his beard, and then turned and waved a wide arm. 'Go ahead,' he said. 'They're not going anywhere.'

Ascha kicked the gelding forward. For a moment, he had the wildest notion that he was on the wrong side. He should be fighting shoulder to shoulder with the Saxons, with his own people, not the Romans and the Franks.

And then he spoke.

'You all know me,' he called out. 'I am Ascha of the Theodi. My father was Aelfric and his father was Osric.'

No sound but the chink of iron and the banners cracking in the breeze.

'My father pledged friendship with the Franks and sealed that pact with a chest of silver. Most of you were there. You swore an oath, a sacred oath, that you would not draw iron against these people. Why now do you take up arms against them?'

The Theodi were silent. Some exchanged glances, others looked at their feet, as if ashamed. He leaned forward over the saddle.

'Have you forgotten how Radhalla's Cheruskkii invaded our land? They murdered my brother and they slaughtered our people. They raped and plundered and burnt our homes. They destroyed us as they have destroyed so many tribes before us.'

There was a low growl from the Cheruskkii.

'We are a free people. A holy people. Guardians of the sacred pool,' he reminded them. 'Generations ago we migrated from the Almost-Island and settled between the two rivers when the Cheruskkii were still sitting on logs in the marshes and croaking.'

The Theodi laughed at that. This was their story and they were proud of it.

Besso kicked the turf with the heel of his boot and looked up at him. 'What does tha want, Ascha?'

'Join us, Besso! Fight alongside the Romans and the Franks as thirty years ago we fought together against the Huns.'

'You want us to take on the Cheruskkii?'

'It's the Cheruskkii who have betrayed us, not the Romans or the Franks. Hanno is dead and you are no longer oath-bound. I am the son of Aelfric, Besso. Join me now against those who stole our honour.'

Besso gave Ascha a fixed and sleepy stare. He ran his fingers through his beard, shrugged and shook his head. And then, with a faint smile as if he was not quite sure what he was doing, he took a step towards Ascha and began to walk slowly towards him.

Ascha waited, heart in mouth.

There was a pause and then Ulfila, one of his father's friends, stepped out from the line. Others followed: Lulla, Hwita, One-eyed Ucca, Odda, red-haired Meoc, old Wada. The boy Morcar grinned and lifted a hand as he passed by. He watched them come, a steady trickle of men. They left the Saxon line and sauntered over as if out for a summer stroll. He counted quickly. Not many. Not enough to make a difference, but better than nothing.

Seeing the Theodi leave, the Cheruskkii raised an angry roar and beat angrily on their shields. The Saxon army shifted like some vast and nameless beast, ready to fall on the Theodi traitors. Now was the hard time. If the Cheruskkii attacked they would destroy the Theodi in moments. Stay calm, he thought. Stay calm.

A sudden boiling in the lines and Radhalla appeared with his big head and powerful stone-crunching jaws. He wore a gleaming chain mail coat held by a war belt as wide as a man's hand and over it a black wolfskin cape. On his arm, a warshield decorated with bronze animals and birds.

Radhalla watched with dark and hooded eyes as the Theodi streamed away.

'Let 'em go!' he bellowed. 'They're all going to die anyway.'

An angry growl from the Cheruskkii, but they lowered their spears. Ascha blew out his lungs with relief. He turned and waved to Syagrius to let the Theodi through and then yanked his horse's head around and followed them.

When he looked back, Radhalla was still watching him.

As he neared the allied line he saw a rumpled figure waiting for him half-way up the slope, accompanied by a young boy. Ascha slipped a leg over the horse's neck and slid to the ground. Besso dipped into his tunic, pulled out an apple and bit into it. The juice ran down his beard, and dripped onto his chest. There was a crooked smile on his face.

'What's tha laughing at?' Ascha said sourly.

Besso scratched his bristly chin. 'The way tha spoke back there. Tiw! But it put me in mind of thi father.'

Ascha threw the boy a suspicious glance. 'What's this?' he said.

The boy looked about fourteen, the age Ascha had been when he went on his first raid. Besso snapped his fingers. The boy ran a pink tongue across his lips and stepped forward. He held a bundle with both hands and offered it to Ascha.

Bemused, Ascha took the gift. It was heavier than it looked. He noticed the boy gazing up at him with a look akin to awe and felt slightly embarrassed. He pulled away a sackcloth covering to reveal a sword, the sword his grandfather wore when he fought the Huns, the sword his mother had hidden beneath the hut floor when the Cheruskkii came. Holding his breath, he ran his hand over the shining blade, gently tracing the wave-like pattern with his finger and looked at Besso, his eyes swimming.

'Thi mother wanted tha to have it,' Besso said. 'She knew I would see tha again. I was unable to give it tha before.'

321

'Tha could have kept this to thiself, and I would niver have known,' Ascha said.

Besso smiled. 'That occurred to me also.'

'I don't want it!' Ascha said suddenly, pushing the sword away.

Besso looked at him angrily. 'It's thi father's sword!'

'My father sent me away to exile,' Ascha yelled. 'He made me an outcast.'

'Thi father had no choice,' Besso said dourly. 'He was a good man and did what he could.'

'But Radhalla...'

'Radhalla is half the man thi father was,' Besso said with a vehemence that took Ascha by surprise. 'He was always jealous of Aelfric.'

Ascha looked at him. 'Radhalla was jealous?'

'Everything Aelfric had, Radhalla wanted. It was always the same with him. But thi father would a been proud of tha. Proud of what tha's done.'

He laid a hand on Ascha's shoulder and held up the sword. 'Take it,' Besso said softly.

Ascha turned and looked at Besso, wanting to believe. He lowered his head and took the sword. He put one arm around Besso's meaty neck and the other round the boy's shoulders and together they walked back up the slope.

'For a moment, I believed you were going over to them,' Syagrius said peevishly.

'I thought about it.'

Syagrius looked at him and gave an uncertain laugh.

'They'll attack very soon,' Ascha said, looking back across the plateau.

'Yes.'

'No word from the Franks?'

'None,' said Syagrius. 'Now, come with me. I want you to translate for the Franks.'

Syagrius rode out in front of the allied line and turned to face the troops.

Ascha looked him over. The King of the Romans, the Franks sometimes called him, although with his grey hair and ill-fitting cuirass, he looked more like a country landowner.

Syagrius spoke in his thin patrician voice. He reminded them why they were there and what they were required to do. He told them they were heavily outnumbered, but that help was on its way. If they died today, they would do so knowing their deaths would be avenged.

'I trust that you will fight with honour and I pray that God will grant us victory.'

Ascha had barely finished translating the Governor's words when there was a wild yell.

'Here they come!'

32

Ascha held his breath. The Saxons held their shields in front of their mouths and boomed their war cry. They hammered their *seaxes* on their shields and then they came on, wardrums pounding. There were thousands of them, covering the plateau from one side to another. The Franks clashed their weapons against their shields and howled like wolves. Ascha felt as if the earth were shaking.

Syagrius flicked his fingers, and archers ran forward into the dead ground between the two armies. Half way down the slope, they knelt and fitted arrows to their bows and drew. They held the shafts to their chins with a look of rapt concentration and then released in one fluid movement.

A dull thrum of bowstrings.

The Saxons raised their shields and went to ground. Ascha saw a dark stain of arrows rise and fall, rattling on shields and thumping into wood and flesh. There were cries of pain and men fell, writhing. The archers fired again and again before withdrawing. Each time the northerners shook themselves like wet dogs and then came on, tramping steadily over a ground littered with arrow shafts and stricken men, bunching up and leaning forward, shields up, as if caught in a storm.

With a wild yell the Saxons broke into a run, dipping down into the lower ground and rushing up the slope like a tidal wave, big bearded faces screaming defiance.

Ascha unlaced the beaded peace-bands that held the hilt of his father's sword and drew it, rasping from the scabbard's throat. He rested the heavy blade against his shoulder, flexed his fingers around the grip and waited, every muscle rigid with tension. A rain of slingshots hummed through the air above his head and crashed onto the Saxons' shields and helmets, shattering skulls and breaking limbs.

He heard Syagrius shout, 'Hold your places. Stand fast!'

'Stand fast!' Ascha repeated in Frankish. 'At my signal!'

He waited until the moment was ripe and jerked his arm down.

'Now!' he yelled. 'Spike them!'

With a grunt the Franks swung their arms up and over. Javelins and *angons*, the cruelly barbed Frankish harpoons, arced and fell, doing cruel damage to soft bodies.

Still the Saxons came on.

'*Franciskas!*' Ascha called. The Franks took two running steps and hurled their tomahawks.

The shields of the Saxon front rank shattered under the whirling blades. Time stood still. And then Ascha felt himself shaken by a bone-jarring crash, like a great oak falling in the forest, as the two armies met.

Twice, against all odds, the allies hurled the Saxons back. The Franks dragged out their dead and injured and closed up the line. They checked their shields for cracks and their blade-edges for chips and wiped their faces clean of blood and sweat. A pause while both sides caught their breath and warily watched each other. Ascha ached all over, and his sword arm felt heavy as lead. Sweat ran down his back and his throat was dry as sand. The first few moments of battle were already a blur. Men swung their weapons, iron thrusts opening the bodies of strangers who died to grunts and curses and the clang of iron on iron. But now the allies' numbers were dwindling. Already more than half were dead or injured. They couldn't take much more.

Syagrius came trotting by, his face drawn.

'We must hold this rise,' he shouted urgently to Ascha. 'Once they push us back we are lost.'

Simple to say, Ascha thought, the difficulty lay in doing it.

There were shouts further down the line. Ascha could see men turning and pointing. He raised a hand to shield his eyes. He saw banners fluttering and the flash of sunlight on iron weapons. There were armed men coming up on their flank.

'Who are they?' Tchenguiz said.

'Franks,' one of the auxiliaries shouted. 'It's Bauto! The Franks are here!'

A ragged cheer went up. Men turned, laughed and threw their caps in the air. Some danced, swinging each other by the arm.

Ascha squinted into the sun.

'It's not Bauto,' he said, his eyesight better than any man's. 'It's Ragnachar and his River Franks.'

He felt a tremor of apprehension but was reassured when he saw that Ragnachar was making no attempt to join the Saxons. Ragnachar rode with his wife and two daughters in a cart pulled by two long-maned ponies, followed by a wagonload of slaves. Behind came a troop of mounted Alani and then the mass of Ragnachar's Franks. Ascha saw Fara among the Alani, riding the same black stallion he had ridden the night before. He wrenched his eyes away.

Some day, he resolved, but not today.

Ragnachar led his Franks with drums beating past the Saxons and toward the allied lines. Ascha could hear bone flutes, a thin and mournful sound, like the keening of kites. He felt a huge surge of relief. Blood was thicker than water after all. Ragnachar had come to rescue his nephew. With Ragnachar's forces they could hold the Saxons off until Bauto's *scara* arrived.

Ragnachar drove to the edge of the plateau. His cart rattled to a halt. The Alani reined in and Ragnachar's Franks came to a standstill. Ragnachar sat in the wagon with his legs wide and his belly drooping over his britches. Banners whipped in the breeze. The cheering faded. The allies turned and looked at each other with anxious faces.

'Why they stop?' Tchenguiz said.

A chill spread down Ascha's back. 'He's not going to fight.'

'What?'

'He's waiting to see which way the wind blows. He'll join forces with whoever comes out on top.'

'It's not true,' someone said.

'It's true,' he said.

The drums thundered once more, the trumpets blared and the horns groaned like a dying bull. Ascha's head throbbed and his eyes stung with sweat.

'They're coming,' someone shouted.

The sun was at its highest. The men buckled down and waited for the onslaught. The rhythm changed. *Rum-pum-ti-ti-pum, rum-pum-ti-ti-pum.* The Saxons were forming up in a deep wedge, axe wielding Cheruskers to the fore, other clans to the sides. They came on baying triumphantly, a dark mass as deep as it was wide, aiming for the middle of the allied line.

'*Cuneus!*' Syagrius yelled. 'Open the front rank! Middle ranks step back!'

Ascha called it in Frankish. 'Boar snout!'

The sound of trumpets shivered the air.

He knew what Syagrius wanted. The only defence to the boar's snout was to pull back the centre of the line to let the Saxons in and envelop them. But they had too few troops to encircle the Saxons. If they were to avoid being penetrated, the allies would have to withdraw.

He screamed at Syagrius. 'Lord, we will not be able to hold them much longer. I must go now!'

Ascha saw a shadow of doubt flit across the Governor's brow, and then his face cleared and he nodded. 'Go!' he shouted. 'And may God go with you.'

Ascha slapped Tchenguiz on the shoulder and they turned and pushed their way through the packed Franks, shouting and banging on the mens' shields to let them through. They ran to the rear and round to the quarry. They moved fast, knowing the way, pushing through chest-high weeds and climbing up over the rocks until they came to where the band of hostages and Pritanni lay hidden in the brush.

They rose when they saw him and looked at him expectantly. He scanned their sweat-stained faces, his weariness forgotten. Far off, he could hear the sounds of battle, rising and falling like the sea.

'Thought you'd forgotten us,' Gundovald growled, and the men snickered nervously.

'Syagrius will hold them as long as he can,' Ascha said. 'But as soon as he pulls back, we go in.'

They drew their weapons and moved up to the edge of the quarry. They squatted and waited, hearing the clash of iron on wood and the screams of dying men. Ascha sheathed his sword and drew his *franciska*. This would be close work and a hatchet would be more use. He heard the brazen call of the Roman trumpets and a hoarse Roman shout, 'Withdraw! Withdraw!'

He peered through the foliage, trying to judge the moment. He waited until the bulk of Saxons had passed before he turned.

'You ready?' Ascha shouted.

Gundovald cleared his throat and spat. 'Ready as we'll ever be.'

Ascha grinned. 'Then let's go tear their arses out!'

The hostages and Pritanni exploded over the lip of the quarry and fell on the Saxons. Ascha swung his shield and whirled his *franciska*. He killed quickly, smashing skulls and hamstringing the Saxons before they knew what was happening. Easy work to kill or maim when a man's back was turned. The Northerners were wedged tight together. Struggling to turn they died in droves, the struggling and the dying, crowded side by side.

A fair-haired Cherusker slashed at him with a murderous deep-bladed stroke. He countered and struck back. The blow cut deep into the base of the Cherusker's neck and he fell with a hollow cry. A Chaussi half-turned and lunged with a spear. Ascha sidestepped, struck and heard the crack as the man's head gave way, spraying him with a fine mist of blood and fragments of bone.

He pressed on, teeth clenched, cleaving bones and shattering shields. He stepped inside a Saxon's guard and pushed his blade deep into soft flesh. He felt a massive blow and staggered, his shield shattered. He slipped in a puddle of human guts and nearly fell. He just had time to see a Saxon smash Hariulf's skull with a single axe blow before the Saxon turned and was coming for him.

He threw the broken shield aside and scrambled to his feet. Hooking his tomahawk over the man's shield, he pulled it away and hacked hard. The man screamed, his severed wrist fountaining blood. Ascha fought on. He saw Rufus, his sword flickering, like a snake's tongue. He was aware of Tchenguiz at his side, his face caked with congealed blood, Gundovald swinging his big axe, Gydda watching his back and howling like a fiend, a *seaxe* in each hand. He heard a cry of pain and saw Hortar the Aleman fall with an axe buried in his chest.

'Where's Radhalla?' he yelled and spat the blood that rose to his throat. Tchenguiz turned and pointed with his long knife. Over the screams and the clash of iron on iron, he could hear Radhalla bellow, 'Come on my grey wolves! The more we die, the stronger we become.' For a moment he saw the warlord of the Cheruskkii surrounded by his *Gesith,* and then he was gone.

The ferocity of the attack took the Saxons by surprise. The Saxon charge began to falter, and they started to pull back, feet slipping on the blood-soaked ground. The allies were too tired to cheer or give pursuit. They rested, bent double, and drew in great lungfuls of air. Ascha saw they were on the point of breaking. They had destroyed the boar's snout, but had nothing in reserve. The dead and the dying lay across the rise like felled logs, the plateau was strewn with weapons and broken shields.

He heard a sudden flurry of drums. He looked up and felt his insides go jagged. Ragnachar's troops were moving against them. Ragnachar stood in his cart, his wife and daughters beside him, waving them on. He let his sword arm fall to his side. His body ached and he felt an acute sense of disappointment. If the Overlord's uncle joined forces with Radhalla, the Saxons would break through and take the town. It would all be over before Bauto arrived.

In front of the Saxon army, he could see Radhalla striding up and down, urging the Saxons on. This time, just one more push, and they would break through. The allies were exhausted and would be unable to hold them.

Ascha tried to get his mind to work but it wouldn't snap to. They had lost, and he wanted to weep with frustration.

But there was another sound borne on the breeze. Horns sounded deep in the forest and there were armed men coming out of the trees.

A shout went up.

Tchenguiz turned to him with a huge grin. 'Them's Franks, boss.'

He looked and looked again, and heard the cry go up, 'It's Bauto! Bauto's here!'

The Saxons looked back over their shoulders, and he could sense their fear. This time it was Bauto's *scara*. He saw Bauto on his horse at the head of his men, captains by his side, the war standard with its six black horsetails carried high, Bauto's Antrustions running ahead, bounding to the kill.

Ragnachar's men paused. They turned to Ragnachar, big-bellied in his wagon. Ragnachar dithered. He looked at the Saxons and at the approaching Franks and then pushed himself to his feet and began to wave them back. Horns blew. Slowly and ponderously, Ragnachar's Franks shifted their angle of march, turning against the Saxons.

The front ranks of Bauto's *scara* hurled their *angons* on the run and struck the flank of the Saxon host like a thunderclap, driving the northerners back onto the spears of the defenders. Saxon horns frantically sounded the withdrawal. But it was too late. Bauto's troops were battle fresh and hungry. Syagrius gave the order to advance and the allies moved forward, squeezing the northerners between Bauto's Franks, Ragnachar's Franks and the defenders of Tornacum.

'They're running,' a Roman shouted.

Ascha saw that it was true. The Saxon host was disintegrating, men throwing away their heavy shields and fleeing in all directions.

'Boss!' Tchenguiz shouted in his ear and pointed. A group of raiders had slipped away from the fighting and were moving along a ditch, not fleeing but moving quickly and deliberately, without panic, towards the allied rear. Ascha squinted, saw chain mail and helmets and a long black cloak.

'It's Radhalla!' Ascha breathed. 'He's heading for Tornacum.'

His war was not yet over.

He jerked his head at Tchenguiz, Gydda and Gundovald and shouted, 'Come on!'

33

Tornacum was silent. Grainy smoke hung over the rooftops and there was a smell of burning. Wherever he looked, houses had been abandoned, the doors mouthing open and tongues of flame licking the shadows. Ascha led the hostages down narrow alleyways littered with discarded panniers, clothes and broken storage jars. Goats wandered and dogs yelped. A basket lay in the street, spilling onions onto the dust.

Rounding the corner of the market square, Ascha stopped. Dead men sprawled on the steps of the Basilica, Franks and Saxons, their limbs entwined. More bodies lay inside. A wounded Saxon sat propped against a pillar, his lips grey and waxy.

Ascha knelt beside him, 'Where is Radhalla, brother?' he said in the dialect of the northshore.

'Inside,' gasped the man, taking Ascha for one of his own.

They ran up the staircase and into the Basilica. The great hall was burning. Thick plumes of smoke swirled and rolled, stinging their eyes and gritting their throats. They lifted their shields and went on, eyes alert, peering into the gloom. He saw that the dirty little fight that had begun in the square had continued inside. Bodies lay crumpled or on their backs with their arms outstretched. Some, he noticed, were clerks who had been caught in the fighting. There was a whoosh of flame and the wall hangings flared, the flames clawing swiftly up toward the roof. The marble statue of a long dead Roman general toppled and crashed to the floor, exploding in scattered fragments. The roof was already on fire, beams smouldering and the stones glowing brightly. He heard the crackle and roar of burning timber and fire smuts danced around his head.

They moved forward slowly. The smoke stung their eyes and scratched at their throats. Two Cheruskkii suddenly came at them from out of the gloom, swinging hand axes. Ascha swung his *franciska* into the leading Cherusker's face and saw Gydda cripple the other. The Cherusker fell with a howl and was killed.

'Come on!' Ascha cried.

At the door to Clovis' chamber, Ascha shouted 'Tchenguiz! Gydda! Guard the door. Gundovald come with me.'

He opened the door and stepped inside.

Four men were in the room. Others lay dead on their faces. Radhalla stood with his back to the fireplace where less than a year ago Clovis had outlined his dream of a Frankish empire that would stretch from the western ocean to the Rhine and the Roman Sea. He turned as Ascha and Gundovald burst in. He had removed his helmet and his tunic was dark with sweat and blood.

Clovis stood on a table with his hands tied and his hair matted with blood and filth. Around the Overlord's throat was a seal hide rope, pulled tight under the jaw and thrown over a high beam. His feet were bare and he stood on his toes. His eyes had a dull look about them, as if he had slept badly. Radhalla's huge bodyguard, his head shaved but for a single hair-tassle, had looped the other end of the rope around an iron stanchion set into the wall. He leaned back, ready to pull on the rope with all his weight. Another raw-boned Cherusker crouched by the table, brandishing a *seaxe*.

Ascha stopped and breathed slowly, taking it all in.

'Hello, Theodling,' Radhalla said in a quiet voice. 'Have you come to watch your Overlord die?'

The big Cherusker with the tassle grinned. He heaved on the rope and hauled Clovis up in the air. Swinging by the neck, the Overlord made a gurgling sound and his face purpled.

'Let him go!' Ascha said.

Radhalla thought for a moment and then gave a careless nod to the Cherusker who reluctantly paid out a little of the rope. Clovis jerked and fell a little way. His toes teetered on the edge of the table and his eyes lurched towards Ascha.

'Help me!' Clovis rasped. 'Help me!'

A dark curl of smoke rose up the wall. Thin flames ran over the door and back again. 'It's over, Radhalla,' Ascha said. 'Bauto's *scara* has come and your men are dying in droves.'

'It's not over,' Radhalla spat. 'It's never fucking over!'

'Let him live, and he may allow you your life.'

Radhalla looked at him with hard, piggy eyes. 'Why should you care what happens to this prick? He deserves to die.'

'I said let him down!'

'You been working for him all along?'

'All along,' agreed Ascha.

There was a sudden whiff of something foul in the air, and they all wrinkled their noses. The Overlord of the Franks had filled his britches.

'Why d'you do it, boy?' Radhalla said. 'Why'd you work so hard against me?'

'You ask me why?' Ascha said, his blood boiling. 'After everything you did? You killed my brother. Sent me to the slavers. Attacked my woman.'

Radhalla lowered his head. 'Hroc got in the way,' he snarled. 'And it was not my idea to sell you to the slavers. Sigisberht disobeyed me. He saw you as a rival when I was trying to save your miserable hide by sending you home. As for the girl,' he shrugged his shoulders, 'these things happen.'

There was something in Radhalla's eyes Ascha had not seen before; a fleeting shadow, not doubt or indecision, but something else.

'Sigisberht suspected me?'

'He did,' Radhalla said.

'And Ragnachar?'

'Fara told me that Clovis had sent a spy but I never thought it was you. Why should I? You were a Theod, one of our own. For years I've been planning and building this fleet,' Radhalla said. 'Is there any Roman or Frankish general who could have done what I have done? It was hard to believe that you would betray us.'

Ascha began to move as casually as he could toward the table, aware of Gundovald at his side.

'Ragnachar sent his Alani to kill me.'

Radhalla nodded. 'After you spoke at the council, he saw you were dangerous and had to be stopped. He sent Fara to warn me. But you were either clever or lucky. I should have killed you when I had the chance.'

'Why didn't you?'

Radhalla looked at him carefully. 'I had my reasons.'

He wondered about that. Why would Radhalla have spared his life? He was sure the Iron Plough wouldn't hesitate a second time. He considered the odds. He had Gundovald, and there were three Cheruskkii. He could kill Radhalla in which case Clovis would die, or try to save Clovis, in which case Radhalla would certainly kill him.

Not much of a choice, he thought. Either way, he was dead meat.

The fire was taking hold. He could hear the flames crackling outside in the hall. Smell the smoke.

'Let's hang the turd,' the ugly Cherusker called and jerked the rope. Clovis, scrabbling to keep his balance, glared at them. Radhalla raised his hand. The Cherusker scowled but held off.

'But you're game, I'll give you that,' Radhalla went on not taking his eyes off Ascha. 'In another life we could a been friends, maybe more. But this thing dies.'

The Cherusker with the rope coiled around his arm, took the strain. The seal hide creaked and a dry choking sound escaped from the Overlord's lips.

'He is a nothing. Why kill him?' Ascha said.

Radhalla breathed in deep. 'Let me tell you a story,' he said slowly. 'And then maybe, just maybe – before I kill him – you'll see what kind of creature you sold yourself to.' His tone was soft and quiet, just beginning to shade into anger.

There was a sudden roar of belching flame. Ascha glanced up. Smoke was billowing into the chamber, and he could see the top of the brick walls glowing red. The high ribbed roof was burning, sparks and blazing embers falling around them in a hot shower. He could feel the heat like a hot blanket pressing on his lungs.

Radhalla placed both hands flat against the wall. 'Six years ago, a high-born Cherusker sails to Pritannia to bring back his bride, a beautiful girl with yellow hair like gold. On the way home, off the coast of Gallia, their ship is caught in a storm and driven ashore. The Cherusker is young, a little younger than you are now, and inexperienced. He sends word to the Franks that he travels in peace and seeks leave to repair his boat. Childeric the Overlord, this one's father, agrees to give him safe passage. But he lies. Childeric sends troops to cut them off. The Cheruskkii are caught unawares and slaughtered. Less than a dozen survive and are taken captive.'

He spoke reasonably as if telling a story in the feast-hall at Radhallaburh.

'What is this to me?' Ascha said.

Radhalla turned to face him, holding up one hand. 'I'm coming to that,' he said with quiet menace. 'The young man and his beautiful bride are taken to Tornacum. Childeric parades them before his friends and guests. The Franks are fearful of the Saxons but they know they must come to terms with them if they are to stop the raiding. They have an opportunity here to be merciful. Help the young man and his bride, and the Saxons might be grateful.' He belched softly and rubbed his belly in a circular movement. 'And who knows,' he went on with a cold smile, 'they might be persuaded to raid Pritannia rather than Gallia.'

'And?'

'Childeric tortures the young man for the best part of a day,' Radhalla said. 'Twists him on a pole and breaks both his legs. Beats him and burns him with hot irons. Then, when he's done, he buries the young man alongside his bride.'

Radhalla picked up a clay bottle from the table. He shook it, pulled the stopper and drank. He wiped his mouth with the back of his arm and let the flask drop on the floor. Radhalla paused and Ascha thought he saw a shadow of sadness pass across the Cherusker's thick face.

He and Gundovald watched without a word.

'Childeric buried them beneath the marketplace of Tornacum,' Radhalla said softly. 'They were alive when he buried them. You walked over their graves when you came in. The rest of the Cheruskkii he spared and sent home to tell the story.'

Ascha shuddered. Buried alive! What kind of monster did that? Even the fire was kinder.

'It's not true,' Clovis croaked. 'He's lying.'

'Shut it!' growled the big Cherusker, jerking the rope.

Ascha ran a hand through his hair. He threw a warning glance at Gundovald. 'What is this to me?'

'The Cherusker was my son, Ceolwine.' Radhalla said. 'And your father saw it happen.'

There was an anguished moan from Clovis but Ascha had eyes only for Radhalla. 'How could my father have seen it happen?'

'Aelfric was in Tornacum that day. It was soon after Clovis found you in the forest at Samarobriva. Childeric would have happily slaughtered Aelfric along with the Cheruskkii, but Besso held his son, Clovis, hostage and so Childeric's hands were tied. Instead, that evil old fuck murdered my boy.' He stared at Clovis with eyes that were full of hatred. 'Murdered him and his bride so he could impress Aelfric and the people of Tornacum with his determination to rid Gallia of Saxons.'

Ascha felt sick to the pit of his stomach. He shook his head. 'There was nothing my father could have done,' he said.

'Na, nothing,' Radhalla agreed. 'But I swore that one day I would have *faida*, I would have my vengeance on the Overlord and his family. I would come back.'

Clovis coughed. 'As a dog returns to its own vomit,' he wheezed.

It was as if a door in Ascha's head had opened letting in light. He realized that no matter how much Radhalla might have wanted to settle in Roman Gaul, it was never his first aim. He had come to Tornacum for revenge. He wanted the blood-price for the murder of his son. And Clovis must have known. Clovis had Cheruskkii blood on his hands. And so did Aelfric. His father had been there when it happened, would have watched helplessly as the Franks slowly destroyed the son of the man who had once been his closest friend. Now he knew why his father had wanted a pact with the Franks. Raddled with guilt, Aelfric had seen that the Franks were too dangerous to have as enemies. Best take the Franks' silver and go home.

'Hang the fuck!' Radhalla said.

The big Cherusker spat on his hands and heaved on the rope. Clovis was dragged up in the air, legs kicking wildly.

Ascha pulled his tomahawk and leapt forward. The Cherusker looped the rope over the stanchion and, with surprising speed for one so big, turned and kicked Ascha in the lower belly. Ascha doubled up and fell to his knees. The Cherusker kicked him in the face. Ascha's jaw seemed to explode. The Cherusker came for him, *seaxe* drawn. As Ascha struggled to get to his feet, he felt a hot pain rip along his belly. The Cherusker stood back to see what he would do. Ascha touched his side and his fingers came up sticky. He started to get to his feet and then allowed his axe arm to slump to his side.

The Cherusker grinned and came at him again.

Ascha twisted suddenly and swung the *franciska*. There was a scream of pain as the curved blade took off half the Cherusker's foot. Rising to his feet, Ascha swung again with both hands. The blade cut deep into the man's neck and the big Cherusker crashed to the ground.

Ascha heard a dry gasp.

Gundovald was standing over the dead body of the other Saxon with a strange and faraway look on his face. Gundovald crumpled and slid to the floor. Radhalla stepped over him, bent and wiped the blade of his sword on Gundovald's shirt.

Ascha had no time to think whether he should kill Radhalla or save Clovis. He couldn't let Clovis hang as his brother Hroc had hung. He leapt onto the table and caught the Overlord's swinging body, gasping as he breathed in his stench. He reached up and sawed at the rope behind Clovis' neck. The rope parted, Clovis fell and the two of them rolled off the table and crashed to the floor.

When Ascha came to, the roof was engulfed in flames and smoke was pouring under the door. He heard a series of loud reports as roof tiles exploded and smashed on the floor by his head. Gundovald stared with dead eyes and the Overlord's body lay slumped some way off. Radhalla stood above him, holding the point of his sword to the hollow in his throat.

He felt little fear, just an overwhelming weariness. He wanted to howl. He had lost everything he had worked for. After all he had been through, to die like this, killed by the man who had done his family so much harm.

His eyes welled. 'Do it,' he gasped. 'What are you waiting for?'

'Don't worry,' Radhalla, said with a grimace like the slash of a knife. 'I'm not about to kill you just yet.'

Ascha stared up at Radhalla. Was he to be burnt and buried alive, like Ceolwine? He swallowed painfully. The pain in his side was like a hot knife against his ribs. He guessed that the new cut had opened Wulfhere's wound. He felt so tired, the blood seeping from him, but before he died, he would know the truth.

'You told Hanno you were going for Syagrius,' he gasped. 'You told him you would make landfall south of Gesoriac.'

Radhalla laughed from deep in his chest. Sparks dropped onto his shoulders but he took no notice. 'My plan was always to deal with the Franks first. I never told him we would land south of Gesoriac, but he had become an embarrassment. After you visited him, he started to question me. So we tied him to a stake and left him for you to find.'

Radhalla was silent for a moment as if trying to give the matter serious thought. 'I think he felt bad about his brother's death. It had been preying on his mind.' He made a circular motion with his forefinger at his temple. 'He thought Tiw was angry with him. Maybe that's why he deceived you.'

'You're lying, you sack of shit,' Ascha breathed. His side was painful and his hand was slick with blood. There was more blood, dark and sticky, seeping through his tunic. Far above the roof was crackling with flame. The billowing smoke filled his lungs and stung his eyes. He coughed, his throat scraped raw.

'Na, lad. Not half as much as you lie to yourself. You see, we're alike, you and me. Peas in a pod.'

'I'm not like you,' Ascha said. Out in the hall, he could hear fighting, the clash of iron on iron.

'But you are, boy,' Radhalla said, his voice dropping. 'You remember when I told you how Aelfric captured your mother and forbade any man to touch her on pain of death?'

He paused and leaned back never taking his eyes off Ascha and then said, 'Later, when your father was asleep, I took her.'

Ascha's heart curled. He felt as if he was choking, a tight fist wound like a snake around his neck.

Radhalla watched him with a faint smile on his lips. 'I'm not proud of what I did, but you can't put shit back in the mule. Your mother was pretty in a strange sort of way and I was used to getting what I wanted.'

'You're lying,' Ascha whispered.

Radhalla smiled and ran his hand over his chin. 'Na, lad, I ain't lying. You and me are closer than you think,' he laughed and slapped his thigh. 'I wasn't sure at first but then it came to me when I saw the hatred in your eyes after we executed Hroc, and when you killed Wulfhere and Sigisberht, and again when you led the Roman horse soldiers against me,' he chuckled softly. 'You're not Aelfric's son, you're mine. You were always mine.'

Ascha saw Tchenguiz slip into the chamber behind Radhalla, a shadow in the smoke. A burning beam fell to the floor with a loud crash and the wall hangings went up in flames with a *whoompf*. He felt a weariness overcome him as if his spirit was draining away. His side was wet with blood and he could no longer feel his legs. Could Radhalla really believe he was his natural son?

But then he remembered Wulfhere's jibes. *Does tha know who tha father is?* And the strange glances Aelfric would sometimes give him, as if he was not sure who Ascha really was.

Tchenguiz stood in the doorway with a bow. Through smoke-stung eyes, Ascha saw Tchenguiz draw a red hackled arrow and fit it to the bowstring.

'We want the same things, you and me,' Radhalla said, 'and we don't give in until we get them. You do as I would do. You keep going. You don't give in. You're my blood and bone. Tiw's breath! We even look alike.' And Radhalla dipped his head to show the profile of his own thick nose.

Tchenguiz drew the arrow to his ear. The Hun tensed, and Ascha knew he was waiting for a clear shot. With a giant heave, he raised himself up on one elbow. He saw Tchenguiz hesitate and then lower the bow. Ascha shook his head, trying to remember how he felt such a terrible pain. His chest was tight and his breathing laboured. 'You're wrong. I'm not like you.'

Radhalla laughed without humour. 'You were born for this. Can't you see? It's in your blood. You could never have accepted life as a simple woodcarver.' He leaned forward and the sword point wavered over Ascha's throat. 'Come on. Join me! It's what I've always wanted, to go through life with my own flesh and blood by my side. Let's finish off this scum and be done with it.'

'I'm a half-slave,' Ascha croaked.

'I don't fucken care what you are,' Radhalla snarled. 'You're my son, and that's all there is to it.'

'And Sigisberht?'

'He tried but he wasn't up to it. But you and I, boy, we could set the world alight.

Ascha looked up at Radhalla. The Cherusker was growing dim again, his voice coming at him like out of some dark funnel. *Set the world alight?* But he had never wanted to set the world alight, he had only wanted to be whole.

'Tell me one thing?' he whispered.

'Name it.'

'Did you kill Aelfric?'

Behind the Cherusker's eyes was a deep and unfathomable darkness. Radhalla shrugged, looked away, and then looked back.

He nodded.

'The slinger was your man?'

'He was meant to injure Aelfric, not kill him. I wanted him out of the way. I didn't want him dead. But Aelfric never was no horseman.'

Ascha looked deep into Radhalla's pale blue eyes for what seemed a long time.

'No,' he said. 'Aelfric was no horseman.' His eyes felt gritty and tired. The pain in his side was welling up and threatening to overwhelm him. Slowly, he shifted the weight on his arm, hesitated for a moment, and then allowed himself to drop back.

'But he was my father,' he murmured.

The blow took Radhalla by surprise.

The warlord of the Cheruskkii lurched forward and crashed to his knees, a bloody arrowhead standing out a full hand's breadth from his chest. He stayed there, sitting back on his heels, without moving and looked down at the arrowhead protruding from his body with a look of dull surprise. His face went through many changes, and then he lifted his eyes to Ascha and his mouth worked silently.

Tchenguiz came up behind him.

'Wah! Radhalla! Are you not yet dead?'

The Hun reached back and swung the hatchet, shattering Radhalla's skull.

Tchenguiz muttered something in his own language and then reached into the Cherusker's broken head and washed his hands in Radhalla's brain.

Ascha must have passed out again because when he came to he saw only blackness. For a moment he imagined he had been buried alive under the market square and the panic rose and gripped him by the throat, and then he saw the shadows move and realized they were black smoke. Tchenguiz had an arm under his shoulders and was lifting him up. Ascha clambered to his feet. He swayed unsteadily and then staggered over to where Clovis lay. The Overlord seemed lifeless. Ascha pulled the rope from his throat and put two fingertips to the side of his neck just below the jaw.

He could not be certain but he thought he felt the faintest flicker of life.

'Leave him,' grunted Tchenguiz. 'We must go.'

'No, I'm not leaving him,' Ascha shouted.

A belch of flame crashed out at him, and he realized that the fire had reached the scrolls and books. With a huge effort, he picked Clovis up and threw him over one shoulder. A burning beam crashed to the floor scattering sparks and firedrops. Wall hangings flared and curled. Everywhere he looked, there was fire. He staggered from the chamber, flames licking his skin and ran heavy-footed towards the door. A shower of red hot ashes fell on his neck and shoulders, stinging the raw flesh. He felt his hair burn.

Halfway down the hall, he stumbled over a burning corpse and would have sprawled if Gydda hadn't appeared and caught him. Gydda and Tchenguiz dragged Ascha to his feet. The way out was a wall of flame. Ascha looked back to see the chamber blazing. A great paw of heat buffeted his face and pushed down his throat. He couldn't breathe.

'The door is that way!' Tchenguiz shouted. 'Now, run!'

Ascha summoned all his strength. Still carrying the body of the Overlord, he put his head down and ran through the fire and out into the sun-splitted street.

A moment later, with a deafening roar, the roof collapsed.

The Great Hall of Tornacum, formerly the Basilica of imperial Rome, was no more.

34

Three months after the Saxon host was destroyed, Ascha travelled home to see his mother. He looked well, she thought, a handsome young man with his dark beard, topknot and fine clothes. He wore a fine wolf-skin cape and carried his father's sword on his hip and was accompanied by Tchenguiz and an ugly Jute with mangled ears.

He sat by the fire and spoke of all that had happened since he went away. He told how he had been rescued from slavery by Octha the Frisian, how he had spoken before the Great Council at Tornacum and how he had led the Franks and hostages during the great battle against the Cheruskkii.

His mother and Budrum listened as if spellbound. They gasped in horror when they heard how Hanno died on the bridge at Tornacum and smiled with delight when Ascha told them how the Overlord of the Franks had shat his breeches while dangling from a rope. And when Ascha told them how Radhalla had died, like a wolf without a groan, they looked at each other and nodded with solemn satisfaction.

One week after the battle, in the burnt-out shell of the Basilica, the Overlord of the Franks gave Ascha Aelfricson his freedom. All the Frankish and Roman lords were there, as well as the Overlord's Antrustions, the Royal Hostages, Rufus and his Pritanni and Besso and the Theodi. The Overlord took Ascha's hands in his and uttered the words *'Maltho thi afrio lito,'* which is in the Frankish language, 'I say to you now, I free you, half-free.'

'Now I am whole!' Ascha said to the two women with a quiet smile.

He told them that Clovis had rewarded him with gold and silver, and had given him a gold neck torc as thick as his thumb, saying it would remind him of how he had saved the Overlord of the Franks from a slow and lingering death. Clovis had wanted to make Ascha a captain in the Antrustions, but Ascha declined. He'd had his fill of Frankish service. Clovis did not seem displeased. After what had happened in the Basilica, they both needed to put some distance between them.

Ascha's mother had no wish to meet Herrad. The girl sounded headstrong and stubborn and she was sure they would have clashed before too long.

After the Cheruskkii were destroyed, Herrad went back to Thraelsted with Octha. It was plain that the girl was with child, but whether the child was Ascha's or Sigisbherht's or Octha's was anyone's guess. Ascha used to visit them. He would go for long walks with Herrad along the beach and, in the evening, he and Octha would get drunk together. By then, Octha knew he did not have long to live. He told Ascha and Herrad that he wanted them to have his wealth when he died.

A curious business to his mother's way of thinking, but it seemed to suit them.

When he was done telling, he sat back in his father's chair, crossed his ankles and closed his eyes. The two women thought he seemed calmer and more at peace, as if the demons that had chased him for so many years had finally been put to rest. He had earned the love of his friends and the respect of his clan, and that was all he had ever wanted.

Ascha never spoke of what had passed between him and Radhalla. But one afternoon, he took Budrum to one side and asked her. Budrum said the journey to the homeland all those years ago had been a trial his mother had tried to forget. The Theodi had used his mother and the other women cruelly, and it was a long time before Aelfric claimed her as his own, forbidding any man to touch her on pain of death. By then a boatload of seed was running down her thighs and she was near despair.

Had Radhalla been one of them?

Budrum pulled a face.

He might have been.

Ascha recovered Hroc's body from the swamp. By some miracle of the marshes in those parts, the body had not rotted and Hroc's face was smooth and unmarked, as if he had died only a few days before. With the help of Gydda and Tchenguiz, Ascha took Hroc to the burial ground and buried him next to Aelfric, overlooking the wetlands they both had loved.

The next day, Ascha picked up his chisels and began carving a monument to Aelfric. He carved him in stone as a Saxon warlord, mounted on a big horse, armed with shield, spear and sword. It was a fine piece of work, perhaps the finest he had ever done. They erected the monument above the estuary where it can be seen by the ships of all nations.

As far as anyone knows it is still there.

After the battle against the Cheruskkii, the Theodi broke up. Some, the old and the faint-hearted, stayed. Others, fearing the storm-floods, went to live among the Frisians, but most emigrated across the Narrow Seas to Pritannia. Besso went with them as their *hetman*. The young women who remained married Cheruskkii boys and moved away, Saefaru among them.

Ascha had wanted to take his mother home to her island, but she refused.

'Pritannia is no longer what it was,' she said. 'My home is where my man is buried, and it is here I will live out my days.'

She told him that others had moved in to occupy the long houses the Theodi had abandoned.

'They are primitive people without history,' she said scornfully. 'Already they call themselves Saxons, as if living in a Saxon hall makes you a warrior. But they know my son is a great lord and they treat me with respect. I heal their sick, I give them advice and, when the nights are cold and damp, I sit the little ones around the fire and tell them stories about the great warrior, Ascha Aelfricson, and how many, many years ago, he destroyed Radhalla, the dark war lord of the Cheruskkii.

And then I tell them I am Ascha's mother.

And for me, it is enough.'

Epilogue

Thraelsted, two years later

Rhine mouth, late summer and a man and a woman are walking along the beach, holding the hand of a small child who walks between them. It is late in the day, and the rain that had fallen that morning has stopped, but there is a fresh wind blowing off the estuary and the air is full of the salt-tang of the sea. Far off the surf booms and hisses.

The child suddenly breaks free and runs off with choppy stubborn steps. The man picks up a handful of pebbles, reaches back and hurls them into the water in long swooping arcs. The woman watches him, one hand drawn up to her eyes. She turns to the child and, at that moment, the little girl falls and sits down on the sand with a surprised expression, as if unsure whether to laugh or cry. The man smiles at her, she looks at him, gurgles with laughter and gets to her feet, bottom first. She shakes herself, rubs her hands together and runs to him with arms outstretched.

The man scoops her up, swings her over his head and drops her gently onto his shoulders. She grips his chin in her tiny hands and beats his head like a drum. He groans in mock despair, and she giggles with delight. The woman stands with her arms crossed, holding her shoulders. She looks at them both and smiles. The wind blows her hair across her face in long floating tendrils like seaweed. She pushes her hair back behind her ear, and then twists it into a roll on the nape of her neck, takes a long pin from the folds of her dress and pins it up. The man watches her until she looks at him, and then he smiles and looks away. The three of them watch the plovers racing over the flat and listen to the shrieks of the gulls wheeling overhead. The woman takes the man's arm in both of hers, bends her head to his shoulder and they turn and walk on towards the west beneath a clear and blue sky.

End

HISTORICAL NOTE

Clovis, Basinia, Ragnachar and Syagrius are actual historical figures. In 481 AD the sixteen year old Clovis succeeded his father Childeric as leader of the Salian Franks and soon after became Overlord of all the Frankish tribes. A few years later, he had Syagrius, Governor of the last Roman enclave in Gaul, murdered. Clovis occupied Roman territory and shifted his capital from Tornacum (Tournai in Belgium) to Lutetia Parisi (Paris, France) and Roman rule in Gaul finally came to an end.

Clovis then turned his attention to his neighbours. One by one, Clovis took on the Germanic tribes who controlled Gaul – the Burgundii, the Thuringii, the Alemanni and Visigoths. He defeated them and overran their territories. While he was about it, he eliminated any Franks he felt might threaten him, including his kinsman Ragnachar, who was arrested, shorn of his long hair and executed. By the time of his death in 511, Clovis (the name became Louis in France, Ludwig in Germany and Lewis in Britain) ruled over most of Roman Gaul and had built an empire that would lay the foundations for modern France. On the continent he is as well known as King Arthur or King Alfred and has become a powerful post-war symbol of Franco-German unity.

The Franks' success in taking over Gaul is likely to have been a major factor in persuading the Saxons and other tribes to avoid Gaul and settle in Britain. In time, the Franks adopted Latin as their language, although there are numerous Frankish loan-words in modern French. In Britain, Roman culture was less entrenched and after Germanic tribes took over the eastern part of the island, Roman culture was abandoned. Latin and the native British languages were replaced by English. It is possible that if Clovis had not succeeded in keeping the Germanic raiders out of Gaul, the British and Americans and other English-speaking nations would today speak a Celtic or Latin-derived language, like French or Spanish.

Few historians now believe that Britain was invaded by mass waves of Anglo-Saxons. Most likely the island was breached by small warbands who gradually assumed political and cultural domination over the native population. Some Britons fled and settled in what we now call Brittany, and this forms the background to Herrad's story.

Although the remains of a basilica have been found in Tournai, the description of the Overlord's Great Hall in *The Half-Slave* is based on the Roman Basilica of Constantine in Trier, which still survives.

The Theodi village is based on the iron-age village of Feddersen Wierde, near Bremerhaven in Germany. Feddersen Wierde was built on mounds raised above the flood plain and was occupied for around 600 years. Despite its remote location, there is evidence of contact with imperial Rome through trading, raids or service in the Roman army. In its later stages, the village was home to about fifty families. One timber-built hall was larger than the others and probably belonged to a hereditary chieftain and his family.

Towards the end of the 5th century, at about the time of the events depicted in this story, the village declined and was abandoned. Some archaeologists believe the inhabitants travelled to Britain as part of the Anglo-Saxon migration and settled in the Thames estuary.

ACKNOWLEDGEMENTS

I would never have written this story without the help of a number of people. Thanks are due to Neil Ferguson and the late Julia Casterton of the City Lit for getting me started; to Peggy Samson, Helen Rowe, John Keane, Alison St Helene, Kyo Louis, Julian Ives and Celia Toler of Covent Garden Writers for their good-humoured encouragement; and to Christian Enders and James Joseph for being such enthusiastic manuscript readers.

Thank you also to Harriet Gilbert, Jonathan Myerson, Jane Batkin, Syd Moore, Barbara Zuckriegl and Olivia Isaac Henry of the MA Creative Writing course at City University, London for their robust but always helpful advice; and to David Stevens for his specialist expertise.

I owe a particular debt to my wife Emma Bloom for her wise guidance and unflagging support. Any historical errors or solecisms that remain are entirely my responsibility.

Finally, special thanks are due to my editor, Yvonne Barlow at Hookline, for her passionate belief in reader power and for guiding me down the long and winding road to publication.

Lightning Source UK Ltd.
Milton Keynes UK
18 March 2010
151587UK00001B/2/P